Split Decisions

Arden Black

Split Decisions
Copyright © 2023 by Arden Black
Cover Design by Arden Black

While effort in providing a certain level of accuracy has gone into the writing of this book, the author makes no guarantees as to the finer legal and educational details of the story. As such, not all references in this book will be strictly realistic and should not be held as complete fact. As much research as possible went into the legal and educational workings contained in this book, but it must be noted this book is a work of fiction; therefore, the novel's story and characters are fictitious. Any resemblance to actual persons, living or dead, is purely coincidental. Any public agencies or institutions utilized in the story are wholly imaginary.

All rights reserved. No part of this publication may be reproduced, distributed, or transmitted in any form or by any means, including photocopying, recording, or other electronic or mechanical methods, without the prior written permission of the publisher, except in the case of brief quotations embodied in critical reviews and certain other noncommercial uses permitted by copyright law. For permission requests, write to the author, addressed "Attention: Split Decisions Permissions Coordinator," at the address below.
ArdenBlackAuthor@gmail.com
www.ArdenBlack.com
Printed in the United States of America

ISBN 979-8-9896944-1-9 (paperback)
ISBN 979-8-9896944-0-2 (electronic book)
ISBN 979-8-9896944-2-6 (hardcover)

First Edition
2024

A teenage prostitute is fighting a war against drugs, poverty, violence, and fear under the heavy fist of her pimp. After running away from home to escape the misery there, she thought she had found a savior in Mack, who took her in, fed her, loved her, cared for her; until he started demanding payment for his kindness. Forced onto the streets to make money, Bitty must fight to survive in her cruel world.

But Bitty has a secret. Throughout the years of abuse and neglect, Bitty had friends. Her alters. They look after each other, support each other, and take turns coping with life. Even though they argue and criticize, at the end of the day, she has someone who loves her, even if they're sharing the same body.

This story follows Bitty's journey from a crucial crossroads. Which path will her decision take her down? Will she be able to survive the consequences of her choice with the help of her alters, or will that ultimate decision be her last? Side by side, Bitty's two paths will unfold, showing the power of the mind, and the strength of a child's will to survive.

DISCLAIMER: The contents of this book may be disturbing to many readers and should be read with caution. The subject matter within references child abuse, human trafficking, rape, homelessness, foul language, and suicide.

Chapter One

"I'm so sick of being cold! Why can't we live in California or something?" Bitty mumbled.

'Half of California isn't warm either, you know.'

"Probably still warmer than here."

It was a lot harder to find customers when it was cold. People just weren't out in this weather, and it was harder to display the merchandise when you risked hypothermia. Winters in the state of Washington weren't as cold as some places in the U.S., but it was certainly cold enough to be uncomfortable without proper clothing or shelter, and could even be dangerous when you were constantly exposed.

She tried to finger comb her long brown hair and make it look a little more presentable, then pulled out the mascara she'd been given a few months ago and caked it on her long lashes to frame her dull, lifeless blue eyes. Her red miniskirt showed off her slender legs and barely covered her virtually naked butt that sported a black g-string. Too-tight, sky-high black heels gave her tiny frame a boost of height that made her look at least a little more presentable and older than her fourteen years, which might—hopefully—attract some more customers. Her black crop top displayed her bare midriff, and the dangly sparkling piercing at her belly caught the eye and drew it to her bare skin like a neon sign. Every car that went by got her hopes up and she'd strut to the street, waving it down. But they all passed her by without a second glance.

"Damn it! Why didn't I ask for that fucking jacket!" she berated herself for the millionth time as she stood freezing at the side of the road.

There were no free passes into the old house she was allowed to sleep in when she wasn't on the street working. There would probably be no meal to fill her aching belly that hadn't seen proper food in days, and no way to avoid the beating she was sure to get for not earning enough. It was almost not worth returning without money.

Almost.

Another several minutes passed before a car finally pulled up. She immediately approached, bending over and leaning into the window to sell her body. Instantly, she could tell what kind of man he was and what he might be into. She'd had a lot of practice reading people, especially in situations like this.

"Hey, big guy. You looking for some company?"

The middle aged man grinned and nodded, unlocking the door. "Aww, yeah, baby. I would really like that. Shall we go play someplace quiet? Just the two of us?"

Finally! She jumped in quickly and buckled up. At least the heat was on in the car! She spread her legs as soon as his hand touched her thigh and she gave him a quick preview before closing them and turning to face him.

"$50 for regular. No weird stuff. That's extra."

He nodded and slipped his arm around her shoulders, stroking and rubbing as he drove. She tried to push the disgust and dread away and pretend she wasn't being forced to be here.

After a few minutes, he pulled over into a darkened parking lot that was big enough to be reasonably private and slid his seat back, turning to stroke her cheek with one hand and slide his other hand back between her legs. "Come on, let me inside you."

She lifted her hips to pull her panties down and off over her boots, then moved over onto his lap.

"$50. Before we start."

He sighed and reached for his wallet, pulling out some bills and slapping them on the passenger seat. "Come on now. I need this."

She eyed the cash, then lifted her hips and sank down on him.

He moaned and immediately began using her painfully hard. His grunts and snorts were disgusting and made her feel sick, but she kept up her script of moans and pleasured cries as he used her, his fingers digging into her skin. She'd have more bruises. That was nothing new.

It always surprised her when it didn't seem to matter to any of them. None of them cared how old she was, or how many marks, bruises or bites she had on her. None of them cared how much it hurt, or how humiliating it was when they did or demanded certain things. She wasn't a person anymore. She was a toy. A tool.

Had she ever been a person…?

"Ooohhhhh, come on baby! I need this! Come on. Beg me for it! Beg me!"

She cringed, closing her eyes and fighting the horrifying memories his words brought crashing around her shoulders like a ton of bricks as she obeyed. Instead, she tried to focus on the money sitting on the seat beside her. The money that would bring her a little closer to her quota. The money that would bring her less of a beating and hopefully earn her the good kind of hit.

A minute later, he made a few disgusting grunting noises as he finished. She obediently moaned as if in pleasure, trying not to focus on what was in her now. It always felt so dirty. Like her body wasn't her own. She was just a container for… that. She hated it so much.

The minute he stopped twitching inside her, she moved off him and pulled her panties on, stuffing her $50 into her little purse and settling back into her seat. At least her purse was a little fuller now. That was worth something, wasn't it?

"Just drop me at Maple, please," she mumbled, looking out the window, already trying to forget.

It took him a minute to put himself back together again and mop his forehead before he started driving. This time, he kept his hands to himself, as eager to be rid of her as she was to be rid of him.

That always seemed to be the way. Well, usually, at least. They were all handsy and lovey-dovey til they got you naked, then it was pain, humiliation, and disgust, and a quiet sort of need to pretend they hadn't just used a child to satisfy themselves. They were all sick, disgusting bastards. Every single one of them.

'Don't even try to act like you don't deserve it.

"Shut up," she muttered.

"What?"

"Nothing. Here's fine. You can drop me here."

"But Maple's still five blocks away!"

"Here's fine," she repeated.

With a shrug, the man pulled over and glanced around as she got out, making sure no one was going to notice a young teen getting out of some middle aged man's car in the middle of nowhere at this time of night. They'd both be arrested! She shut the door and turned to say goodbye, but he was gone the moment it slammed.

For a moment, she stood where she was, watching the car speed off into the night, but the cold soon began to penetrate again and she sighed. It had been nice and warm in there at least.

Once more, she began slowly walking along the street, watching hopefully as a car drove up, then deflating as it went past without even slowing down. A stroll past the bank's big clock told her it was almost 5:00 a.m.. Tired, cold, and jonesing, she'd just have to suck it up and go back without her whole quota and hope Mack would give her the hit she needed.

Mack. He had seemed like a Godsend when she met him after she'd run away from home. He had taken her in, given her some clothes and food. He made her feel special, beautiful, worth something for the first time in her life. It had been so wonderful.

But after a while, the little gifts and sweet touches had started to taper off and he had begun to ask for things in return. At first it had been running errands and little things, but very quickly it had turned into much, much more. She had foolishly opened up to him about some of her past and he had been quick to point out that she was ruined anyway so she had no right to cry about making him some money doing the same thing.

And so began her 'career'.

It was also Mack who had first stuck the needle in her arm and introduced her to something to help make life more bearable. Needing that hit—that chemical escape—kept her coming back to him and made her willing to do anything to anyone, either because she was desperate for her next dose, or she was too strung out to even know or be able to object. It was a miserable existence, and it was showing on her young body.

The youthful skin on her face was growing slack and gray, not just because of lack of food and too many beatings. The drugs were eating away at her from the inside, like a physical representation of the way her existence was killing her. But there was no way to escape. There was nowhere to go; no one to go to.

The house he owned was one of those places that looked like it could have been nice once upon a time. Maybe if it had been cared for, or been in a better neighborhood, it would have still been beautiful. Now, it looked like she felt. Used. Broken. Abused and neglected.

Briefly, her mind flitted to the home she'd left a year ago. At least there she'd had a proper bed, the heat had worked, and there was less chance of the place blowing up. But she pushed that away. Those days were gone now. She couldn't go back there any more than she could be a virgin again.

The stink of drugs cooking assailed her nostrils when she jerked open the door and stepped into the dark hall.

'*Run away. Just run. Somewhere better. Just go. Ask for help.*'

"Shut up. I need a hit," she mumbled, stumbling over the prone form of another of Mack's girls on the floor. Whether she was alive or dead was impossible to tell, and she didn't care. All that mattered right now was getting to Mack, handing over her money, and hoping he'd stick a needle in her arm.

The thin man was sitting playing cards with some of his buddies in one of the back rooms, alcohol and cigarette smell filling the room. His black hair hung down around his face and brushed his shoulders, and a cigarette hung from the side of his thin lips. Three heavy looking black handguns lay on the table within easy reach of him and a couple of his friends. She gulped and approached slowly.

Mack didn't even look at her. He simply held his hand out while studying his cards. She placed every dollar she had in his upturned palm and stepped back just slightly as he drew it in and began to count.

'*Run. Run now. Just run. We can take care of ourself. Just run. Turn around and run.*'

'*Don't be a fucking moron. If she runs now, she'll be shot before she makes it to the door. She's gotta take what she gets now or we'll be in the gutter before the sun's up.*'

Slowly, Mack turned his head to look at her.

"This is it?" he asked in a deadly soft voice.

She swallowed hard and nodded, her eyes on the floor and her head down. "I tried, Mack. Honest to God, I tried. It's so cold. No one's out right now. It's too–"

"THEN WHY THE FUCK DID YOU COME BACK? IF YOU DON'T HAVE THE MONEY, DON'T FUCKING COME BACK! HOW MANY TIMES HAVE I SAID THAT?"

"I..... I..... I need.... I need a hit, Mack.... Please.... I need it.... It's getting bad..." Tears were slowly running down her hollow cheeks.

WHACK

"A hit? How's that for a hit?"

WHACK

She gave a cry of pain as the second one knocked her to the floor with its force. Cowering beside him on her knees, her head ducked and her arms over it, she sobbed and pleaded.

"Mack! Please! I'm sorry! I'm sorry! I didn't–" She broke off with another cry as his fingers wrapped in her hair and pulled her up to look into his face. The blood from her cheek and split lip looked pink as it trickled down her face and mixed with the tears.

"Fine. You come back short, you can pay my pot." He grinned, then turned back to his table mates. "Boys, winner gets her for the day." He tossed her away and laughed at the cheers. "T.J., get her a rig. But not too much this time!"

A young man in the corner, not much older than herself, jumped to his feet and went off to collect a syringe. Bitty didn't dare move without being told to, so she knelt where she was, hunched up, shivering, and crying quietly. She hurt. It wasn't just the pain of the two punches she'd received. It was the all-over ache and chill that was gripping her entire body. It was like the flu, but instead of getting better as time went on, she knew from experience it would only get worse as the drugs left her system.

Soon enough, T.J. returned and knelt beside her, jerking her arm towards him and tying it off above the elbow. Bitty stayed still, her head turned and her eyes closed. She couldn't stand needles, and couldn't watch when they did it, but her fear of them was nothing compared to the grip of the drugs that owned her body just as much as Mack did. T.J. wasn't gentle about any of it, missing the vein a couple of times. Sometimes, Bitty thought he did it on purpose, simply because he knew she hated the needles. But after a few tries, he hit it and a moment later, blissful pleasure coursed through her body.

The shivers became unnoticeable, the throbbing of her head disappeared. Her hunger, cold, misery, humiliation, all faded, washed away by the waves of pleasure that overtook her senses. With a sigh, she sank to the floor and lay down while the game continued above her.

'You're weak, Bitty. You're weak and pathetic. You don't deserve to be here. I would never have let us get into this mess. I would have made sure we were okay. You're pathetic.'

Bitty couldn't even tell her to shut up this time. That was the only drawback to the drugs. It didn't always stop the others. They hated her, she knew that. Well, maybe not all of them. Sometimes the drugs would make her mind so fuzzy they'd be forced back, leaving her alone. At least it let her have a break from their criticism. Other times, it seemed to give them more freedom. Sometimes they helped, but more often Bailey was criticizing her.

She didn't know how long she lay there in her stupor, but it didn't seem very long before she was grabbed by the arm and hauled upwards violently to her feet. She managed to stand and gaze almost blankly into the man's face towering over her.

"She any good?" he asked critically, examining her like a doll.

"Sure. She's young and tight. Do what you want. Just don't kill her. She makes decent money."

She found herself stumbling along with the huge man, his fingers digging into her arm. But it didn't matter. It didn't hurt too much. It was okay. She would be okay. She was always okay.

Mostly.

Bitty was virtually unaware of how loud her screams were that whole day. The hours seemed to melt together and only snatches made sense in the blur of pain and horror. Whatever he'd taken obviously made him go for what felt like forever. His imagination knew no limits it seemed.

Mack poked his head in a few times, but her desperate pleas for his help were met with derisive laughter and an order to keep it down a little because he was trying to sleep.

Sleep.

Yes. Sleep would be good. She needed to sleep. She needed to escape. She should sleep.

Cries of pain faded into moans of pleasure, her body relaxed, her hips met his hungrily, and she reveled in the pain. It was wonderful. It felt amazing. The pain was pleasure. There really wasn't a line anymore.

Her sudden shift in mood didn't seem to faze her abuser, and it was several more hours before he'd gotten his money's worth from her little body and left her bleeding on the bed. Mack came in for a go, then stuck another needle in her arm and called her his good girl. She smiled.

Good girl.

Yes. She *was* a good girl. She had obeyed well. She had enjoyed it. She was a good girl. Mack's good girl. She had pleased him like Bitty never could. It was worth it.

Chapter Two

As the sun began to sink lower on the horizon, Bitty was jerked awake and hauled up off the bed. She blinked, gasping at the pain. What had happened? Where was she?

'It's over. For now. Scarlett took over. Just make some money tonight for fuck's sake.'

Bitty dressed with soft whimpers and gasps of pain, shocked by the marks that covered her thin little body. What had he done to her!? At least she didn't remember it; would never remember it.

"Make sure you don't come back without your quota this time, you stupid bitch," Mack warned as she walked slowly past the doorway to his room. She glanced in briefly and nodded, shocked by the pang of jealousy she felt when she saw his latest 'treasure' sitting in his lap playing video games.

The girl's pretty blond hair was braided and tied with ribbons; her clothes were new, clean, and beautiful. Her cheeks were pink and fresh, and her eyes weren't dead and sunken. Vaguely, Bitty wondered if she'd ever looked like that in her life.

'Fat chance. That one probably thinks her life is shit cuz her mom and dad won't let her have a phone, or stay out late or some kind of bullshit. Mack probably gives her everything she wants and tells her how horrible her parents are. She doesn't know the meaning of misery. Not yet, anyway.'

Bitty ignored the comments in her head and made her way back onto the street. It was colder than last night had been. The wall of chill hit her hard and she was already shivering by the time she reached the end of the block. The cold felt good on the cuts and scrapes, but the chill made the bruises inside ache.

'Bitty, I'm hungry. Can we get pancakes?'

The innocent little voice cut her to the core and she closed her eyes for a moment. "Sorry, Bebe. There's no pancakes right now."

'But I'm hungry, Bitty. I'm so hungry. Why can't we get pancakes?'

Bitty sank down onto the curb, wincing at the bruises she was forced to sit on. "I'll see what I can do, 'k?"

'When? When Bitty? When can we get pancakes? Can you ask Mommy to make pancakes?'

"Mommy isn't here, Bebe, remember? Mommy can't make pancakes. I'll try to find some pancakes somewhere, okay?"

The little internal sigh signaled an assent and she relaxed slightly. She *was* hungry. Bebe had obviously been far more aware of the hunger, and she was shocked to realize she couldn't even remember when she last ate. With that, her stomach growled as if to corroborate that fact.

A pair of headlights came slowly around the corner. Slow was bad. Slow in this area meant police on the prowl. Bitty jumped to her feet and scurried around a dumpster, crouching in the shadows until the cruiser passed.

'Why didn't you just go to them? Just go ask them to help you!' a little boy's voice cried.

'Don't be stupid, Jay! They'll arrest her! They arrest hookers! We'll end up in jail for years! Or worse, they'll send us back home. Can you imagine what would happen if we get sent home?'

'Oh.'

'Geez, how many times have I told you that?'

'Sorry, Bailey.'

"Lay off, Bailey," Bitty muttered irritably.

A homeless man lifted his head from under a cardboard box and glared at her.

She ducked her head and got up, moving back onto the sidewalk again. She had to get a customer; at least ten or she'd never make her quota. And Mack was right—she'd better not set foot in that building until she had all of it.

The problem was, every time she didn't make her quota, she got beaten. But when she did make her quota a few times in a row to avoid the beating, Mack raised the quota because it was obviously too easy. There really was no way to win.

'Just tuck some away somewhere. Take a couple bucks and hide it. Then we can use it to get away.'

"Come on, Jay. Where am I supposed to hide money? Do you know how long it would take just to get a few bucks that he wouldn't notice? And where would we go anyway?"

'I dunno.'

She sighed. He was just trying to help. He was always trying to help. But it got annoying sometimes. Especially when he made it sound so easy. Why not just leave and never go back? Why couldn't they just walk away and not return to beatings and rapes?

'Cuz we have no place to go, no one to help us, and we'd die on the side of the road from withdrawals, that's why!'

"I know, Scarlett. I know. You don't have to keep going on about it."

"You keep talking to yourself and people'll think you're crazy."

The voice behind her made Bitty jump a mile and spin around with a cry of fear. A grandmotherly woman was sitting on the concrete steps of an old Victorian house Bitty had wandered past. She hadn't even noticed her sitting there, wrapped in a colorful knit shawl. Her soft, gray hair was pinned neatly in a bun at the nape of her neck, her dress was old fashioned but clean, and the creases and lines on her face weren't the marks of exhaustion and hardship that Bitty was used to seeing. They crinkled at the corners of her sparkling blue eyes and upturned mouth in a way only frequent smiling could do.

"I…. I didn't."

"Oh, you most certainly did. Who's Scarlett?"

Bitty lowered her head, the unbruised parts of her face going red as she shrugged. "No one. I was just… I wasn't…. It's…" she stammered.

"Do you want to come inside for a cup of hot chocolate? I've got some fresh cookies too."

'Cookies! Bitty, she said hot chocolate and cookies! Oh please let's go in!'

"Shut up, Bebe," she muttered under her breath, hoping the woman wouldn't notice.

"You look like you could use it. Come on, just a few minutes. I'm sure your parents won't mind." The woman was standing up, looking at her expectantly.

Bitty shook her head. "I…. can't. I've gotta… be someplace. I have to–"

"You don't have to stay long. Just something to warm you up. You look freezing."

Bitty stood there for a long moment, gazing up at the woman on the steps who was smiling down at her.

'Pleeease, Bitty? Pleeease can we have hot chocolate and cookies? Please?'

'Yeah, she seems real nice. We could ask her for help. She's gonna give us food. Maybe we can stay with her. She probably won't mind.'

'Don't. It's a trap. She'll probably tie us to a table and chop us up into tiny pieces while we scream. And no one would even care.'

'Bailey!'

"I…. can't stay for long…" she said finally, gazing up at the kind looking woman.

"You can stay as long as you like, dear."

'Don't say I didn't warn you.'

Fighting back the panic and desire to run that Bailey was pounding her with, Bitty slowly climbed the steps to the door of the old house.

Inside, the house did indeed smell like freshly baked cookies. Bitty had never smelled anything so wonderful in her entire life. She could feel Bebe trying to rush forward, wanting to be the first to experience it all. It was warm, too. It felt good and she began to relax. Anywhere that smelled like this couldn't be bad, could it?

The doorway they had entered through led to a flight of stairs and a hallway running alongside it towards the back of the house. Bitty would have liked to get a better look at the room to her left, which seemed to be a living room. The yellow light cast from a lamp on the table near the couch gave it a warm, homey look. But the woman was leading her forward down the hall and Bitty followed. Pictures hung on the wall, capturing a lifetime of weddings, babies, children, teenagers, and pets. It was like walking through a time capsule of photographs.

The kitchen at the end of the hallway was just as delightful as the living room had seemed, maybe even more so because of the heavier scent of baking hanging in the air. It was warm, bright, and clean. Bitty had never been in a kitchen like this. It was like one of those ads for chocolate chips. They had always seemed so fake. Never in her life had Bitty ever thought real people lived in homes like this. And now she was standing in one.

"Why don't you take a seat at the table, dear. I'll get you a cup of hot chocolate. Help yourself to some cookies. Take as many as you like. Lord knows I shouldn't eat them all myself, and my young ones are all grown up. See them mostly at Christmas now. And birthdays. They always come on my birthday, and I'll go to visit on theirs. But it's getting harder, now that my old body ain't what it used to be. Harder to walk and get around, you know."

Bitty sat gazing longingly at the plate of cookies in front of her on the table as the woman chattered on about her family and how many cookies she kept making even though she knew she'd end up eating them all anyway and get fat.

It was so terribly tempting to just reach out and take one, and Bebe certainly was pushing to get at them hungrily. But experience had taught Bitty not to trust it when someone told you to 'help yourself'. That was almost always a trap to catch you being greedy, selfish, or disrespectful. So she waited, watching the plate and the woman alternately, staying silent and still.

Silent and still was the way to be if you wanted to get by with the minimum amount of bruises. If no one noticed you, you were less likely to make them angry with your attitude problem and earn yourself a beating.

"Goodness, haven't you had one yet?" the woman asked in surprise when she placed a steaming cup of cocoa down in front of Bitty. "I told you it's okay. Go on. Have one. They're still warm, I bet. Best way to eat them, you know." She winked at the girl and sat down across the table from her with her own mug.

Tentatively, watching the woman like a wild animal approaching a trap, Bitty reached out and took a cookie. When she didn't get reprimanded, she drew it back and began to nibble on it.

'Ooohh, Bitty! I want to try it! Please, let me try it!' came the desperate plea from Bebe. The desperate tugging for control began to distract her and she didn't notice the little frown that crossed the woman's face.

"Don't you like it?"

"Wha– Oh! No, it's delicious. Really. I just...." She shoved half the cookie in her mouth to prove her point, then promptly choked on a crumb and began coughing.

The woman got up and filled a glass with water, setting it down on the table in front of Bitty as she sat down again. "I didn't mean you had to inhale the whole thing at once! You just made a face, so I thought maybe there was something wrong with it."

Bitty tried to simultaneously cough, swallow, sip, and shake her head, her eyes watering badly. "Oh - *cough* - no - *cough cough* - I just got - *cough, sip* - distracted -*sip* - Thank you."

She wiped her mouth on the back of her hand, trying to contain the rest of the coughs threatening to make her head explode. Every jolt made each bruise on her face throb like new. Her eyes closed for a moment against the pain.

'Open your damn eyes. Don't sit in a strange place in front of a total stranger with your eyes closed, you idiot! Do you want *to be murdered where you sit!?'*

Bitty forced her watery blue eyes open to focus on the woman, surprised to see a napkin being held out in front of her. "Thanks," she murmured, taking it and wiping her face and mouth.

"Better?"

She nodded. "Yeah, thanks."

"Good. Now, why don't you have another one and then tell me who did that to you?"

Bitty froze. "Did..... did what...?" she asked, feigning ignorance.

"You know perfectly well what I'm talking about. Who did it? Parents? Family?"

At least this time, Bitty could shake her head truthfully. "No. They didn't do it. It's nothing, really. I.... I should get going. I have places to be." She stood up quickly, suddenly desperate to get out of there.

'Good one. Now we've got a nosy busy-body on our case. You're fucking useless, Bitty!'

The woman stood up just as quickly, which was surprising, given how she had appeared so frail and weak a moment ago. Panic began to set in when it seemed that the woman had been lying to her, at least about that.

"Don't go. Please. I'm sorry I scared you. You haven't even had your hot chocolate yet. Sit down and finish it, at least. Then you can go."

'Why the hell does she want you to finish that hot chocolate so bad? There's probably something in it. Poison, or drugs or something.'

'Oh, Bitty, please finish the hot chocolate. Can I have it? Please? Bitty, please?'

'Why don't you tell her the truth? Just tell her who did it. Maybe she'll help us? She doesn't look like she'd hurt us. Why don't you just tell her?'

Bitty shook her head wildly and spun around. "I have to go. I have to go." She walked as quickly as possible without actually running, making her way down the hall that had seemed so welcoming when she first arrived, but now seemed like a terrifying trap.

A hand closed around her bruised arm and Bitty yelped in fear, instantly ducking down and shielding herself from the blow that was about to fall.

"Stop. I'm not going to hurt you. I won't even make you stay if you don't want to. Not that I could anyway, as much as I'd like to. I didn't mean to scare you. I'll drop it, okay?"

Bitty looked up at her warily, her heart racing and her head pounding.

'Run! Just fucking run! Don't listen to her!'

"How about we start over? My name is Mildred. Would you like to tell me yours?"

Bitty watched her in silence, a thousand suggestions and orders being thrown at her.

'Run. Just run!'

'I want more cookies, Bitty. Please! Can we have more cookies?'

'Why don't you just tell her? She can help us. She's nice. She makes nice food and her house smells good. Let's just tell her.'

'If Mack finds out we're not working he'll kill us. We've gotta go. Let's go. Just say thanks and get out.'

'Fuck the thank yous and leave!'

"I... I don't..."

The grip on her arm loosened slightly and Mildred smiled encouragingly.

"I.... I have to go," Bitty repeated.

Mildred sighed and nodded. "Alright. Well, why don't you take some cookies with you?"

'Oh yes! Please, Bitty! Please take some cookies! Please! I'm so hungry.'

"K," she mumbled.

Mildred smiled again and bustled off to put some cookies in a bag for her. Bitty was waiting outside on the front step by the time she returned.

"Thanks," she muttered as she took the bag and tried to hide it in her hand.

"You can come back whenever you want. I almost always have something baking."

'Oh, we have to come back! Can we come back, Bitty? Can we?'

Without a word, Bitty just nodded and turned, walking hurriedly into the dark.

Chapter Three

Once they were far enough down the street and around the corner, Bitty finally stopped and leaned against a wall, then opened the bag of cookies and began eating them in quick succession, sighing as the last morsel disappeared. She felt a little better now. The bruises from her beating didn't hurt so much anymore now that her belly had something in it. The problem now was that she was thirsty. Sugar could do that to you. Maybe she could talk the next guy into buying her a soda or something. Her mind returned once more to work and she sighed, her head hanging in defeat once more.

'Please, Bitty. Let's go back to that lady and ask her for help.'

"We can't," she mumbled miserably, pushing away from the wall and putting herself out on the sidewalk, back on display again.

'Why?'

"We just can't, okay? You can't trust people. Mack should have taught you that by now."

Silence.

Luckily, a prospect drove up and she plastered on a smile as she wandered over, trying to sway her hips like Mack had shown her. It was all about displaying the merchandise. It worked, or at least, the guy had decided on picking someone up anyway and she was the first one he saw. It didn't really matter. What mattered was that his car was warm and he had cash. She got in. After the usual spiel about what she would do and how much it would cost him, he agreed and set off.

"How old are you?" he asked casually.

She eyed him uncertainly, trying to gauge what he'd like. His somewhat round face seemed reasonably kind, and the crinkles around his green eyes suggested he smiled a lot. He didn't seem the type to want a younger girl.

"Eighteen," she replied finally, relieved to see the smile on his face. She'd been right, thank god.

'Sick fuck. That's barely more than a kid.'

Bitty tried to ignore the comment and looked out the window quietly as they drove, answering questions as they came.

What was her name? Bitty. Where was she from? Around. What did she like? Everything. Was she hungry?

The last question made her turn her head to look at him. He repeated his question.

"Uhh… kinda…" she mumbled warily, wondering if it meant something entirely different.

"Great. How about pizza? There's a great little place around here. We could have it delivered to the room for us."

"You have a room?" she asked in surprise.

"Yeah. I'm here on business. But I get lonely traveling all the time and sleeping all alone in those big beds." His hands began to explore his new purchase. "I need someone to make me feel a little less lonely."

She nodded in silence.

They reached the hotel, which was surprisingly decent, and he led the way in through a side door. It was your typical queen suite, designed for business travelers: small seating area and a bedroom area, divided by a low wall. Not bad.

"My name is… John," he told her, rubbing his hand nervously over his short brown hair.

She held back the cynical smile. Right. John. Cute.

While he made the call to order the pizza, she used the bathroom, trying to freshen up as best she could. When was the last time she'd taken a shower? She couldn't remember.

By the time she came out, he was already pulling the covers on the bed back. "Pizza should be here in about ten minutes. You like to suck?"

She nodded automatically and he grinned, coming over to her and stroking his hands up and down along her arms. "Eighteen, huh?"

She cringed and focused on his chest as she nodded again. She could hear the grin in his voice as he stroked her cheek, kneeling when he pushed down on her shoulders. He unzipped and pulled himself free, then took hold of her hair and pushed himself into her mouth. Her little hands braced herself on his thighs as he used her roughly, his taunts and grunts playing a sickeningly familiar tune in her head.

He seemed to enjoy the tears running down her cheeks as he choked her, his fingers tight and painful in her hair. But it wasn't anything she wasn't used to by now. This was just an ordinary day. At least he didn't stink. Even his grunts when he pulsed in her mouth and ordered her to swallow it all like a good little girl weren't the most disgusting she'd heard.

"Good girl. Go wait in the bathroom," he told her when the knock came on the door. She nodded obediently and ducked into the little room, hiding from view as he took his order and paid. She was used to that, too. She was an embarrassment, taboo, an illegal object that needed to be stashed out of sight when possible.

Soon enough, though, he called her out and smiled at her, pointing to the couch. He'd been good on his word and had two plates and two cups set out. She sank down onto the seat with a soft sigh and guzzled down her drink once he poured it. When he placed a piece of pizza on her plate and ordered her to eat, she devoured it quickly, smiling gratefully at him when he put another, and another. Four slices of pizza and five cups of soda later, she was finally satisfied.

"Well, I'd say you were hungry!" he said with a chuckle, stroking her bruised cheek with a slight frown. "So, how long can I have you?"

She regarded him cautiously. "How much money do you have?"

"How about $150 for the night? I can drop you off when I leave for my meeting in the morning."

She considered for a minute, then shook her head. As tempting as it was to sleep in a warm, clean bed in a warm hotel room for the night, it wouldn't be enough to cover her quota. "Five."

He frowned. "Five *hundred*?"

She nodded. "I'd make more if I was working the night."

"Well, maybe. But you'd be freezing cold and hungry, too," he pointed out.

'Like that matters. Not like we have a choice.'

"$500," she repeated firmly.

He sighed. "You gonna do what I say for $500?"

She nodded. "Where is it?"

He chuckled ruefully and stood up to get his wallet, pulling out five $100 bills and placing them on the table in front of her. "Good enough?" She nodded again and he grinned. "Good. Now strip, then go shower."

She obeyed, peeling her skin tight clothes from her dirty body in front of him while he watched. Once she was naked, he nodded and she went back into the bathroom. What surprised her was that he followed. With a nervous glance at him, she started the hot water, adjusting the knob until it was perfect. When she glanced back over her shoulder again, he was naked and hard, stroking himself as he studied her.

"Good girl. Now get in and get all wet."

She stepped into the tub and let the water fall down her small body as he watched, stroking, stroking, stroking. A minute later, he stepped in with her. She looked up at him nervously as he held her head gently under the water to get her hair wet.

"Your Daddy isn't taking proper care of his little girl," he murmured, reaching for the shampoo in the tiny hotel bottle and pouring most of it into the palm of his large hand. Smiling at her, he began to tenderly work the liquid into her hair, lightly scooping up the stray strands that escaped his hold and working it into a good lather. All the while, his erection rubbed against her belly button, bobbing with excitement.

'He's nice, Bitty. I like him.'

'GET OUT OF HERE, BEBE! DON'T BE FUCKING STUPID! GET OUT OF HERE RIGHT NOW!'

'But, Bailey, I-'

'GET OUT! GET OUT OF HERE, BEBE!'

Bitty closed her eyes with relief as the child slipped to the back and out of her mind to disappear for a while. She allowed the man to hold her head back under the running water, rinsing her hair out before pulling her back towards him to work conditioner into her hair. It was so...

'Don't. Just don't. It's not nice. It's not wonderful. It's not anything except sick. Don't forget there's a big fat dick digging into your belly right now. Don't get lax cuz he's washing your damn hair!'

Bitty opened her eyes again and looked up into his face when he was done. He was smiling at her. She smiled back.

'Don't.'

But she couldn't help it. No one had been this nice to her for as long as she could remember.

'Mildred was nice.'

'Fuck off, Jay. You shouldn't be here, either. Go play with Bebe or something. Get out of here.'

'But, Bailey...'

'Now, dammit!'

"...then we can get some rest."

Bitty blinked, focusing on his face again. "What?"

He chuckled. "I said why don't you turn around so Daddy can wash your back, and then we can get some rest."

"Oh. Okay. Sorry." She turned around, feeling his soapy hands glide gently over her young body. A moment later, he turned her around again and smiled down at her as he pushed her back against the wall of the tub.

"You know what Daddy wants, don't you?"

She nodded, sighing inwardly, knowing the gentleness was coming to an end.

He grinned and lifted her by the waist, pinning her hard against the wall. Automatically, she wrapped her legs around his waist and her arms around his neck to brace herself. Her cry of pain as he rammed hard and deep into her little body was muffled by his mouth as he kissed her.

When she'd had time to adjust to his size, he broke the kiss and sucked at her neck as he went to work violently on her. Her cries of pain echoed off the smooth walls and she tried hard not to let them get too loud. Her fingers dug into his neck in agony as he used her, tears running down her cheeks.

'Told you.'

Finally, he forced himself as deep as he could and held himself there as he groaned in her ear. "Gooooood girl....." He stroked her hair and pushed her head onto his shoulder as he straightened up, shifting his arm to support her butt as he held her like a child.

After rinsing them both off, he put her down and helped her out of the shower, then wrapped her in a towel, drying her off gently with another kind smile.

The kindness was beginning to confuse her. The pain, roughness, and violence were almost expected, but the tenderness and kindness in between were throwing her off. She didn't know what to expect. She couldn't prepare.

Once they were dry, he led her to the bed and lay down next to her, pulling the blankets up over them both and pulling her against him, almost cradling her in his arms.

"This is nice. You're a good little girl," he murmured, stroking her damp hair.

She closed her eyes, exhausted and full, clean and warm. It felt wonderful.

He sighed softly. "You're not eighteen, are you?" he whispered.

She shook her head very slightly at his question and smiled as he kissed the top of it. A moment later, she was fast asleep.

She didn't hear his soft curse and sigh of regret.

Chapter Four

After his morning romp under the covers, which was surprisingly gentle this time, he helped her dress and brushed her hair, braiding it down her back expertly, his eyes meeting hers in the mirror across from the bed. It was the strangest experience Bitty had ever had. No one had ever braided her hair before. They'd never even brushed it before, as far back as she could remember.

'He's a Daddy.'

"A daddy?" Bitty repeated.

John smiled at her. "Yes, babygirl?"

Bitty paused in confusion.

'No, no. A Daddy Dom. They like to take care of their girls.'

'What the hell do you know about it, Scarlett?'

'Plenty! I talked to another girl one night. She told me about how her Daddy took care of her. Not her real daddy. A Daddy Dom. He really loved her.'

'If he really loved her, why the hell is she selling herself for Mack, then?'

'He…'

'Yeah, didn't think so. Forget it, Bitty. Just get your money and get out.'

"Was there something you needed, babygirl?" he asked again, putting his hands on her shoulders and smiling at her in the mirror.

She shook her head.

"Alright, well, I'll go get us some breakfast." He climbed off the bed and put his shoes on, winked at her, then went out, leaving her alone.

'Take the laptop and go. Mack will love that. And the phone. With those and the $500, we're set!'

"Shut up, Bailey. He's nice. I'm not stealing his stuff. I've got enough that Mack won't be upset. Plus, he bought me dinner and he's getting breakfast. If I leave now, no breakfast."

'He left his wallet. You could take that and get your own breakfast down the street. You could save some of the cash for another day, when you need to make up.'

"Knock it off, Bailey. I'm not doing it, okay? Just shut up about it."

Silence.

She sighed softly and sat down on the couch to wait, turning on the tv to watch some kind of cartoon kid's show. She was smiling when he returned and handed her some orange juice and a couple of muffins. They ate in silence for a while, her eyes almost glued to the screen, his glued to her.

"Stay with me again tonight," he blurted out.

She turned to look at him questioningly and he repeated himself. "Stay with me tonight."

"I..."

'Oh, do it, Bitty! I like him! He's nice! He brought food and he washed my hair and he's so nice!'

'Don't you dare. You'll get attached and then where will you be when he leaves? Don't. Just make a clean break.'

"I.... don't...

"You can stay here for the day, order food or whatever, I'll bring some dinner with me when I'm done with work. You can watch tv, nap, whatever you want. Stay."

She studied him carefully for a long moment, trying to sort out the differing opinions of the others. Finally, she sighed and nodded. "Okay. One more. But you're gonna pay me, right?"

His face fell slightly, as if reality had hit him. "Oh. Right." There was silence in the room. Then he nodded. "Yeah, I'll pay you. $700."

She smiled inwardly and nodded. "Okay. I'll stay."

His grin made her feel warm and she actually leaned against him comfortably when he put his arm around her shoulders and drew her against him. They sat like that for another fifteen minutes before he had to leave for his meeting. After kissing her on the forehead, he left her $40 and the second key card.

"Get yourself a coloring book and some crayons, a stuffed animal, lunch. I should be back around 6:00 and we'll have dinner, okay?"

She nodded, smiling as he left.

Bitty spent a good deal of the morning watching tv and sleeping. She hadn't slept this much or this well for as long as she could remember. She was warm, comfortable despite the background achiness that warned of withdrawals, and even felt relatively safe, which was a new sensation for her. It was nice.

Around 11:00, she was growing hungry and decided she'd go get some lunch and maybe look at some of the other things he'd said to buy. Taking the keycard and the $500, as well as the $40 he'd left for her lunch, she tucked them all into her tiny purse and set off, using the side door he'd brought her through the previous night. It probably made more sense to use that door instead of drawing attention to herself and him by going in and out in front of the reception desk.

It was strange having money in her pocket. She'd never really had that before. At least, not money she was specifically told to spend on herself for something that wasn't food or clothing. It felt like Christmas. Actually, it felt better than any Christmas Bitty had ever known. It was like the movies made Christmas out to be.

There had only ever been one real Christmas. It was almost a miracle really. Her parents had both been sober that year, and on antidepressants thanks to the new outreach clinic that had opened. They had cooked an actual dinner, and even bought her a gift; a beautiful pink and white baby doll.

It was the kind that had a stuffed cloth body, but soft vinyl arms, legs, and head. The thumbs stuck out just a bit, so the baby could suck the pacifier, the bottle, or her thumb. There was a pink velvet blanket with a white, embroidered puppy in the corner, too. Everything about her had been soft and girlish. Bebe had been thrilled. She had been out the whole day, morning to night. No one else had had a chance to experience any of it, though she had regaled them all with the delights of the day for months afterwards, and still did every so often when something brought up the memory of it.

That was before Bitty had learned how to listen for the others. She'd been on her own before that. Or it had felt that way. She couldn't remember much from when she was younger. Only snatches and bits here and there. But it had always felt lonely.

Usually she would end up sitting in the corner, her head down, trying to keep out of her parents' way and nursing the latest bruises and injuries she'd earned from her bad behavior. She didn't dare try to play for fear of making too much noise and bothering them. There was certainly nothing to read, and no one to play with. It was just her. Always just her.

Until the night she'd been curled up in her bed, nursing her shattered wrist and the ache between her legs after daddy had left. That was when she'd first heard the whisper. She hadn't known what it was back then. At first, she had thought she was dreaming. The voice was soft and kind, and somehow made her feel as though she were being hugged. It was the kind of dream a girl like her never wanted to wake up from.

But she hadn't been sleeping. That had been quite obvious the moment she shifted and her wrist sent a stab of agony up her arm. She was definitely awake.

Her next thought was that she was being haunted. She had seen a ghost movie once when her parents were watching it. It had terrified her so much that she had never got over that fear. But the voice didn't sound like the ghost in the movie, and it didn't make her scared.

So then, what was it?

She had started talking to the voice, learning her name was Sarah, and she was there to be Bitty's friend; to help her. She had been someone Bitty could turn to when she hurt, or was scared; the one to cuddle her—at least mentally—when she couldn't move, the one to sing soft songs to her when she couldn't sleep. She had been the one to introduce the others.

And now, Bitty was almost never alone. No matter how much they disagreed sometimes, or distracted her, or annoyed her once in a while, they were her friends. They were her support. They were her family when she had none.

Right now, however, was one of those times when they all seemed to argue.

'Take the money and run.'

'Oh, Bitty, I want to go back. He's nice. He did our hair so pretty.'

'If you tell him how hard it is, maybe he would help you.'

'He sure likes using you.'

"Just stop. Let me think," Bitty mumbled, rubbing her arms as she stood on the sidewalk, looking up and down the street. She had two choices, as she saw it. She could either take what she had in her purse right now and return to Mack, hopefully for a good reward and a hit to tide her over, or she could buy some lunch and go back. The withdrawals were starting to set in, though. She could feel it. That familiar ache and shakiness was beginning to creep through her little body. She'd need a hit soon.

She had to make a decision.

Chapter Five

* Choice One *

"We should get something to eat before we decide anything for certain," she decided.

The fast food chain down the street promised at least warm—if not nutritious—food for a few bucks, so she headed in that direction. It was a lot harder to be out the way she was dressed in broad daylight, and her cheeks burned as she opened the door and drew stares from patrons and employees alike. It took all her willpower to keep walking to the counter.

'Get out of here. You're drawing too much attention. Get out of here.'

'I'm hungry. Can we get chicken nuggets? Ooohhh, Bitty, can we get the princess toy?'

'If they notice, maybe they'll help us. They could help us.'

"I'm not getting a-"

"Hi, can I help you?" the ambivalent order taker asked, interrupting her thoughts.

Bitty nodded and stepped forward. "Uh, yeah. I'll have a...." She could feel the push a split second before it happened, but it was too late. Bebe stepped up. "...princess toy kid's meal with chicken nuggets and chocolate milk."

'You idiot, Bebe! A kid's meal is hardly any food! We could have got a whole box of chicken nuggets for only a bit more!'

But it was too late. Bebe was already fumbling with the money, trying to clumsily count out the amount.

'Five dollars, Bebe! Just give him the one with the five on it.'

"The five?" she mumbled.

The clerk was giving her a funny look. "$4.73."

"Not five?"

'Ooohhh, Bebe, shut up and give him the one with the five!'

"But-"

'DO IT!'

Obediently, Bebe handed over the $5 bill. The server took the money with another strange look and handed her the change, then gave her the receipt with her order number on it and told her to wait to the side.

'Why can't you just listen!? I told you what to do! All you had to do was listen to me! Why can't you just listen!?'

"I did listen," she mumbled petulantly.

Soon enough, their order was up and Bebe smiled in excitement, nearly skipping as she made her way over to the counter to collect the brightly colored box of food. "I wonder if I got the crown! I hope I got the crown!"

'Don't look right now. Just take the box and go. You can look later.'

"But I want to see–"

'DON'T OPEN IT HERE! GET OUT NOW!'

Bebe took the box with a sullen expression and began walking to the door, trying to open the box as she walked.

"Oh! I got the crown!" she cried in delight, pulling it out of the box and settling it on her head.

Bailey groaned internally. *'You'd better hope no one sees us! No, don't sit down here, you idiot! Take it back to the hotel.'*

"But it'll be cold by then!" Bebe objected.

'Fine. Then at least go sit around the corner.'

"Why can't we go sit inside? It's warm in there and I don't feel very good."

'Cuz we're drawing too much attention already, even without that damn crown on your head making us look like we're nuts.'

"But it's beautiful!"

'Relax, Bailey. She's not hurting anyone, and no one is looking anymore. Just let her have her fun for a change.'

There was an internal 'humph' but Bailey fell silent.

"When can we get the coloring book?" Bebe asked eagerly as she took a bite of a nugget. She wobbled in Bitty's high heels, heading for a drug store on the corner nearby. "They'll have crayons here, right?"

Drawing a few more stares, she entered the store and wandered around until she found the toy aisle with a cry of excitement.

"Oh! Look at the toys! John said we can pick one, right? And coloring stuff. I can't wait to color. Do you think they have a princess coloring book?"

There was a scuffle and a shove internally, but the only sign of this outside was the slightly blank look in her eyes as she stood still in front of the coloring things. A moment later, Sarah released a soft sigh, smiled, and bent over to pick up a coloring book with unicorns and princesses.

"There you go, Bebe. This one is good. You can color it when we get back," she said gently, then grabbed a box of crayons. On the opposite side of the aisle was an entire shelf dedicated to stuffed animals with silky soft fur and oversized, sparkly eyes. The gentle smile grew and she reached for a white and pink stuffed unicorn. "How's this?"

'Oh yes, Sarah! Yes! I love that one!'

Sarah took the three items to the check-out and paid for them quickly, then made her way out of the store and back to the hotel to wait for John.

~ Choice Two ~

"Fine, let's go," Bitty said finally. There was a pang of sadness in her heart as she glanced back over her shoulder in the direction of the hotel. It had been nice while it lasted, but it obviously couldn't be forever. It was just setting herself up for disappointment if she stayed there. It had to end some time, so it may as well be now, before she got attached and it was harder.

'Finally, a smart choice.'

"Shut up, Bailey," she snapped, ducking her head and stalking down the sidewalk. "How do we even get back, anyway?"

'Take the bus. Or find another john to drop you off when he's done with you.'

"I like the first suggestion better."

'Can't we get something to eat first, Bitty? I'm so hungry.'

Bitty sighed and eyed the fast food place, then shook her head. "Nah. It's better to take the money to Mack. He'll be happy. I'm sure he'll give us something good when we get back. Besides, I already have to use some of the money for the bus anyway."

'Please, Bitty?'

"No, Bebe. Shut up! I'm not blowing the money on food. It's better to give it to Mack and make him happy."

A police car came down the street and Bitty ducked quickly into the drug store on the corner, hiding until it was well out of sight.

'Oh! Bitty! Can we get the coloring stuff? Please? He said we were supposed to get coloring stuff! It's right over there!'

"We're not spending the money, Bebe. Shut up," Bitty mumbled, slipping back out of the store and onto the sidewalk again. She winced as Bebe began to cry.

She hated it when the little girl did that. It made her feel horrible. She could feel how badly Bebe wanted the childish play things. And honestly, so did she. It was hard to remember sometimes that she was only fourteen. She'd never really felt like a child. But it didn't matter. She couldn't spend the money. It had to go to Mack, no matter how badly any of them wanted the lovely things.

Eventually, Sarah swept Bebe towards the back to cuddle her and Bitty was left with peace and quiet for a while as she waited for the bus in the cold. She couldn't help wondering if she was making the right decision.

Bailey, of course, would say she was. It was always best to placate the one with the big fists, though sometimes she didn't seem to follow that rule completely. But it had been nice with John. Well, most of the time. He'd had his moments, just like the rest, but in between, it had been wonderful. She reached up and gently fingered the braid in her hair just as the bus came.

With a sigh, she climbed on and paid her fare for the bus, then sank down in the first seat she came to and stared out the window. She could vaguely hear Bebe still crying in the back of her mind, but she shoved it away, trying not to cry herself.

Once they reached the stop closest to Mack's house, she slunk off the bus and waited for it to leave before trudging down the street. Again, the familiar feeling of fear and nervousness gripped her as she climbed the steps and opened the door. The drug stink seemed worse now after the extended break in the hotel and the fresh air, and she gagged on it as she entered. It was quiet. Everyone was probably sleeping. She desperately hoped someone would be awake who could give her the hit she needed.

Tentatively, she peered into the couple of rooms Mack usually used. Her heart sank when she saw him. He was sleeping, cuddling that new girl the way John had cuddled her the night before.

'Don't.'

"Don't what?" Bitty whispered.

'Don't start thinking about that. It's finished. Just focus on now.'

"He's sleeping. How am I gonna get my hit? I need it bad, Bailey."

"Talking to yourself again, Little Bit?"

The snide remark made her jump and Bitty turned quickly to find one of the older girls smirking at her, cigarette between her fingers, track marks burning on her arm. Jess was the kind of girl that showed the hardship of her life on her face. She'd probably been pretty once. But life has a tendency to take the prettiest faces and destroy them in the worst way. The hair that had most likely been thick, tightly curled or braided, and full was now stringy, thin, and dull. It framed an equally thin and dull face. Jess's eyes were so sunken into her head she almost looked like a skull now. Even in the past year she had changed a lot from what she was when Bitty first met her. She'd gone on to harder stuff now. It showed.

Bitty immediately looked away and shrugged. "I just... thought..."

"That's a dangerous thing, thinking. Better not to. It just makes trouble. He was looking for you."

Bitty glanced back in the room fearfully, then back at the other girl. "He.... he was...?"

The girl nodded, the smirk growing. "He was pretty pissed. I guess he had a client lined up and you weren't here. You're gonna get it when he wakes up."

Bitty paled instantly. "Jess, please... can you explain that I was working? Please? He'll listen to you."

Jess scoffed and took a drag before blowing it in Bitty's face. "And how the hell do I know you were working? He looked at your spot and you weren't there. If you were working, where were you?"

"I went to a hotel with a guy. He paid me for the whole night. I was working. Honest. Please tell him, Jess. Please?"

"Let me see the money, then. Prove it."

'Don't do it. Don't let her see it, Bitty. Don't do it. It's a bad idea. Bitty, DON'T DO IT!'

She ignored Bailey and pulled out the wad of hundreds, as well as the majority of the $40 and the hotel keycard. Jess actually looked surprised, then smiled and took the wad, fingering through as she counted.

"Wow. You were telling the truth. That's a good haul."

Bitty nodded and held her hand out for the money again. "I told you. So please, will you explain when he wakes up? He listens to you. Please?"

Jess chuckled, took a drag of her cigarette, then folded the stack of bills and tucked it into her bra. "Now, why would I do that, Little Bit? What's in it for me? Why should I risk getting my ass beat for you? I don't think so." She took another long drag and exhaled into Bitty's horrified, devastated, bruised little face, laughing cruelly. "One of these days you'll learn. Maybe today." She turned and left the stunned girl standing where she was in the dark hallway, tears of fear and devastation coursing down her cheeks.

For once, thankfully, Bailey kept her opinion to herself.

Chapter Six

* Choice One *

Once they reached the hotel again, Sarah stepped back and let Bebe out again. The child was thrilled to be allowed out and immediately turned on the tv to watch kid shows while she ate the rest of her meal. Once she'd finished her food, she sat curled on the couch with her new stuffed animal clutched to her chest. After several shows, she got bored and pulled the coloring book and crayons out, tossing the bag on the floor.

'You'd better pick that up before he gets back and sees you made a mess or you'll get your ass beat.'

"I will."

For the next hour, Bebe knelt in front of the coffee table, coloring peacefully while cartoons and preschool programs ran in the background. Every so often, she would get distracted and watch the show for a while, then go back to her coloring with renewed vigor. It felt like a dream. Bebe was best at not noticing withdrawals until they got really bad. Then she was the worst because she whined and fussed the whole time.

In fact, apart from the withdrawals, all of them were beginning to relax for the first time that anyone could remember. They were warm, safe, full, and comfortable. It was a feeling like no other.

"Why do you hate Mommy and Daddy?" Bebe asked out of the blue.

'What?'

"Why do you hate Mommy and Daddy, Bailey?" she repeated.

'Because they're cruel, horrible bastards. That's why.'

Bebe froze, her crayon hovering over the paper. "Why did you say that?" Tears were filling her eyes as she closed them to focus on the conversation.

'Because they are. They've done nothing but hurt us forever.'

"Nu-uh. They cuddled me and kissed me. Daddy loved me best and he always gave me hugs and kisses. And Mommy read me stories and got me cookies for Christmas. I love them."

'You don't know shit, Bebe. The only reason your precious daddy gave you hugs and kisses was cuz he was–'

'Bailey! That's enough. Let her have her memories. She has every right to them. She deserves them. At least one of us should.'

'Shut up, Sarah. She should know the truth about them.'

'Leave it, Bailey. I mean it. Let her be. It doesn't hurt anything to let her remember what she remembers.'

There was an angry huff and Bailey seemed to storm away, disappearing into darkness.

Bebe wiped her cheek gently where a tear had trickled out from under her closed eyelids. "Why is she so mean?" she whimpered.

'She doesn't mean to be, Bebe. She's not trying to be mean to you. She's just… angry.'

"Angry about what?"

'Angry at everyone and everything. She tries to keep us safe, in her own way, and her way is an angry way. She loves you, though. Let's see your coloring.'

Bebe perked up, wiped her cheek again, and spread the coloring book page more flat, gazing down at it happily. "It's the best job I ever did!" she said proudly.

Sarah smiled inwardly, looking past the streaks extending beyond the lines, the purple trees, and the blue hair to the intention behind it.

'It's lovely, Bebe. Nice job.'

"Do you think John will like it?"

There was a derisive snort from somewhere in the back but Sarah nodded slowly, her tone cautious.

'I think he might. But, Bebe… John is going to go soon, you know that, right? He's just here for a little bit. Then we have to leave and go back home.'

"I know," the child assured her, returning to her coloring.

Sarah wasn't so sure, but stayed quiet.

An hour or so later, John returned, bringing with him burgers, fries, and milkshakes.

Bebe jumped up before anyone else could get a handle on her and ran towards him with her coloring book and stuffie.

"John! Look what I got today! I got a unicorn and coloring and crayons and I got a kid's meal and see what it had inside?" She pointed to the plastic crown on her head. "I'm a princess now!"

The man's eyebrows rose in surprise, but a second later he grinned and put the food down to hug her. After sinking onto the couch and pulling her into his lap, he held one side of the coloring book while she held the other, smiling as she showed him all the pictures she'd colored.

"Those are great," he said, rubbing her butt with his other hand. Once she'd shown him the last picture he took the book and set it on the seat beside him, then wrapped his arm around her waist, looking into her shining little face.

"Are you ready to eat now? I brought us the best damn burgers in this town! And chocolate milkshakes! You like milkshakes, right? Of course, you do! All little girls love milkshakes!"

He shifted her off his lap and settled her on the couch, then went to grab the bag and the two drinks.

"Alright, here you go, baby. And what does Daddy's girl feel like watching while we eat?"

Bebe stared at him in utter adoration. "I don't mind."

"Well, let's see what's on for little girls, shall we?" He picked up the remote and began surfing, skipping over things with adult themes and eventually settling on an animated movie which was just starting. "Oh, this one is good. Have you seen it?"

She smiled and shook her head with a sniff, wiping at her suddenly runny nose as she began to eat. "Oh! I heard this song once!" she exclaimed.

He smiled at her as she wiggled on the seat beside him. The tiredness that had been lining his face when he picked her up the previous night seemed to fade, replaced by a warm light that made him look younger somehow.

After they had both eaten, he pulled her close against him and cuddled her as they watched, stroking her hair every so often. Eventually, he moved her onto the floor in front of him and pulled the ribbon from the bottom of the braid, gently loosening it and finger combing it out with his hands, massaging her head as he did so.

Her little body began to go limp and she rested her head on his knee while he played with her hair, yawning every so often. With her back to him, she missed the smile that graced his features every time she did.

Once the movie finished, he kissed the top of her head and hugged her from behind. "How about we take a shower and get to bed, babygirl?"

Bebe nodded tiredly, beginning to feel the achiness now that the drugs were working their way out of her system. "K." She pushed up from where she sat and stretched, the movement lifting her crop top and making the light catch in her belly ring.

He frowned, slightly. "We should get you some clothes. Warmer ones."

She looked at the floor with a shrug. "Mack said we don't need any more clothes."

"Who's Mack?"

"Mack takes care of us," Bebe said innocently.

"Oh? And what does Mack do to take care of you?" he asked carefully, standing up and taking her hand to lead her to the bathroom.

"Oh, he lets us sleep in his house and sometimes he gives us food when we're good and he gives me medicine to make me feel good," she chattered as he undressed her. "I wish I had some of the medicine now. I don't feel so good."

"How about a bath tonight?" he asked as he plugged the drain. He smiled when she nodded, then began running the water.

"Who's we?" came the gentle question.

'Shut up, Bebe! Stop talking! Stop talking right now! Let Bitty out!'

"Oh, Bitty and Bailey and Jay and Scarlett and everyone," Bebe replied, watching the water fill the tub, her hands resting on the sides as she leaned over to see the swirling liquid better.

"That's a lot of friends you have." He stepped into the tub and took her hand, helping her in before he sat down and settled her between his legs, her back resting against his chest.

She relaxed against him, watching the water get higher and wiggling her toes under the running faucet with an innocent giggle as it tickled.

John cupped his hand and scooped up some of the warm water, letting it trickle down over her chest, his cheek resting on the top of her head.

"What's the medicine he gives you to make you feel good?" came the question in a carefully neutral voice.

'BEBE! SHUT UP! DON'T ANSWER THAT! SHUT UP AND LET BITTY OUT RIGHT NOW! BEBE! LISTEN TO ME!'

"Oh, I don't know. It's sparkly sort of, but it hurts to go in. I don't like that part. I hate the needles. But he said it makes stuff better and we get it when we're good. It feels nice after the prick."

Innocent little Bebe missed the tension in his voice when he spoke next.

"I see. And… do you ask him for the medicine?"

She shook her head, ignoring the impassioned pleas of the others inside. "No. He just puts it in me. I cry sometimes. But he gets mad when I cry so Bitty comes and then Sarah gives me hugs."

There was silence as he turned the water off and stroked his hands over her slowly, getting her body wet with the warm water.

"I like your hugs," she announced, tilting her head backwards to look up at him upside down with an innocent little smile on her bruised face.

He smiled back and stroked her hair away from her face. "I like giving you hugs, babygirl."

She smiled more brightly and looked forward again with a sigh and closed her eyes, resting her head back against his chest. The warm water was easing some of the growing symptoms.

He kissed the top of her head, then reached for the soap. As he lathered it, he spoke again. "Babygirl, is Mack your Daddy?"

She shook her head. "No. We went away from Mommy and Daddy. I didn't want to, but Bailey said we had to or she would get mad and do bad things."

"Oh, I see. So, Bailey is your sister?"

"No. Bailey is just… Bailey."

"Does she live with you?"

"Yup."

"I see."

'Bebe, don't say anything else. Don't speak to him about this. Please. Bebe, honey, please listen. Don't tell him. Let Bitty out. Please?'

"Does Bailey know you're here with me? That you're safe? Or will she worry about you?"

She nodded. "Of course she knows. She's…"

For a moment, Bebe gazed blankly at the faucet, then her body hunched up a little bit and she drew into herself with a shrug.

"She knows," Bitty replied softly, ignoring the pitiful cries of disappointment in her head as Bebe tried to push back out to talk to her 'new daddy'. This was getting dangerous. They couldn't afford to get attached, especially not Bebe. If she got attached, she would be devastated when they had to leave.

"Do you need to call her? Let her know where you are?"

Bitty shook her head in silence.

"What's wrong, babygirl?"

"Nothing."

"I see. Well, if there is, you can tell me, okay? I won't be mad."

She nodded in silence and he didn't ask any more questions. When he had washed her and himself, he helped her stand up and reached for the towels, wrapping her in one before wrapping one around himself. Once again, he helped her out of the tub and dried her gently, then combed the tangles from her hair and led her to the bed.

"Did you have a good day, babygirl?" he whispered, pulling her back against his front and stroking her hair.

She nodded, actually honest about it. She *had* had a good day. The first one in… forever. She felt him smile behind her and he kissed the top of her head.

"Good. I'm glad. Sleep tight, babygirl."

She stared at the wall across from her in the darkness, listening to Bebe cry to be let out and cuddled, Bailey screaming that they should run while he was sleeping, Sarah trying to soothe the sobbing child, and Jay whispering that John could help them. Scarlett was either sleeping, or simply had nothing to say. After a while, her eyes closed and she drifted off to sleep, once again warm, clean, and wrapped safely in big, strong arms that had yet to hit her.

~ Choice Two ~

Bitty stood for a long time in the stinking, dingy hallway outside Mack's room, reeling in shock and horror. What had just happened? $535 had just disappeared in the blink of an eye, replaced by absolutely certain punishment. What was she going to do now? Tears trickled down her bruised cheeks and she didn't even bother to wipe them away. It was almost as if moving would somehow make something happen, and by standing still, she could keep time from moving forward and the inevitable happening. But the inevitable did happen. Mack began to wake up. Bitty peered into the doorway in a panic.

'Run. Run for it now. Just leave. Go back to John and leave forever.'

'Don't be a fucking moron. Stay there. Explain. How is Jess gonna explain having all that extra money? If you run, he'll only punish you worse when he catches you.'

Before she could really even process the suggestions, he had opened his eyes and spotted her. With a sleepy growl he glared at her. "What do you want? Why the hell are you standing there staring at me sleeping?"

Bitty shrank into herself even more and began to stammer, "I-I just.... I was.... coming....I was looking for you.... to..... I had some....I-I got.... money...."

"Then give it to me and get the fuck out!"

She flinched when he yelled, amazed that the girl next to him hadn't woken up. Obviously, yelling didn't mean pain and danger to her, so it didn't register. Yet. It would soon enough. "I-I don't..... it's not.... I was... J-Jess..... I.....sh-showed..... I asked..."

"Would you fucking speak like a normal human being? Or are you too stupid to make a complete sentence?"

"Jess took it," she mumbled, hunching up.

"Jess took what?"

"The money."

"JESS!" he yelled. This time the girl beside him did wake up, stretching and yawning, then cuddling him with a smile. He smiled down at her the way he had smiled at Bitty when he first drew her into his fucked up web of destruction and pain. Bitty looked away, trying not to be sick. She was so hungry, and withdrawals were beginning to set in hard. Mack turned to the girl in the bed and stroked her side. "Why don't you get dressed and go wait for me in the kitchen. I have to talk to these two."

The girl nodded and glanced at Bitty in embarrassment, holding the covers over her naked body. With an eye roll the other girl never saw, Mack looked at Bitty. "Turn around so she can get dressed. She doesn't need your filthy eyes on her."

Bitty shrank back and turned around outside the room, tears still trickling down her cheeks. The girl wouldn't be left with any modesty once he was done with her and a pang of sympathy tugged at her heart, but Bailey virtually slapped her internally.

'That's on her. She chose to come here. She can deal with the consequences herself. If she's stupid enough to get sucked into it when she can plainly see what happens, then that's her fault.'

'Bailey... WE got tricked. Don't you remember when he–'

'Shut the fuck up, Sarah. I don't need you being a holy bitch right now.'

'I'm just saying, she doesn't understand. We didn't. We were exactly the same.'

'Fuck off.'

A moment later, the girl slipped out of the room with a look that clearly said what she thought of Bitty.

"Get in here!" Mack called brusquely.

Bitty jumped and obeyed, slipping into the room, Jess coming up behind her with a smug, self satisfied, and perfectly self-assured look on her thin face.

He was sitting up in bed, lighting a cigarette and loading a rig. That surprised Bitty, since Mack had always said he didn't touch the stuff. He sold it, he pushed it on his girls, but he didn't put it in his own body. He was too good for that. He made that perfectly clear. He was worth more than they were. When he was done, he looked up at both girls with an idle, unconcerned look.

"Now, why the hell did I wake up to find your ugly mug staring at me?"

"I.... I-I came to.... g-give you the money..... from..... that I.... I got last night...."

"Then give it to me."

"I-I told you.... J-Jess took it...." she whispered, hunching up in fear.

Mack looked at her for a long moment, then at Jess. "Is that true? She brought me money and you took it?"

Jess shook her head. "Of course not. You know what she's like. She's desperate. She's trying to get mine so she doesn't get her ass whooped for slacking all day."

Bitty stared at her in devastation, but there was very little surprise. She had known it was coming the moment Jess didn't hand back the money. There was no way she was going to admit to stealing it. The tears increased as she turned back to Mack, her eyes pleading with him.

"I swear, Mack. I made money last night. A lot. He gave me $500, plus another $35! I came to give it to you but Jess asked to see it and she didn't give it back."

Mack took a long drag and looked from one to the other. "So, where is it?"

Bitty looked from him to Jess expectantly.

Jess pulled out the wad of cash and handed it to him. "She saw me counting it and she's trying to steal it."

Mack flipped through the stack. "There's $500, not $535."

Bitty looked at Jess in shock.

"You must have seen her counting it wrong. I don't tolerate liars, Bitty. You should know that by now."

Bitty turned back to him, shaking her head desperately. "I'm not lying, Mack! I'm not. I swear! Please believe me. She took *my* money! She's not even giving you all of it!"

The tone of his voice was as cold as steel. "Bitty, admit you're lying and I might go a little easier on you, this time."

Bitty couldn't help it. She couldn't admit to something she hadn't done. She shook her head wildly. "I'm not lying, Mack! I swear. She's the one lying. I'm telling you–"

WHACK

Bitty cried out as his fist knocked her to the floor.

"I gave you a chance to tell the truth, Bitty. You seem to like punishment. Do you like punishment, Bitty?"

She curled up on the floor, holding her head and shaking it. "No. Please, Mack. I'm sorry."

"It's too late now," he growled, a moment before his fist and foot began to inflict her punishment on her for 'lying'.

Jess stood watching, a smirk on her face, absolutely no guilt for what she'd done to the young girl who had made the mistake of trusting her.

When the blows finally stopped raining down, Bitty lay sobbing weakly on the floor, limp and almost unconscious. Every nerve of her body felt like it was on fire. She couldn't think about anything except not throwing up on the floor at his feet. He'd probably kill her for that.

"You did good, Jess," he said calmly, sitting down again as if he hadn't just beaten a child to the brink of unconsciousness. Holding the rig out to her, he nodded. "You earned this. Enjoy."

Jess took the needle with a self-satisfied smile.

"Since you seemed to have such an easy time making $500, you can make $600 tonight," he continued smoothly, taking a drag of his cigarette, watching her closely.

Jess froze in shock. "Wha.... Bu...."

His eyebrow rose. "Is that going to be a problem? You seemed to come by this $500 easily enough. $600 tonight."

Jess shook her head, her face white now as she stammered, "N–no. No problem.... I–I can do that..."

"Then you'd better get to work, huh?" he remarked casually.

She nodded and left, her hands trembling now.

If Bitty could have smiled, she would have. He obviously knew she'd been telling the truth. He'd just wanted to beat someone. Bitty was easier to beat on than the older, bigger girl. But Jess wouldn't be able to make $600 tonight. Not in this weather. She'd get her beating later anyway. With that thought, Bitty drifted off into the welcoming blackness that promised to swallow the pain and horror for at least a little while.

Chapter Seven

~ Choice Two ~

It could have been a few minutes or a few hours later, but eventually, Bitty woke up to a dark room. She was still on the floor where she'd fallen, but someone had put a blanket over her. Vaguely, she wondered if it had been Mack in a rare moment of kindness. Picking her up off the floor, or even not beating her for nothing would have been too much to ask, but a blanket might have been him.

She tried to open her eyes, but her right eye wouldn't open. Probably swollen too much, she thought. With a moan of pain, she uncurled from the position she'd been in since her beating. Every part of her ached. It wasn't the worst beating she'd ever had, but it always felt like it each time.

"Hey," came the whisper in the dark.

Bitty flinched in fear and tried to see through the near pitch black of the room. "Wha...."

"It's Katie," came the whisper.

Bitty tried to recall someone named Katie, but couldn't. Not that she knew all the girls by name. Not everyone was back at the same time, and even if they were, it's not like they socialized or anything. "Who...?" she mumbled finally.

"I.... I was with Mack last night..."

'The new girl. Must be the new girl's name.'

"Oh," Bitty murmured. Was it Katie who had put the blanket on her, then?

"Are.... are you okay...?"

"Just fine," Bitty mumbled, trying to sit up and failing miserably.

"I–I'm sorry...." Katie whispered. "Is he.... Is he always like this?"

Bitty froze uncertainly. Should she tell the girl the truth and give her a chance to realize and run before it was too late?

'Fuck that. If he gets a new girl, then maybe he'll lay off you for a while.'

'Bailey! That is cruel, selfish, and more than a little sociopathic!'

'What the fuck does that mean?'

'It means not caring about other people.'

'Then why not just say that instead of using your big, fancy fucking words?'

Bitty tried to ignore the bickering inside and pay attention to the girl who was slowly coming into focus in the dim room. "Yeah. Always. Except when you're new. When you're new, he's.... so different."

"Different how?"

"Nice. Kind. He made me feel.... special. Like he was the only one who cared about me in the whole world."

"But.... but how can he change so much...?" Katie asked in fearful confusion.

Bitty shrugged and instantly regretted it. "I dunno. He just.... does. He changed with me—started sticking needles in me and hitting me and making me fuck people so he can have the money."

Katie drew in a sharp breath.

"He's done it with two other girls after he stopped being nice to me. You're the third one since me." There was silence for a long moment as Bitty tried to sit up again.

"Why do you stay?" she whispered finally.

"What?"

"Why do you stay here with him if he does this to you?"

"Cuz he's all I have," came the simple reply. There was another long silence as Bitty dabbed at the dried blood on her face, wincing and hissing when it stung. She would have a very hard time meeting her quota looking like this.

"Thanks," Katie said eventually, then left her alone in the dark. It was the last time Bitty ever saw her.

With a whimper of pain, Bitty pushed herself shakily to her feet, feeling to see if anything was broken. Maybe a rib or two? She wasn't entirely sure what was old pain and what was new. Did it really matter anyway? Probably not. She felt sick and weak, it hurt to breathe, she was jonesing, and she was dizzy. Probably a concussion. Though when was the last time she'd eaten?

'It was pizza with John.'

'Like John was his real name.'

'That's completely beside the point, Bailey. We weren't talking about him. We were talking about when we ate.'

"Maybe there's something in the kitchen I could eat..."

'Doubtful. If there is, it's probably off limits.'

'Bitty, can't we go back to that nice lady with the cookies? She said we can come back any time.'

'Don't be a moron. We can't go back there! She'll call the cops on us. She'll try to 'help' us, and we'll end up in jail for prostitution. We can't ever go back.'

Bailey was right, of course. They couldn't go back. Bitty sighed when Bebe's tears started again and Sarah went off to cuddle the crying child. Bitty could have done with one too, but there wasn't anyone to give that to her. Not for real, anyway.

There was, of course, no food she was allowed in the kitchen. Plenty of pots cooking away, but none of them edible—all of them dangerous. Bitty steered clear as she searched for a few minutes for something marked 'girls', then gave up and left.

'I'm hungry, Bitty.'

"Me too," Bitty mumbled as she trudged slowly and weakly down the hallway to the door. She had to work. Maybe that way she could get some food or something. Maybe she'd find someone like John who would buy her dinner. It was a lot to hope for, but it was something to focus on. It was probably all that kept her body moving as she wandered out onto the cold, dark street in search of work.

Once again, the cold hurt some parts and helped others, but she was shivering violently soon enough. She wanted to lie down and sleep so badly. Tears trickled silently down her cheeks, unnoticed in the frigid air. She could hardly feel the parts of her body that didn't hurt. It would have been better the other way around, but that was not the way the world worked. The pain always overrode everything else.

After half an hour, a car pulled up and she wandered over lethargically to try to sell herself. But one look at her face and the guy drove off without another word. More tears fell as she went back up on the sidewalk to wait for the next passerby who might slow down enough for her to approach. Her hopes weren't high.

Another forty-five minutes passed before a sedan pulled up. This one at least barely glanced at her face, his eyes on the rest of her instead. Trying to keep the disgust off her face when he said what he wanted, Bitty nodded and climbed gingerly into the front seat for another nightmare night on the job.

Chapter Eight

* Choice One *

Bitty woke up slowly, then more quickly when she realized she was alone. For a moment, she lay there quite still, listening. The room seemed empty. Sitting up and fighting the nausea of withdrawals, she peered into the other part of the room. It certainly was empty, and the bathroom door was open and empty as well. A sudden panic gripped her chest. What if he'd gone and left her without saying goodbye?

'What the fuck does that matter? You don't need goodbyes. But if he left without paying that other $700, then you can panic. Cuz I don't want to go crawling back to Mack with only $500 to show for the last two and a half days. Don't go getting attached to him. You can't expect anything to last.'

"I'm not expecting something to last," Bitty said with a little pout and a lot of defensiveness in her voice; a sure sign Bailey had hit a nerve. "I'm just thinking about the money."

There was a derisive snort inside, but Bitty tried to ignore it. A feeling of dread still gripped her as she got out of bed, but a second later she relaxed. His suitcase was still tucked in the corner. The relief that washed over her was ridiculous, but once again, she told herself it was because he hadn't left without paying her. Though, when she couldn't find her clothes, she began to worry again.

For lack of anything better to wear, she pulled on one of his shirts and buttoned it up moments before she heard the door beep and open. John came in with another takeout bag in one hand, a carryout tray with two cups on it in the other. She shot him a guilty expression when he paused and his eyes ran over her in his shirt.

"I'm sorry. I couldn't find my clothes and I–" she began unbuttoning the shirt quickly. "I'm sorry. I should have just waited. I'm sorry."

He put the things on the table and hurried over, grabbing her hands and keeping her from unbuttoning any further. "No. Don't take it off. You look…. amazing." He began buttoning the shirt again, then rested his hands on her shoulders for a moment, just looking at her.

Bitty found her cheeks flushing self consciously and she looked down at his chest shyly. "I… didn't mean to just–"

"Shhh, it's fine babygirl. I love that you're wearing my things."

"You do?" she asked in surprise, looking up at him again.

He nodded and stroked her cheek. "I do. You look beautiful. And so sexy."

She flushed and looked down at his chest again with a little nod.

"Can Daddy have you before breakfast?"

She nodded obediently and began unbuttoning.

He stopped her again. "Leave my shirt on." He kissed her and led her to the bed, pulling his pants down and revealing his already hard length.

She lay down and spread her legs, and he smiled, fingering her gently before lowering himself onto her and pushing inside with a groan. She tried not to wince, but she couldn't help it. He was so big in her little body that it hurt, even though he was being gentle.

But he *was* being gentle, which surprised her again. He kissed her, stroked her hair and cheek, and moved slowly and tenderly until he moaned in satisfaction and filled her again. When he finished, he pulled out of her and cuddled her for a bit, stroking her hair and smiling happily.

After a few minutes, he sighed and leaned back slightly to look at her. "Are you hungry, babygirl? I brought some breakfast. I've gotta head to another meeting soon, but I figured I'd get you something first."

She nodded and sat up too, following him to the table where he'd put everything. "Um… I couldn't find my clothes."

"Oh, yeah. I had them sent out to be cleaned. They should be back in a couple of hours."

"A couple of…" she trailed off uncertainly.

He seemed to notice her anxious tone and cocked his head. "Was that not okay? They were pretty… ripe. I figured you'd like some clean ones. I also thought that maybe you'd want to go shopping for some new clothes later."

She stared at him. "Later?"

"Well, once my meeting is over. It shouldn't be as long as yesterday, and then we can have the afternoon to ourselves. I can take you shopping and get you some warmer clothes."

"But…"

'Get the fuck out of here, Bitty. Do it. The second he leaves for that meeting, just grab what you can get and leave. He's being too weird. Just get out. Now.'

'Oh, please can we go shopping, Bitty? I'm so cold all the time. I want some warm clothes. Please, Bitty?'

'He's real nice. Can't we ask him to help us? I bet he'll help us. Maybe we can live with him now. Then we don't have to go back to Mack.'

'It does seem a little strange…'

'Why? He fucks good. He's hot. He's nice. What's there to think about? Stay as long as you can.'

He was watching her expectantly.

"Uh, well…I–I should get back and… hand in my money…." she mumbled without looking at him.

There was silence for a moment until he reached out and stroked her cheek. The bruises were beginning to fade to blackish yellow now. "How much of it does he take, babygirl?"

She glanced up at him, then back down with a shrug.

"He takes it all, doesn't he? He probably never gives you a cent, does he?" She shrugged and he sighed. "Why do you go back? There's shelters, even if you don't want to go home. It would be a much better life."

She stared blankly at him for a moment as a scuffle ensued inside, then suddenly stood up, her eyes on fire. "You don't know anything about it. You live in your own little world where everything is perfect and you fuck little girls. Well I'm not gonna sit here and have you tell me I'm doing wrong! I'm doing the best I can and you don't get to tell me it's not good enough!"

John sat staring at her in shock, his jaw just about in his lap as she ranted.

'Bailey, sit down! Let me out! I can handle it! Please, Bailey. He's not doing anything bad. Please? You're going to ruin everything! Bailey, just let me-'

"No, Sarah! I'm not letting you handle it! I'm done with this sick fuck! We're leaving!"

'Bailey, calm down. Take a deep breath and just sit back down. We should eat before we make any decisions. If you still want to leave after that, we can discuss it calmly.'

"Shut up. I'm in charge now!"

"I'm sorry I upset you. I won't do it again. Let's just eat and we can figure out what to do afterwards."

Bailey glared at him for a long moment, then plopped down on the couch again. This time, she moved to the opposite end and glowered at her food as she ate, her body tense and alert, as if she was ready to jump up and run away at the slightest provocation.

John wisely stayed quiet, letting her eat in peace and silence, though he watched her with interest out of the corner of his eye. When he finished his own meal, he stood up slowly and got his wallet out. Equally slowly, he placed seven $100 bills on the table in front of her and stepped back.

Bailey looked up at him warily. "That's mine?"

John nodded. "For staying last night. Like I promised. Your clothes will be ready in a couple of hours. They're paid for." He fell silent and gazed at her sadly. "I understand if you want to leave. Or feel you have to. But I want you to know, you can stay again tonight. I'll be back around 3:00. If you're still here when I get back, we can go get you some new clothes and find a way to help you. If not..." He sighed and offered her a sad smile. "Well, I'll understand. It's been a pleasure, Bitty."

Bailey frowned, tempted to say that wasn't her name, but the shock of discovering he had remembered the name Bitty had given him was enough to shut her up. Most guys didn't remember or care. And she had figured he was one of them, since he had only ever called her 'babygirl' since they'd met. For a moment, she was speechless. In that moment, Bitty was able to wrest control once more.

Her body slumped slightly and her shoulders curled forward a little, her head falling to a submissive position as usual. She missed the curious look that crossed his face.

"I have to go now. I hope I'll see you later."

She nodded, glancing up briefly when he took his coat. She couldn't bring herself to say goodbye. Not a proper, meaningful one like she wanted to. Goodbyes were for people you cared about. Goodbyes were for weak people.

So why did it hurt so much to stay silent?

'Wait a few minutes, then take the money and whatever else you can grab and leave.'

"Shut up, Bailey. Leave me alone."

'I *will* not *leave you alone. You're too weak to make it without me. I'm the only reason we're alive!'*

Bitty stared at the remnants of her breakfast, then burst into tears. For a minute, she lay curled up on the couch, crying for a reason she didn't understand.

'Oh, what the hell is your problem now? You can't seriously be sad to see him leave? He hurt you! Every time he used you he hurt you! Why do you care?'

'Leave her alone, Bailey. Let her have some time.'

There was an angry huff and Bailey stormed off to the back once more, leaving Bitty to cry until she couldn't cry anymore. When she was done, she sat up and wiped her eyes with a sniffle. Bailey was right. She couldn't stay any longer. She'd already be in trouble for staying away this long, money or no money. Mack would be furious with her. If she stayed away any longer, he'd be angrier than she'd probably ever seen him.

'Let's go.'

Bitty nodded and stood up, then sat down. "But my clothes are gone."

'Oh, yes. I forgot. Well, I suppose we just wait until they get brought back. Then we go.'

Bitty nodded again and sank down on the couch again. "I wish we didn't have to go."

'I know. But what would we really be able to expect? He's not even from here. He's living in a hotel room while he's at a conference. What about when he goes home? We'd be alone then, anyway. At least this way it's on our terms. Sometimes Bailey is right. She may go about it the wrong way, but she has our best interests in mind.'

"I know," Bitty murmured softly, wiping her eyes again. "I just…"

'I know. Me too.'

Neither of them mentioned that they hadn't needed or really even thought about a hit since he'd picked them up…

~ Choice Two ~

Bitty woke up with a whimper of pain. The floor was cold, hard, and filthy. The dirty mattress she'd been 'given' had been given to someone else, along with her blanket. It had been a horrible night. The three clients she'd managed to find hadn't covered her quota. By some miracle, Mack hadn't beaten her for it. He had obviously used his energy and satisfied his desire to hurt on Jess. She had not, of course, reached the $600 he had set her after she claimed Bitty's money as hers, as Mack had obviously known she wouldn't, and her screams and pleas had been audible throughout the house.

Bitty felt a little guilty about that, but she really had brought it on herself. If she hadn't stolen Bitty's money, she wouldn't have been in that position. The older girl still hadn't woken up. It had been hours. Bitty had even gone over to her and checked to make sure she was alive. She was, if barely. But Bitty had been so tired that she had crawled into a corner and gone to sleep herself. Jess was still passed out on the floor, though she'd been pushed or dragged off to one side by someone. The dark mark of her blood where she'd been lying turned Bitty's stomach and she looked away. It didn't do to think about that stuff, especially on an empty stomach. She hadn't been lucky enough to find anyone who would buy her dinner, so John's pizza two days ago was the last thing she'd eaten.

With another whimper of pain, Bitty pushed to her feet and slowly wandered off to see if Mack was in a good enough mood to ask for food. Surprisingly, he wasn't with that other girl, whatever her name was. Katie? He was alone, watching TV. Bitty stood on the threshold for a moment, trying to gauge his mood, then stepped in and approached him slowly.

"M–Mack?" she whispered, her head down.

"What do you want?" he growled without taking his eyes from the screen.

"I.... I'm real hungry, Mack..." she mumbled.

"So?"

She was silent for a long moment, confusion clouding her face. "I-I thought... I hoped you had.... food... or something..."

'Run. Run now. Get out. Get the fuck out right now. RUN!'

But it was too late. Bailey's warning came only a split second before his arm shot out and grabbed her by the throat, squeezing hard and pulling her face towards him. She gripped his wrist, her eyes wide and full of tears and terror.

"Why the fuck should I care about whether you're hungry, you filthy, useless slut. I can't find that bitch Katie! She's fucking run off and I haven't heard from her! Girls don't leave me! Ever! She's gonna fucking pay when I find her!" His fingers tightened around her throat and the fire in his eyes seemed to scream how much he was enjoying that power over her. "You want food, go find some. I don't need your whining!" He threw her across the room and turned back to the TV as if nothing had happened.

Bitty lay on the floor, clutching her throat and trying to keep her tears from disturbing him and earning her another, worse punishment. After a few minutes, she staggered to her feet and left the room. She didn't know what to do. She was so hungry and withdrawing so badly that she felt sick and wobbly. It didn't seem possible to go much longer without at least eating. But what was she supposed to do?

'I'm hungry, Bitty. I'm so hungry.'

'Bitty, let's go to Mildred. She said we can come any time. She has food. She can help us. Let's go there, Bitty.'

'Don't be a stupid fuck, Jay. We can't go there. She'll call the police.'

'She didn't call them last time...'

'Probably only cuz we left in time!'

"Bailey.... I think.... I think we should go back.... I just... can't go any longer. I need to eat so bad, Bailey. Let's go to Mildred."

'Don't you fucking blame me if we end up in jail, then!'

Bitty sniffled, trying to tame her tears as she left the house on unsteady feet, the high heels pinching her cold toes and further hurting her aching back and body. It was dark, cold, and beginning to snow.

'What if she's not home? Or busy?'

No one answered that question. Somehow, it was as if they all knew that if Mildred wasn't home, there were no more chances.

"How far was it? I can't remember which way we went." She seemed to freeze just for a moment, then her shoulders straightened and her head came up almost defiantly.

"I'll get us there. I remember, even if you idiots don't." Bailey set off as quickly as her broken, empty little body could manage.

When they turned the corner a few minutes later, they all breathed a sigh of relief to see the golden aura of lights around the curtains of the building.

'Is this it?'

"Yes," Bailey said, though there was a hint of uncertainty in her voice. Despite that, she squared her shoulders and started up the steps to the front door. Just before she rang the bell, Sarah made her pause.

'Bailey, maybe Bitty should be the one to talk to her first. She's a little less... confrontational. She might give a better impression.'

Bailey was still for a moment, then sighed and let go. As Bitty took control, her shoulders slumped once more and her head lowered as she rang the bell.

'Please answer the door. Please. Please answer.'

"Be quiet, Bebe."

A minute later, the locks on the door clicked and it opened slowly. Mildred looked out, her eyes widening in shock and surprise when she saw Bitty standing on the stoop, shivering violently from cold, the bruises on her face almost glowing in the light against her pale, drawn little face.

"Oh! My dear! Come inside! You look half frozen!" She shut the door and Bitty heard the chain lock slide off, then the door opened again. "Come in. Come in. Let's get you warmed up!"

Bitty couldn't even speak through her chattering teeth. The enveloping warmth threatened to make her pass out. She was suddenly so very tired. When was the last time she'd been warm?

Mildred led her to the couch and wrapped a handmade blanket around her tightly. "I'll be right back. Let me get you something warm to drink."

All Bitty could do was nod, fighting to keep her eyes open. She didn't make it. A minute after Mildred bustled into the kitchen, Bitty's eyes closed and didn't open again, even when Mildred returned with a cup of hot chocolate and a plate of cookies.

Chapter Nine

* Choice One *

Bitty's clothes had been returned with a 'paid' receipt and she dressed slowly. They were clean, probably for the first time since they had been bought, and felt so much better. She smelled good, she looked less gaunt just with the two days she'd spent in the warmth, being cared for and fed. Her bruises were fading without new ones being added to the top, and her hair was less thin and stringy. All in all, she felt better than she'd felt in her entire life.

But she had to go.

Oh, what she would do to stay with John, to live forever as his babygirl; warm, safe, fed, and maybe even loved in a way. But that wasn't practical or realistic. As Bailey had pointed out, they lived in different cities and in very different lives. Cynically, Bailey suggested he was probably even married and maybe even had kids he was imagining when he fucked Bitty. Bitty told her to shut it.

The truth was, she liked John. A lot. Yes, he had been sort of disgusting in the beginning, but he had seemed to change the longer they were together.

'People don't change. You should know that by now. They say they'll change, or they pretend to be something they're not, but they always show themselves for what they are. Look at Mack! He was nice and friendly and everything in the beginning, and now he'd just as soon smash your face in as look at you.'

"Shut up, Bailey," Bitty mumbled, taking the money from the table and tucking it in her little purse with the $500 and the remainder of the $40 he'd given her for lunch and toys.

The toys.

She eyed the stuffed animal and coloring things. She wanted so badly to take them, but how could she? Where would she put them? She had nowhere to keep them. It was just as impossible as staying with John. She sighed and turned away to collect her shoes and leave.

'Bitty! Don't forget the coloring and my stuffie!'

Bitty sighed. "They can't co–"

Mid-sentence, Bitty found herself falling backwards as Bebe shoved her out of the way and scooped up her things, shoving the crayons and coloring book into the plastic bag from the store and tucking the unicorn under her arm.

'Bebe, we can't take them with us! Bebe, please just leave them here.'

"But they're mine! I love them!"

'Bebe, darling. I know you love them, but they'll be safer here. If we take them back to Mack's house, they'll get spoiled. Why don't you leave them here so they can stay safe?'

"But…" She cuddled the unicorn closer to her face, tears filling her eyes. "But I love them, Sarah."

'I know, darling. I know. I'm sorry.'

As the tears spilled from her eyes, Bebe gently set the unicorn down on the coffee table. But instead of leaving, she sat down, pulling the coloring book and crayons from the bag again.

'What are you doing? We have to leave!'

Bebe didn't answer Bailey. Instead, she pulled out some colors and began to fill in one of the pages as carefully as she could, ignoring Bailey's frustrated swears and Sarah's coaxing. When she had finished coloring in the picture, she carefully wrote around the edges of it in her best—though terribly childish—handwriting.

deer jon i haf to go now but i dont want to i like it wif yoo and i miss my yooneecorn plees tak car of her so shee dusnt get hert i luv her and i luv yoo good by

When she had finished her writing, she carefully set the picture in the middle of the table with her precious unicorn sitting on top of it, unable to stop the tear that fell on the paper. That made the tears even worse.

"I ruined it! I spoiled the beautiful picture! It's ruined!" she sobbed.

'It's not ruined darling. He'll understand. It's okay. Come here for a cuddle, darling.'

Bebe slipped backwards into Sarah's waiting arms, sobbing her little heart out as Bailey took control.

'Don't. Please, Bailey.'

Bailey pulled her hand back from the little shrine in the center of the table. She had been about to throw them both away, but Sarah's soft plea touched her and she nodded.

"Fine. I don't care anyway." With that, she grabbed her purse and left the room, the heavy hotel door slamming loudly behind her.

They had to use some of the money to pay for a bus to Mack's house, but Bailey felt they still had a good enough amount to give to Mack that he wouldn't be too upset with her once they returned. Still, the bus ride was tense, and her entire body seemed to be tighter than a drum head by the time they reached their stop. Bailey was obviously scared about what their reception would be like, despite her brave words and callous attitude.

When the door opened, she gagged on the stink of drugs she'd forgotten in her days away. Was it really worse? Or did it just seem that way because they'd gotten used to the clean, fresh smell of the hotel? Either way, there wasn't much to be done about it.

T.J. met her when she went looking for Mack. He looked furious. "Where the fuck have you been? Mack's been looking for you. He's pissed. You were supposed to be somewhere. Now I have to drag your sorry, worthless ass down there. Let's go, stupid bitch."

He grabbed her hard by the arm and dragged her to the back door. His car was parked outside, the engine running to keep it warm. She knew it was for him, not her. His car wasn't as fancy as Mack's luxury car, but it was still high end. A wave of anger washed over Bailey when she thought about who paid for that car and how.

She was shoved forcefully into the passenger seat and she buckled automatically as he came around to the other side and got in. Tires squealed as he tore off. Mack must be upset, or T.J. wouldn't be risking his tires like that. Bailey swallowed nervously.

They reached a fancy house in an upscale neighborhood in the suburbs; one of those communities where the houses were practically mansions and people thought they were poor if they only had eight bedrooms or some crap. This might not be so bad. People in this kind of place paid a lot for younger girls, and the last time she'd been brought to one of these houses, it hadn't been bad at all. Maybe he'd even be more gentle than John had been with Bitty.

But that slim hope went out the window when she heard crying coming from inside. The sound of hysterical sobbing grew louder as they went in. It was coming from an upstairs bedroom T.J. was leading her to. When they reached the doorway, T.J. shoved her hard towards the open door. Swallowing hard, Bailey approached and peered inside.

That new girl of Mack's was underneath one of his more frequent and well paying customers while Mack held her down. Her screams, pleas, and sobs reached every room of the house, but it was nothing new. Just a new voice doing it. Bailey clenched her jaw as the others disappeared further inside, leaving her alone.

Served the girl right, really. She had seen how everyone else was treated, hadn't she? Surely she hadn't been that stupid to think that she was that special? But then again, like Sarah had said, they had thought that too, hadn't they, once upon a time. It seemed such a stupid, obvious thing looking back now. But when it was you being cuddled and loved and praised when you longed for that, it was much harder to look ahead at what might lie in store for you. How could she criticize this girl for being exactly the same way they had been?

Bailey clenched her jaw even tighter when the new girl caught her eye with desperation and terror in her face, then turned away to leave.

"Hey! Get your worthless ass in here!"

Bailey flinched and paused for a moment before turning around and stepping into the room, looking at Mack somewhat defiantly. "What?"

Mack glared at her, his fingers tightening on the new girl's arms. "Don't you speak to me like that, you disgusting whore! I own you! Don't fucking forget it!"

Bailey stayed silent, still looking him in the face.

Mack looked right back at her for a long moment before speaking. "Where have you been?"

"Working."

"Working? For three days? Don't fucking lie to me, you stupid bitch."

Bailey mumbled about it only being two days as she fished in her purse and produced the $1,200, holding it out to Mack, her eyes blazing as if daring him to do something to her. She knew she had given him no reason to beat her. She had money enough to cover her quota. She smiled smugly at the look of surprise on his face when he snatched the money and counted it.

That was her mistake.

WHACK

"Wipe that damn look off your face, you worthless slut! You think you're high class now? Well, I've got some people lined up for later who will put you back in your place, stupid bitch."

Bailey clenched her jaw again, refusing to hold her face where he'd backhanded her. She wasn't going to give up that easily.

He glared at her furiously, then hit her again. "You can clean Mr. J. here when he's done with Katie. Then you can go wait for your next client in the room across the hall. You'd better be naked when they get here."

He spat in her face and turned back to the screaming girl, hitting her square in the face. "Shut up you stupid bitch. You'd better get used to spreading your worthless legs after all I've given you. Time to pay me back."

Bailey turned to go but cried out when Mack's fist closed in her hair and yanked her back.

"Oh no, you stay here and watch. She needs to get used to being watched and Mr. J. likes an audience. May as well make yourself useful."

Bailey clenched her jaw, her hands making fists at her sides as she watched the girl being raped in front of her. It was all she could do not to let the tears show in her own eyes. Anything else she could think of, she did. To her dismay, she found her first thought was John.

That was her happy thought? That wasn't right. But at least it gave her something to think about instead of the girl in front of her.

In a moment of defiance, Bailey simply glared at the man when he ordered her to her knees to clean him, which earned her a punch in the face by Mack which knocked her to her knees anyway. Before she could catch her breath, the other man was in her mouth.

She was startled to taste blood and her eyes flicked to the sobbing girl on the bed. Had she really been a virgin? Mr. J. wasn't that big, so it was unlikely the blood came from tearing or something, though if he'd been violent enough it could have been. She didn't think so. Mack must have sold her virginity for a fortune. Bailey closed her eyes, gagging from the taste and the dick down her throat.

'Scarlett! Scarlett, please!'

Her body relaxed slightly and her throat opened to allow him further, her hands stroking his thighs as she sucked. When he pulled her head off him and smiled down at her, she smiled back.

"Oh, yeah. I remember you. You're a good one. Tight and well behaved. Well, we're gonna have some fun tonight. I'm having a party, so you're going to be busy. You ready to be busy?"

Scarlett nodded her head as much as she could with his fist holding her head still by her hair.

"Good girl." He released her and she sank back on her heels, looking up at him as he reached for his clothes.

A second later, Mack had grabbed her by the arm and was lifting her forcibly, almost dragging her to the door. Mr. J. turned around.

"Oh, Mack, try and get some makeup on those bruises. My friends might be turned off by that."

Mack glowered at her, as if it was her fault her face was bruised.

"My wife has what must be close to a makeup store in the bathroom. She can use that."

Mack nodded and shoved Scarlett towards the bathroom. "Go fix your damn face," he growled, then turned to the sobbing figure on the bed and began yelling at her.

Scarlett went into the bathroom and found the makeup box easily enough. A grin spread over her face when she opened it and saw the contents.

"Wow..." she breathed, picking up some of the soft brushes and touching the tips. This was going to be fun!

For the next few minutes, Scarlett covered her bruises with concealer and foundation, then added touches here and there. The mascara was so much better than her cheap old cakey stuff. By the time she was done, she felt beautiful.

Reluctantly, she left the bathroom and made her way past the quietly crying girl on the bed and across the hall to the bedroom she'd been told to wait in. Stripping obediently, she pulled the covers back and sat down. With her back resting against the headboard, Scarlett looked around the room curiously. It sure was a fancy place.

After a while, she wondered just how much trouble she'd be in if she turned on the massive TV and watched something while she waited. But she thought better of it and left it alone. She was lonely, though. The others had gone so far back to get away from everything that she didn't even have anyone to talk to. Was that how Callie felt when she was out?

None of them could talk to Callie, and they weren't even sure if Callie knew they were there. In the brief, blurred flashes they got of her, she always seemed so surprised when she came out, scared even. She never knew where she was, or what was happening. The worst time had been when Bebe had bailed from a beating and no one else had been in a position to front, so Callie had been pushed out, straight into a beating she didn't know about.

It had taken a long time for her to even move after that. When she could move, she had gone and hidden under the stairs, only to be discovered not doing the chores she was supposed to be doing and ended up being beaten again. She hadn't even known she was supposed to be doing anything, and there had been no way to tell her or help her.

Callie was very truly alone, inside and out. She didn't even talk. None of them were really sure if she *could* talk and just didn't, or if she *couldn't* talk for some reason they weren't aware of. Either way, most of the time it didn't matter because there was no one to talk to and nothing to talk about.

Scarlett sighed sadly and tried to think about something else. She could hear the doorbell ringing every so often and the sound of men's voices echoing in the hall and drifting up the stairs. The party seemed to be getting started.

Curiosity was burning inside her and she so much wanted to go to the top of the stairs and peek. But she knew that would be a mistake, so she stayed where she was, waiting. Eventually, footsteps sounded on the stairs and a moment later, the door opened. A middle aged man stepped inside with a smile when he saw her. He was tall and not completely bad looking for an old guy. Probably some kind of business man or something, judging by the expensive suit and general air about him. Money to burn, probably.

"Oh, yes. Now you're a young one. I hear you're a good girl?"

She nodded.

He came over and sat on the bed with her, winking at her as he pulled out a piece of cardboard, a packet of white powder, and a $100 bill. "You want this money?" he asked with a grin.

Scarlett nodded.

"Good, then you're going to earn your tip like a good girl." He poured the powder into straight lines, then rolled up the bill and winked at her again. "Do what I do." He leaned forward, stuck the bill up his nose, plugged his other nostril and sniffed up the white line. When he sat up, his eyes were closed and his mouth slightly open.

When he opened his eyes, he smiled at her and handed her the bill. "Did you watch what I was doing?"

She nodded.

"Alright. Do it."

"What is it?"

"It'll make what we're going to do feel amazing. Do it."

She regarded him uncertainly, then obeyed, copying what he had done. When she felt the powder hit the inside of her nose, she broke into a fit of coughing and nearly knocked over the cardboard with the last two lines on it.

"Hey! Watch it! That's expensive shit!"

She tried to apologize between coughs and he shook his head. "Not a coke whore, huh?" Taking the bill back from her, he quickly inhaled the last two lines himself, then sat back with a sigh.

For a minute, he simply sat there, his eyes closed, sniffing every so often to keep his nose from running. Finally, he looked over at her, his eyes slightly glazed as they roamed over her naked young body.

"How old are you? Wait, no. I don't want to know. I bet you're tight though, aren't you?" She nodded and he grinned, then began undressing himself. "We're gonna have some fun, baby, aren't we?" She nodded again. "Alright, lay back and spread."

Despite how much she loved sex, something about the way he said that pricked at Scarlett's chest. But she ignored it, pushing her feelings away like she always did. She was here for sex. That was it. The rest didn't matter. She just had to make it feel good.

By the time she had obeyed, he was naked. It took him all of three seconds to mount and penetrate her roughly, his full weight on her little body. At least he wasn't too big, so it didn't hurt too much. But she could barely breathe beneath his weight.

It seemed to go on for hours. At one point, she turned her head to stare at the clock beside the bed, watching the numbers change as he pounded away at her. Eventually, he finished and took a break to snort another couple of rows, then got back to it.

Katie's screams from across the hall started and Scarlett figured she was being sold again, just as Scarlett was. There was no escape. Once you were in Mack's clutches, you were his property. The only way out was arrest or… Well, she didn't want to think about that.

After a while, another man came to replace the first, and then another, and another. Scarlett didn't bother counting. Counting was pointless and sometimes painful. It was better just to lie there and take it, obeying whatever orders were given when necessary. Sometimes it felt good. Most often it just was what it was. You didn't think about it. You just took it. That was the way to survive. Katie would learn that soon enough. Hopefully.

Eventually, Katie's screams faded into hopeless, defeated crying, and then to whimpers of misery. Scarlett felt sorry for her. Katie seemed older than Bitty, maybe eighteen or so, but in this capacity, Scarlett was far more experienced. In fact, Scarlett couldn't remember a time when she hadn't been doing this. If not for Mack, it had been under her father's hand, or his friends'. It didn't matter, really. It just was what it was.

When the clock read 5:02 a.m., the line of men finally stopped. The house was quiet except for drugged and drunken male snores. The one on top of Scarlett seemed to have either fallen asleep or passed out while on and inside her! He was too heavy to move, but she needed to pee so bad. She hadn't had the chance since she'd arrived yesterday afternoon. Not that she'd had anything to eat or drink in that time, either, so that at least helped some. But now she really needed to go.

Desperately, she tried to wiggle out from under him, finally managing to extricate herself and run to the toilet just in time. The guy didn't even wake up! She shook her head with a sigh and finished her business, then returned to the bed and curled up on the other side, falling asleep almost immediately.

Chapter Ten

~ Choice Two ~

The sound of pans on the stove and the smell of bacon were the first things Bitty was aware of. It took her a moment to even register what they were. Her eyes opened slowly, unwillingly, and she stared ahead of her at the room for a moment before she remembered where she was. She felt sluggish and sick, and she needed a hit badly. Her body was begging for it. Her moan sounded strange and far away, but it was obviously loud enough to alert Mildred, who came bustling in.

"Ah, you're awake. Good. I wasn't sure if I should call the ambulance or take you to the hospital or something. No, no, I didn't do that. I knew you wouldn't want that!" she added quickly at the panicked look on Bitty's face. The girl relaxed again and sat up, watching the woman nervously.

"My, my, you're a skittish thing, aren't you? Well, given those bruises all over you, I suppose I can imagine why. Are you hungry? You look hungry. I've got bacon going and I've got eggs all lined up. Do you like butter on your toast?"

Bitty nodded, all without saying a word. It didn't really seem necessary with the way the old woman went on about everything. Quietly, she followed Mildred through to the kitchen and sat down weakly in one of the chairs. The bacon smelled amazing, and Mildred must have known how hungry Bitty was, because she placed a plate full of it down in front of her.

"I'll get you some milk. You like milk, right? I have orange juice too, but milk is more filling and healthy. My mother always said you should have a glass of milk at breakfast to tide you through the day. Of course, back then, they didn't know about lactose intolerance. Hoo, boy! My daddy had it bad. Thank the lord mama figured out something was going on and cut back on that stuff for him. Of course, that didn't excuse us from it. Me and my sisters. I'm the youngest. Youngest of four.

"I don't see much of my sisters these days. Just holidays and the like, you know. But family is important, you know. Well, some families. My family is important to me. But there are some families it's just better to cut ties with. Drag you down, they will. Those types always broke my heart. The kids in those families were never given a fair chance at life. Do you have any brothers or sisters?" she asked casually, pouring a glass of milk for Bitty.

Absently, Bitty shook her head and took the glass, drinking quickly. Her eyes closed in delight as the cold liquid quenched her terrible thirst and put something in her empty tummy. Once she set the glass down, she went to work on the bacon, unaware of Mildred watching her carefully. By the time the girl looked up, Mildred was facing the stove and taking care of the food again.

"You know, I used to be so jealous of only children. My sisters would pick on me sometimes, because I wasn't interested in playing house and whatnot. I'd rather sit with a good book in the corner, studying interesting topics and learning new things. I had no interest in being a housewife and mother. I was the only one of us who went to college, you know. Of course, back then it was almost unheard of for a woman to go to college for anything except transcription and secretarial work, or teaching. But that just wasn't my cup of tea. And sure as molasses is slow in winter, I was not interested in being a stepford wife. Do you want to go to college?"

Bitty shrugged, her mouth full.

Mildred went on. "I met my husband at college, you know. He was so handsome. I thought he was a movie star when I first met him, no lies! Looked just like Gene Kelly. You know who that is? Oh, I'm sure you don't. That's ancient history now. But he was something back in the day. Gene Kelly, not my husband. Well, my husband too, but not the same way. Do you like movies?"

Bitty shrugged again.

"What are your favorite kinds?"

Once again, Bitty shrugged.

"Come now, surely you have ones you like better than others?"

Bitty finished chewing, staring at the table as she tried to remember if she'd ever seen a whole movie before. "I... I saw one, once, with some penguins that talked. And they did funny things." It was the first thing she'd said since she'd arrived.

Mildred nodded. "Well, I can't say I know that much about what it would be, seeing as I mostly watch old movies and TV shows. They just don't make them the same these days." She slid two eggs onto a plate, along with two slices of buttered toast and a few more rashers of bacon, then placed it in front of Bitty.

"Would you like some juice... what did you say your name is?" She smiled innocently down at the girl, knowing full well the child hadn't given her name before she ran out the last time.

'Don't tell h–'

"Bitty," she mumbled, ignoring the groan of frustration inside.

"Bitty? That's an interesting name. Is it short for something?"

Bitty shrugged. Mildred nodded and poured a glass of orange juice, not pushing the subject. She'd learned her lesson the last time and she wasn't going to do it again.

"Well, Bitty, mind if I join you for breakfast?" she asked, placing her own plate of bacon, eggs, and toast on the table across from her.

Bitty shrugged uncertainly, then shook her head. Why would she care if the lady sat down at her own table to eat her own breakfast. She eyed her warily.

"I used to have chickens, you know. When I was younger, we lived on a farm, Beau and I. We had hired the neighbor boy to help around with the chores and such, because both of us worked. Lord Almighty, did that ever ruffle some feathers. People expected me to stop working and stay at home once we got married, but no siree, Beau knew what he was getting into when he married me. He and I both discussed it well before we were engaged. I wouldn't have married him if he'd insisted on that. And he knew me well enough not to." She smiled fondly at the memory.

"Where is he?" Bitty asked softly, unable to keep her curiosity in check at the woman's rambling.

"Ohh… he died. About two years ago." Mildred sighed sadly. "I miss him every day. We were married fifty-three years, you know. It was wonderful. Oh, we had our arguments, of course—every couple does—but we always worked it out in the end." She sighed again. "You want to get married, Bitty?"

Bitty shrugged and looked down, pain flashing across her face.

'Like anyone would want to marry us! We're disgusting.'

'We're way too used up to marry someone. It would be nice though…'

'Mack won't let us marry anyone. Even if there was someone…'

"Well, you're much too young to know that right now, anyway. No sense plotting out your future before you're old enough to know yourself. Besides, people change. Situations change. Who knows, you may find yourself come into money and decide never to work a day in your life, or you may be excellent in school and be a scientist or something you never imagined. The world is open to you."

'Bullshit. She doesn't know anything. She's crazy. There's nothing for us. You gotta be worth something to be something.'

"Shut up, Bailey," Bitty mumbled under her breath. Her head was down to eat and hide her mouth as she spoke, so she didn't see the sharp look Mildred gave her before turning back to her own breakfast.

Mildred chattered on until breakfast was done. Bitty felt so much better, even the aching need for a hit was no longer quite so pressing. When the woman simply handed her the dish towel to start drying, Bitty automatically stood beside the sink and took them as Mildred washed, still chatting amiably.

Without realizing it, Bitty had begun to smile.

Chapter Eleven

* Choice One *

Scarlett woke when she felt the weight of her latest client on her back. She kept her eyes closed as her body was pounded into the bed, her face pressed hard into the mattress by the force of his thrusts and his heavy body. Silently, she bore it until he finished and climbed off to go take a shower.

She sat up with a sigh when she heard Katie crying across the hall. No doubt she'd been woken up the same way. A pang of pity stabbed her chest, and with a glance towards the bathroom, Scarlett slipped out of bed and crept across the hall. Remarkably, Katie was alone, curled on her side in the blood stained bed, crying miserably.

"Hey…" Scarlett whispered, sitting down next to her. "You okay…?"

Katie turned her face into the pillow, her cheeks burning with humiliation.

Scarlett reached out to rub her arm. "It gets easier after a while."

"I don't want it to get easier! I want to go home! I never want to do this again! I want to go home."

Scarlett looked down at the older girl sadly. The fact that she could even want to go home was a sign that maybe home hadn't been that bad after all. Maybe she'd felt ignored at home, or maybe she'd been smothered and overprotected and wanted some breathing room. Whatever the cause, she had decided to get away and find something better. Only, there was nothing but pain going that route.

Maybe Katie had realized that home wasn't the worst place to be. If she was wanting to go there now, when she hurt the most and was scared and miserable, then it had to be decent. Despite what Mack had done to Scarlett and everyone else inside, none of them—well, with the exception of Bebe—had once thought about going back home. Home was no better than Mack. He really was the best she could get.

"Don't try to run. Please. It'll make things so much worse for you. Just… just do what he says and it won't be so bad."

Katie shrugged her arm roughly away from Scarlett's hand. "Fuck off."
Scarlett flinched, then stood up and left.

'Ungrateful bitch. Fine! She can learn it the hard way! She can't say you didn't try to warn her! Fucking moron is gonna get herself beat.'

"Shut it, Bailey."

***

Mack picked them up a short while later, hauling the sobbing Katie along by her arm with a vice grip while Bitty followed, her head down. She'd watched in pain as the 'party host' had doled out several thousand dollars to Mack, who took it all with a greedy grin. That was *her* money. From *her* body. Well, plus Katie's virginity fee. That was probably steep. Bitty was mildly impressed that Mack had held off from taking her first time for himself.

The car ride was silent except for Katie's soft crying. But instead of heading back to the house, they went to another house. A feeling of dread filled Bitty's stomach. She recognized the place. Panic gripped her chest and she looked at Mack. She didn't dare beg, but it was in her eyes.

"Don't you dare, you little bitch. They pay good and you're gonna earn every fucking dime of it, you understand me?"

Bitty's head dropped as her own tears began to fall. Why had she left John?

'You think running off to John for another day would have saved you from this? You know they like you. You'd have ended up here no matter what.'

'Leave off, Bailey. Why do you have to be such a bitch all the time?'

'I just tell it how it is. It's not my fault none of you can take the truth without bawling your fucking eyes out.'

Bitty missed the rest of the argument when Mack parked the car and hauled her and Katie out of it. Their client was waiting for them on the front steps with that smile on his face that Bitty recognized far too well. Her stomach turned and she thought she might throw up. She suddenly realized she'd had nothing to eat or drink for over twenty-four hours. Maybe she'd get lucky and pass out…

At the very least, maybe she would be triggered enough to switch. Scarlett handled this stuff a lot better than she did.

Katie's horror broke her heart, and she reached out to hold the girl's hand, giving it a squeeze before they were pulled apart and handed off to their clients for a long, hard, painful day of 'work'.

***

By the time Mack picked them up again, it was getting dark. Bitty felt sick from hunger, thirst, and pain. She had been lucky enough to pass out twice and switch once. Except, unpredictable as switching was, Bailey had been pushed out instead of Scarlett. That had made everything worse. Bailey kicked, hit, and swore at him, which pissed him off and earned them even more pain and humiliation. It wasn't the worst day she'd had at that place, but it was up there.

Blood seeped slowly through her little top, and the criss cross lines on her body were visible where the cropped shirt ended. Her belly ring had been torn out and her entire body throbbed. She needed at least some water. She had to have water. Her throat was so dry from screaming she couldn't even talk. Katie was no better.

Neither of them said a word as they were shoved into the car, though Katie gave a scream of pain, and Bitty cried out softly when her body touched the seat. Fire shot through her, searing every nerve anew. But hopefully, Mack would have some bottles of water for them or something. Anything. As long as he hadn't forgotten they needed it.

He tended to do that. He just forgot they hadn't been given food or water for days at a time, then got angry when they collapsed. Bitty had learned a long time ago that he didn't see them as people, or even animals. They were tools. Tools that were cheap and easy to replace. Tools that didn't need care.

But they were not going to be so lucky. Mack barely even looked at them, and certainly didn't hand back any water bottles or food. He was on his phone, making arrangements for some other girl. Bitty felt her head spinning. She knew she was going to pass out again. The sick feeling in her stomach and the blackish stuff around her vision were getting worse. She needed something bad.

When he hung up, she risked it. In a croaking voice, she asked, "Mack.... I.... I n-need some water.... please..."

He looked back at them in his rear view mirror, as if suddenly remembering they were there.

"Fuck." Without another word, he pulled into the closest fast food place and ordered them each a meal, then set off again.

Bitty and Katie almost immediately finished their drinks, and despite still being thirsty, they started quickly on their food. It wasn't nearly enough to make up for the days they hadn't eaten, or at least, that Bitty hadn't eaten. She assumed Katie had been treated well right up until she'd been taken to the first house.

Both girls were long finished eating by the time they got to their street. Yet again, instead of going to his house, Mack pulled up along the sidewalk and turned to look at Bitty expectantly.

"Well? What the fuck are you waiting for? Get the hell out and get to work."

Bitty was very nearly on the verge of arguing, saying she'd barely slept in the last two days and had eaten one value meal in that time, but the look on his face made her keep her mouth shut. Wincing and hissing in pain at every movement, Bitty slid out of the car into the cold dark night, barely closing the door before Mack had sped off again with Katie.

For a long time, Bitty stood where she was, staring in the direction he had gone. She couldn't think, her body throbbed with pain, ached with withdrawal, yearned for water, and shook from exhaustion. She wanted desperately to curl up in the nearest dumpster and sleep. But she had a quota to fill, and she couldn't go back without it.

And so began another long, agonizing night of work.

~ Choice Two ~

Once the dishes were washed, dried, and put away, Mildred led Bitty through the house to the upstairs bathroom.

"There now, I bet you'd like a nice warm shower. Or a bath? Do you know how to work the faucet to get the right temperature? Ah, of course you do. You're a big girl. Alright, well, here's a towel and washcloth for you. You can use the soap and shampoo and whatever else you need. I don't mind in the least. Help yourself."

Bitty nodded vaguely and watched her bustle out, shutting the door behind her.

'She's a freak.'

'She's nice! I like her! And she cooks good!'

'I bet she could help us, Bitty. I bet she could. She's so nice.'

'It may be something to consider, actually. She may be the one t–'

'Are you fucking kidding me!? We're not asking her for help! She'll turn us in! We'll go to prison!'

Bitty watched the door for another moment, then turned and started the shower. Once it was luxuriously warm, she smiled, stripped, and stepped in with a sigh. When was the last time she'd had a shower?

'With John, remember?'

"Oh, right," she mumbled, thinking back to that wonderful night she'd spent being fed, being warm, and being clean. It seemed like a dream now. How long ago was that?

'Three days.'

"Three days!" Bitty gasped in shock. "That's it?" It had felt like a lifetime. But then, in that time, she'd been used by a lifetime's worth of guys. So maybe it was understandable. She sighed and turned to the task of trying to clean herself. She almost didn't want to get out, but she was getting tired again. Her body just felt so weak and exhausted!

After she turned the water off and got out to dry herself, there was a knock on the door. She froze for a moment, then opened it slowly, the towel wrapped around her carefully.

Mildred was standing at the door with a smile. "I thought you might like something clean to wear." She held out a neatly folded pile of clothes. "They may be a little big, but at least they're warm."

Bitty took the clothes carefully. "Thanks," she mumbled and ducked back inside. Mildred had given her a blue striped, men's button up shirt, a pair of sweatpants, a pair of underwear that looked rather large, and a pair of fuzzy socks. They were clean and looked warm. Bitty smiled.

The underwear was indeed a little big, but not by much, and the shirt was miles too big and smelled like Old Spice, but it was alright once she buttoned it all the way and rolled up the sleeves. The socks were amazing. She hadn't had socks in a very long time. After attempting to finger comb the tangles from her hair, she left the bathroom and made her way downstairs. Mildred was knitting in the living room and looked up with a smile when she heard Bitty enter.

"Ah, yes. That seems to work reasonably well. How are the pants? Little too loose. Hmm, let's try a rubber band." She stood up and went to a large roll top desk, taking a rubber band from one of the little drawers at the back. "Okay, let's see."

She pulled the waistband of the pants out a bit and bunched it up on one side, then looped the band around the bunch a couple of times and stepped back. "That seems to work alright, doesn't it?"

Bitty nodded with a small smile. "Thank you."

Mildred waved her hand as if dismissing the gratitude and sat back down to pick up her knitting once more. "No need to thank me. It's the least I can do. You need some better clothes than what you were wandering around in out there in the cold of night!" She very carefully did not look at Bitty when she said that.

Bitty stood where she was, looking awkward and uncertain until Mildred gestured to the comfy looking armchair at an angle to the couch. "Do you know how to knit?"

Bitty shook her head.

"Want to learn?"

Bitty debated for a moment. How long did she really want to spend here with this woman? She wasn't making any money hanging around here like this, nice as it was. Mack would be furious.

"Umm...where are my clothes?"

"Oh, I threw them in the wash. They'll be done in a couple of hours. Have a seat." She picked up another pair of knitting needles and eyed Bitty. "What's your favorite color?"

Bitty stared at her in surprise. "My favorite..."

"Color, yes."

"Oh.... uh..."

'Pink!'

'Red!'

'Black, duh.'

'I like yellow.'

'No, blue!'

"Uh.... purple?"

"Are you asking me, or telling me?" Mildred replied, regarding her with an arched eyebrow.

"Telling...?"

"Are you asking me that, too?"

Bitty flushed. "No. I mean, I'm telling you. I like purple," she replied with a decisive nod. "I like purple."

Mildred gave her an approving nod, as if praising Bitty's ownership of her preference.

It gave Bitty a surprising feeling of pleasure; that simple nod. She smiled. Her eyes followed the woman's hands as she picked up a ball of pale purple yarn and began knotting it and looping it over one of the needles, then handed it to Bitty.

"There. Now, hold it like this, your forefingers over the top to hold the yarn and your other fingers back here to keep the string out of the way. Push the right tip under the loop there and make an 'X'... good... now wrap the loose string around that end. No, the other one. There, that's it. Okay, now the tricky part. Use that 'X' to slide the loop over the end and then tug the string gently."

Bitty fumbled with the thin, cool metal needles, her lips twisting into a sideways crease that wrinkled her nose as she concentrated. Her fingers slipped, the soft fluffy yarn tangled when she tried to wrap it, the ball fell, but Mildred was surprisingly patient. In all her life, Bitty had never been treated that way.

Despite that, her frustration began to mount at her ineptitude. She just couldn't make her fingers do what Mildred was doing! She couldn't do it. She was useless. Why had she even tried?

Suddenly, her shoulders flew back and she threw the yarn and needles on the floor with a cry of rage as she stood up. "It's stupid! It's just dumb! I don't want to do some dumb knitting thing! That's for losers!" she screamed.

Mildred had leaned back in her seat in shock, her eyes and mouth both open in astonishment at the girl's sudden flare of anger. "Dear, you don't have to–"

"Don't call me dear! I'm not your fucking dear! I'm not your anything! Just.... just leave me the fuck alone! I don't want to do your stupid knitting shit!"

Mildred's lips pursed into a thin line and her voice was quiet when she spoke. "That's enough, young lady. I will not have that language in my house. You are perfectly welcome to stop the lesson and you're entitled to your opinion, but I will not tolerate rudeness under my roof."

'Bailey! Bailey, stop it! You're ruining it! Please, Bailey! We'll get kicked out!'

"Fine! I don't need you! You know, for a second, I thought you were different, but you're not. You're just like everyone else. I'm out of here! Where are my fucking clothes!"

'Bailey! Please!'

Mildred stood up slowly. "They're in the wash, like I told you. They're wet. You'll just have to–"

"Fuck that! I'm not waiting! I want them now! I'm leaving!"

For a long moment, Mildred stared back at Bailey, as if sizing her up and trying to decide how best to react to the situation. Finally, she pursed her lips and nodded. "Alright. You can have them back."

She led the way down a narrow flight of stairs to the basement. It was cold, dim, and smelled of damp and dirt—typical basement of an old house. To one side, a washer and dryer were set against the wall, a gentle thumping noise coming from the washing machine. Mildred lifted the lid and the noise stopped, then she looked at her guest.

"They're soaking wet. Are you sure you want them?"

Now that they were down here and Bailey was seeing them for herself, it was fairly obvious it would be stupid and ridiculous to take them now and walk out into the freezing cold, even if it was the middle of the day. But what was she supposed to do? She couldn't back down now, could she? She would look weak and indecisive. But they'd die of cold if they wore dripping wet things out of the house in this weather.

In that moment of uncertainty, Bitty slid back in. Shoulders slumping slightly and her head hanging, her voice softened back to a demure murmur.

"I'm sorry. No. I don't want them. I mean... not like that. Not wet. I just... I didn't mean.... I'm sorry..." she stammered.

Mildred watched her for a moment, then she softened as well. "Oh, my dear. I think you and I need to have a talk."

Bitty's head came up fearfully, her eyes wide and anxious. "I... I'm not..."

"Hush now. Let's go back upstairs and have a snack." She shut the lid of the washing machine and it started up again. With a reassuring smile, Mildred put her arm around Bitty's shoulder ever so lightly and guided her up the stairs.

Once they were back in the kitchen, Mildred pulled out a chair at the table and gestured for the girl to sit down, then began collecting some more cookies and pouring glasses of milk. She sat down with the plate and passed Bitty a glass with a smile.

"There. Try that."

Bitty drank obediently, her eyes averted in embarrassment. When she put the glass back down, Mildred nodded.

"Alright. Now, how many are there?"

Bitty frowned in confusion, glancing at the cookies on the plate and counting them. "Uh... nine?"

Mildred chuckled softly and shook her head. "No, dear. I mean with you. How many are there with you?"

Bitty stared in shock, her mind drawing a complete blank in her dismay.

'What is she talking about? Does she know?'

'Of course she doesn't know! How could she know!'

'I think she knows, Bitty. She seems like she knows.'

'Don't say a fucking word! Get out of here right now!'

"I'm fairly sure there's at least two. Are there more?" Mildred continued.

Bitty still hadn't said a word, the jumble of exclamations from inside and her own astonishment causing a disconnect between her brain and her mouth. Eventually, her mouth opened and closed a few times before she managed to speak.

"Uh.... I don't..."

"I've seen it before, dear."

"You... what?"

"My husband, god rest his soul. There were five with him. We got along well for the most part. But I can see it. So how many?"

There was absolute silence inside and out as she sat there staring at the woman across the table from her. What was she supposed to say? Her husband had it? Did she really know? How could she tell?

"Th... there's.... six more," she whispered finally, her eyes on her glass.

Mildred nodded and pushed the plate gently towards her. "And you're Bitty?"

The girl lifted her head to look at the gently smiling woman, then nodded.

"And who shouted at me earlier?"

Bitty's face went bright red and she looked down at the plate once more.

'Don't you dare, Bitty! Don't you fucking dare! Shut up! She'll only get us in trouble! Shut up!'

"Bailey..." she mumbled.

'FUCK!'

She flinched at the internal scream and tried to block out the steady stream of swears and insults now being flung at her for her honesty.

"And who is Scarlett?"

Bitty looked up in surprise. "What? How did you-"

"That's who you were talking to when I first met you." She smiled when Bitty stared at her in shock. "That was my first hint. Either you were a group, or you were schizophrenic. And you didn't show any of the other signs of schizophrenia.

Another long silence ensued before Bitty found her tongue again. "Uh... Scarlett is... well... she's.... Scarlett..." she finished unhelpfully.

Mildred nodded and sipped her milk. "How old are you, Bitty?"

'Don't answer that.'

"Fourteen."

"I see. And you don't live at home, I take it?"

'Don't answer that.'

Bitty shook her head, still not looking at Mildred.

"Do you *have* a place to live?"

'Tell her yes.'

Bitty nodded. "Yes. I have a place to live. It's fine. I'm okay."

'Finally!'

Mildred was quiet for a moment before speaking again. "Do you have to work to live there, Bitty?"

'*Don't answer that!*'

"Yes."

'*Fuck, Bitty! How stupid are you!? She's gonna call the damn cops!*'

Bitty looked up at Mildred quickly. "I mean... no. I mean..."

Mildred was studying her carefully. "Bitty. I would like to help you if I can. But I need to know things to do that. I'm not going to hurt you, and I don't want to get you in trouble."

"I don't.... I mean.... I just...."

'*Don't! Don't do it!*'

"If I don't help pay for things, how can I expect to live there?" she asked finally.

Mildred sighed softly. "Judging by the clothing you were wearing, I can imagine what kind of work he expects you to do."

Bitty's face flushed and she slouched further.

'*She knows. She seems to know a lot.*'

"I'm not judging you, dear. I know how things can be sometimes. It's not your fault. And you don't need people looking down on you for it. I just want to help."

"I'm fine."

"You don't look fine. You look hurt. And cold, and hungry, too. You deserve better than that. What does everyone else say about your situation?"

Bitty shrugged without looking up.

'*Bitty, tell her we want to live here with her!*'

'*Oh shut up, Bebe. We're not living here with her, even if she invited us, which she won't.*'

'*Ask her to help us, Bitty. She can help us.*'

'It might be a reasonable idea to tell her what's going on, Bitty. I, for one, would prefer not to return to Mack.'

"I can't imagine they like it much. Do your parents know where you are? Or is that just as bad?"

Again, Bitty shrugged.

Mildred sighed. "Well, why don't we find something else to do. We'll give knitting a break, shall we? How about we make some little pies or something?" Without waiting for a reply, she stood up and began bustling around the kitchen.

Bitty watched her for a minute, not quite sure what to do or how to react to all this. Mildred hadn't freaked out, called the police, sent her packing, or been angry at her outburst. It was something Bitty had never encountered in her entire life. Always, she had tried to be so careful about not letting anyone know about the others, and they had tried to be equally careful about it when they were out. It didn't seem like a good idea to let people know something like that. As Mildred had said when they first met, people would think she was crazy.

Of course, maybe she was crazy? Well, she was definitely crazy, actually. Just not like that. She was just... broken. But it had helped things. The others had been there when no one else was. They helped her cope with things. They handled things she couldn't. Even when they argued and criticized, they were still there to support each other, most of the time anyway. So, it wasn't a bad crazy, was it?

After a minute or two, she stood up and came over to Mildred, who was browsing a cookbook on the counter. "What kind of pie?" she asked softly.

"Hmm, well, I was thinking apple, because I have several apples left over from the fall, but maybe a savory pie would be better."

"What's a savory pie?"

"Oh, sorry. It's a pie that isn't sweet. Like chicken, or beef, or turkey."

"Oh."

"We could make both, I suppose. The crust is the same, so we can just make a large batch and make several different pies."

"Really?"

"Of course. Do you like chicken pie?"

Bitty nodded.

"And apple?"

Again, a nod.

"Alright, chicken and apple it is. Not together, though!" Mildred said with a wink and a smile. She marked the page for the two pies, then flipped to the recipe for the crust while Bitty watched.

"It's really the same recipe for both kinds?"

"Well, there are different recipes you can use, some are sweeter than others, but I find this one works quite nicely for both. It's the filling that makes it what it is, not really the crust. Of course, I've made this lovely no-bake cheesecake that had a meringue crust. That's something you definitely wouldn't want to use for a chicken pie!"

"What's meringue?"

"It's a sort of sugary... oh, how would you describe it... well, it has a lot of uses really. It's a mixture of egg whites and sugar, and a few other things, that you whip until it's fluffy. Then you can bake it plain like little cookies, or you can make pie crust like I said, or you add it to the top of pies, like lemon meringue pie, or desserts like baked alaska and things. It's quite useful and very sweet. I have rather a fondness for sweets, if you hadn't noticed," she added with another wink.

Bitty found herself smiling at the woman, relaxing as things began to settle back into a calm steadiness.

Chapter Twelve

~ Choice Two ~

For the next couple of hours, the pair of them were busy washing, cooking, cutting, rolling, peeling, and mixing the ingredients for the pies. Mildred had decided they would make small, handheld pies, instead of larger ones, so there were plenty of little trays to be lined with crust and then filled.

"There," Mildred said happily once they were in the oven. "That'll see us for dinner."

"What?"

"Dinner. It's almost dinner time."

Bitty looked out the window in dismay. She hadn't even noticed it was getting dark! "I have to go! It's so late. I have to go. Oh my god."

Mildred sighed. "Bitty, you don't have to leave. You can stay here. He won't find you."

Bitty shook her head quickly, absolute terror in her eyes. "No. No, I have to leave. I have to go back or he'll be so mad. Where's my clothes?"

"I'll go switch them to the dryer. I forgot about them." Mildred gazed at her for a moment, then headed for the basement to switch the clothes into the dryer.

'Oh god, we're gonna get it so bad. What the fuck were you thinking, Bitty?'

"I don't know. I didn't notice. I just... I didn't notice."

'I don't want to go back, Bitty. I like it here. Mildred is nice.'

'No, Bebe! We have to go, or Mack will come looking for us and he'll be so pissed! We'll be lucky not to be kicked out!'

'If we're kicked out, we could come live here. Mildred can help us.'

'Shut it, Jay.'

'Don't be so rude, Bailey. He's just trying to help.'

'We have to leave. Now!'

"But my clothes aren't dry. We can't leave."

Silence.

A while later, Mildred returned looking sad. "I wish you would stay."

Bitty didn't reply. She slumped at the table dejectedly. How could she admit she wanted to stay? She was just too afraid to.

There was an awkward silence for a little while until the timer on the stove went off. Mildred pulled out the tray of little pies and instructed Bitty to collect two plates for them. Bitty had to admit, they smelled divine. Her tummy rumbled hungrily and Mildred chuckled.

"I'm hungry too. They smell wonderful, don't they?" She placed two little pies on each of their plates and sat down at the table with Bitty to eat. Every so often, she would glance at the clock quickly, then back to the food. Her glances grew more and more frequent, and Bailey began to notice from inside.

'Something's wrong. Something's off. Bitty, we have to leave.'

"But..."

Mildred looked up. "What?"

Bitty shook her head and watched Mildred glance at the clock again.

'Bitty, now. We have to leave now. Something is wrong. We gotta go. Something's wrong. Leave. Now!'

"Umm... Could I have my clothes now?"

'Fuck the clothes. We need to get out of here! Just leave, now!'

"Oh, your clothes. Right, uh, give me just a minute, alright?"

Bitty nodded slightly, watching the woman with a growing sense of dread. Bailey was right. Something seemed off. Panic began to tighten its grip around her chest. When Mildred stood up to go to the basement, Bitty stood up too.

'Run. Run, Bitty. Now. As fast as you can, go.'

Bitty ran. Trying to be as quiet as possible, she dashed for the door, sock feet and all. Bailey was right. They had to get out of there. She reached the door and flung it open, then froze.

Horror clutched at her heart like an icy hand and she felt suddenly hot and cold all at once. A sick feeling threatened to make her throw up as she stared up into the surprised face of a police officer about to knock.

'FUCK! I KNEW IT! I KNEW IT! RUN, BITTY! TURN AROUND AND RUN!'

Bitty spun around and made to run the other way, but Mildred was right behind her, tears in her eyes. Bitty shook her head, trying not to sob hysterically.

"You lied! You lied to me! You said you wouldn't get me in trouble! You lied!"

"Oh, darling, no. I'm not trying to get you into trouble. I'm trying to help you. You need someone to help you."

Bitty spun around, aware of someone behind her. The police officer had moved up, another one behind, and a woman in a pantsuit behind them, making her way up the stairs from the sidewalk. For one moment, Bitty stood rooted and rigid on the spot, then her shoulders straightened and her eyes lit with fury.

"NO! NO! LEAVE ME ALONE! LEAVE ME ALONE! I'M NOT GOING WITH YOU! LET GO! LET GO OF ME! YOU SON OF A BITCH, LET GO! I HATE YOU! I HATE YOU! YOU'RE A FUCKING LIAR!

YOU'RE NOTHING BUT A LIAR! I HATE YOU!" Bailey screamed, her head swiveling between the police officer grabbing her arm and Mildred crying behind her.

"Bitty? Calm down. It's okay. Calm down. It'll make everything go a lot easier if you calm–"

"I'M NOT FUCKING CALMING DOWN, YOU BITCH! LET ME GO! LET ME GO RIGHT NOW! I HATE YOU! YOU LYING BITCH! I HATE YOU!"

Bailey struggled violently, but the officer was already putting the handcuffs around her wrists behind her back. Mildred was crying much harder now.

"Is that really necessary? She's just a child."

"She's a violent criminal, ma'am. Prostitution is illegal, and she's trying to attack an officer. Yes, it's necessary."

Mildred covered her mouth, a look of shock and regret on her face. "Oh, Bitty. I'm so sorry."

"FUCK YOU! FUCK YOU! YOU'RE NOT SORRY! I KNEW YOU'D BETRAY US! I KNEW WE COULDN'T TRUST YOU! GO TO HELL!"

Without even looking for shoes, the officers virtually dragged her down the steps and along the path to the waiting squad car, Bailey screaming and struggling the whole way. The cold rain was turning to sleet now, and the sidewalk was slippery and wet. Before she even reached the car, Bailey's toes were so cold they hurt, her socks were soaked through, and her clothes were wet. The hard, plastic seat of the police car was slippery in wet clothes, and it hurt to have her hands trapped behind her as they were with her body bruised as it was.

By the time they reached the station, she was shivering violently and her lips were blue despite the heat of the car.

The station was bright, and at least it wasn't as busy as it could have been. Bailey was led, struggling, into the booking area, still trying to yank herself from the officer's grasp and swearing at them.

'Bailey, please stop. You're just making things worse. Please. If you're polite, maybe they'll let us go.'

"Are you stupid!? Of course they're not gonna let us go!" But she did quiet down a little.

The booking took several hours, and no one seemed to notice—or maybe they just didn't care—that she was still wet and shivering. Thankfully, they switched her arms from behind her back to in front of her, probably for their own convenience in fingerprinting and signing her name. Exhaustion was taking over, from the shivering and the busy day. At least they'd come after she'd eaten.

'Maybe Mildred planned it that way.'

"Don't fucking talk to me about that bitch ever again, Sarah," Bailey hissed angrily.

Two crackheads looked over from nearby seats.

"You talking to me?" one of them asked.

"Is your name Sarah?"

He shook his head with a scowl.

"Then I'm not fucking talking to you, am I?" she snapped, flipping her middle finger at them with a snarky face.

'Bailey, please. Let someone else out.'

"I'm handling it."

'Not very well.'

"What the fuck do you know?"

The crack heads looked back at her.

"You assholes got a fucking problem?"

"Listen, bitch. We know who you belong to, so if you know what's good for you, you'll shut your damn mouth," one of them said.

Bailey glared back at him furiously but once again stayed silent. If Mack caught wind of her being arrested, she wasn't sure what he'd do. It probably wouldn't be good.

'Maybe it's a good thing, Bailey. Now he can't get us.'

"Shut up, Jay," she muttered under her breath.

Eventually, Bailey was taken to a room and her hands uncuffed. A social service worker came in a minute later with a saccharine smile, a folder, and an orange jumpsuit in a plastic bag. She was one of those people who just seemed too perfect to be real. Not a hair was out of place from her neat, auburn bun at the nape of her neck. Her dark brows were perfectly sculpted to frame her blue eyes, her makeup was flawless in the way that it was obvious she was wearing makeup, but not drawing attention to the makeup at the same time. Her pantsuit was pristine. For a government worker, she sure looked spectacular.

"You're Bailey Carter?"

'How did she know it was you, Bailey?'

"That's the actual name, idiot."

The social worker frowned as she slid the packet towards Bailey. "A simple yes would have been fine. My name is Jennifer Wright, I'm one of the social workers for the county. I'm here to ask you a few questions. Would you like to get changed first?"

Bailey glared down at the jumpsuit as if it had just insulted her personally, then back at the woman. "What do you think? You think I wanna sit here freezing my goddamn ass off while you ask your fucking questions?"

"Bailey, I would appreciate some courtesy. I'm trying to be polite, and your attitude is making that difficult. I understand you would rather not be here–"

"Ya think! You must be a fucking genius!"

Jennifer pursed her lips for a moment, probably trying to keep in the words she was dying to say out of anger.

Bailey glared back at her, as if trying to goad her into saying them anyway. It was somewhat satisfying to force people to do what she wanted; making them upset or sad or scared. It was as if she held some shred of control in her life with that power.

Unfortunately—or perhaps fortunately—Jennifer held her tongue and simply nodded. "Alright, then let's get you dried off before we talk anymore. Are you hungry? Thirsty?" Bailey nodded to everything and Jennifer opened the door. "There's a bathroom down this way."

She led Bailey down the hall a little way to a single toilet, unisex bathroom.

Bailey walked in and turned to shut the door but the woman walked in behind her. "I have to supervise you at all times."

Bailey gaped at her. "You can't be serious!?"

Jennifer nodded. "We're both girls. There's nothing to be ashamed of. I'm not going to touch you, unless you need help of course."

Bailey stiffened and backed away. "I don't need fucking help. I'm perfectly capable of dressing myself. You lay a damn hand on me and I'll scream so loud they'll hear me in the next county."

"I have no intention of touching you, Bailey." As if to prove her point, Jennifer turned her body slightly away and examined her beautifully manicured nails.

Bailey stood there glaring at her for a moment longer, then huffed angrily and dropped the plastic packet on the floor. With another wary glance at the social worker, Bailey peeled off her wet socks, pants, underwear, and shirt, dismayed to realize it was virtually see-through from the dampness. Those officers had probably been getting a good look at her the whole time!

Ripping open the plastic bag, Bailey pulled out a pair of one-size-fits-all mesh underwear (if it could be called that), a white long sleeve t-shirt, a pair of orange, elasticized pants, and a baggy orange shirt. Thankfully, there was also a pair of cheap blue slipper-socks. No shoes, no tie strings at the waist, just shit that didn't fit right.

But it was better than cold, wet clothes. Once she was dressed, Bailey shoved the wet clothes into the bag and turned back to face Jennifer. "I'm done."

Jennifer looked up with a nod. "Alright. Let's head back to the room then. I can take your clothes for you."

Bailey handed over the bag with a scowl. "They're not mine. They're that bitch's."

Jennifer quirked an eyebrow but didn't say anything until they reached the room.

"Have a seat, Bailey." Jennifer took a seat on the other side of the table and opened the file folder. "How old are you, Bailey?"

Bailey debated about staying standing simply to be otherwise, but she was exhausted and her legs were trembling. With a rueful sigh, she sank down onto the hard metal seat and crossed her arms over her chest. "Eighteen."

Jennifer looked up at her with that damn eyebrow quirked. "Eighteen?"

Bailey glared at her for a long moment, then looked away. "Fourteen," she muttered.

That seemed to satisfy Jennifer because she went on. "And your parents are…?"

"None of your damn business."

Jennifer sat back slightly and regarded the objectionable teen in front of her. "Bailey, it is my business, because you are my business. I'm here to help you. I want to make sure you have a safe place to live, food to eat, and people to care for you."

"Then don't send me home."

"Why not?"

Bailey huffed and rolled her eyes. "Forget it."

Jennifer wrote something down. "If you don't feel safe going home, then we can find a foster home for you once we get the legal stuff taken care of."

"I'm not going to any stupid old foster home!"

"We don't need to decide that right now. Let's focus on the here and now. Do you have a pimp?"

Bailey stared at her in dismay for a moment, then looked away. "I don't know what you're talking about."

"Bailey, you're a prostitute. An underage one at that. We know that. Please tell us who is making you work so we can handle them."

Bailey stayed silent, looking anywhere but at the woman across from her.

Eventually, Jennifer sighed and stood up.

"I'm sorry, Bailey. I know you're angry, but I can't do anything to help you if you won't help yourself." Her statement was met with more silence.

"If you want to talk, you can let someone know." With that, she left Bailey alone in the room.

'Why didn't you tell her, Bailey?'

'She said she would help us, Bailey. Why won't you let her help us?'

"She's not gonna help us. People don't help. Didn't you learn from Mildred. You can't fucking trust anyone. Just shut up and let me handle this."

Eventually, another officer came to collect her and guided her to a jail cell for the night. It was sparse, and privacy wasn't a thing, but then, that wasn't really anything new. Once she'd been taken in by Mack, she'd hardly been alone for anything. At least in here she had an actual bed, a blanket, and a pillow.

'That's not so bad. It's a lot more comfortable.'

"Shut it, Sarah," Bailey grouched as she dropped down on the bed and stared up at the ceiling. They were really in a mess now. It seemed like everything was just going to shit. "What the hell do we do now?" she mumbled to no one as she drifted off to sleep.

Chapter Thirteen

* Choice One *

There was a needle in her arm. Bitty groaned and tried to move, pulling the thing from her skin with a little whimper of pain. Her entire body hurt and she felt sick. When her eyes finally—grudgingly—opened, she blinked a few times and glanced around uncertainly trying to remember where she was.

The stink was overwhelming and before she even knew what hit her, she turned her head and vomited on the floor next to the ratty old couch. Apparently she had not been the only one, or she had already done so and just couldn't remember, because it was not the only mess on the floor.

Moaning softly again and trying to clear her throat of the burning stuff, she weakly wrenched herself free from where she was pinned between the arm of the sofa and the heavy, toothless man on her other side.

Ah, now she remembered. Yeah, that had been a hard one to accept. But desperate times called for desperate measures, and she had never really been in control of who or what went into her body anyway. He was just another john, after all. Still, she did feel a little more disgusting than usual.

With a shudder at the recollection of the previous night, she glanced around and began gathering her clothes. Other stringy, emaciated users were passed out around the dim, garbage strewn room. Out of the corner of her eye, Bitty was even sure she saw a mouse run along the floor at the wall. At least, she hoped it was a mouse and not a rat.

The room was dim but she could see that it was morning already. As quickly as she could without emptying her stomach again, she pulled her clothes back on and looked around for her purse. As she rummaged around under cushions, chairs, upturned tables, and stinking piles of clothes, panic began to rise with each one.

"I can't find my purse," she mumbled softly. "Oh god, I can't find my purse. Where did my purse go?"

'Look under that guy next to you.'

She did, trying not to cry when it wasn't there.

'What about in the kitchen?'

Nothing.

"Oh, god, Mack is gonna kill me. Oh god. Oh god." She was beginning to panic so much that her eyes were blurring.

'Calm down, Bitty. We'll find it.'

'There! Over there in the puddle of…. eww…'

Bitty gave a shuddering sigh of relief and moved to the spot in the corner, trying not to retch as she gingerly extricated her little handbag from the puddle of… stuff. After trying to rinse it a little in the filthy kitchen and drying it with a scrap of paper towel, she tentatively opened it and nearly sobbed with relief.

It was there. The money she'd earned before her last job. This one.

She glanced back towards the couch and its couple of occupants. "How many did I do last night?" she whispered.

'I can't remember. I think three?'

She nodded and checked her purse. "So none of them paid me yet. Great." With a sigh, she picked her way across the room back to the couch and gently prodded the guy who had been draped over her. "Hey. Hey, mister. I need my money."

Nothing.

"Hey!" she said a little more loudly.

There was a grunt in reply. She shook him.

"Hey! I need my money! Where's my money?" she shouted.

Finally, his heavy eyelids blinked slightly open and he looked at her blankly for a minute before smiling toothlessly. "Hey there, cutie. You wanna give me some of–"

"I already did and you haven't paid me," she interrupted. "Where's my money?"

The man blinked again, then laughed. "Oh yeah… I 'member. It was good. I paid you already."

Bitty stared at him. "No you didn't…"

He nodded. "Sure did. Pushed it into your arm myself."

She gaped at him in horror. "What!?"

"Hell, what I gave you was worth way more than the couple I got out of you. I think you owe me a few more rou–"

"Fuck off! I didn't want that! I told you I didn't!" Bailey was furious. Her back was virtually rigid with anger and she glared down at him. "You can't say you paid me cuz you stuck that damn needle in my arm! I said no! You did it anyway! That's on you! I want my money, you bastard!"

He grinned and reached for her, trying to pull her down on him and kiss her. "Aww, come now. Gimme some of that. You owe m–"

"You fucking bastard! GIMME MY FUCKING MONEY, YOU SON OF A BITCH!"

He pulled harder, gripping her hair and yanking her face to his.

"Now, you listen here, bitch. You took my good stuff, and you owe me for it. You're not leaving here til I get my damn money out of you!"

Before Bailey knew what happened, she had a fist in her face. For a moment, she couldn't even breathe. Stars blinded her and she could feel nothing but a searing pain shooting through her eyes. After what felt like an eternity, she could finally gasp for breath before she passed out. By that time, she was on her back on the filthy, slimy floor. It oozed beneath her and she tried not to think about what was squishing all over her back. Tears, pleas, swears, and fighting didn't help. After a few minutes, Bitty simply lay there and waited for them all to finish.

It felt like forever before they finally left her alone—half naked on the filthy floor—while they went back to their lines on the rickety old coffee table and started shooting up again. She had stopped crying some time ago. It didn't matter anymore. The worst part of the whole thing wasn't the fact that she was being gang raped by disgusting junkies. That was nothing new.

No. The worst part was that she had lost precious hours and would have nothing to give Mack when she came crawling back—if she even dared go crawling back. With a few soft sniffles, she got to her feet and straightened her damp, stinking clothes, trying not to feel what was dripping from her. Without a word, she picked up her purse and pulled her shoes back on, then made her way slowly from the trailer home.

She had absolutely no idea where she was. Well, no idea other than it was a trashy trailer park. The saddest part was the stroller parked outside the front door. Vaguely, she wondered if the kid had been there the whole time. A pang of pity and regret tugged at her heart, but she didn't look back. She couldn't. What could she do, anyway? Nothing. There was nothing to do. Not about the kid. Not about her lost money. Not about the rape. Not about her whole fucking life.

Trying not to cry at the hopeless feeling that was beginning to wash over her like a heavy blanket, she began counting. Counting anything she could think of. First, she counted steps, then lamp posts, then puddles. Anything to keep her mind from drifting to the dark place.

It was the drugs. She knew it was. They felt so good for a while. They made you forget how miserable and sore and sick and worthless you were, just for a bit. One, blissful moment. But then you crashed. That was usually what got people hooked. Not so much the hit itself but the aftermath. It was such a stark difference, that low point, that you wanted more of the high to balance it out. So you took another hit. And every down felt worse and every high felt not quite as good, so you took more, and more, and more. Until you looked like those guys back there, or Jess, or any of the other thousands of miserable people trying to forget their misery for a little while.

Eventually, she reached a street she recognized. By that time, she wasn't sure how much further she could go. Her entire body felt like she had the worst bout of flu she'd ever experienced. She was crying without even realizing it now. It just came, unbidden. A desperate desire to release the misery and pain.

"I don't feel good…" she mumbled miserably. "I don't feel good." She couldn't keep going. She just couldn't. With a heart wrenching sob, she stumbled into the tiny space between two old brick buildings.

It was full of trash, of course, and was barely as wide as she was. But it was out of the frigid wind and hopefully away from any prowling police cars. It was the best she could do at that moment. With another sob, she sank down with her back to one wall and her knees tight to her chest. Resting her forehead on the top of them and tucking her arms between her body and her thighs, Bitty closed her eyes and slept.

~ Choice Two ~

The lights went on, bright and cold white, and Bitty blinked quickly. With a moan, she rolled over onto her side facing the wall and pulled the blanket up over her head. Much as she would like to have denied it, she'd had a pretty good night. Certainly the best since she'd left the hotel the other day. It was warm and soft, and blankets always felt nice.

She'd often wondered about that. Why did blankets feel so good? It wasn't like they had ever been able to protect her, or keep anyone from touching her or ripping them away. They weren't always warm enough to keep the freezing cold air from numbing her skin. They couldn't hide her from prying eyes or pummeling fists. But it still felt so much safer to be able to wrap a blanket around herself and feel covered. Blankets were wonderful things.

"Bailey. Bailey, time to wake up." It was Jennifer, she was sure of it. God, even her voice was smooth and posh. How the hell was a woman like her a lowly social worker?

She pretended not to hear.

"Bailey?" The door unlocked and slid open and heeled footsteps approached. Bitty felt someone looming over her. "Bailey, wake up. It's time for breakfast and then we have to go to your hearing."

That got her. Bitty rolled over and looked up into the crystal blue eyes of the social worker. "What?"

"Your court hearing. We need to talk to the judge about where you're going to be put for now."

"A judge?" Bitty asked fearfully, sitting up slowly when the woman stepped back.

"Yes, the judge will decide where to place you and what course of action we'll be taking to help you. I'll be with you during the hearing."

'Oh no, Bitty. A judge! We have to see a judge! We can't see a judge! He'll send us to jail! Bitty, we're going to jail!'

'Bebe, calm down. It's going to be alright. Come here and let's have a cuddle. It'll be okay.'

Bitty felt, more than saw, the child moving to the back and fading out with Sarah, still crying in fear.

With a deep breath, Bitty stood up and followed Jennifer slowly from the cell she'd spent the night in. For one brief moment, she wanted to grab the blanket and bring it with her.

'Pathetic.'

Bitty ignored the jibe. Bailey always got meaner when things were harder. It didn't make it easier to take, but it was at least consistent.

The cafeteria was a bright, noisy place. Surprisingly, Bitty wasn't the only young girl there. Jennifer left Bitty at the door, saying she would be back to collect her for her hearing. Trying not to look at anyone, Bitty took a tray from the pile and slid it along the counter so the food could be put on it. Her stomach rumbled. Ahead of her, an older woman complained loudly about the shit they were trying to feed her.

Sure, the eggs were probably that artificial or powdered or liquid stuff, or whatever institutions used to make their yellow rubber 'scrambled eggs', and the sausages were kind of black. But to Bitty, they were food, and she rarely had that luxury. She wasn't about to complain. If it was reasonably edible, she was happy.

'We could stay here, Bitty. They've got food and beds and clothes and stuff. It's nice.'

'Shut the hell up, Jay! You don't know shit! This is fucking JAIL! Jail isn't nice. It's jail.'

Once her tray was loaded up, Bitty scanned the room carefully, looking for a spot where she stood the least likelihood of being beaten up for looking at someone wrong. She settled on an empty section of the bench near the door, which seemed to be less desirable because of its proximity to the guards watching the room. The two girls on either side of her were both older than her, and one even smiled at her.

As she approached, Bitty even managed to flash the girl a tiny smile in return. "Can I sit here?"

"Do you see a place card?" the older of the two growled without looking up. She was a big black girl with wild hair and a scar across the side of her neck that looked like it had probably been nearly fatal.

"Sure, have a seat," the other girl said, smiling again and showing a mouthful of straight white teeth. Her face was bright and rosy, her eyes glittered, her blond hair shone in the harsh light of the cafeteria, and she looked just beautiful to Bitty. In fact, she seemed like she could have been a model! "Don't mind Tess. She doesn't like kids."

That stung. It had been a long time since Bitty had considered herself a 'kid', and the fact that this other girl thought she was one and held it against her ruffled her feathers.

"I'm not a kid," she mumbled as she sat down and put her tray on the table. It was bolted to the floor.

Tess snorted. "If you're not a kid, then I'm the president's personal bitch."

"Ignore her. I'm Mel. When did you get here?"

"Last night," Bitty mumbled, glancing apprehensively at Tess.

"Figured. Didn't see you yesterday so you must have come after dinner sometime. How long are you here for?"

Bitty shrugged.

"Oh, haven't had a hearing yet, huh?"

Bitty shook her head.

"Oh. Well, it'll be okay. It's not so bad. How old are you?"

"Fourteen," Bitty mumbled around her mouthful of eggs and sausage.

"Wow. Really? What did you do? Shoplifting?"

Tess snorted and Mel looked over Bitty's head at her. "What?"

"Look at her. She ain't no shoplifter."

Bitty felt her face flush as Mel looked down at her appraisingly. "What then?"

"She a damn whore, girl! You know what that is, doncha? Fucks for money? Spreads her legs for sick fucks what like to do lil' kids?"

Bitty dropped her fork and her head, desperately fighting the tears of pain and humiliation that threatened to spill down her face right then and there.

"Tess! That's enough. Leave her alone." Mel wrapped her arms around Bitty's shoulders to give her a reassuring hug.

"NO TOUCHING!" one of the guards called out.

Mel yanked her arm back with a sigh. "Just don't mind her. It's okay. I'm sorry I brought it up."

The rest of breakfast was eaten without speaking, though Bitty was aware of Mel glancing at her every so often and even thought she saw Tess look at her once or twice. She wasn't really sure how she felt about that.

***

The courtroom they stood outside was quite different from what Bitty had imagined. Everything she knew about courts and judges and court stuff came from tv crime dramas; big, dark, wood-filled courtrooms with wooden benches, high judges' stands, and lots of people. This was....not that.

For a start, it was bright. Actually, it was very bright. And warm looking somehow. It wasn't dark and scary like the tv courtrooms. There was carpet on the floor and the seats were like conference room chairs, not benches. The tables were laminated and even the judge's podium wasn't high and intimidating. It was higher than they were, but not by much. There also wasn't a panel of people on the side like on TV.

In fact, the only ones there were her and Jennifer, some other guy in a suit at another table, and the overweight bailiff. She eyed his gun warily, the instinct to duck threatening to make her huddle under the desk. A minute later, the judge came out of a door to one side and went to sit at the podium. She knew it was the judge before he even got to his seat because he was wearing the familiar black gown. That was about the only thing that was like tv. But even that was a little different. It looked more like a long robe than anything.

'*It is a robe, moron.*'

She ignored the jibe.

The other man in the suit stood up from his table and began talking to the judge about who she was, where she'd been taken from, all that stuff. When she was spoken to, Bitty said what the social worker told her to say; mostly 'yes, sir', about her name and age. She was too scared to listen to much, but a few words penetrated the fog of fear.

Prostitute. Trafficking. Jail.

That last one sent a spike of absolute terror through her and she swayed slightly. Jennifer put a hand on her back and rubbed gently. Bitty looked at her with tears in her eyes and a silent plea on her little face, then back at the judge when he said her name.

"Bailey, at this point we're not trying you for anything, do you understand?"

She nodded and he continued.

"I am just ruling about where to put you until you actually do go to trial. My ruling right now is that you will be confined to the juvenile detention facility for the duration of your stay unless your parents will agree to take you home under certain conditions."

'Not likely.'

He said a few more things, but after the mention of juvie and her parents, Bitty had tuned it out. She couldn't listen anymore. She could barely breathe. She couldn't think. She couldn't be here! She closed her eyes and tried not to scream. She needed to not be here right now, mentally, if not physically.

She disappeared. She wasn't aware of who took over or what happened next. She wasn't really even aware of not being out anymore. It was just so wonderful to be quiet and dark. She needed to sleep. She would sleep now.

Bitty slept.

The trial continued and Sarah was a model of perfect behavior and manners. No one was any the wiser.

As usual.

Chapter Fourteen

* Choice One *

Once again, the moment she became aware of anything, Bitty needed to throw up. It was remarkable, really. How could you throw up so much when there was nothing in your stomach to throw up? But it didn't seem to matter.

When she was done, there were other bodily functions to see to, but that was *not* something she wanted to attempt or risk in an alleyway. With a moan of pain and objecting muscles, Bitty pushed up to her feet and stumbled out of the alley. Luckily it was still light. There was no way to tell how long she'd slept, but at least it hadn't been *all* day.

'Can we get pancakes, Bitty?'

She sighed. "What is it with you and pancakes, Bebe?"

'They're yummy. I like them. Can we get some?'

"I don't have any money."

There was a little internal sigh but Bebe didn't push.

"Maybe we can find a couple more clients and make up some of the money we lost..." Bitty mused. There was an indelicate snort from inside.

'Are you fucking kidding me? The kind of guys who look for a whore during the day aren't gonna want a stinking slimy mess like you.'

Bailey's words stung, but they were the truth. She was filthy and stinking.

'Perhaps if we find a quiet bathroom and wash up a bit, Bitty?'

'A bit!? We'd need to run through a fucking carwash!'

"A bathroom sounds good, thanks Sarah." She ignored Bailey's snort of contempt. Thankfully, there was a gas station across the street and down a little, but unfortunately it was the type that needed a key. That meant you had to walk into the store, speak to the cashier to ask for the bathroom key, be handed a wooden plank with the key attached to it, walk through to the back of the store and use the bathroom, then return to the cashier and thank them for the use of the key while trying to avoid the glares when you didn't buy anything. It was humiliating and dangerous. If you got the wrong cashier, they just might call the cops.

Mack had been furious once when he stopped at a gas station like this to let a couple of his girls wash up between jobs. The cashier—or someone in the store anyway—had called the police. Mack had pulled out of the lot without even getting out of his car. He just left the girls to take the fall. Bitty had never found out what happened to them. Someone said they had been released, probably because they weren't kids and served a little while in jail or something, but Bitty had never seen them again. Not in Mack's house, not on the street, nowhere. But you really couldn't worry about those kinds of things when you had to look out for your own neck 24/7.

The problem now was whether or not to risk going into the gas station. Bitty stood outside across the street for a minute or two, watching. Just as she had decided to risk it, she felt Bailey grab at her mind.

'STOP! Check the cars.'

Bitty froze and glanced nervously at the three cars at the pumps. One was a rusty red sedan with a green door and a sheet of plastic over the back window. The driver had his back to her while his car filled, his head down as he texted on his phone that probably cost more than his car.

The second was a bulky brown conversion van very obviously filled with kids of various ages. Their screaming was audible from across the street as the large woman who was presumably their mother headed inside and they called out the things they wanted from the store. The father, equally heavyset, was fiddling with his card in the pump reader and muttering to himself when it seemed not to be reading.

But the third was the one to notice. Not because it was noticeable, but because it wasn't. There was nothing notable about the car. It seemed to be in good condition and was a nondescript navy blue. The windows were tinted, but not illegally like many around here. No flashy hubcaps or bumper stickers. Nothing. Not even a vanity plate. No scratches or dents, no ornaments on the dash. It was so unobtrusive it was almost obvious.

And the driver was sitting in his car. There was no pump handle in his car. His engine was running.

And he was looking at her.

'Walk. But not too fast. Just get the hell out of here. Go!'

Bitty obeyed, turning and trying not to run. After a short way, she risked a glance over her shoulder and her stomach twisted. He was pulling out of the gas station. In her direction!

'Find somewhere to get inside. Quick.'

Bitty didn't really even need Bailey's instruction. Her survival instincts had already kicked in big time. She was in trouble. The moment she reached the corner of the block, she ran. But after a few strides, she nearly fell as she twisted her ankle in her ridiculous heels. Kicking them off, she ran barefoot, glancing over her shoulder again to see the car turning the corner. Now he was on a radio!

'I knew it! He's a cop! Go!'

Bitty didn't have the breath to say, 'I AM'. She just kept running, looking wildly for somewhere to duck into and disappear. Just when she thought she was out of options, she spotted a low cost, chain grocery store that looked reasonably busy.

With a final glance back at the approaching car, she ducked inside and made straight for the back. It was all she could do to keep from running through the store, but she was already drawing looks and wrinkled noses from her appearance and smell. She couldn't risk drawing more by running. When she reached the 'employees only' door, she glanced around, then pushed it open just enough to slip inside.

She could run for the bathroom maybe? No. Then she'd be trapped if they came looking through the store. The best bet was to try and slip out the back. As long as he didn't expect that and swing round the back to wait for her.

For a moment, she stood near the back door, panting and trying to decide what the best idea might be. Finally, she opted for the back door anyway. If he was out there, she'd just run back in and figure something else out. If he wasn't, then she'd make her escape. All she knew was that she couldn't get caught.

Almost holding her breath with fear, she opened the heavy metal back doors and peered outside. Nothing except a delivery truck that was empty. With a quick look over her shoulder back inside, she slipped through the door and dashed around the building along the alleyway between it and the Chinese food place next door.

No one was following her each time she looked back and by the time she was four or five blocks away, she began to relax. Once the grip of terror eased and her adrenaline dropped, she was suddenly very aware of her throbbing bare feet and her pounding head. She felt sick again. She had to get back to Mack.

Without stopping, she took a weary look around, trying to figure out where she was and how to make it back. She looked awful, she felt worse, and she smelled so bad she couldn't possibly take a bus. Tears began to trickle down her dirty cheeks as she walked on and on, wincing as a piece of broken glass sliced her bare foot. But she couldn't stop. If she stopped she was afraid she would either get caught again, or not be able to get up.

Gradually, as she walked, her mind began to drift. Once again, she was thinking of anything but her current position and the misery of her existence. But she was even too tired to count cracks or light posts or anything else anymore. She just walked mindlessly until it all seemed to fade away.

Sarah sighed when she found herself limping along the freezing cold sidewalk in the chilly afternoon. This was bad. She paused and leaned against a building, lifting her bleeding foot to see just how bad the damage was. At least it wasn't so bad that it would need stitches, but she could already see flecks of dirt and stone ground into the wound. She wiped away a tear that threatened to spill off the end of her nose onto it as a sob tore from her throat.

What she wanted more than anything in the world right then was to rest somewhere clean, warm, and safe. But she'd never had that.

'John was like that.'

"Oh, Bebe. Please. Not now."

'But he was so nice. And he took good care of us.'

Sarah sobbed again and tried to blink the tears from her eyes. "John is long gone, Bebe. He was just traveling. He doesn't even live here. It wasn't real." When she didn't get a reply, Sarah sighed and straightened up. Sniffling uselessly, she limped off in the direction they had been going.

Things were beginning to look familiar now. As she was able to recognize places, Sarah began to relax. Almost there. They were almost there. Mack might be in a good enough mood that he would fix her foot up for her. Or at least give her something to ease the pain. That would be nice. Something to forget the last few days. Though she wouldn't admit it, Sarah's mind flitted to the days they had spent in the hotel. If she was honest with herself, she wanted that again too, no matter how ridiculous or impossible it was.

~ Choice Two ~

Once the hearing was over, Sarah was led back to her cell to wait for preparations to be made. She sat cross-legged on the bed, gazing down at the floor uncertainly, her mind running over the last few minutes. Gradually, Bitty began to surface again.

"Welcome back," Sarah said softly.

'Sorry...'

"It's alright. I understand." She sighed softly. "We're staying here for a few days until they process things and send us home."

'Home!? They're sending us home!? They can't do that! Oh god. What do we do?'

'We run away again, obviously. We just get through the next few days, then we're gone as soon as they drop us off. It's no big deal. Quit your damn whining.'

"Bailey, please. She's scared. And, quite frankly, so am I."

'Why? We got away once, we can get away again. We just survive until then. We did it before, we can do it now.'

Chapter Fifteen

* Choice One *

For at least a minute, Sarah stood at the bottom of the steps that led up to Mack's house.

"I think maybe we shouldn't have come back here," she repeated to the others arguing inside.

'What the fuck is wrong with you, Sarah? Of course we had to come back! We've got money and we need a place to rest. Mack's gotta be okay with what we've got. It isn't bad, even without the money that son of a bitch didn't pay us for the last couple hours last night. We have no reason to be scared.'

'Since when does Mack need a reason to beat on us?'

'Shut it, Scarlett!'

A moment later, Bitty felt herself shoved hard and found herself in control of the body once more. In a sudden rush, every ache and pain came crashing down on her and she actually gave a sobbing gasp of shock. It took her a minute to recover, but it was pretty bad.

"I gotta go in, Sarah. I'm sorry. I need to lay down. It hurts so bad." When there was no response, Bitty limped up the steps and opened the door carefully.

Screams greeted her along with the stink of the place. She winced and shut the door behind her before limping slowly down the hall towards Mack's room. Except, that's where the screams were coming from. Dread sank its cold teeth into her chest and she paused just around the corner, debating whether or not to check in and turn over her money right now or not.

The rule was, the minute you walked in that door, you found Mack to turn in your money and tell him you were back in case he had any jobs lined up. If Mack wasn't around, it was one of his guys. Either way, the rule was hand it in before anything else. If you didn't have anything to hand in and were gutsy -or stupid- enough to return before you *did*, you went to take your punishment.

But the screams coming from that room made the hair on her neck stand up. A blind, horrified panic began to threaten to choke her. There was something about those screams that was beyond terrifying. She'd heard them twice before. Each time, there had been a body left when they finally stopped.

She didn't want to step out from behind this wall. She didn't want to see who it was. She didn't want to face him after being gone for so long without a *really* good stack of cash for him. She didn't want to be here

"Oh, God… please help me…" she breathed, tears spilling down her cheeks and sobs threatening to make her presence known anyway. She didn't even know why she kept begging to God. There was no God. She had learned that a very long time ago. There was nothing in this world that could ever save her. Nothing could protect her. Why send a desperate plea to a deity that wasn't there? What was the point?

Maybe if she stepped out now, whoever it was being beaten might be given a little reprieve, though? Maybe she could distract him just enough that he'd forget what he was doing.

'Yeah, and he'd go the fuck after us instead! Great idea. Let's do that.'

'Oh Bailey, come on. We have to try to help them. Please. The longer we stand here, the more trouble they're in. If we go now, then we can give him the money and he'll be happier.'

Bailey didn't reply, which either meant she was too angry to speak, or she was letting them get themselves into trouble by doing what they wanted. Bitty took a deep, shuddering breath to at least try to calm her nerves, then stepped forward into the doorway.

She wished she hadn't.

Katie lay in a bloody heap on the floor, her face almost unrecognizable. Bitty only knew it was Katie because of her clothes. Mack was kicking and punching at her as if she wasn't even a living being, swearing at her madly with the vicious, crazy glint in his eyes that meant he wasn't even really there. She wanted to scream, or throw up, or run, or beg him to stop, or *something*. But she just stood there, horror and terror etched on her thin face.

A half choked sob must have escaped without her realizing it because Mack looked up, glaring at her blankly for a moment before straightening up and giving Katie another hard kick.

"Where the fuck have you been, you stupid bitch?"

Bitty flinched at his words and looked down, doing her best not to look at the moaning, bloody heap on the floor. "I… was…. I was working…" she mumbled softly.

"What? I can't hear you. What were you doing?"

She flinched again. "I was…. whoring…" she whimpered, closing her eyes in misery, her head hanging so low her chin was nearly touching her chest.

"Damn right you were. But I asked *where* the fuck you've been, you stupid shit, not what you were doing. Of course you were whoring. That's all you're good for, isn't it?"

Tears trickled down her face and she nodded, trying not to sob when Katie tried to move and cried out in pain. That brought Mack's attention back on her and he kicked her in the side, making her scream again. Bitty cringed and cried harder.

"Where the fuck is my money?" Mack snarled, stepping closer to Bitty.

She didn't look up at him. She didn't dare. She just reached into her little purse and pulled out the money to hand to him.

He snatched it and began counting. "This is it? What? You couldn't find anyone to fuck your ugly cunt?" He spit in her face. "Look at me."

When she didn't lift her head fast enough, he grabbed her by the throat and forced her head up.

"I said look at me!"

He moved his face down an inch from hers, his fingers gripping her with a fist that said in no uncertain terms that he could snap her neck right then and there if he felt like it and she was only alive because he allowed it.

"You wait here, you keep quiet, and you take a lesson from this. I have some business lined up from online for you when I'm done. You understand?"

Bitty tried to nod but his hand prevented it. He finally released her and she fell backwards, landing with a hard thump on the floor. It knocked the wind out of her for a second and she sat there, stunned.

Mack had already moved back to Katie. Crouching down next to her, he took a fistful of bloody hair and lifted her head to look at him. For just a moment, there was the hint of the tenderness he showed his new girls to hook them, and he stroked a strand of hair from where it stuck to her bloody face. He made a soft 'tut tut' sound with his tongue and shook his head.

"Katie...I don't like it when one of my girls calls the police on me. Did you really think calling the police would get you out of this? You're mine. And I do what I want with my own damn things. And I don't tolerate my things getting me in trouble." He punched her in the face again. After two more blows, Bitty threw up and disappeared.

Callie sat frozen to the spot for a moment, then covered her ears with her hands and closed her eyes. Hunched up with her thighs to her chest, her eyes pressed to her knees as if it would rub out the images she'd just seen, she sat there, too terrified to move. Moving brought attention. Moving was bad. Moving wasn't safe. She didn't even bother trying to figure out where she was. It was never a good idea to move. Ever.

But the beating continued in front of her, the sounds still penetrating her blocked ears. The sickening wet cracking of knuckles on flesh and bone, the smell of blood, the gurgling screams that began to dwindle to whimpers. Callie just sat still and silent, crying quietly. She had no way to tell if she was next, or what she was supposed to be doing, if anything. She didn't know where she was, or when it was. All she knew was that she was here, witnessing yet another murder. How many was that now?

Her mind began to wander, trying desperately to escape the horror in front of her.

There had been that nice girl Daddy had in his bed once when Mommy went away for a while. After they got naked, she had said to Daddy that she wouldn't do anything while Callie was watching. That girl had been nice. Callie had liked that girl. Callie didn't want to watch. Callie hated watching. It meant Daddy was practicing for having Callie later. Callie hated that. But Callie had sat still like Daddy said. Callie was a good girl. Callie was sad when that nice girl was carried away. It hadn't been as messy as this though. Callie missed that nice girl.

There had been that little baby. Callie liked the baby. He was cute. He smelled good after she changed him and got all the poop off. He even smiled at her once. Callie had smiled back. Callie dressed the baby and played with the baby and cuddled the baby all the time. But the baby cried sometimes. Callie thought he was hungry but the can with the white stuff to put in the bottle was empty so Callie just put water in for him. But he still cried too much. Mommy didn't like it. It made Mommy mad. Callie had liked the baby. Callie missed the baby. Callie had cuddled the baby for a long time after Mommy made him go to sleep. But the baby didn't wake up again. He smelled bad after a while. He didn't smell good like he used to. Callie had really liked the baby before he smelled bad. Callie missed the baby the most.

Callie had a friend once too. They didn't talk. They weren't allowed to talk. But they went places together for the parties. Callie didn't like the parties. The parties hurt. They hurt her and her friend. Sometimes Callie held hands with her friend while they got hurt by Daddy's friends. But her friend bit someone when they put their thing in her mouth and she couldn't breathe. She had hurt Callie's hand squeezing so hard. After she bit him, the man got angry. He hurt her friend a lot. Daddy made her watch. Daddy said that would happen to her if she was bad. Callie didn't want to watch. It hurt Callie's insides to watch. Callie had gone to her friend when Daddy and his friends went to the other room. Callie held her friend's hand until her friend let go. Callie had to get a garbage bag to put her friend in when Daddy said. Friends shouldn't go in garbage bags. Callie missed her friend.

There had been the lady with all the pictures on her arms. Callie didn't know her but she seemed nice. She gave Callie a sucker once when she was so hungry. Mack got mad at her for something. She said it was her money and she could spend some to give Callie a sucker. Callie had to cover her ears that time too. Her insides hurt again when she saw Mack hitting her. Callie didn't like it when her insides hurt. It made her cry. Callie missed the picture lady.

There was that man who hurt Callie but he didn't give Mack any money for it. And he didn't pay for the white sugar Mack let him put in his nose, either. Callie had covered her ears that time too, but it had been too late. The bang was so loud it made her ears ring for a long time. And wet red stuff sprayed all over her too. It was gross. Callie didn't miss that man.

There was another girl who made Mack mad. Callie didn't know why that time. She didn't remember anything before that. She only remembered sitting in the corner covering her ears and eyes as the girl screamed.

She didn't like those times. The times she couldn't remember anything before. It was scary to just suddenly be there when someone was getting hurt in front of her. Callie didn't like that. It made Callie so very scared. Callie didn't know that girl, but Callie's insides still hurt when she didn't move anymore.

And her insides hurt now. Callie didn't know this girl either. But it still hurt her insides to see her getting hurt so bad. Callie didn't want to see it or hear it. But she didn't dare move. She cried silently into her knees, trying hard to press her palms tightly enough against her ears to stop the screaming from getting in. But after a while, it was quiet except for the smacking, cracking noise of Mack's fist and boot. Finally, even that stopped and she heard the creak of the couch as he sank down on it.

Callie slowly lifted her head and opened her eyes just enough to see, then closed them again tightly. Callie felt sick. Callie didn't want to see. Callie stayed still and quiet, her eyes closed and her ears covered. Eventually, Callie lay down on the floor, curled up in a ball while Mack watched tv. Callie was tired. Callie hurt. Callie wanted to sleep for a while. Callie slept.

Chapter Sixteen

* Choice One *

An hour later, Mack hadn't even bothered to move the girl's body before dragging Callie out of the room to go somewhere. Callie stayed quiet, shooting one last, sad glance over her shoulder at the still form of the other girl. It had been a long time. The girl hadn't moved once. Mack had kicked her one last time on his way over to grab Callie. There hadn't been a sound. Callie wondered if the girl would be gone when she got back. Probably.

Callie was tired. Callie wanted to sleep in the corner with a blankie. But Callie didn't have a blankie. Callie had to sit still and quiet in the car. Callie looked out the window as they drove fast on the busy road. Callie imagined what it would be like to ride in the other cars. She made up stories about the people in the other cars as they drove.

The big gold car with the pretty lady and all the kids looked like a nice car to be in. There was even a tv playing while they were driving! The lady looked kind. She didn't look like she would hit Callie. She looked like a mommy. A nice mommy. Callie wished she had a mommy like that.

There was a pickup truck with a trailer. It was loud. But when she looked into the trailer, there was a horse inside! Callie imagined riding that horse. Callie would ride it far away. They would run fast together. The horse would take her far away from all the mean, sad things. Callie would be best friends with the horse. Callie thought the horse's name must be Blackie. It was a black horse. Callie liked the horse.

After a long time, Mack stopped the car at a hotel and pulled Callie out of it and to a side door where another man was waiting. Callie felt tears stabbing her eyes when the man looked at her. Callie didn't like men. Men hurt Callie. Callie wanted to run away with the horse. Callie imagined the horse while the man took her to his room and did things to her. He did things to her for a long, long time. But Callie thought of the horse and the places they would go together. Callie went far, far away with the horse. They went so far away, the men couldn't hurt her anymore. The horse was kind and gentle. The horse liked Callie. Callie liked the horse.

***

Bitty was exhausted, aching, and thirsty. There had been a lot of men during the night. One of them had brought her a fast food combo at least. She had been grateful for that. But that had been hours and hours ago. She'd barely been given time to use the toilet between customers. She had no idea where they were other than a generic, unidentifiable hotel room. She wasn't even sure how long they'd been here. It seemed they'd been here for a while before she was out fronting again. It had been just one customer after another. They didn't even say hi. Why do you say hi to a chair when you walk in the room? Or a toilet? That's pretty much what she felt like. A toilet. Bitty was simply an item in the room to deposit bodily fluids into and leave again. Except that when the toilet broke, they would fix it. When Bitty broke, it didn't matter.

Sometime after the sun was up, Mack came back to collect her, shoving her clothes at her to put on and watching her closely as she dressed.

"God, you're an ugly bitch. I can't believe people actually pay me to fuck you. I should be paying them to do it."

A tear trickled down Bitty's face and she hung her head, her heart cracking even more.

If you've never felt your heart break, you're lucky. It really does hurt. A lot. It starts as a tightness in your chest, then instantly spreads like electricity through every nerve in your body before rushing back to your chest equally quickly. It leaves your fingertips tingling and numb, and your body ice cold and clammy. You feel sick to your stomach and your heart feels like it's stopped beating for a minute. You can't breathe. You can't think of anything but the shattering, tearing feeling in your chest. Then it sinks into your stomach to settle there with the nausea, and you grudgingly begin to breathe again. But you wonder why you bother anymore. Eventually, it goes numb, and it just sort of sits there, like a lump in your chest. It hurts more than you can imagine.

Once she was dressed, Mack led her back to his car for another few hours' worth of driving to another city and another hotel. Apparently, he really had lined up some work for her. Bitty took the opportunity to sleep a little during the drive. She hadn't had any sleep for a while and she was exhausted.

There was no way to tell how long she'd been asleep or how far they'd driven except that the sun was much lower on the horizon. But it didn't matter. Time didn't matter. Time was just a way for people to know when to wake up, go to work, eat, go to bed, meet friends, and relax. There was no other reason. And none of those reasons mattered to Bitty. She had none of those reasons. Time wasn't a thing for Bitty. She just existed.

Bitty existed for another two days and a night before Mack finally drove back home to his usual place the second night. Surprisingly, he even allowed Bitty to stagger inside and collapse in a corner to sleep for a few hours. Her body throbbed and ached, her head was spinning, she was hungry and thirsty, sick and exhausted.

~ Choice Two ~

"I didn't stay away, so I guess that's what got me in trouble. They said they were just running in for some stuff. I didn't know they were gonna empty a cart of DVDs and games into the back of the car and tell me to floor it. I wouldn't have done it if I had. But the police didn't care. So I'm here for a couple months and I have probation for a year after." Mel was sitting on the couch in the common room, braiding Bitty's hair while the girl sat between her knees listening.

"It's not so bad, though. I'm taking online classes so I can finish high school at least. I got a special exception for that I guess. What grade are you in?"

Bitty shrugged. "I dunno."

"Oh. Sorry."

"It's okay."

Over the last couple of days, Mel had swept Bitty under her wing, and even Tess seemed to be watching out for her unobtrusively. Bitty had seen her intercept a group of girls on their way over to Bitty during dinner later that first day. She hadn't been able to hear what was said, but she'd caught a lot of glares in her direction and Tess stepped up in front of one of the girls in the group, towering over her and glowering, her chest out menacingly. The group had backed off with a few swears and rude gestures. Tess had glanced back at Bitty, scowling when she caught her eye, then stalked off to get her tray for dinner. No one said anything about it when she sat down next to Bitty, Mel on her other side.

It was hard not to focus on the fact that they were warm, fed, and relatively safe—thanks to Mel and Tess—for the first time in their lives. Despite the dread of being sent home looming over her head, Bitty was almost happy. Only once, on her last night in the facility, did her mind drift to Mack and how furious he was going to be with her once she got back.

'Why do we have to go back? I'm sure word has gotten out that we've been arrested. Why not just let him think we're in jail and go somewhere else?'

"Like where?" Bitty mumbled, laying in bed and gazing up at the ceiling.

'I don't know. We could work for ourselves. We don't need a pimp. Then we could keep all the money we make.'

'Oh there's a great fucking idea! And where are we gonna get clients that he won't find out about? If he sees us on the street not working for him he'll kill us! Genius, Sarah. Fucking genius.'

'It was just a suggestion...'

'Well it was stupid.'

"Well, they're coming tomorrow to get me."

"What?" Her cell mate lifted her head to look at her blearily.

"Nothing. Sorry." Bitty rolled over and faced the wall. She'd been too loud. She really had to watch that. It might pay to practice talking to the others without having to say it out loud. Then she might not be caught so much. Mildred had been right. People probably thought she was crazy.

Chapter Seventeen

* Choice One *

Scarlett woke up on the floor to find someone already using her. She recognized the guy by sight. He was one of Mack's gaming buddies. He'd probably won something. This one wasn't so bad. He was still kind of old, but he wasn't disgusting like a lot of the others. And he wasn't too rough. Scarlett actually kind of liked him sometimes. She smiled and lifted her knees to let him deeper.

He lifted his head in surprise, then grinned when he saw her smile and kissed her hard, giving her a hard, deep thrust. "Morning. You like my dick inside you?"

Scarlett nodded and wrapped her arms around his neck. "Mmmm… yeah. You feel sooo good." Her hips lifted to meet his thrusts which picked up in excitement.

"Ohhh… yeah. Tell me again," he demanded, picking up speed.

"You feel amazing. So good." She almost wished she hadn't, because in his excitement he began going faster and more violently, and her back was scraping along the filthy hard floor, scratching on the splinters in places. But she was proud of how she was making him feel. Only she could do that. She was a lot of Mack's friends' favorite girl and she knew it was her and only her that did it. Not Bailey. Not Bitty. Scarlett. She was the one guys loved to be inside. She was the one who made them all feel amazing. She was the one who was their best lay. She was the best. It filled her with a certain pride. Not many other people could ever claim to be someone's best fuck.

He didn't last long after she woke up and participated. Soon enough he was groaning in her ear as he finished inside her. Her satisfaction was momentary, though. Almost immediately he'd winked at her and gotten up, leaving her sprawled on the filthy floor with her skirt up around her hips, alone and dirty once again.

Scarlett hated those moments. They felt cold and disgusting. She did her best for them. She made them happy and satisfied them. But then she was alone again. Dirty, used, filled, and alone.

'You're not alone, Scarlett.'

She smiled sadly and pulled her skirt back down before sitting up with a sigh. "I know. Thanks, Jay. It's just... never mind. You're right. I'm not alone." She wiped the tiny tear from the corner of her eye and stood up, shoving the hurt deep down and ignoring it. She was a whore. She was good at sex. She had no right to want anything more than that. She was good at what she did, she made people happy, and that made her happy. That's all she needed. Wasn't it...?

~ Choice Two ~

The morning Bitty had been dreading arrived with a discordant amount of sunshine for a day that threatened to be horrific. She went through the motions of dressing, brushing her teeth, combing her hair, and going to breakfast. Mel was waiting for her, and even Tess was watching her with something close to concern on her life-hardened face. Bitty hadn't told them what her parents were like, she hadn't said she didn't want to go home, she hadn't mentioned the fact that she was not entirely sure she would live to see tomorrow. But they seemed to know. Both were quiet and serious, as if sensing that Bitty just couldn't think clearly enough to have a conversation. Mel guided her onto the bench between her and Tess once they had their trays, and all three ate in relative silence.

Not that Bitty wanted to eat. She felt sick, cold, and sluggish, as if she was crawling through the sludge of terror that was threatening to drown her. How could she go to someone and tell them that she didn't want to go home? Would they even believe her? No one had before. And they would probably just say she was trying to get out of being punished or something. But it might be the last good meal she got for a while, so it would probably be best to eat anyway.

After she'd forced down as much as she could, she sat numbly until they were released into the common room, then sat down to wait. She had nothing to pack or prepare, so she simply had to wait. Wait for the executioner almost. Though, it couldn't be worse than what she'd get if she went back to Mack, could it? That helped a little bit. Just a little.

An hour later, she was called to the door where she was met by the social worker, Jennifer. The woman smiled warmly at her and Bitty tried to smile back, though she wasn't entirely sure it didn't come out more like a sick grimace than a smile. But she didn't care. She didn't need to worry about how she looked to Ms. Perfection.

Jennifer led her down the corridor to the front of the building and the desk near the exit. Her parents were waiting for her. Neither of them looked happy to see her, or even slightly relieved that she was okay. She hadn't seen them in over a year, but no one would have been able to tell that. Neither of them even smiled. They had probably had to pay to get her or something, Bitty figured. They probably thought it was a waste of money getting their daughter out of jail.

The guard at the desk went through her restrictions with her parents and Jennifer, noting the date for her court appearance on the paper her parents had to sign, then handed over her belongings. Her parents hadn't brought her anything else to wear, so Bitty was forced to wear the clothes Mildred had given her. She didn't want to put them on again. She wanted to forget about that woman and how she had betrayed the girl who had wanted so badly to trust her. The guard gestured to a bathroom nearby and said she could go in there to change, and that she had to return the uniform and throw away the underwear. Bitty shrank into herself at the look her father gave her at the mention of underwear and quickly lowered her head.

Once she'd slunk off to the bathroom to change into the street clothes and handed back the uniform, Bitty waited silently near the desk. The look of greed that flashed across her parents' faces when they spotted her little purse in the bag now that it was empty made her stomach clench. At least there was no money in it. It wouldn't have lasted long if there had been, she was sure.

Finally, everything was signed, returned, noted, and paid for, and Jennifer shook all their hands with a warm smile, then turned and left Bitty with her parents.

Once again, Bitty risked a glance up at their faces and shrank back at the look on them. They were silent as they led her from the building to the car and gestured for her to get into the backseat, but once they started the engine, they both turned around in their seats to look at her.

The expression on her mother's face was disgust and greed. It made Bitty want to cry. The look on her father's face, however, made her feel sick. It was a very different kind of greed. She pressed herself back into the seat with her head down and her arms around her waist.

"So you're a whore, huh?" came her father's voice, thick with something disgusting. "You been fucking a lot of men, huh?" Her mother didn't even seem to notice. "You been making money doing that? Where is it? Where's the fucking money?"

When there was an expectant silence, Bitty realized she was supposed to actually answer that. "I..... g-gave it all.... to m-my.... to.... Mack...." she whispered.

"Who's Mack? Your pimp?" her father asked.

Bitty nodded. He spoke again but Bitty tried not to listen. She couldn't even look up at him.

There was the certain knowledge that she had escaped one pimp, only to return to her first; her parents.

Chapter Eighteen

* Choice One *

Mack hadn't lined up jobs for today like he had the last few days. Today, Scarlett was back out on her own with a quota to fill as usual. She didn't feel good today. She felt hot and uncomfortable, but shivering. Her throat hurt, her head hurt, her entire body ached, and she couldn't stop coughing. She was miserable. Well, more miserable than usual.

Her foot hadn't had much time to heal, but the last couple of days of work, she'd spent most of her time on her back or stomach, so she hadn't had to be on it much. But now she had to be out walking on the streets today and it hurt a lot.

She hadn't had a chance to even really look at it despite Sarah's urging to do so before it got infected. She hadn't really thought much about anything except sleeping, drinking, and eating when she wasn't being used over the last few days.

Mack hadn't been very happy about her lost shoes, either. He'd given her another pair -well, thrown them at her head- and told her if she lost that pair he'd make a new pair with her own skin. They looked horribly like the ones Katie had been wearing when she…

Scarlett shivered and whimpered softly, trying not to cry from misery. She didn't want to be out here in the cold working, trying to please men so they would give her money she couldn't keep. She wanted to sleep, curled up on a soft bed with a warm blanket over her. A car drove by and she wiped the tear from her cheek and limped over to sell herself again.

~ Choice Two ~

Bitty hadn't spoken since answering her parents' questions in the car on the way home. Now, she sat on her father's lap on the stinking couch while he watched tv and fondled her, his disgusting hand down her pants right in front of her mother. Bitty had stopped even wondering if her mother would notice, let alone protect her. She'd realized a long time ago that her mother didn't care.

Her father's prickly chin brushed against her neck as his fingers pressed deeper into her. She cringed, turning her face. Her mother was on the phone, a glass of something golden and a cigarette in her other hand, talking to someone about the cost of something.

"So you fucked a lot of men without my permission, huh? Lots of guys used this?" he asked, wiggling his finger.

Bitty didn't respond except to wipe a tear from her cheek, her shoulders hunched tightly.

"Sure. Fine. $50. Tell your friends." Her mother hung up and glanced at Bitty, down at her husband's hand in her daughter's pants, then away to the tv. "Be quick. I've got guests coming."

Bitty stared at her in horror as her father licked her neck and pushed her off his lap and between his knees. He wasn't even trying to hide it anymore as he pushed his filthy sweatpants down and pulled out his dick.

She couldn't help the sob of disgust when he grabbed her by the hair and pushed her down on him. Her mother didn't even look over again, despite her father's sickening moans and grunts.

Bailey hated them. She hated them with every ounce of her being. She wished they would die. She wished she could kill them. She would kill them if she ever got the chance! They were her parents! They were supposed to protect her, not do this to her! She struggled against his grip, but his fingers tightened painfully in her hair and he pushed her harder.

"You're just gonna make him mad. Just suck it you stupid bitch. Any whore daughter of mine should know how to suck her Daddy's cock."

He half chuckled, half grunted at that and continued to use her mouth. But if that had been all, it might have been something she could tune out and block. If only he hadn't started talking.

Anger, disgust, and fury rose in Bailey's chest as he talked about her and the things she'd done or probably done. He was getting off on it. It was sickening. She hated him so much. All she had to do was....

'DON'T BITE HIM, BAILEY! DON'T! I KNOW WHAT YOU'RE THINKING! DON'T BITE HIM! HE'LL KILL YOU!'

As much as Bailey wanted to ignore the desperate plea from Sarah, she knew she was right. If she bit, she'd be dead. For a few more minutes, she bore the humiliation until he was finished. But that was all she could take. The second he released her head, she lifted it and spit her mouthful all over his face and chest, then stood up abruptly.

"DON'T YOU EVER FUCKING TOUCH ME AGAIN, YOU SICK SON OF A BITCH!"

Dead silence greeted her unexpected outburst and there was instant sobbing inside.

'Ohh, Bailey! What have you done!? Oh God. We're in so much trouble!'

'Why would you do something like that, Bailey!?'

'Bailey! Oh, Bailey, why!?'

Bailey simply stood stock still, glaring at her father and mother, defiance shining brightly in her eyes, fury and hatred seething inside her like a volcano about to erupt. She didn't care about consequences anymore. She was finished. She wasn't going to be anyone's toy anymore.

Chapter Nineteen

* Choice One *

Four hours since she'd started that day, Scarlett had only made $120. She knew she wasn't exactly selling herself very well, coughing and shivering like she was. Her bruises stood out on her pale face and her hair stuck to her forehead with sweat despite how cold she was. Her foot was throbbing and felt hot and tight in the high heel she'd forced it into. And she couldn't stop crying.

Twice, she'd approached a car only to have them give her a nervous, disgusted look and shake their heads before driving away quickly. The second time, she'd just sunk down onto the curb and burst into miserable tears.

'I wish we could go home.'

'Shut up, Bebe. We can't go home! You don't know what it was like. It was a nightmare! Worse than this! We're not going home. Moron.'

'Bailey. That's enough. Let her be.'

'Fuck off, Sarah.'

'I wish we could find someone to help us.'

'Oh, grow the fuck up, Jay. No one is ever going to help us.'

'John was nice. Why can't we live with John?'

'Oh, Bebe, dear. John is probably far away by now. He doesn't live here, remember?'

'Oh. I miss him. He was nice.'

'I know. Me too.'

"I..... can't s–stay....." Scarlett muttered between chattering teeth. "I can't.... stay out...h–here. I'm g–going... back." Without listening to the gasps of dismay from the others, she pushed herself to her feet and hobbled back along the darkening streets to Mack's house.

"You met your quota already?" Mack growled suspiciously when he saw her.

Scarlett shook her head as she coughed hard. "N–no. I just... I need to... to lay down, Mack..."

He hit her hard across the face, sending her sprawling to the floor with a cry of pain. She huddled there weakly, unable to stand up right away.

"You wanna lay down, you can get out there and lay down on your back. Don't you fucking come back without my goddamn money!" He kicked her as he passed.

Scarlett lay gasping and sobbing on the floor, trembling and coughing. She couldn't do this. She couldn't. She needed to get away. She needed out.

Bitty's sobs were more quiet than Scarlett's had been; less heart wrenching and pathetic. She was used to being sore and miserable and wounded. Scarlett wasn't. Not outside of sex, anyway.

After a few minutes, Bitty pushed herself to her feet, gasping in pain as her weight came down on her injured foot. Scarlett hadn't let on just how badly it had hurt! No wonder she'd needed a break!

It felt a lot harder leaving the house tonight than it had the last time. It was taking everything she had just to keep going and not turn around to curl up somewhere and sleep. Without realizing it, she was crying as she walked. She just had to make some more money, then she could rest. Just a little more. She could do it. Just a little more.

~ Choice Two ~

The silence seemed to stretch forever after Bailey spat on her father. Her heart raced and a sick feeling gripped her stomach, icy and dark. In a remarkably calm manner, her father wiped the combined spit and semen from his face and stood up, but when he fixed his eyes on her, there was death in them. Bailey swallowed and tried not to shrink back, but it obviously didn't work because a sneer marred his face and he stepped closer to her, looming over her like a tower.

She didn't even see it coming. Before she even knew what hit her, Bailey was on the floor, blood filling her mouth. Her father could hit as hard as Mack any day of the week and he seemed to enjoy it just as much.

He stared down at her, his jaw hard and his eyes cold. "You do that to me again, you stupid bitch, and I will make sure you never live to do it to anyone else, do you understand me?" he said, his voice dangerously quiet.

Bailey looked away, her own jaw clenched against the rebuttal she was desperate to throw at him.

"Paul, leave off. You shoulda made her swallow it before you let her head up. It's your own damn fault."

Her father turned to glare at her mother angrily. "You want my next load?" He sneered when she looked away and shook her head. "Then keep your damn mouth shut, Laura."

He turned back to Bailey. "You're gonna make that up to me and you'd better do it good. You're mine and I won't be treated that way. Now get your sorry ass into that bedroom and stay there."

Bailey wiped her mouth with the back of her hand and stood up, glaring at him but staying silent for a change. She didn't even look at the woman sitting on the couch beside him, though she was fairly sure her mother wasn't looking at her, either. Without a word, she turned and walked down the hall to her old bedroom. She wasn't surprised to find it untouched. She doubted they'd even gone in there when she'd disappeared.

With an angry sigh, she sat down on the bed and crossed her arms, glaring around the room. It wasn't much. It never had been. But she'd tried to make it her own as she'd grown up. Over the years, she'd cut out pretty pictures from magazines and taped them to the peeling walls; photographs of horses, dogs, cats, happy families...

There was a doll—or at least, the remnants of a doll—in the corner. Bailey felt Bebe give a sharp cry of dismay when her eyes landed on it and she felt a pang of sympathy for the child. It had been the only thing Bebe really ever owned and she loved it. It had been that Christmas gift from the one nice Christmas they'd ever had. She very carefully made sure Bebe couldn't see the memories Bailey had of that night, after all the pleasantness came to an end. The visions of drinking, screaming, hitting, and her father angry at her for closing her legs against him as she tried to play with the doll that night raced through her mind and she closed her eyes with a shudder. The doll had been the last straw.

Bebe had adored that doll. And her father had known that when he destroyed it right in front of her face; although, he didn't know it was Bailey by then. She had glared right back at him as he did it while laughing, torturing the toy and his daughter by doing so. She had stayed quiet as he'd taken his use of her and left her with the mangled pieces of the beautiful doll, but inside she had been seething. More than once, she'd pictured that knife being stuck in his own chest and not the doll's. The worst part of that moment was the realization that she wouldn't feel sorry if she did it. That was the moment she had realized they needed to get out.

So they had. When she could hear her parents' drunken snores from the other bedroom, she had put on her boots and jacket and she had left. She hadn't even cleaned up the pieces of the doll. She had just run.

The hope—or perhaps the desperate aching need to believe—that there was something better out there for her drove her to run. She just needed to get away. And she had. But all she had managed to do was get them into the same situation with a different person. She had just changed their location. She had failed. She had failed then, and she had failed now. They were back where they started, worse for wear, and there was nothing they could do about it.

Bailey turned and buried her face in her pillow and sobbed. She sobbed like she'd never done in her entire life. She had always been the strong one. The one who stood up for them all. The one who knew what to do and how to get out of things the best way. The one who could take care of them. The one who could save them.

But she couldn't. She was helpless. In all her life, Bailey had never felt the way she felt right now. Bailey was broken.

Chapter Twenty

* Choice One *

There didn't seem to be any distinction between days anymore. There wasn't usually, but at the moment it was worse. Bitty slipped in and out of it, the others taking turns as she faded into the back when things got too much. None of them could take much for long anymore. Everything hurt fifty times more. Even being straight up fucked by a small dick hurt like she was being rammed by a monster. Her body was hot to the touch, her muscles were tender and trembling, and she was so weak it was hard to stand upright.

Things blurred into nothing more than tableaus of moments. A car. A man. A cigarette. A hot meal. Snow. A man. Another man. Pain. Mack. Pain. A man. Money. Mack.

Over and over again, in a seemingly endless rotation, Bitty went through the motions of her existence.

Obey. Obey. Obey.

Just a little more, then we can lie down. Just a little more, then Mack won't be angry. Just a little more, then we can eat. Just a little more. Just a little more. Just a little more.

Her foot got worse. It swelled up and began to ooze greenish brown stuff when she pressed on the hard, hot spot where the cut was. It smelled bad and the pain was enough to make her throw up once. But it did feel better when some of the pressure was gone. Of course, it was right back within a few hours. And it was beginning to spread up her foot into her ankle now. She just wanted to curl up until she stopped hurting. She couldn't even remember what that felt like anymore. What was it like to not hurt…?

~ Choice Two ~

For four miserable days after her parents had taken her home from jail, Bitty was put through just as much as Mack ever did. But somehow it had always been a thousand times more disgusting when her father did those things to her than when anyone else did. It hadn't felt this horrible when Mack had sold her, used her, beat her. But when it was her parents doing the selling and using, it felt like a white hot poker was stirring her insides and making her sick and angry.

"Bailey..." she whispered on the fifth day of being home, "we should leave again. I want to leave again. Bailey... please help me leave."

'What's the point. This is it for us, Bitty. This is all there is. We can never escape, we can never be more. This is all there is.'

"Bailey, please!" she whimpered, curling up on her bed in a ball. "Bailey, I want to leave. How do we leave?"

There was silence.

After an hour or so of crying, Bitty wiped her eyes and sat up. "Fine. If you're not gonna help me, then I'll do it myself. We can just–" She broke off abruptly when her father's head poked into the room and she shrank back.

"Get dressed and quit talking to yourself, you crazy bitch. You gotta be in court today and I'm not getting the cops dragged down on my ass cuz you're not there. Hurry up."

Bitty sat frozen on the bed for a moment after he left, her head reeling.

'Bitty! Bitty, we can tell the police or the judge! They can help us! Bitty! They can take us away from here! Please, Bitty! We can get out of here!'

Bitty didn't say anything as she dressed and walked out to the living room to meet her parents. They looked remarkably decent, dressed up as they were. Probably wanting to make a good impression with the judge or something. In silence, she was escorted out of the house to the car and shoved in, buckling automatically.

If she did tell someone, would they believe her? Would she be able to talk to anyone alone? She didn't think she could tell anyone with her parents standing right next to her. But if she asked to talk to someone in private, her parents would know something was up anyway. Either way, she'd be in trouble. And if whoever she spoke to didn't listen, or didn't believe her, she'd be in even more trouble.

But she had to get out of here. And Bailey wasn't helping anymore. Bitty wasn't sure what had happened while she'd been inside, but Bailey had barely talked to anyone over the last four days. And when she did, it was nothing good or even helpful. It was just… hopeless. And no one knew why. Bailey had always been the strongest of them.

Bitty still hadn't decided what to do when they reached the courthouse. Her parents escorted her into the building, one on either side of her. With her arms wrapped around her waist and her shoulders hunched, she would have looked like a prisoner if she'd been wearing the uniform. As it was, people seemed to think she was just feeling bad for being in trouble. They didn't even look twice at her.

Not that there was anything to see. Her parents had been very careful after that first night to keep the bruises in places clothes would cover. They had bathed her, brushed her hair, and chosen her clothes for today. There was no reason anyone would have to think she was being abused. No one would believe her.

The hearing went quickly and quietly, with no opportunity to speak to anyone. The judge asked her parents if they felt she was safe at home, unlikely to run away and get into trouble again, and of course, they nodded quickly. Both promised she was happy now and they had worked through the teenage angst that had caused her to run away in the first place. Bitty was never even given a chance to speak in private.

She walked out with them in the same silence she'd walked in with, fighting tears of frustration, betrayal, and hopelessness. There was no one to help her. No one would ever help her. She was alone.

'You're not alone, Bitty. We're here. We're still here.'

She nodded slightly and hugged herself a little more tightly as she sank into the back seat of the car and drove back to her nightmare realm. This time, as they drove, Bitty was thinking more clearly now. Bailey might not be there to plan and help her with an escape, but Sarah was right. She wasn't alone. She was never alone. Just because Bailey wasn't going to help, that didn't mean that she couldn't do it with the others' help. They would do it tonight. As soon as her parents were asleep, she would run.

Chapter Twenty-One

* Choice One *

The last guy who had dropped her off had given her half of what he was supposed to have paid for the things she did. She had argued, but she was just so tired, and sore, and weak. And he knew it. He could sense it. There was nothing she was going to do about it and by the time she reported him to Mack, the guy would be long gone. All that she could do would be give Mack his plate number so that if he came back the other girls would steer clear and Mack might be able to go after him then. But for now, Bitty was screwed.

Limping down the sidewalk towards the house, Bitty's tears began to flow faster in fear and pain. Mack was going to be furious. She had almost nothing to give him. She was in so much trouble. But she couldn't stay out any longer. She had to sleep! She needed to sleep!

Once they reached the house and she hauled herself up the stairs, Bitty paused at the door, her hand resting on the handle as she braced herself to enter. "I can't..." she whimpered.

'Maybe he'll understand you're sick...'

Sarah's voice didn't sound hopeful and Bitty knew the chance was slim to none. But she was desperate. With a sniffle and a cough, she turned the handle and entered.

Mack was snoring in his lounger in front of the TV, one of his other girls passed out on the floor at his feet with a needle in her arm. Waking him up would not be a great idea. Not at all. Especially not with only this much money. So she limped over to the corner, kicked off her shoes, and curled up on the floor, crying herself to sleep softly.

~ Choice Two ~

After another long, horrific day of 'working' for her parents, Bitty curled up and cried miserably. She didn't feel good. She'd been feeling sick all the time lately, and she was just exhausted. She wanted to rest. She just wanted a break from life for a little while. Maybe her father wouldn't come tonight. Maybe he'd know she was exhausted after the seemingly endless parade of men they had sold her to today. It was more than it used to be before she ran away.

But a few minutes later, her door opened. She lay still, pretending to be sleeping, hoping that might make him leave her alone. But of course not. Why would he care whether she was asleep or not. He just wanted her body. A moment later, she felt him.

Her tears flowed unchecked and she sobbed into her pillow. She didn't worry about being quiet anymore. It didn't even matter. There was no one to hide it from. He had always threatened her to keep quiet or her mother would kill her for doing those things to him, but her mother knew. She had presumably always known, if her behavior the last few days was anything to go by. So there was no reason to keep quiet. He didn't even seem to care anyway. Not anymore. He just kept going until he satisfied himself with her body and left her again.

For a long time, Bitty just lay curled up where she was on her bed, crying miserably into the pillow, hoping she could just go to sleep and never wake up. Eventually, she managed to stop crying and simply lay there for a while, staring at the wall.

'Bitty, if we're going to go tonight, we should get ready. I think I heard them going to bed...'

Bitty didn't move or answer.

'Bitty? Did you hear me? We should go soon if we're going to go.'

After a minute or so, Bitty finally nodded and wiped her cheeks. "K." For a little while longer, she lay still and silent, listening to the sounds outside her room. When she was certain she could hear two distinct snores, she slowly and carefully got up and tiptoed as quietly to the door as possible. Her mother's winter coat was dropped on the floor by the door where they had walked in earlier and Bitty picked it up to put on. At least she had a coat now. For a while.

There was a noise from her parent's bedroom and she froze, her heart racing and her breath stuck in her chest. What if they woke up, or one of them came out here for something? What if they caught her trying to leave? She'd be dead. She knew she'd be dead.

It felt like forever that she stood frozen next to the door, holding her breath and waiting to be discovered and beaten. But nothing happened. No one came. With a sigh of relief, Bitty gently tugged the door open and slipped out the moment it was wide enough, shutting it quietly behind her. Without looking back, she hurried down the steps and away from that hell hole for the second time in barely more than a year. Maybe this time she could stay away...

Chapter Twenty-Two

* Choice One *

WHACK

A boot to her ear woke Bitty from her fevered sleep. She cried out and curled up with her hands over her head, sobbing.

"What the fuck is this!?" Mack shouted at her. He stood over her with her purse in his hands, the measly income she'd managed to make that night obviously already counted. He was furious, as she'd expected.

"I'm sorry! I'm sorry!" she sobbed, cowering from him. "I tried. I just had to lay–"

WHACK

"I told you, you stupid, worthless whore! If you wanna lay down, you go lay on your back, spread your fat legs, and get me some fucking money for it!"

WHACK

His fist impacted on her throbbing skull, then grabbed a handful of hair and pulled her head up to look at him. "You come back here again without that damn money and I will use you as an example, do you understand me!?"

"Yes!" she sobbed, closing her eyes and trying not to cough in his face. He dropped her and turned on his heel, tossing her purse back at her. She pushed to her feet once more and sobbed as she forced her foot back into the shoe again, then limped back out onto the street.

~ Choice Two ~

'Do we have to go back to Mack?'

"Where else would we go?"

Bitty had slowed down once they got a good distance from the house and was now walking quietly along the silent sidewalk, the jacket pulled closely around her.

'I don't like Mack. Can't we go to Mildred?'

'DON'T YOU EVER FUCKING SAY THAT NAME AGAIN!'

'Bailey! There's no need to talk to her like that! Bebe, remember it was Mildred who got us sent back home. We're not going back to her.'

"There's nowhere else to go, Bebe. Anywhere else we go will probably just send us right back again. Mack is the only option. I'm sorry," she added when the child began to cry. To be honest, she felt like crying too. She didn't want to go back any more than Bebe did.

Once they reached the house, Bitty stood at the bottom of the steps, looking up at the front door and swallowing hard. She felt sick and scared. She had no money to bring back and she was being watched by the authorities now. If anyone saw her, she'd be a liability to Mack and his whole crew. What if he took one look at her and kicked her out, or worse...

'At least it would be over. We could get out of this miserable existence...'

Wiping a tear from her cheek with a trembling hand, Bitty took a deep breath and climbed the steps to the front door. Before she could open it, though, it opened itself. Before she knew it, she was looking right up into Mack's face as he almost ran her over.

"What the–" he started, then glared. "Bitty! Where the fuck have you been?" He grabbed her by the jacket collar and hauled her inside, throwing her against the wall and scowling down at her furiously.

"I got arr–"

"I know you got arrested! T.J. told me! You're so fucking useless! But he said you got released a fucking week ago! Where the hell have you been!?"

She shrank back at the anger and violence in his voice. "I.... I was.... my parents.... They.... they picked me up and.... I–I was... They were..."

"I don't care, you stupid bitch. It shouldn't have taken a week to get back here! You're in a hell of a lot of trouble, you know that, don't you?"

She cringed and nodded.

"Then gimme that fucking jacket and get ready to start paying me back."

Slowly, Bitty slid the jacket down off her arms and handed it to him. She'd never see that again. He'd probably pawn it or something. Tears began to roll down her cheeks and her head hung miserably. Bebe's crying was just making it worse. Part of her felt the child was right. They shouldn't have come back. Why did they come back? Why did they always come back?

Chapter Twenty-Three

* Choice One *

She just couldn't keep going anymore. She'd done four guys during the night, but it wasn't enough to make her quota. She told them she didn't do a lot of the things that they would have paid well for. She just couldn't face it right now. So she'd made barely anything. But she couldn't go back to Mack's or she'd regret it big time. With a sob, she collapsed in a heap on the sidewalk, her back to the closest building, her arms wrapped around herself in a desperate attempt to keep herself warm. Her entire body was shivering violently and every part of her hurt so badly she wanted to scream. Except her throat burned and scratched too much to really be able to do that anyway.

It was almost tempting to go back to Mack's and let him finish her for good. Then she wouldn't hurt anymore. Except that he'd probably just beat her to the brink and let her live. That was the way her life worked. Nothing she wanted ever worked out. If she wanted Mack to kill her to put her out of her misery, he'd just make her more miserable without actually killing her.

It was impossible to tell how long she lay there, shivering violently. At one point, another girl came over, someone she didn't recognize. Not that Bitty could really open her eyes properly to look at her anyway. The girl poked her gently.

"Hey, you okay?"

When Bitty didn't answer, the girl pulled the purse out from under Bitty's shivering little body and walked off.

Bitty couldn't even call after her to stop.

'That bitch stole our money! Get up! Get up and go get it! What the fuck are we gonna give Mack!? Get the hell up off the fucking ground, Bitty!'

But Bitty couldn't. She couldn't move, or speak, or think. She just lay where she was, curled into a tight, trembling ball as her body seemed to shake itself apart.

"Hey. Hey, you okay? Are you-" the gentle voice broke off abruptly. "Bitty? Bitty, is that you?"

Bitty tried to open her eyes or give some kind of response, but she just couldn't. She could barely breathe.

"Oh my god," the voice said when the cool hand brushed her forehead. "You're on fire! You're sick!"

Whoever was there left, but she couldn't open her eyes to see who had abandoned her again.

But a second later, the footsteps returned and she felt a blissfully warm blanket wrapped around her, then felt herself lifted into strong arms and cradled against a firm chest. She whimpered softly. Even the pressure where his hands held her aching body was painful. But it was nice to be a little warmer.

"Shhhh… it's okay. I've got you. We'll get you someplace warm. It's okay, babygirl."

'Babygirl?'

'He said babygirl! He said babygirl! It's John! Oh, I know it's John! Open your eyes, Bitty! I know it's John!'

'Why the fuck would John be here? He left.'

Bitty tried to open her eyes, but they just wouldn't obey her. She felt herself placed gently on the seat and the back was laid down so she was almost horizontal. The seat was warm! Warmer than it should have been just by the heat of a vehicle.

'I bet he has heated seats.'

'But why the hell is he here in the first place!?'

The door shut and a second later the driver door opened. The car dipped slightly when he got in, then they set off. Every so often, his hand would rest on her cheek or forehead.

"Hang in there, babygirl. I've got you. It's going to be okay. Hold on for Daddy."

'It is John! He came back! He came back for me!'

'Oh, Bebe… Don't get your hopes up, please, darling.'

'I know he came back for me! I know he did!'

Bitty missed the rest of the conversation. She slipped off into unconsciousness with the gentle rocking of the car and the warmth wrapping around her.

~ Choice Two ~

"Obviously I can't trust you not to get your sorry ass arrested if you're out on your own, so you'll be sticking with me from now on, you useless bitch."

Mack went through the pockets of her mother's coat as he spoke, pulling out keys and a wallet. Bitty's heart sank. Not only had she stolen clothes, but she'd stolen a lot of things without even knowing it.

When he'd finished emptying all the pockets, he hooked the jacket over one arm and grabbed Bitty, hauling her off towards the door. "I was just on my way to a job. You're the lucky girl who gets to do it."

Without another word, Mack dragged her out of the house and shoved her into the car, slamming the door behind her. Bitty shrank into the seat as he peeled out of the driveway and traveled through town. She was on a leash again. The first few months she'd been with him, she'd been on a leash. It had been awful. But other girls either stayed on it longer, or never got off that leash. She'd been privileged. Until now. Now he'd never let her out on her own again.

Half an hour later, they pulled up at a nondescript motel and Mack hauled her out of the car. "You'd better behave yourself. You know what you'll get if you don't."

He knocked on the door and another man—Bitty recognized him as someone Mack often worked with, but she couldn't remember his name—let them in.

"How old?"

Mack frowned, then turned to Bitty. "How old are you?"

"F-fourteen..." she mumbled.

The other man nodded and began undressing her as if she were a doll. "Well, I've got a couple lined up for a young one. They don't mind what she looks like. This one isn't too bad, though. That last one you sent was disgusting. You really need to take better care of your girls, Mack."

"Yeah, whatever. I can get more."

"What happened to that juicy one you had with you when I came over last time?"

"Hmph. Katie?"

"Yeah."

Mack scowled darkly. "She fucking ran off. She was doing just fine and then suddenly she's just gone. I shouldn't have let her out of my sight. She was close to being mine."

Bitty stood naked in the center of the room, her arms around her waist and her head down. For a moment, she felt happy for the other girl. At least she'd managed to escape. That didn't help Bitty, or any of the others. But there was one less girl trapped in this nightmare with no escape.

"Get on the bed. The first one will be here soon. You give him whatever the hell he wants, you understand?"

Bitty nodded without looking up, a tear trickling down her cheek. She wanted this to stop. She needed this to stop. It felt like a thick, cold hand was gripping her throat, strangling her with panic and disgust. She hated it. She hated Mack and his friends. She hated the johns. She hated sex. She hated.... herself....

The rest of the night was more of what her entire life seemed to be meant for. Scarlett eventually came to take some of the customers, getting into it with a fervor Bitty couldn't understand. None of them understood her, really. Scarlett could enjoy things none of the rest of them could. Very often, Bitty wished Scarlett could come out more reliably for things like this, instead of only being triggered when Bitty absolutely couldn't handle any more. Scarlett enjoyed it, so why couldn't Scarlett take it more often?

But it didn't seem to work that way. Sure, sometimes they could agree amongst themselves who might be allowed to come out for a certain time, but so often it just sort of happened. None of them really knew how or why, except that it seemed to happen when the one out couldn't take anymore. It helped, yes, but it wasn't ideal. Then again, none of this was ideal.

Chapter Twenty-Four

* Choice One *

When Bitty woke up, she felt warm, clean, and comfortable. That didn't make sense. She frowned as her eyes opened. For a moment, she wasn't sure what she was seeing. Everything seemed blueish. She blinked a few times and shifted, glancing down at her hand when it felt stiff to move. To her shock, there was a needle in her hand. But not a drug needle. A hospital needle. An IV.

She blinked again and finally looked around, able to focus a little better now. It *was* a hospital. The walls, blankets, ceiling, curtains, and hospital gown were all blue.

'No wonder everything looked like an ocean!'

'Grow up, Jay! It doesn't look like an ocean. It's just blue. Don't be stupid.'

'Bailey, leave him alone.'

'What's he *doing here!?'*

At that remark, Bitty registered what Bailey was talking about.

John was sleeping in the blue guest chair next to the bed. His chin was resting on his chest, his arms crossed and his legs out in front of him, crossed at the ankles. It didn't look very comfortable and Bitty was rather impressed he could sleep like that.

'Why? We've slept in all kinds of fucked up positions before! We gotta get out of here, though. Now. While he's sleeping.'

'Don't be ridiculous, Bailey! How are we going to do that? There's a needle in our arm and we're in a hospital!'

Bitty looked down at her hand again, wondering how hard it might be to pull the thing out of her. Probably not that hard. But then what?

"Sarah's right," she mumbled, then started to cough.

John gave a snort and his head came up instantly. He blinked once, then smiled brightly at her. Bitty could have sworn there was a look of relief in his face.

"Hey! You're awake!"

'Genius.'

'Shut up, Bailey!'

John got up and moved to the bed, stroking her forehead gently. "How are you feeling? It was touch and go there for a while. You were pretty sick. Well, you *are* pretty sick." He reached for an insulated cup that looked like a small jug emblazoned with the name of the hospital on it. "Here, have a drink."

Bitty gazed at him in silence for a long time, then took the cup and drank from the straw. The water was delightfully cold and clean and it felt amazing on her sore throat. When she'd had enough for the moment, she handed it back to him and he put it back on the tray table.

"Why are you here?" she whispered finally.

To her surprise, a small blush spread over his cheeks and his eyes flicked to the pillow beside her head for a moment, as if he was debating what to say.

"I... was worried about you. I know. I know. It's none of my business. I'm just a nobody to you. Just like all the rest. But I was concerned. When you left, I tried to forget you. When the meeting ended, I headed home. But I was worried. You just seemed so... alone.

"I'm glad I came back though. I don't think you would have made it much longer if I hadn't found you. Why didn't you go home? Or inside somewhere?"

It was Bitty's turn to look away. "There wasn't anywhere to go."

A thought occurred to her and she looked back at him curiously. "How did you find me, anyway?"

"I just... figured I'd swing by the area I'd found you last time to see if you were there. I was hoping you would be. I saw you curled up like you were hurt. I didn't even realize it was you until I moved your hair back. I would have taken anyone to the hospital. I just might not have stayed all night with them," he admitted.

She looked at the wall clock and frowned slightly, trying to figure out what time it was. But she'd never been able to learn that stuff and it was just a circle of numbers. She looked away. "You didn't have to."

John sat down in the chair again, scooting it closer to the bed. "I know. But I wanted to. Does that bother you?"

She glanced at him uncertainly, then shrugged. "I... don't know," she replied honestly. "Kind of. It's sort of creepy."

John sighed and nodded as he sat back in the chair tiredly. "Yeah. You're right. I'm sorry. I should have thought more clearly. I'll leave."

He stood up and smiled sadly at her, then took a winter coat from the seat of another guest chair against the wall.

'NO! NO, BITTY! NO! DON'T SEND HIM AWAY! MAKE HIM STAY! PLEASE, BITTY! PLEASE! DON'T MAKE HIM LEAVE!'

'Shut up, Bebe. He's a creep! He needs to leave!'

'Bailey, we don't-'

"John…" Bitty whispered uncertainly.

He stopped and looked at her. "Yes, babygirl?"

"I… I don't… You don't… Could you stay…?"

A smile that would have put the sun to shame spread across his face and he put the coat back down. "Of course, babygirl. Whatever you want. I thought you'd prefer I leave you alone. I'm more than happy to stay."

He returned to the chair beside the bed and sat down, reaching out to hold her hand. "I would leave if you asked me to. But, honestly, I'm really glad you asked me to stay." He squeezed her hand gently and smiled at her.

Before either of them could say anything else, there was a knock on the door and a nurse poked her head in. When she saw Bitty was awake, she smiled warmly and entered the rest of the way, bringing in a tray of food.

"Well! Good afternoon! How are you feeling?" The woman set the tray on the table and moved to Bitty's side, lifting her hand with the bracelet.

"Last name and birthda–" She broke off with a small frown at the label.

John stood up. "She was unconscious when she was brought in, and we didn't know either of those things."

"Oh, okay." She let go of Bitty's hand and took a thermometer from the rack of equipment on the wall behind the bed, then ran it over Bitty's forehead and temples.

"Still a fever, but it's gone down a lot. That's good. How's your foot feeling?" she asked, replacing the thermometer and lifting the blankets on the side to access her leg.

"My foot?" Bitty repeated blankly.

"Yes, dear. You had a nasty gash on your right foot that was infected. They cleaned it out and stitched it up." She lifted Bitty's foot to examine it, nodding. "Looks good to me."

She put Bitty's foot back down and covered it up again, then checked the IV bags.

Bitty watched warily.

"Don't worry, dear. It's just some fluids because you were severely dehydrated and some antibiotics to fight that infection." She turned to John with a smile.

"Dr. Matthews, Dr. Graham will be in to discuss things with you on his rounds soon."

Bitty's head whipped around to look at John in shock and she could hear the outcry of dismay from the others inside as well.

'Doctor!? He's a fucking doctor!?'

'Is he a doctor, Sarah? She called him a doctor. Is he gonna make Bitty's foot better?'

'It's your damn foot too, you idiot!'

'Bailey! That's enough! I don't know, Jay. Maybe.'

'Daddy John is a doctor? Cool!'

'He's not your daddy, Bebe! Shut up.'

John noticed her look but simply nodded to the nurse, staying silent until she left. When they were alone again, he sighed and sank into the chair once more.

Bitty simply stared at him expectantly.

She wasn't sure why. It wasn't like he owed her anything. But somehow it felt different that he was a doctor and not just some guy. He seemed...like he should have been a better man than he was. Good men didn't pick up underage prostitutes on the street and fuck them hard.

'But he is a good man, Bitty. He gave us food and let us stay in the hotel with him and stuff. And he brought us here...'

'You should report him. Turn him in for soliciting a minor.'

'Oh shut up, Scarlett. What the hell do you know? If we do that, then we go to jail for it too! You moron. He probably knows that or he wouldn't have brought us here. He knows he's safe.'

'No, Bebe is right. He seems to be a good man. He has faults, certainly, not least of which is buying an underage girl for sex. But he seems generally decent...'

After rubbing the back of his neck, John finally looked at her. "I'm sorry, Bitty. I really am."

The use of her name caused her to blink in surprise. It was not a normal thing to hear her name said in such a gentle, apologetic tone.

"I feel like I betrayed you. No. I *did* betray you. I shouldn't have done what I did. I'm a doctor and I should never have done those things to you, or anyone."

"You really are a doctor?" she asked tentatively.

He nodded and rubbed the back of his neck again. "Yeah. I practice across state. I come here to do consulting and other things for their... well, for one of the departments here."

She watched him for a long time, then looked away, uncertain how to feel about any of this. A wave of exhaustion washed over her suddenly and she closed her eyes. They flew open again when she felt his cool, gentle touch on her burning forehead and he withdrew his hand.

"Sorry."

"It's okay," she whispered, gazing at him. "I... I liked it."

He smiled gently and reached for her again, brushing the hair back from her bruised little face. "You should get some more sleep. You're still a very sick little girl. We can talk more when you wake up."

"You're... you're not... leaving...?" she mumbled, trying to stay awake.

He shook his head. "Not unless you want me to."

Her eyes closed and she couldn't open them again. "No."

~ Choice Two ~

"I can't anymore, Mack. Please. I just can't. It hurts so much."

WHACK

Bitty landed on her naked butt hard on the floor, her cheek throbbing. She burst into exhausted, agonized sobs and huddled in a ball.

"You'll fucking do what you're told and you'll do it quietly." He went to his jacket and pulled out a needle.

Bitty looked up and whimpered. "Please don't. I don't want it. Please, Mack. Please, no more."

He ignored her, gripping her wrist tightly and pinning her against him. "You're hurting? Then I'll fix it. You just keep fucking my clients until I tell you to stop."

The needle pierced her skin and she cried out in pain, sobbing as he pushed the plunger down and the chemicals flowed into her bloodstream for the third time in the last day and half. It only took a moment for it to begin working.

Mack released her and patted her cheek almost tenderly. "Good girl. Good girls get to feel good. Mack makes his girls feel good. Now get up on that bed and spread your legs."

The drugs helped. They really did. Her body didn't hurt so badly and her mind didn't think too much about what was happening. She wasn't as desperately exhausted from being awake for two days without a break or food. She could take her mind away from it all so much more easily. She could be free...

She barely noticed when the next client climbed onto her bruised, broken little body and began to use her. She barely noticed the pain as he forced himself into places men didn't belong. She barely registered the humiliation or disgust when she cleaned him off and tucked him back into his pants again, or when she lay back and spread again for the next one. None of it mattered anymore. It didn't make her sad anymore. It didn't fill her with a lifetime's worth of self loathing. She could cope now.

Maybe the drugs weren't so bad afterall. She was starting to see why the other girls begged him for more and more. This stuff was different than the stuff he'd given her before. This stuff was way more enjoyable. This stuff took her mind away almost as well as when she switched. She could escape the horror of her life for a while. The pain wasn't so bad. Her mind wandered away from the misery. She felt floaty and... good.

No. That stuff wasn't so bad after all.

Chapter Twenty-Five

* Choice One *

Over the next day and a half, Bitty's fever went down. Her foot stopped throbbing and her nausea vanished. She had good food, good medicine, and John—to her surprise—never left her side except to use the bathroom or get his own meals. He read to her from a children's book he bought for his Kindle and his voice was calm and warm. More often than not, it put her to sleep with a small smile on her face.

By the afternoon of her third day in the hospital, she felt like a completely different person. She smiled more easily and didn't flinch quite so badly when he made sudden movements. She couldn't remember ever feeling this way in her entire life. She didn't want it to end. Her heart sank when the doctor came in to examine her and decided she could be discharged.

'What? Did you think we were gonna live happily ever after in a fucking hospital room? Get over it, Bitty. This is the real world, not one of John's fairytale books.'

'Leave off, Bailey.'

John must have seen the fear and disappointment on her face because he brushed the hair back from her forehead and smiled at her as he sat down next to the bed again. After taking a deep breath and watching her carefully, he spoke.

"So look, I was thinking... I can't send you back out to whoever it is did this to you," he gestured to her bruised face and body, then held up a hand to stop her from interrupting, "But, I have a proposition for you. Social Services is coming to talk to you- Wait!" he cried, grabbing her arm as she tried to leap out of the bed. "Bitty! Stop! Let me finish! I want you to come home with me!"

She froze, then turned around to look at him. "What...?"

He loosened his grip but didn't let go. "I'm a licensed foster parent. I talked to them about you coming to live with me, if you'd like. I'm not going to force you, but I'm giving you the option."

She sank back onto the bed and regarded him warily. "You're not sending me to jail?"

"Of course not! Why would I do that?"

"Cuz I'm a whore."

He flinched at the word and shook his head sadly. "No, Bitty. I'm not sending you to jail, and I'm not even going to tell them about what you… do. I'm hoping it will be a 'did' if you'll come to live with me. We don't even have to do any of the things we did in the hotel. Never again, if you don't want that. I won't take advantage of you again. I really am sorry. But it's up to you. They can find another foster home for you until the court sorts out your family situation." He tightened his grip when she moved to run again.

"Bitty, please stop! You'll hurt yourself! You'll tear your stitches!"

"I'm not going back! I'm never going back to them! I'm not going to some foster home either! I'm not going! You can't make me go!" she screamed.

"Shhh…" he stood up and moved to her side, gathering her in his arms and holding her against his chest. "Shhh… It'll be okay, babygirl. It's okay."

When she began to sob, he stroked her hair gently, rocking her back and forth and kissing the top of her head. "It's okay."

Bitty wanted nothing more than to stay there like that forever, wrapped in his arms as if nothing in the world could touch her while she was there. But there was a knock on the door and a moment later, a well dressed woman with a briefcase walked in. She looked simply elegant in her slim gray pantsuit, her auburn hair drawn back in a bun at the nape of her neck, her blue eyes rimmed with just the right amount of mascara and eyeshadow to make them stand out but not look gaudy.

The woman put her hand out to shake Bitty's, offering it to John instead when Bitty didn't move. "I'm Jennifer Wright, I'm a caseworker with Social Services. Is everything okay?" she asked gently, her eyes resting on Bitty's tear-stained, miserable face.

'No, bitch, everything is not fucking 'okay'. What kind of moron is she!?'

'Bailey, just leave it. She's being nice.'

'Bitch.'

John continued to stroke Bitty's hair. "She's scared. We were talking about options."

Jennifer nodded and pulled up the other chair. Seating herself and crossing her legs neatly, she gave Bitty a warm smile. "I know it's a very scary thing to be in this situation. It's my job to help you with that and find a way to make you happy and keep you safe. We contacted your parents and they're on their way to s–" She broke off abruptly when Bitty once again struggled to leap out of the bed almost hysterically.

"No! No, I'm not going back there! You can't make me go back there! I'm not going! I'm not going! I'm not going!"

John held her tightly to him, pinning her against his chest in a firm, but somehow gentle embrace. "Bitty! Bitty, it's okay! No one is making you go anywhere! Bitty, calm down. We're not sending you back there. I promise. Look at me!"

He bent so his face was in front of hers and she was looking into his eyes; her wild, panicked ones met his calm green ones. "Bitty, look at me. Take a deep breath. No one is sending you back there yet."

She looked back at him, terror etched in every line of her little face. But his words began to register as she gazed into his eyes. Finally, she tried to take some deep breaths and move past the hysteria like he was urging her to do.

"I... I'm not...g–going...b... back?" she gasped finally.

He shook his head and stroked her hair. "No, babygirl. We're not going to send you somewhere that isn't safe, and I don't think your family is safe, is it?"

Her eyes flicked away and he nodded. "I thought so. I mentioned that to Jennifer when we talked on the phone. We're not sending you anywhere that's not safe. Okay?"

For a long moment, she gazed back into his eyes, then finally nodded slightly.

He smiled and released her, straightening again and turning to Jennifer.

The social worker glanced from him to Bitty with a gentle smile. "I was just going to say that your parents are going to sign off on transferring custody. You don't even have to see them if you don't want to." She nodded when Bitty shook her head. "Alright, then we'll keep them out of the room. The other thing I was going to talk to you about was placing you somewhere. I know that's scary, and I don't blame you. I'd be scared if someone came and told me I had to go live with a stranger."

She looked at John for a moment, then back at Bitty. "So I was talking about it with John, and he's happy to take you for as long as necessary. Since you know him already, it might be less scary that way. Would that help things?"

'His name really is John? He gave you his real name?'

Bitty tried to ignore Bailey's surprise and looked from Jennifer to John and back. "I can really… choose?"

Jennifer nodded. "In this case, yes. Usually, we don't have a registered foster parent that a child would already know, so there wouldn't be much of an option for that. But since John is already a licensed foster parent, you can choose to live with him if you'd like. You don't have to, if you'd rather go somewhere else."

She smiled when Bitty shook her head violently. "So you'd like to go home with him, then?"

"Yes."

"And that's still alright with you?" Jennifer asked, turning her head to John.

When he nodded, she nodded in return and pulled out some papers. "Then I'll get the signatures I need to have you discharged into his custody. I'll be back in a little while." She smiled at Bitty as she picked up her briefcase, then nodded to John and left them alone again.

~ Choice Two ~

She felt sick. Her head was pounding. Every inch of her body hurt. She had no idea what time it was or how many men had used her, or even how long she'd been stuck in that motel room. The curtains were always drawn so there was no way to so much as tell day from night. It was just john after john endlessly.

It was strange how you could feel sick enough to throw up when you hadn't even eaten anything in who knew how long. She'd even thrown up once when a client moved her around too fast. Mack had at least waited until the client had left before beating her for it. That only made it worse of course.

'Like we wanted to puke our guts out! Fucking asshole. We didn't have anything to even puke out!'

'Please, Bailey. Not now.'

That had probably been the point Mack had decided she might actually need food because when he'd left her alone with the next client he must have gone to get it. He shoved the bag at her when he came back and told her to eat fast. He'd brought her a hamburger and fries and she'd virtually inhaled it, but strangely enough, she had begun to lose her appetite. She knew it must have been a long time since she'd last eaten, but she was feeling less and less hungry, especially after he dosed her.

She needed to rest. She just wanted to sleep so badly. When the next john arrived, she actually cried from sheer exhaustion and hopelessness. It didn't matter, of course. It had never mattered. Some guys even liked the tears.

It continued that way for several more johns, each paying Mack directly and barely even speaking to her beyond telling her what to do. Every so often, she would stumble to the bathroom and splash some water on her face, rinse the stuff out of her mouth, and get a drink after using the toilet, but that was about all the time she had.

The only highlights were the times Mack would come in and dose her. The pain would disappear for a while, pleasure taking over. She would float through the horror on a cloud of relief. It didn't matter. None of it mattered. This feeling was the only thing she needed to pay attention to. She just needed to keep this feeling and everything would be alright.

After what could have been hours or days, Bitty heard shouting outside through the closed door. She turned her head towards it just as it flew open and men with guns flooded in. The man inside her leaped off her and tried to run but he was vastly outnumbered and didn't stand a chance. She tried to sit upright, debating her chances of escape in her condition and watching them as they cuffed him and read him his rights. But she was just too weak and too drugged to manage much movement at all.

Once they realized she had been alone with the john, they calmed down and holstered their weapons, then began looking around.

Two more came over to her—a man and a woman—and helped her to sit up, then handed her a blanket to wrap around her naked body. Once she was sitting without assistance, they began asking their questions back and forth.

"What's your name?"

"How old are you?"

"Who brought you here?"

It took a few moments for their questions to penetrate the fog of drugs and longer for her to manage to form words that were understandable through her sheer terror.

"B... Bitty... Fourteen..."

'Bitty, we gotta get out of here! They'll take us back home! Bitty, please! Get up and run!'

'Bitty! Listen to her! Bitty, run!'

She blinked, frowning and trying to think. "I.... have to go. I have to go," she mumbled. Another officer stood beside her and she looked up nervously.

"It's going to be a while before we can get you out of here," the man sitting beside her on the bed informed her. "I have an officer getting you something to wear."

The man's brows were furrowed in what looked like a disgusted grimace and she shrank back.

"I can't... stay. I have to go. I have to go." She was getting hysterical as the thought of what was waiting for her began to register properly.

A big, strong hand gripped her upper arm tightly and she looked up at the man towering over her.

"Just sit still. Calm down." Someone shoved a handful of clothes towards him and he, in turn, shoved them at Bitty. "Get dressed."

Automatically, as if by remote control, she pulled the sweatpants on, then tugged the sweatshirt over her head. They were just gray clothing with no undergarments, but they were still warmer than anything she'd had to wear since she'd been in jail the last time.

'It's not so bad, right, Bitty?'

'Oh, shut the fuck up, Bebe. Just cuz they gave us clothes doesn't mean they won't screw us later by sending us home!'

Bitty's attention was snapped away from the child's crying when she was spun around and her arms were pulled behind her back. In that split second of helplessness, Bailey was thrust forward in full-on protection mode.

She yanked at her arms and tried to twist away as the cuffs were put in place, pinning her arms behind her uselessly. Panic and vulnerability flooded her.

"LET ME GO! LET ME GO! GET THEM OFF OF ME! LET ME GO! FUCKING BASTARDS! LET ME GO!" she screamed.

Two pairs of strong arms grabbed her by the shoulders and forced her to sit on the bed, but that only triggered her further.

Arms bound. Men standing over her. Helpless. Trapped. On a bed. About to be raped. That was always what happened.

She began to kick, scream, and struggle desperately, hysteria driving her.

"SIT DOWN!" the voice boomed in her ear. She flinched violently and glared up at the absolutely huge officer towering over her. He looked like he wouldn't hesitate to hurt her, and his hand rested on his gun threateningly.

For a split second, Bailey thought about kicking him and trying to run, but self preservation got the better of her terror and she shrank back, turning her tear stained face away from him. It took everything she had just to sit down quietly on that bed again; the bed where she had spent the last few days on her back with her legs spread. She wanted to run; to escape. But she would be more hurt if she did. So she sat, her head down and her shoulders hunched, while they investigated the room as if she wasn't there.

Chapter Twenty-Six

* Choice One *

Jennifer had returned with the nurse and stood to the side as the woman went over the discharge instructions with John and Bitty and showed her how to use the crutches she was to use until her doctor cleared her to walk on her injured foot again. Once they signed her out and were given the written instructions and the prescription for the antibiotics and withdrawal medications Bitty would continue to take, the nurse left and Jennifer stepped forward again.

"Alright. We've got everything taken care of. You'll be going home with Dr. Matthews and we'll arrange everything else over the phone. Do you have any questions?"

Bitty shook her head in silence, a strange mixture of excitement and terror swirling in her stomach. Could it really be that she'd be going home with someone who wouldn't hurt her?

'Don't be a fucking moron. Of course he's gonna hurt you. Everyone hurts you. It's the way it always is.'

She tried to ignore Bailey's comment, focusing on John as he handed her two large store bags.

"Here. I got you some new clothes to wear home. I mean, home to my house. It's going to be a new start, Bitty. A new life."

With a wary expression, she took the bag and peered inside it. She had been expecting lingerie and skimpy clothing, but from what she could see, it was neither. With a glance up at him, she began pulling the things out of the bags.

First came a big, pale pink, puffy coat lined with soft, warm white fleece. The hood was also lined with the same fleece and had a white fuzzy trim around it.

"You… you got me a jacket?" she breathed, looking from it to him in amazement.

He grinned. "Well, of course. It's winter. You can't go outside without a good jacket. You'll get sick again." He nodded towards the bag. "Keep going."

Next came a pair of pink fuzzy boots with pink fluffy socks tucked into them. She glanced up at him for a moment, her mouth open in shock before she turned back to the bags again. Beneath the boots was a pink scarf and pink, knit mittens.

The second bag was just as thrilling; a pair of thick leggings with a pale pink and gray snowflake pattern on them lined with some kind of super soft fleece that felt like heaven, a big gray sweatshirt that covered her to mid-thigh, thick and warm and comforting, and finally, there was a package of regular, normal kid underwear and a bra. It wasn't sexy stuff. It wasn't see through, or thong, or even revealing. It was just cotton briefs with rainbows and unicorns on them, and a plain white cotton camisole bra. It was all just regular kid clothing.

She lifted her face to look at him, tears shining in her eyes. "These… are for me?"

He nodded. "Of course, babygirl."

"But they're not… I mean, they're just regular clothes."

"What kind of clothes would they be? Did I get the wrong kind? Is there something I missed? Don't you like the colors? We can go shopping together another day. These are just to go home in. You don't have to wear them again after today. Oh god, what's wrong?" he asked, his voice full of dismay and concern when she began to cry. He wrapped his arms around her and held her, stroking her hair gently and crooning softly.

"No! No, I like them. I love them. They're so perfect. They're just so perfect. I thought they wouldn't be so normal. I thought…." She hugged him tightly as he held her, burying her face in his chest. "I thought they would be less cozy," she murmured finally.

"Oh, you mean you thought I'd buy you clothes like *he* made you wear?"

When she nodded, he sighed softly and tightened his arms. "Oh, babygirl. You don't have to live like that anymore. You're going to have warm, comfortable clothes, a place to live, food to eat, everything little girls need. And you can be just that; a little girl. Come on, why don't you get dressed so we can go home. I'll wait outside."

With another tightening of his arms around her, he kissed the top of her head and straightened up. He smiled down at her for a moment, then left the room so she could change in private.

For a minute, she simply sat where he had left her, staring at the door he had just shut. Could things really be different now? Was her life really about to change?

~ Choice Two ~

For several hours, Bailey had sat on the bed, her hands cuffed behind her back, nothing to eat, drink, or do besides sit there in silence. They tried to ask questions, but she refused, clenching her jaw tightly and staring at them in defiance. Eventually they gave up.

After a while, Bitty switched back in again and sat quietly, her shoulders hunched and her head down. She really wasn't feeling good. She felt like she was getting the flu or something. Her body ached deep down in a way that had nothing to do with the bruises all over her. She felt feverish and sweaty and her heart felt fluttery and fast. She tried to wipe her running nose on her shoulder in an effort to keep it from trickling down to her chin. She wanted the cuffs off so she could lie down. All she wanted was to lie down and rest her aching body. But no one was even paying any attention to her. She didn't even exist, it seemed.

When they had finished collecting whatever information they needed from the hotel room and staff, the officers hauled her unceremoniously up off the bed and led her out to the waiting squad car.

Bitty stumbled along beside them, her head still down so she didn't have to see the gawkers standing around to glimpse what all the police cars were doing there. It was humiliating. Once again, she slid into the hard plastic seat of a police car and shrank down.

'How come there's no seatbelts? What if the police car got in a crash? What would happen to us? We don't have a seatbelt on. How come there's no seatbelts, Sarah?'

'Probably so no one can strangle us with them!'

'Bailey! That's enough! It's probably to do with being in handcuffs and not being able to put it on properly or something, Jay.'

Booking was faster this time, since she was already in the system from the last time. It was more a matter of adding to her list of crimes now. She was processed and sent back into the jail and found herself looking around for Tess and Mel.

'What the fuck is wrong with you?'

"Nothing," she mumbled, looking back at the floor.

'Do you think they're really your friends? Like they actually care about you?'

Bitty stayed quiet, ignoring Bailey's jibe and pretending it hadn't hurt her. Yes, she *had* thought they were her friends, as much as anyone ever had been, at least. They had been kind to her when no one else in the world had been. But Bailey didn't trust anyone, so she could never understand. It was sad, really.

Either way, neither of them seemed to be there, though it didn't stop her from looking around hopefully at breakfast. Eventually, she simply took her tray and retreated to the farthest corner, bent over her tray. By this time, withdrawals were really beginning to overtake her and the last thing she wanted was food. She was trying hard not to puke.

'See? It's not so bad. We got good food and nice clothes.'

'Oh, grow up, Jay! They're not nice clothes or good food! They're prison issue rags and garbage on a plate!'

'It's still food....'

Bitty had to agree with both of them! Food was food, and she hadn't eaten enough for a very long time, but even the thought of eating was making her sick. She just wanted to lie down in a tight little ball against the cramps that were beginning to tear at her insides. Thankfully, she was given a cell by herself so Bitty actually had a shred of privacy. It was kind of nice, actually, and it made it a little easier to cope with the pain and nausea of the withdrawals.

'Don't you start that shit now too!'

"Start what?" she mumbled into the pillow as she cried in pain.

'Start thinking it's nice here cuz we got a bed in a fucking cage!'

"I'm not...."

'Whatever.'

Rather than reply, Bitty curled up more tightly under a nice, warm blanket and tried to ride out the waves of shivering and puking.

Chapter Twenty-Seven

* Choice One *

For the first time in as long as she could remember, Bitty felt pretty. Not sexy, or hot, or attractive. Just pretty. Like a fourteen year old girl should be. She still felt like hell, too, but it was a lot better than it had been when she'd collapsed on the sidewalk.

Once they reached John's car in the parking structure, he and a nurse helped her out of the wheelchair and into the car, sliding the crutches into the back seat as the nurse headed back to the hospital with the wheelchair. She sank back in the passenger seat with a sigh, shocked by how exhausting the short trip from the building to the vehicle had been. It felt like she'd just run a marathon, not been pushed a few hundred feet in a wheelchair.

"You okay?" he asked as he slid into the driver's seat.

She nodded slightly, her head resting on the cold glass of the window. "Yeah. Just tired. Sorry."

"Hey, don't apologize. You were a very sick little girl. You still are. You need to rest. I should have brought the car around to the door. I'm sorry."

She lifted her head to look at him in surprise. He was apologizing to her?

"It's fine. It's no big deal."

"It still seems stupid to have overlooked."

He put the car into gear and pulled out of the spot. "It's about five hours from here to home, but we can make as many stops as you need. And we'll grab some dinner on the way, too. Sound okay?"

"You live five hours away?"

"Yeah. It gets to be a pain in the butt, but I don't have to do it all the time. And sometimes I take a flight, if I'm staying for a short time. I'd rather not drive ten hours round trip for a one day meeting, as you can imagine."

He winked at her and she found herself smiling back at him.

"What kind of music do you like?" he asked, reaching for the radio. "I've got CD's too, though they're mostly classical and a bit of jazz."

Bitty shrugged. "I dunno. Whatever."

John hit 'play' and the soft sounds of some orchestral piece floated from the speakers into the car. It was remarkably quiet inside. Much nicer than Mack's car, even though his was a pretty expensive looking vehicle. John's smelled nicer, too. It wasn't 'new car smell' or anything, it was definitely lived in, but it was sort of like a mix of vanilla and… John. It was a comforting scent and soon Bitty was fast asleep as they rolled along the highway into the setting sun.

About three hours later, she jerked awake when she felt herself being shaken gently.

"Hey sleepy bunny, let's get something to eat and use the bathroom." John was leaning over to her from the driver's seat with a reassuring smile.

Blinking, Bitty looked around and sat up.

They were parked outside a truckstop diner, neon signs glowing in the dark, snow falling gently around them. It was actually sort of pretty. She nodded and rubbed her eyes, suddenly feeling the need to use the restroom now that she was awake.

John stroked her hair just briefly, then turned and got out of the car. After retrieving the crutches from the backseat, he opened her door and helped her out, making sure she was steady before letting go of her and shutting the door.

The diner was moderately busy and Bitty automatically shrank back. Fear washed over her at the feeling of exposure the bright lights brought with them. Then John's big, steady hand was at her back and she looked up to find him smiling down at her encouragingly.

"It's okay. You're safe. Bathrooms first, then dinner?" he asked, as if he could read her mind.

She nodded. "Yeah, thanks."

It was difficult maneuvering into the stall with the crutches, but she managed it, and within a few minutes, she came out to find him waiting for her with a patient smile. She smiled back and followed him into the restaurant.

John found them a secluded booth in one of the darker sections of the place and seated her with her back to the room, giving her a sense of seclusion which was simultaneously comforting and mildly scary. For quite a while, she kept glancing over her shoulder every time she caught movement out of the corner of her eye. Finally, John had her switch seats so she could see the room, and she relaxed.

After returning with their drinks—black coffee for John, root beer for Bitty—the waitress pulled out a notepad. "Ready to order?"

John looked to Bitty and she felt her cheeks flush. "Uh... I... guess I'll just... have... that," she mumbled, pointing to a brightly colored picture of a hamburger.

"How do you want it done?"

"What?"

"Your burger. How do you want it cooked?" the waitress repeated impatiently, scowling slightly when Bitty continued to look back at her blankly.

"She'll have it medium well," John supplied.

The waitress nodded. "And what sides?"

Again, Bitty looked at her blankly.

"Sides. They're listed below the burgers. You get two. What do you want?"

Bitty's face burned as she gazed down at the menu, wishing the floor would open up and swallow her.

"She'll have fries and chicken noodle soup."

Bitty looked up to see John give her a gentle smile before he ordered his own food.

Once the waitress had taken their menus and left, John regarded her. "I can help you with that."

"With what?"

"Reading."

"I can read!"

"Alright, read better then. We can work on that together. There's programs and things to help, too."

Bitty's cheeks flamed and she looked anywhere but at him. Her eyes landed on two sheriff's officers as they walked in and she automatically shrank down in her seat, her eyes flicking to the nearest exit.

"Bitty, look at me."

The use of her name again made her look automatically.

"You're safe now. It's okay. You don't have to worry about them anymore. You're safe," he repeated.

She nodded slightly and tried not to look back at the officers.

John tried for a few minutes to talk to her, asking her questions to engage her, but when she stayed virtually mute, he gave up and let her be. Their waitress refilled their drinks and a few minutes later brought their food out.

Bitty's stomach growled and she began to eat hungrily. She'd had food at the hospital and it hadn't been horrible, but this was so much better, and it seemed like the more she ate, the hungrier she was. She'd had steady meals for three days now, but it seemed like she was somehow more hungry every time the next meal came around. It didn't make sense.

They both ate in silence, John watching her with a smile, Bitty looking around her warily out of habit. When she couldn't eat anymore, John had the leftovers boxed up and paid their check, then helped her retrieve her crutches from under the table and stand up.

"Bathroom stop before we get going again?"

She nodded and they made their way slowly to the restrooms. It was getting a little easier to navigate with the crutches and she found herself finishing more quickly than she had the first time. He was still waiting for her when she got out though. How did men go so fast?

Within minutes of getting back on the freeway, Bitty was asleep again.

***

Several hours later, Bitty woke again when John gently shook her. "Hey, babygirl. We're home."

She blinked and sat up, rubbing her eyes and glancing around the garage they were parked in. It was neat and organized, almost like a magazine garage. Peg board lined one wall, hung with various tools and equipment. Another wall sported lawn equipment; shovel, rake, snow shovel, shop broom. Below them on the ground was something under a canvas cover which was probably a lawnmower. Plastic tubs were stacked against the third wall next to the doorway, each numbered with big black numbers. It smelled like sawdust and oil. It smelled nice.

John had come around and pulled out the crutches while she'd been looking around and she turned her attention to getting out of the car.

"Ready?" John asked with a smile. She nodded and he led the way through the small door on the side into a mudroom that looked just as neat and organized as the garage. A wooden bench lined one wall with three cubbies underneath that held different kinds of boots. One looked like ski boots, another rain boots, a third snow boots. The coat hooks took up the opposite wall and held a raincoat and a thick ski jacket.

John took off his long black wool coat and hung it on an empty hook, kicking off his loafers before turning to her to take hers. "You can leave your boots under the coats here."

She nodded and sat down on the bench to take off her snuggly new boots, sighing softly when the cold air swirled around her feet. It had been nice to be warm. Not that it was cold, but the boots had been really warm!

John led her from the mudroom and flipped the lights on to reveal a kitchen that took her breath away. She halted in the doorway and stared around in amazement.

Everything was warm, reddish wood tones, golden light, and a sort of understated luxury that came with taste and talent. Deep cherry wood cabinets lined the walls above and below the cream colored countertops, giving the room a sort of comforting glow. The floor matched, also a deep red wood. The ceiling was high and there was a gap between it and the top of the cabinets of about a foot. That space was filled with greenery. She presumed it was artificial, but it was well done and looked as if it very possibly could have been real. The stove, fridge, microwave, and dishwasher were all black, and there was a black coffee maker on the counter near the big sink. The center island had four bar stools on one side and cabinets around the other three sides. Warm golden light came from track lights along the ceiling that highlighted accent points throughout the room; stove, sink, fridge, island, and various points along the counters. It was neat, clean, and absolutely wonderful. All Mack's kitchen had really been good for was cooking meth.

John put the boxes from the diner into the fridge, which was surprisingly almost empty, then turned to her. "Are you thirsty? Hungry?"

"Kind of thirsty," she admitted, still gazing around the room.

"How about apple juice?" he asked, examining the contents of his fridge. "Or ice water?"

"Apple juice, please."

John nodded and took a glass from a cabinet next to the fridge, filling it for her and offering it, then paused, eyeing her crutches.

"Oh, never mind. I'll carry it. Why don't we go sit down in the living room." He replaced the bottle and led the way through to the living room with her glass.

This room was just as warm and welcoming as the kitchen. The dark floors carried through the house but there was a deep, fluffy warm rug in the center of the large room. Bitty almost wanted to go right over and lie down in it! The warm cream-toned couch was massive and stretched in a horseshoe shape around the rug. Cozy yellow lights around the room lit it from recessed sconces on the walls and a fireplace crackled to life when John turned a well concealed knob on the wall beside it. It gave the room a glow that seemed to radiate the most wonderful warmth Bitty had ever felt.

"Why don't you have a seat," John suggested, gesturing to the couch. He brought a large footstool over as she obeyed and he propped her foot up on it with a smile.

"It's so beautiful," she whispered.

"What is?"

"Your house. It's like… a magazine or something."

John chuckled and looked around as he sat down beside her. "Yeah, my ex-wife did a nice job. It's a little fancy for just me, but it's not like I'd change it or anything. I'm not really home that much."

"Why not?"

He shrugged. "Oh, just working a lot. It gets lonely all by myself, so I may as well spend my time helping people instead of sitting around alone."

"Oh."

He smiled at her. "But you're here now, so I'll have some good company." He watched her for a moment. "Why did you agree to come stay with me, Bitty?"

She shrugged one shoulder. "Cuz you've been nicer to me than anyone. And I didn't want to go home, or to some foster home. It seemed as good a choice as any."

'Yeah, that's what you think!'

'Shut up, Bailey.'

His face suddenly lit up. "Oh, hey! I have something for you."

She tilted her head curiously. "You do?" She watched him fairly leap out of his seat and rush from the room. While he was gone, she looked around again.

A tall bookcase built into one wall was absolutely full of books. She'd never been in a library before, but she imagined that's what it would have looked like. The TV above the fireplace was also the biggest she'd ever seen, and Mack had a big one!

John returned in a moment and held something out towards her with a smile.

She gasped and reached for it instantly, her face glowing. "My unicorn!" Bebe cried, her face alight with an enormous smile. She immediately cuddled it to her chest and began to cry as she stroked it. "I thought it was gone! I thought it was gone! They said I couldn't take it but I wanted to so bad!"

John watched her closely as he sat down again, his eyes smiling but also contemplative.

"Thank you so much! Thank you! I love her! They said I couldn't take her."

"Who said?" he asked gently.

"The others. Mostly Bailey. She said it would get ripped up."

"I see." He turned on the couch slightly to face her, trying to keep the frown from his face. There was a sudden flip flop of mixed dismay and excitement in his stomach.

"Who are the 'others'?" he asked cautiously in as nonchalant a tone as he could manage.

"The others with me. All of us."

John tried to quell the sudden inkling of understanding that was threatening to overwhelm him and cause him to react too strongly. If what he thought was going on was indeed the situation, he didn't want to blow it by overreacting, even in excitement or comprehension. "What's your name?" he continued, his voice calm and steady, belying the eagerness he felt.

"Bebe," she replied, still cuddling the toy and rubbing it against her face.

'Hell, Bebe! Don't say that! What are you thinking?'
John nodded slowly, the feeling growing. "How old are you, Bebe?"
"I'm five," she said with a smile.
"I see. That's very nice. So the others said you couldn't keep the unicorn?"
She nodded.
"I see. Are they your friends?"
She nodded again.
"How many friends do you have, Bebe?" he asked, repeating his question from the hotel that second day.
'Don't answer. Don't say anything. Stay quiet! You'll get us locked up! Keep your mouth shut, Bebe!'
"There's me, and Bitty, and Bailey, and Scarlett, and Jay, and Sarah, and Callie," she answered, counting off on her fingers. "So… I have six friends."
'Fuck, Bebe! What is wrong with you!?'
"That's a lot of friends!" he said with a gentle smile. "And are they with you all the time?"
She shook her head. "No. Sometimes they go to the quiet place by themselves. I go there too sometimes. I don't like scary things. I hide in the quiet place when I get scared."
John nodded. "I don't like scary things either," he agreed. "Bebe, when you hide in the quiet place, does someone else take care of things for you while you're gone?"
She nodded and reached for her drink on the side table. "Yeah. Lots of times Bitty or Bailey takes care of stuff. But not always."
He regarded her thoughtfully for a long time.
"So, Bebe, when I'm talking to you, can your friends hear me?"
She shrugged. "I dunno."
"Do you hear them when I'm talking to you? Or when other people are talking to you?"
"Sometimes. Sometimes I'm by myself. I don't like being by myself. It's scary."
John nodded sympathetically. "Do you hear what they say when I talk to them?"
"Sometimes. Did you keep the coloring book, too?" she asked hopefully.

He smiled. "I did keep it. I'll be right back." He stroked her hair for a moment as he passed.

'Damn it, Bebe! He's probably going to call the cops right now! Or the mental hospital! You can't tell people about us! You have to pretend you're Bitty!'

"But he's so nice…" Tears filled her eyes and she gazed down at the unicorn. "He asked me what my name was."

'He was probably already suspicious with you acting like such a baby and all the shit you and Bitty told him at the hotel!'

'Don't be mean, Bailey. She didn't mean to. We'll just…'

'What? Pretend Bitty was just pretending? Run away? What, Sarah? What will we just?'

Sarah's reply was cut off as John came back with the coloring book and crayons.

Bebe's face lit up and she reached for them eagerly. "Oh, thank you! Thank you!"

"I think we should get to bed, though. I'll carry those and show you to your room."

"But I want to color."

"You can color as soon as you wake up. Come on. Let's get to bed." He held his hands out for the things.

Her head jerked slightly and her eyes flashed as she stood up abruptly, her jaw set.

"Don't you fucking touch me!" Bailey screamed.

John yanked his hand back, his eyes wide. "I… Woah… Easy! I'm not going to hurt you."

"Like hell you're not! You want to go to bed!"

He stared at her blankly for a moment before shaking his head as understanding registered in his eyes.

"No! Well, yes. But, not like that! I just meant I'll show you your room and you can rest. I'm not trying to pull anything. I just wanted to take you to your room." He stepped back to give her some space, watching her with his hands up in a gesture of surrender.

She glared at him, a wary expression on her bruised face.

"I swear. If you don't want me to take you there, I can tell you which door it would be and you can go by yourself. I'm not trying to hurt you."

After a long moment, she relaxed; her shoulders slumped, her head lowered, and she brushed her hair back from her face nervously, though she wasn't quite able to hide the look of confusion on her face as she took in his posture.

"What?" Bitty asked softly.

John stared at her in dismay for a second before lowering his hands. "I was asking if you'd like me to show you to your new room, or if you want to find it on your own?"

"Oh. I'd… yeah. Could you show me?"

He nodded, smiling with a slightly relieved look and made a gentle gesture for her to follow as he led the way into the hall. "There's the bathroom," he said, gesturing to the first door, "And that's the linen closet," he added, pointing at the second door. Further down the hallway he paused in front of the third door and opened it. "This is your room."

Chapter Twenty-Eight

* Choice One *

Bitty hobbled in awkwardly, but didn't get far before she stopped and looked around in wonder. The hardwood floor stopped at the doorway to the bedroom and lush white carpet covered the floor. The walls were a pale blue that was almost impossible to see but managed to give the room a soft sort of glow. To her right in the center of the wall was the bed. A thick, soft looking pale blue comforter gave the queen sized bed almost a cloud-like look and for a split second she wanted to jump on it to see whether she would bounce or sink into it. The top of the white sheets were folded down at the head of the bed, accenting the blue fabric on the headboard. A pale blue bedskirt hung down around the edges of the bed completing the look. A tall white dresser and a white bedside table faced each other from across the room, white curtains hung over the windows with pale blue window scarves draped like flowing water over the top. The gorgeous room was finished with a blue chair that matched the headboard, tucked at an angle in the far left corner.

"If you decide to stay, you can decorate it however you like. Posters, or pictures or whatever. We can get different bedding too, if you'd like."

Bitty slowly made her way into the room, a smile on her face. "It looks like a cloud."

John grinned. "I didn't even think to get you any pajamas, but you can use one of my t-shirts for now. I'll be right back."

He hurried out and returned a moment later with a dark blue t-shirt, along with the bag of toiletries they had brought from the hospital. "Do you need anything else? I'll put them in the bathroom for you so you don't have to worry about carrying them."

She shook her head and followed him back down the hall to the bathroom, watching while he set her things on the counter by the sink. Once again, she caught her breath, though the decorating was becoming less of a shock than it had been at first. Here, too, the wood floors stopped at the doorway and cream and gold colored tiles picked up. The countertops to her left and the walls were also cream, and a gold ivy pattern swirled over the walls around the room. The cabinets and woodwork was the same deep cherry wood color that the kitchen cabinets were made of and they seemed to glow with warmth, set off by the soft cream. A massive cream colored bathtub was ahead of her against the far wall and Bitty thought she could probably lie down in it and stretch out without either her head or toes sticking over the end! To her right was a large shower stall surrounded by glass, though calling it a stall was a little understated. It was more like a small room of its own! There were even two shower heads, one on each side.

"Wow," she whispered. "This is… wow."

John smiled. "Brush your teeth and then we can get you tucked in. You can have a shower tomorrow. Just leave your clothes on the floor. I'll get them later."

Bitty nodded and watched him leave, then hobbled over to the sink and gazed at herself in the mirror. The bruises stood out starkly against her pale skin and her eye was swollen, though the marks had begun to turn a grayish yellow in some places. It was like looking at a dead fish on the side of a beautiful pond; she was ugly and didn't belong in this exquisite room.

She looked away quickly and pulled out the toothbrush and toothpaste. It had been nice to be able to brush her teeth more often. It seemed such a simple thing, but somehow it had made her feel more alive and clean. Even more than a shower, having her mouth feel less disgusting made her feel the most different. It was probably not something most people would understand.

After she changed into the t-shirt which came down past her knees, used the toilet, and washed her hands, she opened the door expecting to find John standing outside waiting for her like Mack used to do. But the hallway was empty. It surprised her so much it took her a moment before she got herself moving again and headed for her new room.

John was just pulling the covers on the bed back when she walked in. The unicorn stuffed animal was propped against the pillows and he gestured to it. "You forgot him on the couch."

There was a moment of blank confusion on her face, then her eyes fluttered and her face lit up. Instead of moving both crutches at the same time, however, Bebe tried to move one at a time, like she was walking, and promptly fell down hard on her knees with a cry of pain. Immediately rolling to sit up, she brought her knees up to look at them, crying quietly. There were red carpet burns on each knee and she cried harder when she saw them.

John was next to her in a heartbeat, rubbing her back and examining the red marks with sympathetic noises.

"Aww, dear. That looks like it hurt. Ssshhhh… we'll take care of it. I've got some bandages. Come on, let's get you up on the bed and I'll go get them."

He scooped her up and cuddled her as he carried her to the bed, putting her down with her head on the fluffy pillows. With a gentle smile, he handed her the unicorn and stroked her cheek. "I'm going to go get something to make that better. I'll be right back."

He hurried out of the room, returning a minute later with a box of bandaids. "I'm afraid they're not fun patterns or anything, but we can get some tomorrow."

He sat down on the bed by her feet and took out two bandaids in their little paper wrappers. After he peeled one open, he leaned down and kissed her knee, then stuck a bandage over it.

Bebe's tears slowed to a silent trickle.

He did the same with the other, and when he had finished, she smiled at him. He smiled back and pulled the covers up to her shoulders.

"Better?" he asked, sitting beside her and stroking her hair.

She nodded and he smiled.

"Good." He turned away and took a glass of water and a pill off the bedside table, holding them both out to her. "Can you swallow a pill? This will help it stop hurting. It'll help your foot, too."

She nodded and sat up with his help, popping the pill into her mouth and swallowing it with a drink of water. Then she lay back down again.

"That's a good girl. Now, why don't you get some rest and I'll see you in the morning, okay?" She nodded again and he leaned down to kiss her forehead. "Sleep tight, babygirl." As he left, he smiled at her from the doorway, then turned out the light and closed the door.

Bebe tucked the stuffed animal close to her body and turned on her side, gazing at the wall across from her for a moment, rubbing her cheek against the soft fur. The bed was so soft. It was the most wonderful thing she'd ever lain on. Her eyes grew heavy almost immediately and she sighed softly, letting them close and drifting off to sleep, ignoring the soft remark from Scarlett.

'He didn't try to use her...'

She sounded surprised. And confused.

~ Choice Two ~

The following morning, Bitty woke up in agony. Her entire body felt achy and sweaty and she began retching the moment she was conscious. The guards were calling everyone for breakfast but every muscle in her body was cramped tight and she couldn't have moved even if she'd wanted to. Instead, she simply lay on the bed in a puddle of puke, choking and crying in a strangled little croak.

A guard banged on the open door.

"Hey! Get up! You better– Ugh!" He broke off at the smell and the sight of the ragged looking bundle under the covers. Once he got himself under control, he approached and leaned over her with a smirk.

"You jonesing?"

Bitty couldn't answer beyond a little whimper.

"Off what?"

"Dunno," Bitty mumbled into the vomit-soaked pillow.

The guard regarded her for a minute. "You a whore?"

Bitty didn't answer. The man seemed to take that as confirmation and nodded.

"Probably heroin." He studied her for another minute, then asked, "You want a dose?"

Bitty looked up at him through teary, blurred eyes.

He smirked at her. "I can fix it. I can get you a hit if you cooperate."

'Don't do it, Bitty! Just let it get out of your system. We wanted to get off it. This is the way. We weren't like this until the last couple weeks. We just have to ride it out.'

"Well?" the guard demanded.

Bitty closed her eyes against Sarah's pleas and nodded, turning her face away with a little sob.

The man smiled. "That's a good girl. I'll get it for you.'

'BITTY! WHAT THE FUCK ARE YOU DOING!?'

'Oh, Bitty! Don't do this!'

"I... I need it," she gasped, sobbing again as another knife-like cramp tore into her belly. "I can't d-do this!"

'Yes you can, Bitty! You can do this! We can help you. We can take turns. We can get out of this. Please.'

Before she could respond, she cried out as another stab of agony ripped out her insides.

The guard returned in a few minutes. Bitty vaguely felt him wrap something around her arm and a prick, then heaven flowed into her veins. It took a minute or two for it to really take effect but even the first hints of relief felt like the best thing in the world.

The cramps relaxed, she could breathe again, some of the nausea began to fade a little bit. The pain faded into the background and everything grew softer and further away. She sighed at the reprieve.

The guard pocketed the syringe and band, then yanked back the filthy blanket.

"Clean yourself up and get that shit down to laundry, then get your ass to breakfast. I'll find you later to collect."

Bitty groaned softly and pushed herself up off the bed, gathering the vomit and diarrhea soaked bedclothes. It was then that she realized she didn't have any clean clothes. She didn't even know who to go to to ask for some.

A sob broke and she hung her head. She was disgusting.

A moment later, another guard stopped at the doorway to her cell.

"Why are you still here?" the guard demanded, then registered Bitty's state and wrinkled her nose. "Infirmary. Let's go."

Bitty shrank into herself a little more and followed the guard with her bundle of stinking things. She was fairly sure she wouldn't have been able to walk without the hit from the guard earlier since she was having trouble even now.

The infirmary was locked up, just like everything else, and the guard had to escort her all the way in. There was no way Bitty would be able to get there if she needed help without a guard to take her; and that didn't seem likely to happen easily. She was pretty sure the only reason she was being taken now was because she stank so badly they couldn't tolerate it. Once again, she was at the mercy of those stronger than her.

Chapter Twenty-Nine

* Choice One *

For the first time in a long time, Bitty woke up slowly; warm, comfortable, and not aching from a beating. She couldn't remember a time ever feeling like that in her life. At first, she wasn't even sure she *had* woken up, it was like a dream. A smile tugged sleepily at the corners of her mouth as she opened her eyes and gazed up at the clean, white ceiling.

'Don't.'

"Don't what?" Bailey's surly order had slightly soured the delicious awakening.

'Don't get all home-sweet-home *about this place. We're not staying.'*

"What do you mean, we're not staying?"

'It's temporary, you moron. Foster home. Not home. Foster homes are short term. Temporary. They're not a home. They should be called kid shelters or something. They're not home. We're not staying.'

The wonderful euphoria that had wrapped around her when she woke was in shreds now. She wasn't entirely miserable, and she was trying not to let Bailey's bad mood ruin her day, but it had certainly impacted it.

With a sigh, she sat up and noticed her clothes folded neatly on the little blue chair. Another tiny smile touched her lips. Clean clothes. *New* clothes. She couldn't remember ever getting new clothes.

'Mack bought you new clothes. Remember?'

Bailey's comment felt like a punch in the gut. She did remember. She remembered how nice he had been and how lucky she had felt when she'd been taken under his wing. New clothes, kindness, food when she was hungry.

'Just like now.'

"Shut up, Bailey. He's not like Mack."

'How do you know?'

"I just... I just know."

A derisive snort met that response and Bitty closed her eyes to keep her heart from lurching with fear. What if Bailey was right? After taking a deep breath, Bitty dressed quietly and tiptoed to the door as silently as possible with crutches. The clock said 9:32, but she wasn't sure if John would be up yet and she didn't want to wake him if he wasn't. That was always a sure way to get a beating.

'He's not like that. You said so.'

"He's not. I know he's not," she assured Jay, though she wasn't sure she was doing it completely for his benefit alone.

To her relief, John was awake and cooking something that smelled like heaven. She paused in the archway between the kitchen and the hallway and watched him for a minute, trying to decide if this was real or another repeat of Mack.

John turned away from the stove to get something from the fridge and caught sight of her. He smiled and beckoned her over.

"Morning! How are you feeling?"

Bitty took a few tentative hopping steps into the kitchen.

"Okay."

"Do you like eggs and bacon?"

'Bacon! Bacon, Bitty! I want bacon! Oh, please, Bitty. Please say you like bacon!'

'Jesus, Jay! What the hell!'

Bitty's smile grew and she nodded, almost breaking into a full grin at the whoop of excitement inside.

"Of course. Who doesn't like bacon, right?" John teased as he turned back to the stove.

'I hate bacon.'

'Oh, shut up, Scarlett. No one asked you!'

'He was talking about people who don't like bacon. I was just saying...'

'Shut up.'

"...and get you some other stuff while we're there," John was saying. He looked over his shoulder at her and paused at the blank look on her face.

A moment later, Jay tugged at the front of his shirt and grinned, his whole body relaxed and happy. "I *love* bacon! Bacon is my favorite. I like bacon on hamburgers and eggs and sandwiches and by itself and everything!"

John blinked a few times, then smiled. "I agree." He held out the plate of bacon. "Help yourself. What's your name?"

Jay reached for a handful of bacon with an eager grin and began eating as quickly as he could without choking.

'Don't be such a fucking pig!'

"Jay," he said through a mouthful, trying to slow down at Bailey's command.

John nodded. "Jay, it's nice to meet you."

There was a string of curses from inside as Bailey raged at his stupidity and Jay's eyes filled with tears of fear. He paused, his hand halfway to his mouth with another strip of bacon, a look of terror on his face.

"I... didn't mean... Bitty. My name is Bitty. I don't know why I said Jay. I... wasn't thinking. I thought you said... I was just..."

John shook his head and offered a gentle smile.

"It's okay, Jay. I understand the situation. You don't have to be afraid."

Jay stared at him nervously, confusion on his face.

John sat down on one of the bar stools at the counter and leaned on the flat surface.

"Do you know what kind of doctor I am, Jay?"

Jay shook his head.

"I'm a psychiatrist. Do you know what that is?"

'Stop talking, Jay! Stop talking right now! He's a shrink! He'll have us locked up!'

'Oh, Bailey, stop it. He hasn't done anything so far, and I'm pretty sure he's known for a while. It would be easier if he does understand.'

'You're all fucking insane! Don't blame me when we end up in a fucking straight jacket!'

Jay stood still, watching John as everyone argued inside. After a moment, John's question registered and he shook his head again.

"A psychiatrist is a doctor who helps people with things in their minds. Sometimes it's a sickness, and sometimes it's something like you. You're not sick, no matter what some doctors think. But sometimes it's good to have someone who can make things a little easier to handle.

"I'm not going to try to change you or make you leave, okay? I'll help you manage everything a little better, but no one is going to get pushed away, alright?"

Jay nodded uncertainly. He wasn't quite sure what all of this meant, but judging by Bailey's reaction and her snort of derision, it didn't sound ideal.

~ Choice Two ~

"This one's a mess. I think she's jonesing," the guard muttered in a bored tone to the nurse practitioner as she thumbed over her shoulder at Bitty.

The male nurse practitioner sighed as if Bitty had set out on purpose just to annoy him and pointed to the exam table. "Get up. Wait," he snapped, eyeing the bundle in her arms and pointing to a bin in the corner, "that stuff in there first."

Bitty obeyed, her shoulders hunched in embarrassment as she stuffed the soiled laundry into the plastic lined bin.

"Strip."

She flinched at the harsh command so much like what she'd been told to do for years and looked over at the nurse practitioner in fear.

"Come on. Now. I'm not having that mess on the table. Put the clothes in the bin too." He poked his head into a back room and called to someone.

An older woman who was probably in her sixties waddled in.

"This one messed herself. Wash her up, please."

The nurse shot Bitty a disgusted look and nodded.

"Why are you still in those clothes?" the N.P. demanded.

Bitty flinched again and began to strip with trembling hands. She'd been naked in front of hundreds of men, but this felt somehow worse. She felt more exposed in this open room with the three of them watching her like she was an annoyance. Tears filled her eyes and she turned her back as she undressed.

The minute she'd taken off the last of her clothes, the nurse grabbed her arm with a gloved hand and pulled her to the center of the room. At least the N.P. seemed to have left while Bitty's back had been turned.

The nurse was none too gentle about cleaning the mess off Bitty's bruised and aching little body and muttered impatiently the whole time. Bitty felt guilty, disgusting, and humiliated.

When she had been scrubbed off, the nurse motioned to the exam table and Bitty climbed on. She had been expecting to be given a gown, or a blanket, or *something* to cover herself, but she was just left to sit naked in front of everyone. She hunched up and wrapped her arms around herself, her ankles crossed to try and hide herself a little more.

Apparently, this annoyed the practitioner when he returned.

"How am I supposed to examine you if you're all bunched up like that? If you're not going to cooperate, this is a waste of my time."

Bitty shrank into herself and slowly uncrossed her arms, tears in her eyes as the N.P. began to check her eyes and the nurse took her blood pressure and temperature. Without even bothering to move past her eyes, he looked at the nurse expectantly.

"85/40," she announced grimly.

The N.P. clenched his jaw briefly and pulled his gloves off.

"Fine. You're an addict. You'll just have to deal with it until it's over. Shouldn't have started in the first place. That's what you get."

Bitty hung her head as tears trickled from her eyes. She hadn't *wanted* to start! She hadn't ever wanted to start using drugs! She had never had a choice! Mack just stuck the needle into her arm until she needed it—and him.

The nurse shoved a stack of clean clothes at her with an order to get dressed.

Bitty obeyed with her head down and her heart aching as her thoughts darkened even more. She was a drug addict and a prostitute. That's all anyone was ever going to see her as. Nothing more. Not even the N.P. cared what happened to her. No one did.

'We care, Bitty.'

'Yeah. We don't think you're disgusting.'

Sarah and Jay's words of encouragement managed to ease a little of the pain and she managed to dress without sobbing.

After thrusting another stack of clean clothes into Bitty's arms in a surprising moment of kindness, the nurse beckoned to the guard and practically shoved Bitty out the door.

"Don't mess those ones up," the guard informed her as she led the way back to her cell to drop off her clothes.

She had missed breakfast. The rest of the girls were all either doing their chores or occupying themselves in the common room. Once again, Bitty wished Tess and Mel were here. They had been people she knew and had seemed to look out for her. Now she was on her own again.

More than anything right now, Bitty wanted to curl up on her bunk again, but she knew she'd be in trouble if she didn't go where everyone else was, so she sighed and put her extra clothes on the bare mattress before following the guard down the corridor.

Coming the other direction was the male guard from earlier. He stopped when he reached them.

"Where's this one going?"

"Common room," the female guard replied in a bored tone. "Then I'm on break. Late, thanks to her. Had to stand around in the damn infirmary."

"Why don't you go on break. I'll escort her."

"Really? Thanks. I'd appreciate that." The female guard turned slightly, jerked her head towards the male guard, then trudged down the hall in the other direction again to take her break.

The other guard smiled a sickening smile at Bitty and took her upper arm. Without a word, he led her down a side corridor away from the common room. Bitty's stomach did a flip flop when he paused in front of a locked door and opened it.

It was a guard toilet, apparently, and he shoved her inside before shutting and locking the door again. When he turned to her, she shrank against the wall and wrapped her arms around herself at the way he looked at her.

"Turn around," he told her, stepping closer to her and unbuckling his pants. "And be quiet," he added when a whimper broke from her throat. "You owe me, and you know it. Turn around."

Bitty obeyed. What else could she do? She did owe him for the hit he'd given her earlier, even though it was already beginning to wear off.

The minute she turned around, he pushed her against the wall. She braced herself on it with her hands flat against the cool tile at her shoulders, her forehead pressed to it as tears began to trickle and the familiar tightness clutched at her chest. She flinched when she heard his zipper, then again when he pulled her pants and underwear down.

A choked little sob forced its way out of her and he grabbed her hair in a tight fist, his lips beside her ear.

"You better be quiet or you'll regret it. Who do you think they'll believe? A drug addicted whore, or an upstanding man of the law?" he hissed.

She turned her face in the opposite direction and clenched her jaw to keep from crying out as he thrust into her roughly and began collecting his payment. All she could do was stand there and try not to make any noise.

Nothing had changed. She was still a thing. She may not be on the street anymore, but she was no better off, really. Worse, because she was facing withdrawals with nothing to help her cope and no sympathy to be found.

Chapter Thirty

* Choice One *

Jay sat down on the barstool one over from John, watching him and the bacon alternately.

John smiled and pushed the plate closer. "You can have as much as you want. If you finish it and want more, I'll make more. If I run out, we'll buy some more when we go shopping today."

"Shopping?" Jay asked, reaching slowly for another piece of bacon.

"Of course. We have to get you some more clothes, and some school supplies and things."

"School?"

John nodded. "When was the last time you were in school?"

Jay shrugged. "I dunno. Not since Bailey ran away and we met Mack."

'Shut UP, Jay! Shut up! Shut up!'

Jay froze uncertainly, trying to distinguish who to listen to. John was being so nice. Was it really that bad to answer his questions? He was helping them, wasn't he? But Bailey was always right about how mean people were when they seemed nice. Maybe she was right about John and he really wasn't as nice as he was pretending. But it was just questions. That couldn't hurt, could it? John was speaking again and Jay turned his attention back to him.

"...and tomorrow we can register you, okay?"

"Register for what?"

John chuckled. "For school. Today we'll hang out, do some shopping, get to know each other, and tomorrow we'll get you settled in at school."

"But can't I stay here with you?" Jay asked nervously.

"I'm afraid not. For one thing, it's the law that you have to go to school, and for another, I have to work. I'm going to be careful about cutting back on my hours so I can be here with you guys, but I still have to work. There are other people who need me at the hospital and I can't let them down, either. I took some vacation days to be with you last week, but I'll need to get back to my patients."

"Oh."

John smiled at him. "We'll have plenty of time to hang out, okay?" For a moment, it looked like he was about to reach out and touch Jay, but he simply stood up and went back to the stove. "Eggs are on their way!"

***

Once they had been eating for a while, John cocked his head.

"So, Jay, Bebe said she has six friends. Does that mean there's seven of you?"

Jay nodded and Bailey swore as she stomped away towards the back, muttering and cursing about no one listening to her and not to blame her when they were in trouble again.

"So, you're all different, right? Bebe said she was five, but Bitty isn't five, so you're different ages and things?"

Jay nodded again.

"How old are you, Jay?"

"I'm ten."

John nodded and ate a few more mouthfuls before asking more questions.

"Do you look different than Bitty, Jay?"

Jay nodded emphatically. "Of course!"

John chuckled. "Of course. Sorry. Do you want to tell me what you look like so I can see you how you really are?"

Jay smiled in surprise and sat up a little more. "Really?"

John nodded. "Of course. I want to know what you each look like."

"My hair is short and sort of reddish but not like red like Scarlet's hair cuz it's not so dark. Sarah said it's called ginger like hers and that's why we got freckles too cuz that's what happens when you got ginger hair. Except I saw ginger once and it was white, so I don't know how it's called ginger but that's what Sarah says and she knows stuff like that."

John had pulled over a small notepad and had been scribbling notes as Jay rattled on, a smile tugging at the corners of his mouth.

"You're right. Real ginger root tends to look white, but there are some kinds that are reddish."

"Oh. Well, anyway, I got short hair and freckles like Sarah. The freckles are like Sarah, not the short hair. Hers is long."

John was starting to grin now. "Okay, short ginger hair and freckles. Anything else? How about your eyes?"

"Oh. Um, they're brown."

"No special color brown?" John asked playfully.

"No. Just brown?" Jay replied, perplexed.

John chuckled and made a note. "Okay, brown eyes, check. Anything else?"

Jay shrugged and took another big bite of breakfast.

John nodded. "Alright. So, do you think the others want to tell me how they look, or would you like to tell me?"

"Well, you already know what Bitty looks like. Umm, Bebe has the whitish yellow color hair."

'Blonde.'

"Blonde hair," Jay amended after Sarah's helpful comment. "It's short but not as short as mine. It's sort of round and goes to her ears."

"And her eyes?"

"Umm…" Jay thought for a moment, trying to remember.

'They're blue!'

"Oh, right. They're blue."

John chuckled and made a note. "That's not really something you pay attention to much, is it? Not like in all the books where they tell everyone what color people's eyes are before what they're wearing, right?"

Jay nodded, his mouth full again.

"No freckles for Bebe?"

Jay shook his head and swallowed. "Nope. But Sarah has freckles."

John chuckled. "I think I've got that. Anything else about Sarah? Besides freckles and ginger hair?"

"It's long. Down to her shoulders. And it sort of ripples but isn't really curly but it's not straight like Bebe and Bitty. Bailey's hair is sort of like that too. Not really straight but it's not curly either."

'Don't you fucking tell him about me!'

"Oh. Bailey doesn't want you to know about her," Jay said apologetically.

John nodded. "It's okay. Maybe she'll tell me herself sometime. So that's… three and a bit descriptions. Who am I missing? I've got Bebe, you, and Sarah. I know what Bitty looks like, and Bailey doesn't want me to know, so that's five."

"Um, Scarlet and… I don't remember her name. We can't talk to her. She doesn't talk to anyone even when she's around. But we can't really even see her. Only Bailey can see her, and not when she's out. When that other girl is out, it's scary, cuz everything goes black and we have to be sleeping but sometimes I can't sleep and it's dark."

'Her name is Callie, Jay.'

"Oh. Sarah said her name is Callie."

John cocked his head and listened carefully. "So, when the other girl, Callie, is out, no one knows what's happening, but when the others are out, you do?"

Jay shrugged. "Sometimes. Sometimes not. It's different all the time."

"I see. Well, why don't you tell me about Scarlet, and then we'll go get ready for shopping?"

"Scarlet has dark red hair. It's pretty. And it's sort of a tiny bit curly and it's fluffy and so pretty. She doesn't have freckles even though she's got red hair. It's not fair."

John laughed and nodded. "No freckles, check. What about her eyes?"

"Um… green."

"Okay, got it. Are you finished eating?"

Jay nodded and pushed his plate away.

"Okay, let's get the dishes into the dishwasher and we'll go."

~ Choice Two ~

When the guard had finished with her, she was dumped in the common room without even a minute to clean herself up. She wanted to curl up in a corner and cry. But he had promised to visit again with another needle for her before he left that evening, so that was at least something good. No doubt he would be collecting his payment at the same time, of course. It would be a lot fewer doses than Mack had been giving her the last several days, but it should be enough to see her through without severe withdrawals. Maybe she could even get herself off it. Then she wouldn't be so sick *and* she could get out from under the guard, literally.

Once again, she was looking around for Tess and Mel before she realized and forced herself to stop. They had probably been released or sent somewhere else. She didn't think she'd be released anytime soon. Not that it was much different from her life with Mack in here, though she did have meals and a bed, at least.

'That's good stuff, right? It's not so bad.'

'Shut it, Jay.'

'Don't be mean, Bailey. He's right. It's better than being out there.'

A group of girls was approaching and Bitty found herself searching for a dark corner to escape to. There wasn't enough time though and soon the girls were surrounding her.

'Well, well. You again. I notice your friends aren't here to protect you this time."

Bitty suddenly recognized them as the ones that had tried to approach last time, before Tess and Mel intervened. She got a sinking feeling in her stomach and she shrank into herself, fighting to keep Bailey back as her escape was cut off.

"You need to understand who's the boss in here, kid. I am. So you can either do what I say, or you can regret it. Choice is yours."

She reached out and played with the ends of Bitty's long, brown hair simply because she could, then flashed a fear-inducing smile and left with her posse, leaving Bitty trembling where she stood.

'You should have let me handle it.'

'I'm sure that would have gone so well!'

'Shut up, Scarlett. Go fuck yourself. You do it so well.'

"Stop it," Bitty muttered, looking around for a chair in a corner somewhere. There was an over-used looking lounger free in front of the TV. A couple of girls were watching some kind of animated movie. A glance at the movie shelf showed it was the majority of choices for movies. Probably 'kid safe' she figured.

"Anyone sitting here?" she asked softly.

The others shook their heads and Bitty sat down with a grateful sigh. She was already tired and desperately wanted to just lie down. She knew a lot of it was most likely the drugs, but some of it was probably the effects of the last few days with Mack.

It was actually kind of nice watching the movie. Bitty drew her feet up in front of her and rested her chin on her knees, losing herself in the show for a while. She'd never seen it and vaguely wished she could have caught it from the beginning, but it was a nice distraction all the same. She even smiled in parts. She couldn't remember the last time she'd watched a movie. A long time.

***

For the first time in longer than she could remember, Bitty actually found herself relaxing. She was warm, wearing clean clothes, inside on an actual chair, and watching a movie. Almost like a real person. It was more than she had ever thought possible given the situation. Maybe things weren't so bad after all.

After a while, a bell sounded for lunch and the guards lined them all up and escorted them to the cafeteria to eat. Her tray was piled high with food and she smiled a little to herself. This was more food than she'd had since... the last time she was here, and before that, the hotel room with John.

That thought brought a tinge of sadness, but she pushed it away and focused on finding a seat at one of the long tables. She didn't want to sit anywhere near those girls from earlier, but she wasn't sure if any of the others would be any better. The last thing she needed was to get on the wrong side of everyone here. They could make life miserable for her.

Luckily, there was a girl towards the far side of the room who offered her a smile and Bitty returned it shyly, then headed over with her tray.

"Can I sit here?"

"Sure." The other girl moved over just a tad so Bitty could squeeze in beside her.

"You're new." She wasn't asking, but Bitty nodded anyway.

"Yeah."

"I've been here for a few months. Not sure when I'm gonna get out. The social worker isn't exactly big on spending time explaining stuff. My mom says they're overworked so she doesn't have time."

Bitty was surprised the girl mentioned her mother. She almost never heard anyone talk about their parents.

The other girl held out her hand. "I'm Rebecca. Please don't call me Becky."

Bitty nodded and shook her hand. "Bitty."

"Bitty? That's your name?"

Bitty shrugged. "A nickname, I guess. My full name is Bailey, but please don't call me Bailey," she said, mirroring what Rebecca had said with a small smile.

Rebecca laughed quietly. "Nice to meet you, Bitty."

"No talking!" the guard called out.

Rebecca sighed and turned back to her food. "They're so grumpy," she mumbled.

"Why can't we talk?" Bitty asked under her breath.

"I dunno. I guess they just want us to eat."

"Oh." She glanced at the guard, then quickly down at her tray when she realized it was the guard from earlier.

"Are they all like that?"

"Who? The guards? I dunno. Not really. Some of them are okay. Fowler isn't that great, though. He sorta gives me the creeps."

Bitty looked at Rebecca sharply. "Does he... do stuff to you?"

"What? Like, creep stuff? Nah. He just gives off that vibe, you know? Like you just get that weirded out feeling from some people. He's one of them. But he can't be that bad or he wouldn't be a guard, right?"

Bitty gave a noncommittal grunt and went back to her food feeling a lot less hungry than she had a few minutes ago. Why couldn't she be like regular kids? Why couldn't she be someone who didn't get used by every guy on the planet.

'We should have stayed with John.'

'Don't fucking start, Jay.'

'I was just saying...'

'Yeah, well don't.'

Chapter Thirty-One

* Choice One *

By the time they had finished the dishes, Bitty had switched back in. It only took a few minutes for John to notice the change in her behavior now that he was watching for it, and he managed to address her as Bitty.

Her expression when he did earned him wide eyes and a look that could have been dismay or awe; or perhaps both.

'How did he know, Bailey? How did he know it was Bitty. How?'

Bailey was silent, stunned.

None of them commented on it out loud, though. That would have been much more of an admission than they were willing to give at this point, despite Bebe and Jay's mistakes. At least John didn't mention it, either.

The drive to the store was quiet, but it wasn't an awkward or fearful silence. More like the silence that comes when you're too busy taking things in to be able to talk. Bitty looked out the window, watching the things outside fly by about as fast as her thoughts were moving. So much had happened in such a short time. She wasn't sure how long it had been since she'd met John, but it couldn't have been more than a couple of weeks, surely. And yet, her life seemed to have gone to hell and back again.

Her gaze wandered to the man beside her. If he hadn't come along when he did, she'd probably be dead by now. It was a morbid, cliche thing to say, but it was what it was, she was sure. If Mack hadn't killed her, the weather and the infection would have. It was only a matter of time.

"So, I made a list of things we need to get while we're here," John said, making her jump a little. He showed her the lined notepad with a neat list of items on it in funny, scribbly handwriting. "What would you like to start with? Clothes, toiletries or school supplies?"

"Clothes, I guess," she mumbled, a pang of fear stabbing her when he brought up school supplies. She *really* didn't want to go to school. She was too stupid for school. She never understood what the teacher was trying to explain, she could never concentrate, and she never seemed to fit in.

Bitty was quiet the rest of the way to the store, chewing on her lip anxiously and looking out the window until they parked in front of the department store.

"Here? We're shopping here?"

John frowned. "Is this not okay? I figured they have a decent enough selection and they're not too expensive. They're not brand name or anything. Did you want that? I won't be able to get as much for the price, but we can go if you'd rather."

She shook her head quickly. "No. No, I just...didn't realize we would come to a store like this. I thought we were going to a thrift store."

John smiled. "Ah. Well, I'm not exactly broke, and I'd like to spoil my little girl."

She eyed him briefly as he got out of the car and collected her crutches.

"We can get you a wheelchair while we're in the store. That way it won't be so tiring. You still have some recovering to do."

She nodded and followed him inside without objection. It was actually rather a relief to know she didn't have to hobble around the whole store looking for clothes on crutches. She was getting the hang of it, but it was still awkward and tiring.

After John settled her in a store wheelchair and they left the crutches with the customer service desk, he pushed her to the girl's department.

"Okay, how about pj's first? Let's see…" He began browsing the racks looking for pajamas. Bitty was staring at him with a disconcerted look on her face. He paused when he looked back at her with a flannel pajama set in his hands. "What? You don't like it? You can choose whatever you want."

She shook her head. "N… no. I just… never had pajamas."

John sighed sadly and squatted down beside her. "Babygirl, things are going to be different as long as you want to stay with me, I promise. No more sleeping on the street. No more beatings. No more going hungry. You're going to be treated the way you should have been all along; like a treasure."

Her face flushed and she looked down at her lap, tears filling her eyes. He stroked her cheek and she looked up.

"I'm going to take care of you, Bitty. All of you."

She nodded and gave him a teary smile which he returned. Then he stood up, ruffled her hair gently, and held up the pajama set.

"How about these?"

She nodded and he put them in the basket of the wheelchair.

"Hmm, we might have to get a cart. Not sure we can fit a whole wardrobe in that little basket." He winked at her and turned back to the rack.

For the better part of an hour, John wandered around the girl's section with her, pointing out things and asking her opinion. After a while, he got better at judging which things she actually liked, and which things she was just agreeing with out of habit.

Dresses, skirts, tops, pants, sweaters, underwear, and socks all began to pile up in the cart he'd gone to get. Once again, she'd been surprised when he'd grabbed regular underwear and soft, plain cotton bras in black, tan, pink, and blue. He winked at her when he caught her expression and she smiled.

'Just wait.'

'Oh, Bailey. Come on. Have a little faith. Maybe he really isn't going to want sex from her.'

'And Scarlett's not a dirty slut!'

'Hey!'

'It's true and you know it.'

"...a sock on that one for now."

Bitty looked up at him blankly. "What?"

He smiled. "I said, we'll go get you a couple of pairs of shoes, but until your foot heals you'll have to use a sock on that one for now."

"Oh. Right. Sorry."

"No need to apologize." He got behind her and began pushing the wheelchair, pulling the full-sized cart behind him until they got to the shoe department. After trying on a couple of pairs of amazingly comfortable shoes, she ended up with a pair of black Mary-Janes and a pair of pink and white sneakers.

As they headed for the checkout, Bitty felt like the luckiest girl on the entire planet. She had new clothes, a warm, beautiful place to live, her own room with an amazing bed, and someone who seemed to genuinely care about her.

'*He only wants sex, moron. You're his fucking child mistress. Wake up!*'

"I don't care," Bitty murmured happily while John paid. "He's nice, and mostly gentle, and I'll never find anyone like him ever again. He treats me like I'm worth something."

'*Yeah, worth fucking.*'

'*Stop it, Bailey. Leave her alone, at least for now. We'll see how things go, okay? Nothing could be worse than where we've already been. Maybe this is a good thing. Who cares if he wants sex? It wouldn't be any different anywhere else. But it certainly won't be as bad as anywhere else. It's probably worth it.*'

Bailey made a snorting noise and disappeared to the back, leaving Bitty to bask in the joy of John's attention, however it would come.

~ Choice Two ~

The rest of the day, Bitty stayed close to Rebecca, trying to learn the ropes of the institution. It was scary in a different way than it had been with Mack. Here it wasn't the fear of being beaten that drove her to desperately try not to make a mistake, but the fear of what she didn't know would happen. The guard, Fowler, watched her all day whenever she was near him. It felt like his eyes were roaming over her like hands, slimy and disgusting. She felt so trapped. Sure, she had been trapped with Mack and her parents, but this was different. With Mack, she hadn't been able to get away because she had nowhere else to go and he would beat her if she tried. Here, she *couldn't* get away, trapped as she was by walls and fences and guards; guards who hated her, were disgusted by her, and who wanted to use her. It made her chest tighten every time she thought about it.

Not only was Fowler watching her, but the group of girls had eyes on her too. She had no idea why they felt such animosity toward her, but it emanated from their group like heat waves. She kept wishing Tess and Mel were still there.

After lunch, she and Rebecca were split up. Rebecca was on dish duty in the kitchen and Bitty hadn't been assigned a job yet, so she ended up sitting in the common room by herself.

Her solitude didn't last long. A few minutes in, she found herself surrounded before she even had time to react. Two girls had grabbed her arms and the third had her hand wrapped in Bitty's hair, pulling it back so she could look up at their ringleader.

"I hope you've decided to be smart. Let's find out, shall we? I want–" She broke off as Fowler appeared in the doorway, looking them up and down in that disgusting way of his. The girl's face flushed angrily and he sneered.

"Problem, Nat?"

They immediately released Bitty and stepped back.

"She was trying to attack me."

Bitty stared at her in horror. "I... I didn't... I wasn't..."

Fowler took her arm, looming over her while Nat stood behind him with a smug look on her face.

"I think you and I need to have a little talk about your behavior. Let's go."

Bitty's eyes filled with tears as she looked from Fowler to Nat and back while he dragged her from the room. As she rounded the corner, she heard Nat and her friends laughing.

As she'd half expected, he took her to the bathroom he'd used before. This time, though, he practically threw her inside before shutting and locking the door.

"I don't tolerate bullies on my watch," he growled, approaching her with a menacing scowl.

Bitty shrank back against the wall. "I–I didn't do–" She broke off when Fowler grabbed her throat and pushed her against the wall, just like Mack used to.

"I could report you, have you put in solitary confinement. But I'm feeling generous today. You can take care of me, and I'll keep quiet about your behavior," he whispered in her ear, grinding against her.

Bitty couldn't help the choked little sob of despair that escaped, causing his hand to tighten around her throat. At this point, being put by herself away from everyone sounded very good and she began debating her options.

As if reading her mind, he growled, "If you go into solitary, you won't get your hit before I go home."

At that, Bitty capitulated. Her eyes closed and her shoulders sagged.

He smiled and released her throat, stroking her cheek in a way that made her want to gag. "That's a good choice. Get on your knees."

Bitty obeyed miserably, silent tears running down her cheeks as she opened her mouth for him.

Chapter Thirty-Two

* Choice One *

Once the clothing was stowed in the trunk, John drove them to a drug store and helped Bitty out. Together, they wandered the aisles slowly, choosing a hair brush, hair ties, face wash, shampoo, conditioner, shower gel, soap, toothbrush, and toothpaste.

Bitty grabbed a fresh mint flavor after her typical glance at John for approval, but a second before she put it in the cart, she froze, staring blankly at it for a moment. Her eyes fluttered briefly and she made a face, her entire body suddenly shifting into a different position before she shoved it carelessly back on the shelf.

"I hate that! It hurts my mouth! I don't like it to hurt my mouth! I don't want it!"

John stared at her for a moment before tilting his head gently. "Bebe, right?"

She nodded.

"I see. Well, I think Bitty likes that kind, but I'll tell you what," he added quickly as her face began to scrunch up, "We can get two kinds. There's strawberry flavor right here, just for kids, that doesn't burn mouths. We can get that one for you and Jay, and we can get the minty kind for Bitty and whoever else wants it. Would that be okay?"

Bebe gazed at him in surprise. "Two kinds?" she repeated in amazement.

He nodded and she grinned.

"Thank you!" she cried, suddenly hugging him tightly.

He grinned back and wrapped his arms around her, kissing the top of her head. Once she stepped back, he reached for the minty flavor Bitty had chosen, then showed Bebe the children's flavors below. It took Bebe a while to decide between the bubblegum flavor or the strawberry, and finally settled on strawberry when John promised they could buy the other kind when the first was finished.

It was a very happy little girl who wobbled up to the checkout and then to the car. After buckling up, she looked at him hopefully.

"Are you my new daddy?"

'Bebe! Don't be a moron. Of course he's not your daddy! He's a fucking per-'

'Bailey, please! That's enough. Let her be. I'll talk to her about it later.'

Bebe looked down at her lap miserably as Bailey and Sarah argued inside.

John paused in the middle of putting the key into the ignition, then finished and turned on the engine before answering.

"Well... that depends."

Bebe looked up hopefully. "On what?"

John sighed and turned his body to face her. "I wanted to talk to one of the older kids first, but I'd *like* to be your Daddy, if you'd all like that."

'We don't *all want that, you fucking dirty bastard!'*

'Bailey!'

'It's true, Sarah! He's a sick fuck and he only wants us to fuck us!'

'He hasn't wanted that with Bebe."

'Yet.'

'Oh, Bailey... Can't you just-'

'NO!'

"I do! I do!" Bebe cried happily, her face wreathed in smiles. "I want you to be my daddy!"

John couldn't help but smile. "It makes me really happy to hear you say that, Bebe. Thank you. It means a lot to me."

"It does? Why?"

His smile grew somewhat sad. "Well... because I..." He sighed and ruffled her hair gently. "It's something I need to discuss with the others. For now, yes, I'd like to be your Daddy for however long you'll let me."

She grinned and leaned over to hug him, reveling in the comfort his arms provided for the first time in a very long time.

John sighed softly and rested his cheek on the top of her head for a moment, then took a deep breath and pulled away.

"Okay, time to get school stuff."

"I get to go to school?"

"Yup. We'll get you registered tomorrow."

"Do I get a backpack?"

He laughed softly and pulled out of the parking space. "Yes, you'll get a backpack. And pencils and notebooks and all kinds of things." He laughed again at her cry of glee.

She ignored the comments from the others inside.

~ Choice Two ~

By the time the guard finished with her, it was time for dinner. Bitty had been assigned a job now; helping in the serving line. All in all, she was rather relieved to have something to do that would keep her from the clutches of Nat and her gang. The food had already been cooked, so it was her job to help put it out on the line over the warmers and help serve it. She kept her head down and did what she was told, scooping mashed potatoes onto trays as they went by, then ladling gravy over it.

"No gravy."

The request came a split second after she'd poured the gravy over the pile of potatoes and Bitty looked up to apologize. Her face went white when her eyes met Nat's glowering blues.

"I said no gravy, you fucking moron. Do you not understand English? Or are you just that incompetent you can't think for yourself?"

Bitty shrank back and lowered her head again.

"I'm sorry. I didn't hear–" She broke off and in the space of a heartbeat her head snapped up and her shoulders straightened. She leaned forward with the spoon clenched tightly in her fist.

"You don't get to talk to me like that, bitch. You said it too late, and you did it on purpose. I'm not gonna deal with any more of your shit, do you understand me? Now *back off!*" Bailey hissed, her jaw tight and her eyes blazing.

Nat looked like she'd been slapped for a moment before her eyes narrowed and she, too, leaned forward.

"You're gonna pay for this. You just dug your grave." Her eyes on Bailey for as long as possible, she picked up her tray and stalked away to sit with her friends.

'Oh Bailey! What did you do!?'

"I stood up for us, Scarlett, that's what. I'm not gonna be pushed around by a prissy bitch like her," she muttered under her breath as she went back to scooping potatoes, slapping them on the trays angrily.

'She's gonna kill us!'

"I'll handle it."

***

Throughout dinner, Bailey kept her eyes roaming over the cafeteria like a hawk, every muscle in her body tense and ready to fight at the slightest provocation. No one came near her, not even Rebecca, but Bailey didn't care. She didn't want anyone around anyway. She caught Nat glaring over at her every so often and she glared right back, righteous fury in her eyes. Her lips quirked into a smirk every time the other girl looked away first.

"See? Told you I'd handle it."

'I don't know, Bailey....'

***

Luckily there was no time to run into Nat and her posse after dinner, because the guards lined everyone up for inspection before sending them to their cells. Bailey returned Fowler's sick wink with a defiant jerk of her head, her jaw clenched in anger.

When she reached her bed, she threw herself onto it and drew her knees up, resting her forearms on top of them and her back against the wall, frowning angrily at the opposite wall. Rage and impotence warred within her, threatening to make her explode. Why did it always seem like she was trapped no matter where she went?

'*Maybe someone will help us?*'

"Grow the fuck up, Jay. No one is gonna help us. Ever. How have you not learned that by now? This entire fucking world hates us. We may as well be dead. It's the only way we'll ever make it stop."

Her jaw tightened when she heard his crying as he ran further back, retreating into his safe place.

'*Bailey. That was cruel and you know it. He's a kid. At least one of us should have hope.*'

"Why? It's pointless. Hope just hurts."

There was no reply; just the quiet tears of more than one little child inside.

Chapter Thirty-Three

* Choice One *

Bebe was chattering happily the whole way home, gushing over the pink unicorn backpack he had bought for her in addition to the more traditional backpack in pink and gray. Besides the required school supplies, he also bought Bebe another coloring book and a box of sixty-four crayons, as well as a less princess-y coloring book for Jay. Bailey spent the rest of the trip sulking in the background, muttering every so often about 'grooming' and 'bribery'. Everyone else ignored her.

For dinner, he stopped at a fast food restaurant and ordered them both a combo meal, plus a kid's meal with a toy for Bebe. She was delighted to find hers contained the tiny stuffed white pony that went along with her princess crown from the one she'd bought the very first day with the money he'd given them.

At John's house—which Bebe was already referring to as 'home'—he helped them inside and put the leftovers in the fridge.

"If anyone else can hear, I'm putting the second meal in the fridge if any of you are hungry later. Bebe's meal wasn't very big."

At that, a flicker of a blank look passed over her face before she smiled gently.

"Thank you, John. That is very considerate of you."

He blinked a couple of times, then leaned on the counter in what he hoped was a non-threatening posture. "Well now, I'm pretty sure you're not Bailey because I haven't been screamed at," he said with a wink, earning him a slight flinch on her face as Bailey set about screaming internally. "I know you're not Bebe, and I don't think you're Jay or Bitty. So that leaves..." He paused. "Hmm... Scarlett, or Sarah, or... I can't think what Jay told me about the last name. Cassie, was it?"

Sarah smiled and nodded. "I'm Sarah. I must say I'm quite impressed that you can already see differences in us. No one has ever seen that. They just assume Bitty has 'moods'."

John shrugged. "They just didn't pay attention. Not that you'd have wanted that anyway, I'm sure. Don't worry, I'm not going to say anything to anyone or do anything to you. It can be just between us."

"Thank you."

"Why don't we go sit down in the living room and relax for a while? Get that foot up and resting."

"Okay. Thank you."

He gave her a bright smile and led the way slowly to the other room while she followed carefully. Once they were seated, he turned to her curiously.

"How old are you, Sarah? If I may ask?"

She regarded him before answering. "I... don't have an age. I'm just... an adult, I guess."

He nodded. "I have to admit, I've obviously got some things I need to discuss with you all, but I'm not sure who would be best to discuss it *with*. Since you're the adult, I would be inclined to talk to you about it, but it's legally Bitty's body, so maybe she should be the one to make the decision, if that's how it works."

"What do you want to discuss?"

'Fucking us, moron! He wants sex. That's all he's ever wanted. Why can't any of you see that!'

"Our situation," John replied, unaware of Bailey's internal outburst. "I know our relationship is... awkward, and I thank you for keeping that from everyone. When I first met you, I just wanted... well... a physical encounter; someone to take the boredom and loneliness away. Obviously my feelings on that changed and I want more than that now.

"I want to know how you feel about things; all of you. I like certain... things. I don't know how much you know of that." He blushed and looked down at his lap briefly before looking back at her. "I never intended it to be with an underage girl, I swear. But now that I've... been with whoever I was with, it's all I can think about. I'll understand if you don't want that ever again, and I'll respect that. I just want to know what the general... thought on the subject might be."

Sarah watched him silently while he spoke, trying to focus on what he was saying and filter out the internal flurry of dialogue.

"I don't understand. Are you asking if we want to stay here, or if you can have sex?"

John flushed and looked away again. "Both, I guess."

Sarah opened her mouth to speak but seemed to pause. Then a smile spread over her face and she scooted closer to him on the couch.

"You are one of the best I've ever had. Of course I want that. You're a Daddy, aren't you? A Daddy Dom?"

John closed his mouth and recovered from his shock in a reasonable amount of time. "Uhh, yeah. I didn't know you… Well, I didn't expect… Yes. I like to take care of my little and treat her well, but I–"

"Like to fuck a whore, too, right?"

John flushed deeply. "Sarah?" he asked carefully.

Scarlett shook her head with a laugh. "I'm Scarlett. I got to be with you sometimes in the hotel. You are amazing. I really enjoyed what we did. Even the parts where you were rough were still great. Usually it hurts, but with you it was okay."

He smiled and gently wrapped his arm around her, pulling her against him and resting his cheek against her head.

"I would love it if you would be my little," he murmured.

"A little is the girl a Daddy takes care of, right?"

He nodded against her. "Right. Well, usually it's an adult who likes to just let go of responsibility for a while and be taken care of like a child, except when there's sex involved. All my littles have been adults. I didn't realize you weren't until I got all the makeup off you and really saw you underneath all that. I should have stopped then and there, a big part of me wanted to, but I…" He trailed off and she tucked herself against him as much as her foot would allow.

"It's okay. I liked it a lot. I wanted more."

He hugged her gently. "I want to take care of you, Bit-… Scarlett. Even if it can only ever be a platonic relationship. I know it really should be anyway. I just can't… forget what it was like with you."

"What about when Bitty grows up?" she asked quietly. "Won't we be too old?"

He sighed and hugged her again. "Of course not. Like I said, all my littles were adults of various ages. It's not really about sex with a real child. I'd *never* be with Bebe like that. It's the caring and protecting part that matters."

"What if Bebe comes out while we're fucking?"

He shook his head. "Then we stop. Immediately. I stop. It won't be like that."

She shifted so her head was in his lap and she was looking up at him. "John," she murmured, "I want to be your little. I want to be with you the way it was in the hotel. I want everything. All of it."

He smiled sadly down at her. "What about the others?"

She snorted. "Well, Bailey hates you. But she hates everyone, so that doesn't count. I think the rest of us really like you and want to stay with you. It's never felt like this for as long as anyone can remember."

"Felt like what?" he asked with a frown.

"Having someone love us like this. No one ever cared before."

"Ever?"

"Never ever."

He closed his eyes and sighed sadly. "I'm so sorry, babygirl." He opened them again and looked down at her for a moment, then lowered his head and kissed her softly.

She returned the kiss willingly but he pulled his head away after a moment. A look of confusion clouded her face. "What?"

He shook his head. "I think I need to discuss it with everyone first. We need to work things out between all of us."

She looked away. "Why? I want it. Isn't that enough?"

"I wish it was. But everyone needs to have a say in it. I need to know what everyone wants; how everyone wants to be treated." He stroked her hair softly.

"How long can we stay here?"

"As long as you want, I think. If you like it enough, we could file for semi-permanent placement. In a few years you'll be an adult anyway and then you're free to do whatever you want. You won't need to be in foster care anymore."

"Will we have to leave here when we're eighteen?"

He shook his head. "Not if you don't want to. I'll never force you to leave."

"Okay." She suppressed a yawn and he smiled.

"Time for bed, young lady. Your own bed," he added when she smiled at him in a suggestive way.

She sighed and sat up. "Fine."

"You'll have to come to work with me tomorrow, since you're not registered for school yet. Then on Tuesday you'll go to school while I'm at work. I'll be changing my hours so I can be home earlier."

"Really?"

He nodded and helped her stand. "Gotta be here for my little girl."

She smiled and he returned it as they made their way to her bedroom. When they reached the doorway she paused. "Can I just finish that meal you got? The extra one?"

He chuckled. "Putting off bedtime already? How about I let you eat it in bed. Just this once," he added quickly.

She grinned and nodded, hobbling into her room while he went to get the bag. So far, things seemed absolutely perfect.

'It's never perfect. Good stuff doesn't last. You know that.'

"Come on, Bailey. Give it a chance. Maybe things will be different now."

There was a derisive snort and then silence for the rest of the night.

~ Choice Two ~

Just after the lights went out, Bitty's door opened and a figure stood silhouetted in the doorway before entering. Her stomach contracted in fear. No matter who it was, it wasn't going to be good.

Fowler stepped up to her bed with a smile.

"I'm heading off duty, so I came to collect and give you the dose I promised."

Bitty closed her eyes miserably and tried to fight the nausea and heartache that washed over her.

Without another word, Fowler was already getting himself ready, then her. She lay still and tried to be quiet as he mounted and took what he wanted from her, his hand over her mouth to muffle the little whimpers of pain he was causing.

She cringed when he finished and climbed off, adjusting his clothes again and grinning down at his work he'd left exposed to admire for a minute.

When he'd tucked his shirt in, he pulled the syringe from the pocket and stuck it in her vein. Relief washed over her and her eyes closed as he finally pulled her pajamas back into place and tossed the blanket over her again.

"Sweet dreams, slut. I'll be back in the morning."

She barely heard him as she slipped into the welcoming abyss.

'You're fucking weak, Bitty.'

She barely heard Bailey's taunt as she drifted off to blessed sleep.

Chapter Thirty-Four

* Choice One *

"Hey, sleepyhead."

Bailey groaned and rolled over in bed, pulling the covers closer. "Fuck off."

There was a soft chuckle. "Good morning, Bailey. It's time to come get some breakfast before we leave."

"Fuck off," she repeated.

"I'll call you again in five minutes. Then it's time to get in the shower, get dressed, and come for breakfast. I can't be late today or they'll make it a lot harder for me to change my hours."

She grunted and he left her alone.

'Why do you have to be so rude, Bailey? He's being nice. He cares about us. Why do you have to antagonize him all the time?'

"Cuz he's a sick fuck."

'Come on. He's the best we've ever met. Probably the best we will *ever meet. He's certainly the best we could ever hope to have care about us. And I like being cared about, Bailey. Even if you don't need anyone, the rest of us do. The rest of us just want to be cared about, and John cares. A lot. Please, just let him care about us. Please?'*

She didn't answer but she did get up and snatch some of her new clothes from the bags on the chair in the corner before hobbling down the hall to the bathroom.

'We're not supposed to be walking on that foot.'

"Fuck off, Sarah. I'll do what I wanna do. You can't take that away from me."

***

John had made pancakes for breakfast, which instantly caused Bebe to shove her way to the front in excitement and made John chuckle.

"You like pancakes, Bebe?" he asked with a grin.

She nodded, syrup dripping from her chin.

'Ugh. Grow up, Bebe. You're eating like a slob! I'm surprised you're getting any of that in your mouth. You're gonna ruin our new clothes.'

'Oh, Bailey, she's enjoying herself. Leave her alone.'

"Mommy made pancakes once. She was smiling that day. She said it was a good day. I ate all the pancakes! She was happy with me."

John smiled and sat down with his own. "I'll have to remember to make pancakes more often. Does everyone like pancakes?"

She nodded eagerly.

'I fucking hate pancakes!'

'Oh, Bailey, you do not! You're just being otherwise.'

'What do you know, Scarlett? When did you ever see me eat pancakes? Huh? You think you know every fucking thing but you don't! You know how to fuck and that's it! Fuck off!'

Bebe paused with her fork halfway to her mouth as the tears and argument grew louder.

"Bebe? Are you okay?" He frowned. "Bebe?"

Bitty set the fork down carefully on the plate and tucked her hair behind her ear with her head down.

"I… don't feel very good."

"What's wrong? Did I do something wrong?"

Bitty shook her head, then burst into tears.

John stood up and hurried to her side, hugging her close to him and stroking her hair. "Shhh, what's wrong? What happened?"

"It's been so wonderful here and Bailey hates everything so much and she's making everyone cry and being mean about everything and she even got mad about pancakes and I don't know what to do anymore or who to listen to and nothing makes sense!"

"Ooohhh. I see." He hugged her a little more tightly. "Bailey's upset because she doesn't know how to help anymore, right? She's used to being the one to keep you safe, and now she's not?"

She shrugged, still crying into his chest.

"Shhh. It's alright, babygirl. We'll figure this out. It'll take some time, but we can do it. I'm sure of it. You're all strong and brave, and I know we can work through it."

He held her until she stopped crying and pulled away from him. Then he smiled at her gently and sat down to finish eating.

"We'll be leaving soon to register you for school and head to my office. You'll spend the day with me there," he said, trying to change the subject and get her mind off the internal conflict.

She nodded and tried to finish her pancakes, but her appetite was gone. She had thought things would finally be like she'd always dreamed they would be, but they were fighting more than ever and it seemed like everything was falling apart.

~ Choice Two ~

The lights came on suddenly and Bebe blinked and squinted her eyes in the glare of the fluorescent bulbs. Her eyes hurt and she didn't feel like moving. All she wanted to do was roll over and go back to sleep, but a guard came and banged on her door making her flinch.

"Wake up! Shower time."

Bebe whimpered and tried to sit up, rubbing at her eyes. Her arms felt so heavy and droopy it was hard to make them work right.

"I don't feel good," she mumbled miserably. Tears filled her eyes and she rolled out of the bed in slow motion to gather her uniform and toiletries.

"Where do I go?" There was no reply from anyone. Bebe's heart began to tighten in fear. "Where do I go?" she repeated. She jumped as the guard who'd called her spoke from down the hall.

"That way. The door that says 'showers'."

Moving sluggishly, she trudged down the hall, opening doorways along the way until she finally found the door to the shower room and pushed it open, then paused. "It's scary," she whispered.

A guard was standing at a second doorway that led from a changing area to a large group shower area. There were no curtains and no privacy. She was watching them all with a bored, tired expression. When she spotted Bebe standing in the doorway to the hall she scowled.

"Get in here! It's shower time."

Bebe jumped and stepped inside, letting the door swing shut behind her as she moved to the spot the guard had pointed.

"Strip and find a shower."

"But... there's people there."

"So? We're all girls. Get in there before I make you."

Bebe's eyes filled with tears and she was trembling as she took her clothes off.

"Bailey," she whimpered, "I need help. Please. Sarah?" She didn't know what was wrong! She couldn't hear anyone properly. There was something thick and dark covering the spot where they usually were and she could only hear muffled voices. She was suddenly very alone. Tears began to trickle down her cheeks when the guard virtually shoved her into the large, echoing room.

Some of the girls turned to look at her but most were keeping to themselves and carefully avoiding looking at anyone else. Bebe hunched up and wrapped her arms around herself in a futile attempt to hide herself.

"So that's what a whore's snatch looks like? I thought it would be wider!" came the taunt from the girl she thought was called Nat.

She began to cry harder, hunching up even more.

"Jackson!" the guard shouted, making Bebe jump.

Nat glared at Bebe. "You're gonna pay for yesterday, bitch," she hissed before turning back to her shower.

Bebe's tears increased yet again as she stepped under a shower another girl had just vacated. The water was nice and warm, but she couldn't make herself move her arms from around herself to wash. Terror gripped her and she just wanted to hide.

She caught the glare from Nat as she and her friends left the shower to get dressed. After waiting as long as she possibly could, Bebe finally turned the shower off and made her way to the changing room. The guard was standing at the main door now and girls were lining up. Bebe dried and dressed as quickly as she could, but her arms and legs just felt so heavy it was hard to move.

By the time she was finished, she was the last one left and everyone was glaring at her. Apparently they couldn't go to breakfast without everyone. With her head down and her arms around her waist again, Bebe took her place at the end of the line and followed as they made their way to the cafeteria.

It was loud in there, too, and Bebe started to turn and escape the noise but a guard stepped behind her and barricaded the way.

"I'll see you after breakfast," he whispered, stepping closer to her as if herding her like a sheep.

Bebe shrank back and turned back to the noisy room to get her tray. Her spirits lifted somewhat when she saw it was pancakes for breakfast and she was beginning to feel a little less scared as she made her way to the furthest, most quiet looking table in the room. It was so loud!

Before she knew what was happening, she tripped over something and went down hard on her hands and knees with a cry, her tray flying and its contents spilling everywhere. Crying hard, she shifted onto her butt and held her knees in pain.

"Carter!" the guard from the showers shouted. "Get up and clean up that mess!"

It took Bebe a long time to stand up and trudge to the front of the room to get cleaning supplies, crying the whole time and occasionally rubbing at her bruised knees. Several of the other girls were laughing at her childish behavior, calling her a baby and a whiner.

"Sarah!" she whimpered, doing her best to stop crying and clean up the sticky mess. Her precious pancakes were spread over the dirty floor and everything was covered in syrup and milk. Even her delicious bacon was ruined. Nothing had survived the fall. "Sarah, I need help."

There was no answer.

"Who's Sarah? Your babysitter or your pimp?"

Bebe looked up into the cruel face of Nat. The girl was smirking down at her as she leaned casually against the table, her feet stretched out lazily.

"You really should watch where you're going," she taunted, waggling her foot with a cruel laugh.

Bebe turned away, tears coursing down her cheeks a little harder again. That mean girl had made her fall! Now she'd have to go ask for more pancakes.

Finally, she finished cleaning up the mess and took it and her tray back to the front.

"Can I have some more pancakes?" she whispered to the woman in the kitchen.

"No seconds. Besides, breakfast is over. You'll have to wait for lunch."

Bebe couldn't take any more. She burst into fresh sobs and hunched up on the floor with her knees to her chest and her face buried in them.

"Get up!" a disgusted voice ordered.

When she didn't immediately move, a big hand gripped her tightly around her upper arm and hauled her to her feet before dragging her from the cafeteria and down the hall. It was the guard who had yelled at her to clean up. She led Bebe to a virtually empty room which contained only a padded mat and a blanket.

"I think you need some time in the quiet room. Calm down and stop acting like a baby," she snapped, giving Bebe's streaming tears a derisive look before leaving and locking the door.

Bebe curled up on the mat with her sore knees against her chest and sobbed.

"Sarah! Bailey! Bitty! Please help! Please let me in! I don't wanna be here! Please help me! Where are you?"

Chapter Thirty-Five

* Choice One *

Bitty slipped out to 'front' on the drive to the school two blocks away, trying to get her bearings when John pulled into the parking lot.

"This is the school?" she asked softly.

He nodded and unbuckled. "Yup. It's a good one. Come on. Let's get you registered."

Once she'd struggled out of the passenger seat and had settled her crutches comfortably, she followed him into the building. There was a second set of doors with a button that John had to press.

"John Matthews. I'm here to register a new student," he said into the speaker.

The door buzzed and he opened it to let Bitty hobble inside before leading her to the office.

"Hi. We're here to register a new student," he repeated to the woman behind the desk.

She gave them both a warm smile and stood up to shake their hands.

"It's great to meet you. What's your name?" she asked, turning to Bitty.

"Bitty Carter," she mumbled.

The woman nodded. "I'm Trudy Simons, the school secretary. Why don't you both come with me and you can sit down while I get the paperwork?"

They followed her around the desk to a little room with a table and six chairs around it.

"I'll be right back."

John nodded and pulled a chair out for Bitty, then sat down.

"She's nice, huh?" he asked with a smile.

Bitty nodded silently, her eyes scanning the room nervously.

"It'll be okay, babygirl," he said softly, taking her hand. "You're safe here. The doors are locked and no one can get to you here. You'll be okay."

Trudy returned with the papers and a pen, then left to deal with a student who needed to call home. John began filling out the forms, asking questions every so often.

"I guess I should have thought to bring the folder from the social worker," he said with a chuckle when Bitty asked what a social security number was in answer to his question.

"I'll just have to come in and fill out the rest tomorrow when I drop you off."

Her stomach flip flopped at the thought of being here alone.

***

An hour later, John and Bitty climbed back into his car and headed for his office. Bitty was still nervous about school, but John's reassurances helped ease some of her fears. The locks on the doors meant that even if Mack did somehow find her in a town five hours away, he wouldn't be able to get in anyway.

John's office turned out to be on the third floor in one of the buildings of a large hospital complex. It looked like the hospital she'd been in for her foot and she wondered if all hospitals looked the same as she followed him along what felt like dozens of identical corridors.

When they reached his office, Bitty smiled. This part was different. For one thing, the reception area had toys in one corner and a small fish tank near the check-in desk. The receptionist smiled at them both.

"Hi, Dr. Matthews."

"Morning, Joan. I'd like you to meet Bitty. She'll be living with me for a while and she's staying at the office today."

Joan gave her a warm smile. "It's nice to meet you, Bitty."

Bitty just nodded quietly and stayed slightly behind John as if trying to hide.

"Alright, I'll get her settled in the break room and then I'll be in my office. You can send in my next appointment." He smiled down at Bitty and led her along a hallway. "I'll show you my office first and get you some things to keep you busy in the breakroom."

When they got into his actual office there was an even larger aquarium than the one in the reception area, filled with a variety of large and small fish of all kinds.

"Wow!" she breathed, heading over to it.

He grinned. "Pretty, huh?"

She nodded, watching them swim peacefully.

John rummaged in his desk for a minute, then joined her. "Ready, babygirl? We'll get you settled, then I have to work for a while. I'll check on you between clients, okay?"

She nodded and turned away from the tank to follow him down the hall to a room with a tiled floor, a fridge, sink, cabinets, a table, and some chairs. John pulled one of the chairs out for her and she sat down, then put her foot up on the second chair he pulled over for her.

"Okay, here's some coloring stuff, blank paper if you want to make up your own stuff, and some magazines. There's some juice boxes in the fridge and some crackers in the drawer next to it if you get hungry." He kissed the top of her head and smiled. "You okay?"

She nodded. "Yeah. I'll be okay. Thanks."

He nodded, ruffled her hair, and left.

Bitty sat there for a minute, looking around nervously.

'Now's our chance. We could leave.'

'Bailey, stop it. Where are we supposed to go? And how? We're not exactly very mobile right now, in case you hadn't noticed.'

'It would be a start!'

"I'm not leaving," Bitty mumbled, opening the coloring book and the box of crayons. They were almost new, which wasn't what she'd expected. She spent some time coloring, ignoring the quiet bickering inside until John checked in fifty minutes later between appointments.

~ Choice Two ~

Bebe had no idea how long she stayed curled in a ball on the mat in that empty room. All she knew was she was lonely and frightened. She had never been so lonely in her whole life. Everyone had always been there for her when she'd been out like this. This was the first time no one had answered when she'd called.

Eventually, the door opened and she sat up, wiping at the slow trickle of tears that refused to stop. A big man stood in the doorway, then stepped inside after checking up and down the hall. Bebe watched him somewhat curiously as he smiled and pulled something from his pocket.

"Ready for your hit?"

Her stomach lurched when she saw him take the cap off a needle and she began to cry harder and crawl backwards against the wall.

"I don't want that! I don't want that! It hurts! It hurts!" she cried. "Stop!"

Fowler scowled and grabbed her face, putting his close in front of her. "I don't know what the fuck your problem is today, but you shut the fuck up. I risked a lot bringing this in here for you and you're gonna take it and pay me for it. And *be quiet!*"

Bebe screamed and tried to pull her arms from his grasp but she still felt heavy and weak. Before she was able to even twist away, he had the needle in her and she felt a strange wave run through her. She stared at him as the feeling spread through her little body and her arms and legs went more limp than they had before. Her tears slowed and she couldn't think straight.

The man smiled and put the cap back on the needle, shoving it back in his pocket before grabbing her ankles and pulling her toward him until she lay flat on her back with her legs spread.

Bebe could only whimper pathetically as he pulled her pants off and climbed onto her. She had no idea what was going on and the fear felt like it was strangling her along with the stuff he'd put in her arm. Quiet tears trickled into her hair as he did things to her she didn't understand. All she knew was that it hurt, she couldn't stop him, and she was alone. She needed to get away! She didn't want to be here. She didn't want to hurt anymore! She didn't want to be scared anymore!

Callie lay very still and quiet, her eyes shut tightly as the man finished hurting her. She had to keep quiet or he would hurt her more. She learned that a long time ago. Be quiet. Don't move. Don't cry too loud. It would stop sometime. They always got tired sometime. Or hungry. Sometimes they stopped when they were hungry. They didn't care if Callie was hungry. Callie was always hungry it seemed. Callie was hungry now.

Callie opened her eyes slowly when the man got off her. She felt icky. It was always icky. Callie hated it. She closed her eyes. She felt dizzy. It didn't feel like the dizzy that came from being so hungry your whole belly hurt. The man laughed and she opened her eyes again slowly.

"That looks good on you. Now pull your damn pants up and you can get out of here."

Callie blinked and looked around. Callie didn't know where she was supposed to go. Callie didn't even know where she was.

"Hurry up!"

Callie jumped and did her best to pull her clothes back on and sit up, but she felt even more dizzy. The big man didn't care. He grabbed her arm and pulled her up. It hurt her arm. Callie cried softly. She didn't mean to. She shrank back, expecting the big man to hit her. He didn't. She looked up carefully as he took her from the room and down a strange hallway.

There were other people going into a room and the man took her to the room. It looked like a kind of school room. He shoved her into a seat and went to talk to the teacher. The teacher looked nice. Callie thought maybe she would like the teacher.

The teacher came over and Callie shrank into her seat. The teacher smiled and crouched down beside Callie.

"Hi. I'm Mrs. Barnes. What's your name?"

Callie looked down at her lap quietly. It wasn't good to make noise. It was bad to talk. Callie didn't talk to anyone.

"It's okay. You're shy. I'll give you some time to get more comfortable, okay?"

Callie looked up at the smiling teacher as the lady stood up and went back to the front of the room. This was a different school than the last one she was at. The last one was more colorful. Callie had liked the colors. They were pretty. She wished they had colors like that at home. Mommy and Daddy didn't like colors. They tore up Callie's colors and hurt her. Callie didn't make colors anymore. But she liked to look at them.

The teacher talked for a while and wrote things on the board and the other kids started talking and handing out books. Callie jumped when a big girl slammed a book down in front of her and laughed. Callie didn't think that girl seemed very nice.

Callie looked down at the book while everyone started opening theirs. Maybe she was supposed to open hers, too? She opened it and stared at all the numbers. The whole book was full of numbers! So many numbers! Too many numbers. Callie didn't even know all the numbers.

The teacher kept talking and the other kids started writing things. The teacher put a pencil and paper in front of Callie and went back to the front of the room. Was Callie supposed to write, too?

The teacher wrote numbers on the board and Callie tried to write them on her paper, but they were hard numbers and she didn't do them right. The girl next to her laughed and Callie scrunched up her paper and hunched up, crying quietly. The teacher came over and took her paper.

"What's this supposed to be?"

Callie stayed quiet, her head down. She did her best! She didn't know what all the numbers were. She tried to write the numbers too.

"Why did you do this? This is not a time for jokes. You need to take this seriously or you're going to have a hard time when you get out of here. Now do it right."

Callie wiped at her tears and picked up the pencil, trying to hold it right while the other kids laughed. The teacher got mad.

"Bailey, that's enough. You and I will have a talk in a little while. Just stop messing around."

Callie wiped her cheeks and looked around to see who she was talking to. Everyone still seemed to be laughing at her. Maybe Bailey was laughing and the teacher was mad at her? Callie hunched up when the teacher went back to the front and started talking again. The teacher had taken Callie's things away. Callie couldn't do the numbers anymore. Callie just sat still and quiet. That was best. Always still and quiet.

Chapter Thirty-Six

* Choice One *

Bitty colored for a while, then Jay wanted to make paper airplanes and the breakroom was soon littered with his attempts. By the time John returned, Jay was frustrated.

"I can't make them fly right!" he pouted when John commented on them.

"Ah. Well, I can help you really fast, then I have to go back to work, okay?"

Jay nodded and John sat down beside him to start folding a plane. Jay watched and copied with his own paper. When they'd finished, John flew his across the room perfectly.

"Wow! Let me try!" Jay stood up and tossed his plane. It did a half loop and skidded along the ground, but went farther than any of the others had. "Oh WOW! Did you see that? Did you see how far it went!"

John laughed and stood up. "Way to go. I have to get back to my office, but I'll be back in a little bit. Have fun. Maybe you could color your plane and make it look cool while I'm gone?"

Jay nodded eagerly and sat down with his creation.

***

John checked in three more times, each time giving whoever was out something new to do. At one point, Bebe wanted a snack and helped herself to some crackers and juice before coloring the paper dolls John had shown her how to make the last time he was in. By the time he came in the fourth time, Bitty was back and coloring the picture she'd started before.

"Lunch time, babygirl. Are you hungry?"

Bitty looked up with a smile and nodded.

"Great! How about subs? There's a little shop down the street that delivers. Or do you want to get out of here for a while?"

She looked out at the snow falling gently outside and shook her head. "If it's okay, I'd like to stay here." She'd had enough time outside in the snow to last a long time.

John nodded. "Absolutely. What do you like on your subs?"

"Anything is fine."

He sat down beside her and smiled. "I know you'll make do with anything. I want to know what you *like*."

'I want salami, Bitty! Can we get salami! And tomatoes?'

'No tomatoes! I hate tomatoes!'

'Can you ask for roast beef, Bitty?'

'Just get a fucking turkey sandwich.'

Bitty stared blankly for a moment before tucking her hair behind her ear. "Uhhh…"

John laughed. "Do you want a bunch of little sandwiches? We could have them put a little of everything and cut it up into small pieces."

Bitty's jaw dropped. "They can do that?" she asked in surprise.

"I'm a regular. I'm sure they will for me. Tell me what everyone wants."

Once he'd written down what they all told her to say, he gave her a wink and pulled out his phone to order, adding a packet of chips and a soda to each of their orders.

"They'll be here in about fifteen minutes. Can I see your pictures?"

Bitty smiled a little more and showed him the page, glowing with pleasure at his praise.

'How can you be falling for his shit? It's all crap and you know it! He doesn't give a fuck about your damn coloring in a baby book!'

'Bailey! Knock it off! He does care! I told you, he's a Daddy Dom. They care about stuff like that!'

'Fuck off, Scarlett. You don't know shit. I know how men are. You only know how to fuck. So fuck off.'

"…and marshmallows."

"What?" Bitty asked with a jolt.

John stroked her cheek. "Are you okay?"

She nodded. "Yeah. Just… I'm okay."

"Okay. Well…if you need to talk, I'm here."

She nodded and looked down at her coloring page, suddenly not so happy with it. Was John really just saying all those things to get her to like him? Was he really just going to turn into another Mack? Was that the way all men were, like Bailey said?

John nodded and stood up to get some plates from the cabinets. "Anyway, I was thinking we could rent a movie tonight and have some hot chocolate with marshmallows after dinner, if you'd like."

"Okay."

"Is there a movie you'd like to see?"

Bitty shrugged. "Not really."

"Well, how about Despicable Me? I really like that one."

"Okay."

"Babygirl, are you sure you're okay?" he asked as he placed the plates on the table. "You look like you're upset."

She shrugged.

"Is it Bailey?"

She nodded without looking at him.

He sighed and sat down again. "Look, I know Bailey has spent a long time keeping you all safe. I'm really proud of her. And I also know it's going to take her a long time to let go of that. It's okay. We'll work on it together."

She nodded again just as the receptionist came through. "Your lunch is here, Dr. Matthews."

"Thanks, Joan." He smiled at Bitty and tousled her hair as he stood and headed for the reception desk to collect the food and pay the delivery driver.

~ Choice Two ~

The teacher finished with the other kids and they packed up their books to leave. Lots of them made faces at Callie, but Callie just looked down at her lap. Stay quiet and still. That's what you had to do. Quiet and still.

The teacher came over and sat down on the table in front of Callie. Callie didn't look up. She stayed very still and quiet.

"Bailey."

Callie stayed very still and quiet.

"Bailey. Look at me." She sighed. "I don't know what you were playing at earlier, but this isn't a joke. You need an education, and while you're in here, you're going to get one. I expect everyone to work to their potential. I know you probably haven't done that in the past, either because you haven't had a chance, or you haven't bothered. That needs to change. I'll give you another chance, but I expect you to make an effort. Understand?"

Callie stayed very still and quiet. Was the teacher talking to *her*?

The teacher sighed again and stood up. "Come on. It's time for lunch."

This time, Callie looked up at the teacher. She didn't look mad anymore. Callie felt a little less scared. Maybe the teacher really was nice? Maybe she was only angry because of that Bailey girl. Callie stood up and followed the teacher back into the hall.

The room the teacher brought her to was so bright and loud it hurt Callie's ears. She stopped quickly and covered her ears, her eyes wide and instantly filling with tears. She wanted to run and hide from all the people and the noise. It was scary!

"Bailey? What's wrong?"

Callie closed her eyes and tried not to cry so loudly. She would be in so much trouble for crying! But it was so loud and scary!

A big hand grabbed her arm and started to pull, and Callie flinched and covered her head.

"Stop. She's terrified!" the teacher said.

"Bullshit. She was fine yesterday and this morning. I don't know what she thinks she's doing today but it's not fooling me!" the man in the uniform said. It was the man from earlier. He was hurting her arm. He was going to hurt her again.

Callie cried harder as the teacher and the man argued. Callie didn't want the teacher to get hurt like everyone else who was nice. Callie followed the man into the loud room so he wouldn't hurt the teacher.

There was food in there. Callie's tummy made the hungry noise and she took her hands away from her ears slowly, staring at the food. There was so much food! Callie had never seen so much food. The man pushed her at the food and a lady gave her a tray with something on it that smelled so good. Callie stopped crying a little bit and took the food.

"Bitty. Come sit by me," a girl said softly, nudging Callie with her elbow.

Callie flinched away and nearly dropped her tray of food. She was really glad she didn't. She wouldn't have had any food and she would have been in so much trouble.

"Bitty. Come on!" the girl said again. She was looking at Callie.

Callie looked around, then followed the girl. She didn't get mad when Callie followed. Callie sat down by the girl and listened to her whisper things while she ate. Callie stayed very still and quiet. Callie was good. Callie liked the food.

Chapter Thirty-Seven

* Choice One *

Bitty really liked the sandwich that had the things she liked on it. She still couldn't believe John had ordered something for everyone. It seemed like so much money! The only problem was she didn't know if anyone else would be able to come out to eat theirs and she didn't like what was on the other sandwiches. Hers was gone really fast and she sat debating whether or not to just eat them anyway. Just when she decided to eat one anyway, her eyes fluttered briefly and she made a sudden grab for the one with salami.

"You got me one!" Bebe cried in delight before taking a big bite and grinning at John.

He smiled back. "Are you hungry, babygirl?"

She nodded and took another bite, a look of contentment coming over her face. "It's so good!" she said through a mouthful.

John smiled and ate his sandwich quietly, watching her with pleasure.

All too soon, it was time for his next appointment and he stood up to throw away his wrapper.

Bebe finished her sandwich and gazed at him. "Can't I sit by you? I'll be real quiet."

He smiled and crouched down beside her chair. "I'm afraid not, babygirl. I'm a doctor, and these are my patients. I can't have someone who's not a doctor in there with me. I'll be back in a little while, just like last time, okay?" She nodded sadly and he ruffled her hair, then stood and left the room.

'Get over it, Bebe.'

"But I want to be with him."

'Fucking hell, Bebe. You're such a–'

'Bebe, it's okay. We know you like him. He'll be back soon. Just like he has been the whole day.'

Bebe sniffed and nodded, propping her chin on her hands with her elbows on the table. "I'm bored."

"You're bored?"

Bebe looked up to see Joan walking into the room. "I miss John," Bebe mumbled.

Joan nodded and took a plastic lunchbox from the fridge, then came to sit across the table from Bebe. "How are you settling in with him?"

Bebe smiled. "Good. I have my own room and strawberry toothpaste and new clothes and a stuffie and coloring books and all kinds of stuff!"

'Bebe! Stop! That's enough! You can't act like this around her. We'll get in trouble and then we'll have to leave John! Is that what you want?'

Bebe froze in dismay, then looked down at the table. "It's good," she finished quietly.

Joan smiled even more. "It sounds like it. He's a good man. Everyone loves him. You're in a good place."

'What the fuck does she know?'

'Bailey. That's enough. Bebe, we have to be careful, okay?'

Bebe studied her hands for a moment, then her shoulders hunched and she brushed her long hair from her face.

Joan seemed to sense the change in atmosphere and left off the conversation, eating her lunch quietly for a while.

Bitty eventually looked up and pulled her coloring book closer.

Joan smiled. "That's a lovely picture. Did you do that today?"

Bitty nodded, studying her picture critically. She was glad no one else had colored it. Bebe would have ruined it completely while thinking she was making it beautiful. Thankfully, the younger girl had chosen another page of her own to color earlier and Bitty went back to work on this one.

After a while, Joan got up and put her lunch things away, then went back to work leaving Bitty alone for only a moment before John came back in to check on her.

The rest of the afternoon went by just like the morning had, with John checking in every so often between appointments and Bitty staying busy with things of her own. It wasn't so bad, as long as she didn't think about school the next day…

~ Choice Two ~

Callie finished all her food and her tummy didn't make the hungry noise anymore. It didn't hurt, either. It felt good to not hurt. When the other girls got up to put their trays away, Callie followed slowly. It was still so hard to move her body. But it was getting better. Like the tiredness was wearing off. That was nice. Callie didn't like the fuzzy feeling in her like that.

When the other girls left the room, Callie followed them again. This time they went into a room that looked like a living room. It was also loud in here, but not as loud as the lunch room. It was nicer in here, too. There were soft places to sit, and the lights weren't so bright for her eyes. She followed the nice girl to a couch and tucked her feet up when one of the other girls turned on the tv. It worked! And there was a nice show on. Not one of the naked shows that made Daddy and his friends hurt her. This show made her smile.

Callie watched the show until it finished and another one came on. She watched that one too, until the nice girl said she had to go do chores. Callie watched her go, then turned back to watch the show again. It felt good to smile.

"Move."

Callie looked up to see a big girl frowning at her. Callie shrank back and hurried to move off the couch. The girl looked mad. Callie didn't understand why.

"Smart move. I see you've decided to make the right choice," the girl said as she sat down. Her friends sat down around her and one of them pushed Callie out of the way. The others laughed.

Callie hunched up and turned away, confused. She didn't know what to do now. She didn't feel good. She wanted to lie down. Where was that room with the mat? Could she go back there?

Callie looked around for a minute, then moved to a corner and sank into it, huddling with her knees to her chest to keep out of everyone's way. Callie cried. Callie hated it.

Chapter Thirty-Eight

* Choice One *

"Ready to head home, babygirl?"

Bailey didn't bother to look up from the geometrical design she was drawing on a blank sheet of paper.

"That's pretty," John said, looking over her shoulder.

Bailey scowled and twisted so he couldn't see it anymore.

"Ah. Bailey?"

"Fuck off."

"Please don't speak like that in here. If you need to curse, then wait until we get home."

"You don't fucking own me. I'll do what I want."

"Well, I'm heading home. Are you coming for dinner?"

She stayed silent until he'd gathered her activities, turned, and left the room, then she stood up and followed sullenly.

"Goodnight, Joan. See you tomorrow. Did you make a note of my new hours?"

"I did. I also rescheduled most of your patients. The ones who couldn't come during the day are moved to Thursday nights."

"Thanks, Joan. You're an angel."

Bailey snorted softly behind him but he didn't turn around and Joan didn't seem to notice.

John gathered his coat but left Bailey's hanging on the hook. She looked up at him, nonplussed. She had been expecting him to hand it to her and she was prepared to go off on a rant on how she could take care of herself and didn't need him treating her like a toddler. But he hadn't.

It took her a moment to recover, then she clenched her jaw at the loss of the expected argument and snatched her coat from the hook. She seemed to take her time putting it on, but as soon as he was around the corner, she hurried to get it on and follow. She did her best to stalk after him, but that was a little difficult on crutches, so she finally gave up and just focused on getting from here to there without falling. That's all she needed; to fall and him freak out and try to help her.

On the other hand, that would give her an outlet to vent her anger on him. She felt like if she didn't find some reason to scream at him, she'd explode soon. Anger bubbled inside her, clawing at anything that might free it. So much anger and fury. It would never leave. It was always almost too much. Never crossing that line, but always, *always* pushing and tearing at her until she felt it must break at any moment and everything would explode.

She was so tired of holding it back all the time. It got worse when she held it back and couldn't do anything with it. Now was one of those times. She was angry, but there was no real reason and there was nothing she could do to release it. Tears pressed at her eyes but she clenched her jaw more tightly and refused to give in to them. She would *not* lose this battle.

~ Choice Two ~

'How could you let that happen?'

'ME? I didn't have any fucking control over it, you bitch! What about you? You could have done something, too!'

'Like what? I couldn't get out of my house!'

'Yeah, well why the fuck do you think I could, Scarlett?'

"Stop it," Bitty mumbled, trying to block out the screaming match between Bailey and Scarlett, and the heart wrenching sobs from Bebe while Sarah tried to comfort her.

No one really knew what had happened that morning except that no one could do anything for a long time. Bailey blamed Bitty for being weak and taking the drugs the night before. Scarlett blamed Bailey because she was supposed to protect everyone and she hadn't protected Bebe from being raped. Bailey blamed Sarah for not having let Bebe and Jay know about the possibility of being in that situation. Sarah blamed Bailey for not caring about the littles having any chance at never having to live through it.

All Bitty wanted was for everyone to shut up and leave her alone. She was back in the dinner line and getting ready to serve. She had no idea how the day had gone and she wasn't really sure she wanted to. The part Bebe had experienced was no different than usual, but to Bebe it had been horrendous. She had never been raped before. Even the drugs weren't something she usually experienced. It had all been new, and terrifying, and she'd been alone. They all assumed Callie had come out after that, since no one else remembered anything.

Poor Callie. Not for the first time, Bitty felt sorry for her. Whoever she was.

"Cry baby," Nat murmured as she moved in front of Bitty's station.

Bitty kept her head down. "Corn?" she whispered.

"Of course I want corn, you moron."

Bitty flinched but carefully put a scoop onto the girl's plate, being sure to check with each of her friends before doing the same for them. When they left for their usual table, Bitty lifted her head enough to watch them. What must it be like to have friends that stuck with you like that? For a moment, Bitty wished she had friends.

'They're not friends, Bitty. They're probably just as scared of her as you are, but they found it easier to go along with her and pretend than to stand up to her. They're weaker than you are. Don't wish to be like that. You're better than that. And you've got us."

Bitty nodded, grateful for Sarah's reassurance as she turned her attention back to her job. Rebecca came through, but when Bitty smiled at her, the other girl gave her a strange look and left without a word. Bitty was left watching her go in confusion. What had happened that day? They'd probably never know. They'd just have to pick up the pieces and try to make it work.

***

Bitty ate her dinner in silence; alone. Rebecca glanced over at her every so often, but didn't so much as smile. It made Bitty want to cry. She hated it when it was like this. Sometimes she could understand what was going on when she came out. Some information might leak in when the others were out, or it was a short enough length of time that things weren't so drastically different. But this time, *no one* knew what had happened, and Bitty had been gone all day up until twenty minutes ago.

It was terrifying. Like a piece of her was missing; ripped out. Having that gone was like knowing you know something, or should know something, but instead of even a fuzzy recollection, there's just a black void. Nothingness. You know there should be something there, but you can't reach it, see it, or grab it. Bitty imagined it was what drowning felt like, a little bit. Knowing you need to breathe, but not able to reach anything to help you do it and just floating right below the surface. It didn't hurt quite like drowning probably did, but it was that same sort of desperate need to grab something that you just can't grab. There was no other way to explain having that piece missing from you. Or if there was, she'd never heard it.

'Bitty, can you try to go without the drugs tonight? Please? Just give it a try. If we can get off it, it would help things a lot. And we wouldn't have to... you know... do stuff with that Fowler guy.'

"But I need it, Sarah," she whimpered under her breath. "It hurts so much without it."

'I know. But we're all here to help you. And it's cut down a lot since what Mack was putting into us at the hotel. It might be easier now that we've been having less. Let's just go down to maybe once a day and try it, okay? Try not to have it tonight, please?'

Bitty stood up slowly and put her tray away before following the other girls to the cells. She didn't answer Sarah. What was she supposed to do? If she didn't have it, she'd be in pain, but the more she had, the more she needed it. And she'd never wanted to start it in the first place. Didn't continuing it just keep giving Mack power over her? But she *needed* it. It hurt so badly when it began to wear off. It scared her. She didn't know what to do.

She still hadn't decided what to do when Fowler came to her after lights out.

"Pull your pants down and spread," the guard whispered.

Bitty cringed and in that moment made her decision. "I....I–I don't want it tonight, sir."

"What?" he hissed. She could hear the anger in his voice.

"I don't want the... the drugs tonight, sir. Please." She gasped when his hand flashed out and grabbed her face.

"You don't have to have the drugs, whore. Cheaper for me. But I still get that hole. Do you understand? You don't get to just walk away from this."

Tears trickled down Bitty's cheeks and she tried to hold back her whimpers of hopelessness and despair as he once again climbed onto her to take what he wanted. There was just no way to stop it. Any of it. She never could before. And she never would. She closed her eyes and cried silently, her heart breaking yet again. Vaguely, she wondered how many times a person's heart could break before there was nothing left to break.

Chapter Thirty-Nine

* Choice One *

Bailey stayed quiet the whole way home and John didn't try to talk to her. Again, she wasn't sure whether she was relieved or frustrated about that. Part of her wished he would say something so she could attack him for it. Part of her was just glad he was leaving her alone. She was confused and she hated it. This whole situation was confusing.

Why weren't the others listening to her about him? Why did they keep thinking he was such a great person? He was no better than any of the others. He'd still fucked them after he knew how old Bitty was. Just because he was nice to them, suddenly they all thought the sun shone out of his ass. They acted like she was in the wrong.

Was she wrong? If every guy *was* an ass and a pedophile, was it really so wrong to at least accept being with one who wasn't as bad as the rest? He'd been gentle since he'd found out, at least, even if he hadn't stopped while they were at the hotel. And now he'd done a lot to help them. Stuff Mack or Bitty's parents would never have dreamed of, let alone done. Maybe he really was the best they could ever find. Maybe he was the only one who'd ever take someone like they were; broken, disgusting, used, worthless. Maybe choosing to stay somewhere where they hadn't been hurt, at least yet, was the better move for now.

She sighed softly and stared out the window into the falling snow. Christmas decorations lined the roads and trees lit up display windows and people's living rooms. Bailey hated Christmas, and she wasn't the only one. Only Bebe really looked forward to Christmas, and they had to work so hard to keep her from being disappointed. Bailey sometimes wondered why they even bothered. Maybe it was only cruel to keep letting her believe. But no matter how much shit she talked, Bailey just couldn't bring herself to crush Bebe's best memories. If she did, she'd be no better than anyone else who'd hurt them. Tears stung her eyes again and she closed them, her jaw clenching hard. She needed to breathe. She needed to get out of here for a while. She needed to think.

Bitty brushed her hair back from her face and tucked it behind her ear, watching the lights in the dark until they reached John's house and pulled into the garage. When he smiled over at her cautiously, she smiled back and he relaxed.

"Hungry?" he asked. She nodded and he got out to help her with her crutches and getting into the house. "I was thinking of having spaghetti and garlic bread for dinner. What do you say?"

"That sounds nice."

"I'll have to go grocery shopping tomorrow. I don't have much in the way of food for decent meals. You can come with me after school and tell me what you like."

Once they had taken off their boots and hung up their coats, he led her into the kitchen and pulled a stool out for her at the counter.

"Do you like meatballs? I think I have some in the freezer."

She nodded and leaned on the counter to watch him. He chatted to her while he cooked, asking questions that she couldn't always answer, but was surprised that she was actually happy to answer the ones she could. It was peaceful and comfortable, and Bitty felt more relaxed than she'd felt in a very long time.

Dinner was delicious. It might have been easy and quick, and it certainly wasn't gourmet, but it was hot and fresh, and Bitty was suddenly starving.

Before she knew it, dinner was over and they were having hot chocolate in the living room on the couch in front of the fire. John sat beside her and put his arm around her shoulders, holding her against him gently. It wasn't the tight, possessive kind of grip Mack had used when 'cuddling' with her in the beginning. This was a warm, kind embrace that was just loose enough that she could sit up to get away if she wanted to, but also gave her a sense of protection and safety. It was the most wonderful feeling in the world.

Her head began to nod and she didn't hear the far off warning from Sarah about her cup tilting. She barely noticed when John took it from her and set it on the coffee table before tucking her closer against his chest and lightly stroking her hair. Within a minute, she was asleep in his arms.

He smiled down at her, content to sit with her like that for a while longer until he finally got up and carried her to her room. As tempting as it was to climb in with her and hold her all night, he just tucked her in and kissed her temple before going to his own room for the night.

For the first time in a very long time, John felt completely whole. He just hoped it would last.

~ Choice Two ~

Scarlett woke up the next day when the lights came on, groaning at the foggy, flu-like feeling in her head and the ache in her body. She knew it was withdrawals but that didn't help it feel any less miserable. They had all discussed it after Fowler left, deciding that they would try to make it through the day without another hit. But the way she felt right now, Scarlett was already somewhat eager to see Fowler and get the next hit from him. This was awful.

Somehow, she hauled herself out of bed and grabbed some clothes to get dressed. A female guard stuck her head in the door and scowled.

"Why aren't you in the showers yet?"

"Showers?" Scarlett repeated blankly.

"Showers. You know, water coming down, washing filth off you, getting rid of stink, showers? You gonna pull this every morning?"

"N–no. Sorry. I... forgot."

'Sorry, Scarlett! I forgot about that! I was... all the other stuff just...'

"It's okay, Bebe," Scarlett mumbled, following the signs to the showers.

Scarlett took a quick shower, actually enjoying being able to get clean. It felt good to get some of the slime from Fowler off her from the night before, and while it seemed like so much effort, it really did help the way she was feeling from the withdrawals, too. It was surprising how exhausting it was though. She wished she could go back to bed when she'd finished, but she had to follow the guard down the hall to breakfast instead.

The smell of the food in the cafeteria nearly made her throw up and she closed her eyes for a moment, trying to keep herself together. An elbow jabbed her hard in the back and she looked up in shock to see Nat smirking at her.

"Get out of my way."

Scarlett flushed but stepped aside, looking away from Nat's triumphant grin until she and her hangers-on were past her and in the food line. After taking a somewhat calming breath, Scarlett took a tray and collected her own breakfast. Rebecca was sitting at the table she'd been at the day before and Scarlett went over there.

"Can I sit here?"

"Talking to me again, are you?"

Scarlett frowned. "What?"

"You didn't say a word to me all day yesterday, and now you suddenly wanna be my friend again?"

Scarlett's face fell when she realized what must have happened. "I'm sorry, Rebecca. I didn't realize it came across like that. I was just... having a bad day and I wasn't exactly myself. I'll sit somewhere else. I'm sorry."

Rebecca sighed and moved over. "No. You don't have to. Sit down."

Scarlett turned back and gave her a grateful smile. "Thanks. I really am sorry."

"It's okay. Sorry you were having a bad day. You don't look so good today, either."

Scarlett shrugged and tried not to gag on the spoonful of scrambled eggs she was trying to put in her mouth. "I'm not feeling very good."

"Do you wanna ask to see the nurse?"

Scarlett shook her head. "No. It's okay. I'll be alright."

Rebecca eyed her for a moment, then nodded and went back to her breakfast.

Scarlett followed along when it was time to leave, emptying most of her tray into the garbage after being unable to eat it. She expected to go to the common room like they had the first day, but Rebecca headed the opposite way and into a room that sort of looked like a conference room or something. There were large tables with several chairs around them, and a chalkboard on one wall behind a desk. Suddenly, Scarlett realized it looked kind of like a different kind of classroom. A woman -presumably the teacher- came over as she sat down beside Rebecca.

"Bailey. Are we going to have a better day than yesterday?"

Scarlett swallowed nervously and nodded, wondering for the hundredth time what had happened that day. "Yes, ma'am."

The teacher smiled and went back to the front of the room to start passing out books and Scarlett turned to Rebecca. "Did I do something wrong yesterday?" she whispered.

Rebecca frowned at her. "You're kidding, right? You scribbled a bunch of numbers on your paper super huge and wouldn't talk to the teacher when she called on you! That's not very cool in any school."

Scarlett flushed and looked down at the desk. "Oh."

"What was up with that, anyway?"

"Bad day," Scarlett mumbled.

Rebecca snorted and took a paper and pencil from the pile being passed around as the teacher began speaking.

'I guess Callie can't write.'

'What the fuck gave you that idea, genius?'

'Bailey, leave off. It was just an observation. No one knows anything about her.'

'Fuck off.'

Scarlett frowned and tried to focus on the reading assignment the teacher was talking about, following along as best she could in the book. The woman called on several girls to read out sections, but thankfully she didn't call on Scarlett. It was hard enough just to keep up with where they were. There was no way she'd be able to read any of it herself.

After the reading was finished, the teacher moved on to math and Scarlett felt even more like she was floundering. Eventually, the teacher came over.

"Which school did you go to before you came here?" she asked quietly.

Scarlett shrugged. "I don't remember."

The teacher frowned. "What grade were you in?"

Scarlett turned red and shrugged, looking down at the book. "I... I don't...."

"Bailey. When was the last time you were in school?" she asked softly. Scarlett's cheeks reddened even more. "What grade were you in last time you were in a school?"

Scarlett stared at her pencil for a long time before whispering, "3rd grade, I think..."

The teacher sat staring at her in stunned silence for a moment, then sighed and nodded. "I see. Well, thank you for answering me. That helps me know how to help you. We want to give you the best support we can before you leave."

Scarlett just nodded.

'Best support? The fuck does that mean? Like we have any options when we get out of this hell hole. Fucking stuck up bitch.'

'Bailey! Stop it! She wants to help us learn.'

'What's the point?'

"I'll give you some quick tests so I know what level you're at, okay? Just do your best and hand them in when class is over."

Scarlett nodded and the teacher went to her desk to collect some sheets of paper.

'What the hell are we even supposed to do with all her dumb school stuff? What good is being able to multiply the fucking exponents of the god damn alphabet gonna be when we're trying not to get our heads bashed in by Mack or the next guy? Why doesn't she just teach us how to cook or some shit so we can get a real job and someplace to live where Mack doesn't fucking sell us all the time?'

"Shut up, I'm trying to think," Scarlett muttered under her breath, scowling down at the tests the teacher had placed in front of her as she tried to concentrate.

She had to admit, though, that it really didn't seem to have a point. Whores didn't need to know how to read anything except the names of streets and hotels and the numbers on the rooms, and the only math they needed was the ability to count cash.

Chapter Forty

* Choice One *

Scarlett had wanted to choose their clothes for school but Bitty had vetoed the outfit. She'd wanted something that wasn't going to grab anyone's attention. Scarlett liked people to look at her. That was the last thing Bitty wanted. In the end, everyone else agreed that Bitty's outfit was the better one for first impressions. A simple pair of jeans, the pink boots John had given them, and a long, cozy sweater that went halfway down her thighs over a t-shirt with a dreamcatcher design on the front of it. She left her long brown hair loose around her shoulders; it gave her a place to hide her face if she needed it, though John offered to braid it for her again.

"Could we do that tomorrow?" she replied nervously when he'd asked.

"Of course, babygirl. Whatever makes you more comfortable."

Bitty had given him a shy smile and that had been that. She was virtually silent all morning while she got ready and ate breakfast. John tried to make small talk and psych her up for the day, but all it did was make her withdraw more. He finally stopped trying and just let her be while they ate.

When they had finished eating and the dishes were rinsed and loaded in the dishwasher, he gave her a reassuring smile and gathered up her school things.

"Alright, babygirl. Let's get going so you're not late."

She followed him slowly, her stomach twisting into knots of nervousness as she got her coat and boots on.

"It'll be okay, babygirl. You'll see. You'll settle in in no time."

She nodded in silence and followed him to the car, trying not to puke on the passenger seat and her new clothes.

***

"I'll walk you to your classroom if you'd like?" John said once he'd parked the car.

"You will?"

He nodded quickly. "I'd love to, if you'd like that."

She nodded back. "Yes."

His smile virtually lit up the car and he jumped out to get her crutches. While she got out and adjusted them under her arms, he grabbed her backpack for her and locked the car.

"Alright, let's see," he murmured, pulling out the schedule the principal had given him the day before. "Homeroom and your locker are this way, I think."

They headed slowly down the echoing halls full of rowdy students, Bitty trying to keep her crutches from being kicked out from under her by a stray boot or backpack.

"Here's your locker. Your combination is in your backpack, remember?" he whispered.

She nodded and he smiled.

"Okay, is there anything you want to leave in here?"

She shook her head, and he led her a little further to a nearby classroom.

Bitty suddenly felt the almost overwhelming urge to run as a security guard turned the corner and began strolling down the hall. She made a sudden lunge to get away, to hide, to escape or *something*. But she forgot about her crutches in that moment and caught one on the typically overlarge-seeming sneaker of a nearby boy which sent her crashing to the floor with a cry of shock, fear, and pain.

John was immediately down beside her helping her up. The boy gathered her crutches for her and held them while John righted her.

"Are you okay? Sorry about that. I didn't see you there."

She kept her head down and took them from him. "I'm okay. Thanks. Sorry."

"You're new, aren't you? I'd remember someone as pretty as you."

'Oh for fuck's sake. Tell him to fuck off.'

Bitty's cheeks went pink but she still didn't look up. She felt John tense very slightly beside her and his hand tightened almost imperceptibly.

"Today is her first day. I'm taking her to her classroom."

Bitty looked up at the tone of John's voice. It was more gruff than she'd ever heard it. Was he being... protective? Because of a random teenage boy who was being nice to her?

'That's what predators do, moron. They don't like other predators coming in on their catch.'

'He's not a predator, Bailey.'

'The fuck he's not. Why can't any of you see that!'

'Because he's nice, Bailey.'

'Shut up and go away, Jay. No one asked you.'

'That's enough, Bailey! Everyone else likes him. You're out-voted.'

'Fuck you all! Fuck this whole mess! You'll see!'

'Oh, Bailey...'

"...help you out today."

Bitty looked up at the boy. "What?"

"I said I'd be happy to help you out today, since you're new and everything."

"Oh. I... uh... thanks."

John took a quiet, deep breath and his hand relaxed slowly on her arm. "Thanks for offering. I'm sure it will be appreciated. What was your name?"

"Oh. Sorry. I'm Cody Masters."

John put his hand out. "Nice to meet you Cody. This is Bai–" he glanced at Bitty briefly, "Bitty, and I'm John."

Bitty looked up at John in gratitude. It would have been weird being called Bailey all day, even if that *was* her 'real' name.

"It's great to meet you, Bitty," Cody said over the ringing of the bell.

Bitty flinched at the noise and John's hand tightened protectively again.

"You in Crandall's homeroom?" Cody asked.

Bitty nodded.

"Cool. Me too. Come on, I'll help you."

Bitty looked up at John nervously and he nodded.

"Go on." He hugged her gently and smiled at her. "Have a good day, babygirl."

She gave him a weak half smile and nodded, then turned to follow Cody.

"Your dad seems really cool," Cody said as he walked with her.

Bitty nodded and glanced over her shoulder at John. He was watching her go. When he saw her looking at him, he smiled encouragingly and gave her a little nod before turning back to the entrance.

"You can sit next to me," Cody offered, jerking his thumb at another boy who was already sitting at a desk. The other guy got up immediately and Cody sat down in the seat beside the newly empty one. "Go on. Have a seat."

Bitty glanced at the other boy who had moved to the next row, seemingly unperturbed by being ousted from his seat. "Uh… he was–"

Cody waved a hand dismissively. "Don't worry. That's Petey. He doesn't mind. You'd better sit or you'll get in trouble."

With some misgiving, Bitty slid into the seat and tucked her crutches and backpack alongside her out of the way as the teacher began roll call.

"Baxter."

"Here."

"Bryant."

"Here."

"Carter. Oh." The teacher stopped and smiled around the room. "Class, we have a new student joining us. Her name is," she consulted the roster, "Bailey Carter. Bailey, would you stand up and tell us a little about yourself?"

Bitty's face went bright red and she felt the panic begin to rise in her chest suddenly. Her eyes automatically flicked to the door and she had to work hard to keep herself in her seat. Before she could even open her mouth, however, Cody spoke.

"Ms. Crandall, Bitty has to use crutches to walk, so it's probably not a good idea for her to stand. And she's shy," he added.

Bitty's face went hotter, if that were possible.

"Oh. Well, thank you, Cody. Don't worry about it, Bailey. Let's continue. Cranz?"

"Here."

Bitty looked up at Cody with deep gratitude. "Thanks," she whispered.

He winked and leaned back in his seat with his hands behind his head. "No probs."

***

It had been a long time since Bitty had been in a classroom, and she'd never been in one like this. She supposed it was because it was high school. They probably did things differently with the older kids. The homeroom wasn't even like being in school. Bitty had expected it to be a lesson or something, but once the teacher finished talking, the whole class sort of split up into groups of two or three and seemed to be doing their own thing! Some were reading or writing, but others were just sitting around talking or eating.

Her confusion must have shown on her face because Cody frowned.

"What's wrong?" he asked, looking around at everyone else. "Is it different than your old school?"

Bitty looked at him for a moment, then down at her lap. "Yeah," she murmured. It was true enough. He didn't need to know that her 'old school' had been 3rd grade in elementary school!

"Yeah, this school is pretty cool. Besides," he leaned forward so his lips nearly brushed her ear and Bitty tried not to flinch or pull away, "I can pretty much do what I want here, anyway."

She looked at him silently and he shrugged as he sat back with a grin, putting his hands behind his head again.

"I'm the star quarterback *and* captain of the football team. I rule the school, baby. Stick with me and you'll be a queen."

'Tell that stuck up bastard to fuck off.'

'Bailey! He hasn't done anything!'

'He will!'

'You think everyone is out to get us! Just because he's popular doesn't mean he's a bad person.'

'Then what does he want anything to do with Bitty for?'

'Maybe he's being nice?"

'Shut it, Jay. You don't know shit.'

'Bailey, leave off! Stop being so paranoid all the time!'

Bitty closed her eyes for a moment against the barrage of arguing inside, then opened them again to see Cody smiling at her.

"Lemme see your schedule. Hopefully you can eat lunch with me."

She dug it out of her folder and handed it to him in silence. He scanned it and nodded.

"Yup. We got lunch and social studies together." He handed back her paper with a wink. "I'll make sure you settle right in."

Bitty smiled back a little bit and tucked her hair behind her ear nervously. "Thanks."

Cody reached for her hair and Bitty instantly ducked away nervously and hunched her shoulders as if preparing for a blow.

"Woah," he said with a chuckle of surprise. "Chill, girl. I was just gonna tuck the other side back. You're beautiful. You shouldn't hide your face."

Bitty looked up at him again. "Oh. I... didn't... mean..."

'He's hot. And he's into her! We should totally stay on his good side. He could make things great here. Plus maybe he's looking for a girlfriend or something.'

'For fuck's sake, Scarlett! Back off!'

The bell rang for next period, drowning out whatever Scarlett's response was. Bitty checked her schedule, then tucked it into her folder and shoved it in her backpack before slinging that over her shoulder and standing.

Cody had already stood and was holding her crutches for her with a winning smile and she smiled back a little more warmly.

"Thanks."

'See? Hot and sweet!'

'Go to hell, Scarlett.'

~ Choice Two ~

It took Scarlett until lunch to finish the tests the teacher had given her and she felt like her brain was going to explode by the time she stood up to hand them in when the others began to line up.

"Thank you, Bailey. I'll work out a study plan for us to start tomorrow. Have a good lunch."

Scarlett just nodded and followed the rest of the girls to the cafeteria.

'Us to start tomorrow? What the fuck does she mean us? She's gonna do homework too? I don't fucking think so. Where does she get off saying us!'

'She's trying to make it less obnoxious, I guess.'

"Fuck that, Sarah. She's being a condescending bitch.'

Scarlett sighed softly and shook her head. She was glad to be off the streets and away from Mack for a while, but Bailey really seemed to be looking for any kind of fight or trying to find anything she could complain about. It was one thing when they were counting on her to help them stay as safe as was reasonably possible out on the street, but in here, it was getting old, fast.

"Carter." Scarlett turned her head to see the guard, Fowler, coming toward her. "With me."

"But I–"

"Now, Carter."

Scarlett swallowed hard.

'Tell him to go fuck himself.'

'Just say we don't want it anymore, Scarlett. We can do it. We're doing okay, right?'

Scarlett shook her head slightly. "We're not okay, Jay," she whispered miserably. "I feel awful. I need it or we'll be sick like we were when we got here the other day. What difference does it make anyway? It's all we're good for," she mumbled in defeat as her head fell and she followed the guard.

This time, he led her to a locker room and made her stand behind the door while he rummaged through a duffle bag. A moment later, he pulled out a syringe and stalked back over to her, taking her arm roughly.

"You want this today? Or are you still on your high and mighty refusal horse? Too good for a hit?"

Scarlett shook her head without looking up. She could almost sense his smile.

"Alright, then."

She winced as he spun her so her arm was bent behind her back and her front was pressed to the wall. In that position, she couldn't have changed her mind if she'd wanted to. A moment later, she felt the needle and winced again, but her body relaxed into the wave of relief that flooded her a second after the prick.

Fowler's chuckle in her ear would have made her clench her jaw in disgust if she hadn't just been filled with heroin. Now it was only a vague discomfort in the back of her mind. She barely noticed him pulling her pants down and taking his payment. She just stood where he pinned her to the wall, her eyes closed and her mind a delicious fog.

It felt so good not to care for a while; to just be able to exist without fear or disgust or hatred or self loathing. It was the only time the physical and emotional pain didn't make her want to completely stop everything forever. She knew rationally that it didn't make anything better, it only made it worse, but for those brief few minutes, she could escape the horror of her life and be free for a little while. Sometimes, afterwards, she wondered if that's what it felt like to be a regular kid.

***

By the time Scarlett got back to the cafeteria, lunch was almost over. Everything had been put away except the fresh fruit. She took a banana before floating slowly toward Rebecca and sinking onto the bench. With the drugs in her system, she wasn't hungry anymore, anyway.

"What's wrong with you?" Rebecca asked warily. "You look like you're on drugs."

Scarlett shook her head. "I'm fine."

"Then why are you taking so long to open a freaking banana and why are you talking so weird?"

Scarlett looked up at her in surprise. "I'm not taking a long time. I just started! How fast do you want me to go?"

"You're kidding, right? You are moving like a snail and all your words are slurred and your eyes look like they're just huge blue circles. It's weird. Are you on something?"

Scarlett looked away and focused on peeling her banana. Rebecca might have been kind of right. She felt a little sluggish. But she couldn't be as bad as the other girl was suggesting. It didn't feel that much more different from how she felt all the time. She was probably exaggerating.

"I'm fine," she snapped irritably.

Rebecca's eyes widened, then she scowled and stood up. "Fine." She snatched her tray from the table and went to put it away before Scarlett even realized what had just happened.

Before she could react any more, the guard called for everyone to line up to go to their chores or the common room. Scarlett shuffled along behind everyone else, then made a beeline for the couch.

The fist came out of nowhere.

Scarlett doubled up and hit the floor hard as more blows from fists and feet rained down on her. Instinctively, she curled up with her arms over her head like she'd learned to do since she was a child. Her confused brain was suddenly trying to figure out how Mack had got in and how she hadn't even noticed.

Several hands hauled her up and Nat put her face right up to Scarlett's.

"So *you're* the reason I'm not getting my cigarettes? You fucking turf-stealing BITCH!"

Another fist landed in her stomach from one side and Scarlett would have doubled over if she hadn't been held up by her arms.

"You're horning in on my supplier with your slutty ass pussy and getting jacked up on some shit so that he 'forgot' to get my cigarettes? I *told* you when you got here that I rule this place. You didn't listen. Now you can pay, you slutty, whoring, tweaking *bitch!*"

Nat's fist contacted Scarlett's mouth at the same time two more fists hit at random places on her front and sides. After a minute, the hands holding her arms let go and she fell to the floor when the beating continued despite her screams. Where were the guards!? Why couldn't anyone hear her!?

She had no idea how long the beating went on for, but it seemed to blur into one blob of ongoing pain and fear that stretched on forever. Then, suddenly it was over and she was left sobbing and panting alone on the rough carpet, bleeding from several cuts on her face and hands, and everything inside throbbing painfully.

For a while, Scarlett just lay there, trying to catch her breath and stop crying so hard. She couldn't move, and even if she could have, it hurt too much anyway. The unfairness of it all began to penetrate the fog of drugs and pain.

How was she supposed to have known? Fowler had come to *them! He'd* been the one to offer the drugs. There was no way any of them could have known there was something going on with Fowler and Nat. They'd just been trying to get by. But that's how it always was, wasn't it? Everything *always* had a price. There was never anything in this world that was given freely. Everything cost something, whether you were aware of it at the time or not.

"Bitty? Bitty, are you okay? What happened?"

Scarlett tried to open her eyes but one of them just wouldn't open.

"Bitty. Come on. Let's go to the infirmary."

Gentle hands slipped under her arm and Scarlett hissed in pain. But she did her best to sit up and wipe at the blood in her eyes.

"Oh my god. Who did this?"

Scarlett sniffed carefully -her nose didn't feel broken at least- and shrugged. "Nat," she mumbled. "I pissed her off."

"Come on. Let's go get you looked at." Rebecca helped Scarlett up and let her lean against her shoulder as they walked slowly down the hall.

"Where are you going?" a guard asked.

"Infirmary. Bitty got beat up."

The guard got on the radio and told the nurse they were coming, then began helping Scarlett down the hall. "You go back to the common room until dinner," she told Rebecca.

"But she's-"

"Now. She'll be fine. I'm sure she'll be back by dinner."

"I'll see you soon, Bitty," Rebecca called after her in concern as the guard opened the door to the infirmary.

"Who beat you up?" the guard asked when she'd seated her on the exam table and the nurse practitioner began checking her over.

"No one," Scarlett mumbled.

"Come on. If you don't tell us we can't stop them or punish them."

"I don't know," Scarlett lied, wincing when the N.P. touched one of the cuts on her face when he held her head up.

She could tell the guard wasn't happy about her answer, or lack thereof, but Scarlett pretended not to notice while the N.P. examined her and the nurse's assistant washed and dressed the injuries.

By the time she left the infirmary, she had a total of six stitches on her cheek and forehead, and she ached badly. The N.P. had given her a suspicious look after he shone a light in her eyes, but he didn't comment on it. At least that was something.

***

Due to her injuries, they had given her the evening off from serving dinner, and Scarlett gratefully sank onto one of the benches at a table in the corner. Rebecca was allowed to get her a tray of food and returned to sit beside her with her own dinner.

"Did you tell them it was Nat?" she whispered.

Scarlett shook her head, poking at her peas. "No way. She'd kill me if I told anyone." She suddenly froze and turned to Rebecca. "You didn't tell anyone, did you?" she asked in a panic.

Rebecca shook her head. "No. I was waiting to talk to you about it. When they asked me who did it, I said I didn't know."

Scarlett relaxed a little. "Thanks. Hey... I'm sorry about getting mad at you earlier."

Rebecca looked down at her tray quietly. "You are on something, aren't you?"

Scarlett sighed and nodded, sagging in her seat.

"What?"

"Dope," she whispered.

"Oh my god. *Heroin*?" Rebecca hissed in horror. "Where did you get that? *Why!*?"

Scarlett hunched even more and hung her head, tears filling her eyes. "I needed it, Rebecca. It was hurting so bad and I was so sick. I tried to do it by myself but I couldn't. He... someone offered me some to help me and I... I needed it."

"He?" she repeated. "Was it one of the guards?" She gasped. "Was it Fowler?"

Scarlett flinched and hushed her. "Shh. He'll hear you. You can't tell anyone, please. Please, Rebecca? Please don't tell anyone."

Her friend studied her for a moment. "Do you have to give him something in return?" she asked quietly, but the tone of her voice suggested she already suspected what the answer would be.

Scarlett shrugged, then nodded.

"He wants sex, doesn't he?" Rebecca whispered.

Scarlett closed her eyes and nodded again.

Rebecca let out a tiny whimper of pity and sorrow. "It hurts that bad that you'd do that to get some?"

Once again, Scarlett nodded miserably. "I tried. I honestly did. We-....I didn't take any last night. But it's just too hard, Rebecca. It hurts so bad and there's nothing I can even think of to describe it. I just... can't go without it. I'm sorry."

"Why are you apologizing to me?"

"Because you probably think I'm a worthless drug addicted whore."

"Bitty! I wouldn't think that. I didn't know it was that bad. Did you tell the nurse? I thought they had medications that would help with that kind of thing."

Scarlett snorted. "That's for rich people in expensive detox facilities, not whores from the streets."

"You're not a whore, Bitty," Rebecca said softly.

Scarlett actually laughed derisively. "That's what I've been my whole life, Rebecca. I'm a whore. A filthy, worthless, disgusting whore. I've never not been one. That's why I'm here. I've been used by so many men I'll never be old enough to make it even out to one a week even if I stopped doing it right now. I was arrested with one inside me, Rebecca! They didn't even think to let me clean him and all the other guys out of me before they dumped me in here in the middle of withdrawals! I'm nothing but a slut and I never will be."

Tears were running unchecked down her swollen cheeks but Scarlett didn't even bother to wipe them away. She was hurting, physically and emotionally. She didn't want to see the way Rebecca was looking at her. She didn't want to see the disgust and revulsion on the other girl's face. It would be too much. Rebecca was the closest thing she'd had to a friend besides Tess and Mel, and they were mostly Bitty's friends, however briefly.

The silence—even amid the noise in the cafeteria—seemed to stretch for a long time while Scarlett slumped on the seat with her head hanging. A soft sniff broke the quiet between them before Rebecca spoke.

"I'm so sorry, Bitty. I had no idea. I can't even imagine what... I just... You're not worthless, Bitty. Honest. What they did is disgusting and horrible, but you're not. And maybe if you tell the nurse how it's making you feel, maybe... maybe they can help you?"

Scarlett looked up at Rebecca's kind, earnest face. "I wish I could believe that. I really do. But I saw how he looked at me the first day when I made a mess all over everything and they knew I was in withdrawals. He didn't care. He looked at me like I was some kind of disgusting creature that should be locked away far from anyone I might contaminate."

"Oh, Bitty...." Rebecca murmured in a choked voice. "I'm so sorry."

Chapter Forty-One

* Choice One *

Bitty tried her best to keep up with the lessons, but every class felt like they were talking way over her head. The teachers didn't push too hard, obviously giving her time to adjust to the 'new school' and because it was almost at the end of the semester, but they did start handing out homework. Basically though, as Bailey said, they were here for daycare.

Cody was there for her second class of the day; social studies, as he'd said. He sat beside her which thrilled Scarlett, and she spent the whole lesson pushing to be out and around him. So much so, that Bitty missed most of the class and ended up staring blankly at the homework that was placed on the desk in front of her.

'Great. Nice going, moron. Now we have an assignment due and no one has a fucking clue what's going on cuz you were drooling over foot boy.'

'He's not foot boy. *He plays football. And he's cute. And nice. And popular.'*

'Foot boy is close enough.'

Scarlett made a disgusted sound at Bailey's comment as Bitty hobbled out of the room to her next class. Again, she was given homework for this class as well, and her panic began to mount. She could barely read the instructions detailing the assignments. How could she ever complete them?

Gym was next, and thankfully she had a good excuse to sit it out. In an effort to catch up a little, she sat down on the bleachers and pulled out her assignment sheet for the first class; English. She wished she hadn't. It was just a wall of words that swam in front of her eyes. She wasn't even sure what the name of the book was, let alone how she was ever going to read up to the point she was supposed to be at! She'd opened the first page and had been able to understand about ten words total.

As a flash of terror strangled her throat, she scrunched the paper up and shoved it into her backpack abruptly, then rested her elbows on her knees and buried her face in her hands, trying desperately not to cry from the overwhelmingness of it all. And she still had half a day left! After she tried to catch her breath again, she pulled out her schedule and found lunch was next. Some of the terror flowing through her veins subsided a little.

For the rest of the period, Bitty watched the rest of the class throwing balls from one side of the gym to the other, laughing when they got hit or hit someone.

'Why are they laughing if they get hit, Sarah? How is it funny?'

'I think it's part of the game, Bebe.'

'But why are they having fun getting hurt?'

"I… don't… think they're getting hurt… I think they're just… I don't know.'

'I don't get it.'

'Yeah, Einstein, we get that you don't get it. Shut up.'

'Bailey! She's just asking!'

'Well, why does she have to ask over and over and over again? She's driving me nuts.'

'She only asked once.'

Bitty sighed and tried to drown out the bickering. Truthfully, she didn't understand it either, and was *very* glad she didn't have to 'play' a game that would earn her a beating for fun. It didn't sound very fun. It was the kind of thing her parents would have laughed at; throwing a ball at her and laughing when it hit her in the face and knocked her down. Why would they teach that at a school? Was that where her parents learned it? Were they really just playing with her when she thought they were trying to hurt her? Confusion and doubt suddenly began to swirl in muddied patterns in her head as she tried to recall the times her parents had hurt her. Maybe she had misunderstood all those times. Maybe she *had* been whining about nothing, like they had always accused her of doing. Maybe when she'd cried about being hurt all the time, it really had been her fault.

Guilt joined the confusion and doubt.

***

If she'd expected to be relieved to go to lunch, she was sorely mistaken. The lunch room was crowded, rowdy, and loud. It felt like running into a wall of noise when Cody opened the door for her.

"Come on!" he laughed, reaching for her back.

She automatically arched slightly away from him before forcing herself to relax.

"Skittish, aren't you?" he teased.

She gave him a weak smile and hobbled after him to the lunch line.

"I'll carry your tray. Just tell me what you want."

She nodded and shuffled along behind him, pointing to a slice of pizza, a banana, a cup of jello, and a bottle of apple juice. She'd begun to relax until they reached the cashier.

"$4.25."

Bitty froze in dismay, her cheeks going white and her eyes stinging with tears. She didn't have any money!

"I… I don't… I haven't got…"

"Did your parents put money in your lunch account?" Cody asked.

She looked up at him blankly. "My what?"

"Your lunch account, honey. Put your number in on the keypad. It comes out of a food account if your parents put money into it," the cashier said.

"O-oh… I… I don't…"

"Check your information sheet. It's probably next to your locker combination."

"Come on! Hurry up!" someone yelled behind her.

Bitty's eyes almost overflowed and she flinched at the shout as she tried to hurry.

"Back off, jerkwad! She's new! Give her a minute. You're not gonna starve to death. You should be on a diet anyway, lard butt. Give it a rest," Cody snapped.

Bitty's face was burning when she pulled her folder out and looked at her information page. Sure enough, there was the 'food service account code'. With trembling fingers, she punched the numbers in slowly, unaware she was holding her breath.

The machine made a beep and the woman smiled at her. "There you are, honey. Enjoy your lunch!"

Bitty nearly passed out with relief and even returned Cody's big smile with a small one of her own.

"Thanks," she murmured as they made their way to a table amid shouts of greeting and playful challenge from people all across the lunch room.

Cody slid into a seat and pushed her tray toward her with a grin. "Told you I'd have your back. Trust me."

'I'll trust you to climb up the backside of a donkey and kiss its-'

'Bailey! STOP IT!'

Bitty looked down at her food and just nodded. It bothered her how much Bailey seemed to dislike Cody. But she didn't like John either, and John had done nothing but take care of them since he'd picked them up and taken them to the hospital. Bailey was just being irrational. Like she always was. Surely.

***

The rest of the day went by much the same as the morning had; Bitty was given more and more homework and her panic and dread began to mount higher and higher with each one. How did anyone have time to do any of this, let alone before the following day. More and more, Scarlett and Bailey were pushing to be out; Scarlett to seek out Cody, and Bailey to tell the teachers where to shove their homework. It took everything Bitty had just to hold onto a shred of reality for the rest of the day.

The only class that didn't make her want to cry or run from the building screaming was art. The room was luxuriously quiet and it smelled wonderful. It was the sort of smell that came after a rain washed away the worst of the smell of decay on the streets and left just the muddy aroma of dirt and gasoline behind. They were the only things she could think of to describe the earthy aura. The lights weren't as harsh in here either, and everyone in the room seemed somehow more relaxed and less chaotic and frenzied. For the first time all day, Bitty felt she could breathe.

And she did.

She took a deep breath and a tiny smile played at her lips as she pulled out a metal stool splattered in various shades of paint and globs of clay. It was beautiful.

To Bitty's delight, the class had just finished up what they had been working on the week before and were moving onto sculpting. Bitty was able to start fresh with the rest of the class and was given her own chunk of clay to work with. They were given the freedom to design what they wanted and were shown where resources for inspiration and ideas were, then set free to work. The teacher wandered up and down among the tables offering hints and tips to them as they worked.

Bitty felt like she'd slipped and fallen into heaven. The rest of the day melted into oblivion and she lost herself in the art. It felt amazing to knead and sculpt the clay however she wanted and watch it obey. It wasn't perfect, by any means, and even compared to the rest of the class, hers left much to be desired, but it was *hers*. It was the first thing she'd ever made that felt like it was real and tangible, and she was disappointed when it was time to go.

"You can place your pieces on the tray here with a slip of paper with your name on it. We can continue working on it tomorrow," the teacher told them.

Bitty's face lit up. "We don't have to be done with it?"

The woman smiled. "You can take your time, within reason, of course. You'll have ten days to complete your sculpture before it goes into the kiln."

Bitty left the art room feeling like she was walking on clouds. It was the perfect way to end what had not been a great day overall.

John was waiting outside in the pickup line and she hurried over to him with a smile of relief. He helped her into the passenger seat and put her backpack and crutches into the back seat.

"How did it go?" he asked as he pulled the car out of the line.

She shrugged.

"That good, huh?" he said with an expression of understanding. "I'm sorry, babygirl. It's probably going to take a little adjustment to get used to being back in a normal life. Was it terrible, though? Or just overwhelming?"

Without a moment of warning, she burst into tears and covered her face.

John pulled over into a store parking lot and drew her into his arms, stroking her hair and making soft shushing sounds.

"Oh, babygirl. I'm sorry." They sat like that for several minutes before she finally stopped crying. Then he released her and gave her a tissue.

"I've got so much homework and I don't understand anything they were talking about and it's all due tomorrow and I don't know how to do any of it and I can't do it by then!"

"It's okay, babygirl. It's okay. I'll help you tonight, and I'll talk to the school about changing some of your requirements. We'll work through it. It'll be okay."

She nodded and blew her nose. "K."

He stroked her hair and gave her a gentle smile, then pulled back onto the road and headed home.

"What's your favorite food?" he asked as he helped her out of the car.

"I... don't know?"

"Well, we'll have to work on that, won't we?" he said with a grin.

As they made their way inside, he began listing off possibilities for dinner. Finally, they settled on ordering in some pizza because he had forgotten to go grocery shopping.

"Do you want to come with me after school tomorrow and help me choose some things you'd like?"

"Okay."

He sighed. "It'll get better, babygirl. I'm sure."

She sank onto the couch with an exhausted sigh while he ordered the pizza and brought her a glass of juice before sitting beside her.

"What homework do you have?"

Bitty hunched up and hung her head, fighting tears of exhaustion and misery again. "Everything."

John opened her backpack and pulled out her folder to look through. "It's not too much. We can do it. I'll help you. Hold on."

He got up and left the room, returning a moment later with some kind of lap desk thing which he placed on her lap, then handed her a pencil before sitting down beside her again.

"Okay. Let's start with math, huh?"

She shrugged and he studied the worksheet.

"Okay, this isn't too bad. Linear equations."

He put the sheet on her lap and twisted to face her a little more. "Okay, let's work on the first one." Slowly and patiently, he began to explain the technique to her, trying to find different ways to help her understand. But Bitty didn't even understand multiplication, let alone the work she'd been given.

The pizza arrived fifteen minutes later and Bitty breathed a sigh of relief. She had barely been holding it together and she felt like her head was ready to explode. It was impossible to understand and she hated it.

John brought it through with plates and napkins, as well as the bottle of juice to refill her glass. For a few minutes, Bitty was able to push the anxiety from the forefront of her mind and focus on eating while he told her some funny stories of previous clients.

Chapter Forty-Two

~ Choice Two ~

After dinner, Scarlett made her way back to her cell, carefully avoiding Nat and her group when their backs were turned. The last thing she wanted was another run-in with them. When she reached her bed, she lay down and curled up on her side.

Why did everything have to be so hard all the time. Other people seemed to be able to catch a break now and then. Why couldn't they? It wasn't fair. She was so tired of fighting the never ending battle of their miserable existence.

Fowler must have assumed she wouldn't want the hit again that night, because he didn't show up after lights out.

'At least we get one night without him using us.'

Scarlett nodded. It was a difficult position to be in. On one hand, she knew what she 'was'. She had been created for sex. That was her role. That was what she was for and she was good at it. It was virtually all she knew. On the other hand, there were times she wished she could be something else. Everyone expected her to take it all the time if it was at all possible to switch, and sometimes she was okay with it. But nights like this, nights when the misery and hopelessness washed over her like a blanket, she wished she could be something more than a fuck toy. She was tired of being used by every man who laid eyes on her. She was tired of being an object put there solely to fulfill someone else's fantasy. She was tired of being a whore.

But if she wasn't a whore, what else was she? Nothing.

***

The withdrawals weren't quite as bad the following morning and Bitty was able to open her eyes without too much pain.

'He came later yesterday, so it's not gonna wear off for a while, genius.'

'Bailey, please, can't you just be a little less negative for a few minutes?'

'What the fuck am I supposed to be positive about, Sarah?'

'You don't have to be positive, just not so negative.'

'That doesn't even make sense!'

"Please stop," Bitty mumbled, hauling herself out of bed to get ready for the day. "I'm tired of all the fighting. Please just stop."

Every bruise hurt and every movement felt like her body was screaming with resistance. She was stiff and achy, and even though the withdrawals weren't as bad as they could have been, they were still there, adding to the achy, tired, sick feeling.

Nat glared at her from across the room when they reached the showers, and Bitty tried to keep her eyes averted. At least with the guard on watch, Nat couldn't try something in here.

'Let her try it. I'll kick her ass.'

'Stop it Bailey. No one's kicking anyone's ass.'

Bitty hunched up a little more as she walked past Nat to get a towel and dry off, wincing in silence as an elbow jabbed her in the small of the back when she passed.

'Why is she so mean to us, Sarah?'

'Same reason everyone is, Jay. The whole fucking world hates us. Get used to it.'

'Bailey, leave off. He's just trying to understand.'

'There is no understanding. It's just the way it is. Adjust.'

Bitty kept her head down while she dressed and lined up, but it didn't stop a foot impacting her ankle as she walked past. It wasn't even breakfast and she felt like crying.

Little 'accidents' kept happening to her throughout breakfast and on the way to class. It seemed Nat had a lot of 'friends' who were more than willing to torture Bitty for her at every opportunity. Bruises were added to the bruises Nat and her gang had inflicted the day before, and the ache of the injuries and the withdrawals seemed to swell deeper and deeper until it was everything Bitty could do to keep from crying.

When they reached the classroom, she sank into the chair farthest away from anyone and hunched up miserably, grateful just for the time in a place where Nat couldn't get to her.

The teacher—Bitty discovered her name was Mrs. Barnes—came over after giving the class their assignments and crouched down beside her.

"Bailey, I put together some ideas for us to work on to help you get a little caught up with your school work. I talked to my boss and she's going to give me some extra time in the afternoons with you, since I saw you don't have chores until dinner. That way, we can work on some things just the two of us.

"For now, I'd like you to try reading this book for me as much as you can, and then fill in the worksheet, okay? If there's a word you don't know, I want you to write it on this sheet of paper here, and then we can go over them when we're together. How does that sound?"

'Why the hell would she ask us that? It sounds like bullshit, that's what! She doesn't really want to know how it sounds. Fucking bitch.'

'Bailey, please stop. She's trying to help us and she's being nice.'

'She's a bitch.'

Sarah sighed internally and Bitty could practically see the smug smirk on Bailey's face at 'winning' the argument.

Bitty just stayed quiet and opened the little book. It was a young children's book and she sincerely hoped no one was looking or had noticed. The words were large and there were bright pictures everywhere. The worst part, though, was that there were still quite a lot of words Bitty couldn't read.

The story turned out to be a rather nice one about a mouse and a fairy living in a garden and helping other animals. Bitty could sense Bebe peering over her shoulder with interest as she read. The girls on either side of her pulled their chairs a little further away with frustrated noises because Bitty was whispering out loud as she read, but she couldn't read it otherwise! That didn't make it easier to imagine what they must think of her.

Half an hour later, she finally finished the seven page book and looked down at the worksheet for the first time. It was a series of pictures with some instructions before them.

"Number... the... the pic...pictures... in the or... order they... ha... happen in the s... story." She looked down at the page trying to understand.

'I think it means write number one on the picture of what happens first, then number two on the next one and on and on.'

"Oh. I can do that!" Bitty murmured with a relieved little smile. She picked up her pencil and began looking through the pictures on the page. She had to erase a few of them when she remembered that something had happened before another she'd already marked, but on the whole, she felt like she'd done a good job.

By that time, Mrs. Barnes was going around with the math worksheets for the rest of the class. When she reached Bitty, she placed a page down that held much simpler problems on it than the day before. This one also had pictures and Bailey made the snide comment that it was probably from a Kindergarten book. Bitty ignored her as best she could and listened to the teacher's instructions before picking up her pencil again.

Bailey was probably right, of course. There were a lot of questions about how many apples could Jack buy from Jim and how much money would be left, and how many times could Jack go to the movies with the money he got for mowing the lawn.

"Money," Bitty murmured in surprise. "I know that!" With another smile of relief, she bent over the worksheet and began figuring it out slowly and carefully. For the first time in a long time, she felt like she could actually do something other people could. It felt good.

When the rest of the class lined up for lunch, Bitty actually had something to hand in that didn't seem like a sheet of nonsense. Mrs. Barnes smiled warmly at her.

"Thank you, Bailey. I'll look these over and then we can discuss them after lunch, okay? You can come right back here when you're done eating. One of the guards will bring you."

Bitty nodded with a small smile and followed the others to the cafeteria. She'd done something that was somewhat worthwhile. The teacher hadn't looked at it and yelled at her for her bad handwriting, or instantly found ten things wrong with it and thrown it back in her face.

'She just didn't want to bother before lunch. She'll tell you all the things you did wrong as soon as you get back. You'll see. She'll give you an even baby-er book.'

Bitty sighed as her fleeting good mood evaporated at Bailey's words. Why did she always have to do that? Couldn't she just be happy for five minutes without Bailey bringing everything crashing down to reality. She just wanted to be proud of herself for something, even if it was only a short time.

Just like at breakfast, Bitty found herself the target of veiled abuse and hurtful words, but she did her best to ignore them, focusing instead on not tripping over the multitude of feet that suddenly appeared in her path on the way to a table near the back.

Rebecca was waiting for her.

"You looked a little happier after class. I heard her say she was going to change some stuff for you yesterday. Did it help?"

Bitty nodded. "Yeah. It's stuff I can kind of understand better."

Rebecca smiled. "That's awesome. I'm really glad she's helping you."

"I have to go back after lunch to work with her some more."

Rebecca glanced in Nat's direction. "That'll be nice. Then you can get away from Nat and her friends. I don't know why she hates you so much."

Bitty stayed silent and took a bite of her cheeseburger. Rebecca didn't need to know it was because the guard was fucking Bitty and not Nat for contraband and Nat was pissed. It was bad enough her friend had found out about the drugs in the first place.

Her train of thought led her onto the track she'd been trying hard to avoid all morning. Drugs. She needed another hit and it was getting worse by the second. She'd done her best to think of other things and keep her mind from how she was feeling and how badly she needed a dose, but now it had slammed right into her, front and center, and the need and craving felt a hundred times worse. She nearly moaned out loud in pain, and crumpled slightly over the table, her appetite gone in a rush.

She had thought for a minute that she might be able to work her way through the withdrawals and focus on other things. She'd managed to keep it at bay for a seemingly long time. But it was too late now. All she could now was wait for Fowler to arrive with his precious needle and take his payment so she could be out of pain for another day.

But he wasn't in the cafeteria when she looked around. She frowned and hunched up against the cramps in her stomach. Maybe he would come find her after lunch. She certainly hoped so.

'But Bitty, if we have that medicine, how are we gonna do school?'

Bitty sighed and closed her eyes miserably. She honestly had no idea. She couldn't think clearly from the pain and withdrawal fog in her head, but Jay was right, once she had the drugs in her system, the pain might be gone but the fogginess would be even worse. It was a lose/lose situation. As usual.

When lunch finished, Bitty slowly stood and followed the others to empty her tray, hissing in pain as a tray 'accidentally' missed being put on the high pile and 'slipped' down onto her head, just missing her stitches.

"Oops. Sorry. I guess your big head got in the way," Nat's skinny friend taunted, causing several other girls to laugh. Bitty just lowered her head again and put her tray away before moving to the side to wait for her escort back to the classroom.

Her eyes scanned for Fowler, her need becoming more desperate by the minute. Finally, one of the other guards came over and led her back to the classroom. By that time, Bitty had begun to shake, but she managed to hold it back enough that neither the guard nor Mrs. Barnes seemed to notice.

"Bailey, have a seat. I'll get your sheets out so we can go over them."

Bitty nodded and sat down, wishing she could ask the woman to call her Bitty. It felt weird and uncomfortable to be called Bailey all the time, but how could she explain that? And what happened when it was someone else out? At least this way, they could all agree that it was the 'official' name, so they all had to use it for now. But it still didn't feel very good.

The teacher sat down beside her and put the papers down. To Bitty's surprise, there were only two red marks on each paper.

"Well done, Bailey. You did a very good job on these. Let's go over the ones you missed and address the words you listed that you couldn't read."

Bitty nodded slightly, trying desperately to keep her mind focused on the praise and encouragement, and off of her growing pain and misery.

Chapter Forty-Three

* Choice One *

After they finished eating, John pushed her homework back in front of her and Bitty sighed miserably. Despite his gentle encouragement and patient instruction, Bitty still didn't understand it at all!

"No, no," he said again after she got another problem wrong. "You're trying to balance the numbers, so you have to do the same thing to both sides. You're trying to eliminate this number on this side and move it to the other side. That's why you have to-"

He broke off abruptly as the lap desk, paper, book, and pencil went flying across the room and Bailey abruptly leaped to her feet.

"I'M NOT DOING THIS STUPID CRAP ANYMORE! IT'S POINTLESS AND USELESS AND I'M NOT DOING IT! FUCK IT! WHEN THE HELL WOULD I EVER NEED TO KNOW HOW TO MOVE IMAGINARY NUMBERS TO OPPOSITE FUCKING SIDES ON A FUCKING SHEET OF PAPER! I'M NOT DOING IT! GET AWAY FROM ME!" she screamed. She'd tried to storm off and forgotten her foot. When she stepped on it, pain shot through her leg and she stumbled. John jumped up and tried to catch her and Bailey nearly hit him as she snatched her arm away from him.

"Bailey? Calm down. If you're going to leave, at least use the crutches. Don't hurt yourself."

"I DON'T NEED THEM! I'M FINE!" she screamed, limping away from the living room toward her room. It hurt terribly, but she wasn't about to admit pain or weakness in the middle of storming out in a rage. That would have ruined the effect quite badly.

For a moment, John was tempted to go after her with the crutches, but he thought better of it and sat back down with a sigh. He would take them in once she calmed down a little. Her reaction had taken him off guard, as it seemed to come from nowhere, but he realized belatedly that it had probably been building all day and it had just been too much so late in the evening. In the meantime, he just hoped she wouldn't split her stitches.

Bitty was back the following morning and no mention was made of Bailey's outburst from the night before. Whether Bitty was aware of it or not, John decided it really didn't matter. She'd been through a lot that day and he would let it be.

"How about omelets for breakfast?"

She nodded and sat down at the table, laying her crutches on the floor beside her. Her foot hurt and she assumed she'd been on it too much the day before.

"John," she began tentatively.

"Would you call me Daddy?" he asked gently.

She looked down for a moment and nodded. "Daddy," she tried again, looking up once more.

"Yes, babygirl?" he replied with a big smile.

"Do you have... I mean, could I... my foot hurts."

"You want some Tylenol or something?"

She nodded and he nodded back.

"Of course. I'll be right back." He hurried off to the bathroom and came back with a bottle of pain meds. "Can you swallow a pill?" Bebe had said she could when he'd given her some, but he didn't want to assume Bitty could as well.

She nodded again and he went to get her a glass of juice to take it with.

"Prop your foot up on the chair next to you. Get it elevated for a little bit. That might help too."

She did so, leaning back in her chair to get comfortable while he went back to cooking breakfast.

After a few minutes he glanced back at her for a moment before saying casually, "I emailed your teachers about your homework and got you an extension for it. We can work on it through the week and weekend and you can take it in on Monday."

Bitty's stomach did a somersault and she stared at the table. She'd forgotten about the mountain of homework waiting for her and the sudden reminder slammed into her like a bus. Her appetite was abruptly gone.

"K."

"Hey, babygirl. It'll be okay. We'll work through it. I promise. You're not alone anymore, okay? I'm here to help you. You don't have to do it by yourself anymore."

"K," she murmured, though she looked up at him slightly with a tiny flash of a grateful smile, then fell silent again.

Breakfast was quiet and she barely managed to finish the food on her plate, though she was still not used to all the food she was getting now. John had told her it would take a while for her stomach to adjust to having a constant and plentiful supply of food. She didn't understand it, but he was probably right.

That day, she opted for sneakers instead of boots, since it had stopped snowing and it was fairly warm in the building, though she still kept an extra, thick sock on her right foot to keep it a little warmer without a shoe. Once again, John helped her into the school with her backpack and walked her to homeroom. To her surprise, Cody was waiting for her at her locker.

"Hey, Bitty. Figured you could probably use the help again today."

She gave him a small smile and glanced at John. This time she was sure the look on his face was jealousy. Confusion set in. If he was jealous, did that mean she was *his*, or was he just being protective, like a father would be?

'Moron, he practically bought you with the hospital visit and bringing you home and shit. Of course you're his. I'm only surprised that he hasn't taken you yet. It'll be hell when he collects, though.'

'Oh, Bailey, stop it. He's a nice guy. He didn't buy *us. He was just taking care of us. He said he didn't expect anything.'*

'That's what they always say, but they're all liars. He's jealous cuz some other animal is moving in on his girl.'

'Yeah, yeah, you said that already.'

'Shut it, Scarlett. I'll say it again and again until maybe one of you will listen to me.'

"...by nine."

"No. It's a school night and she has homework."

Bitty looked up at John's carefully neutral face in confusion, trying to catch up to the conversation.

"Nine isn't that late and I can help her with her homework before it starts. Come on."

"I said no. Don't push it."

Cody scowled but wisely dropped the subject and turned to Bitty. "Ready for class?"

She nodded. "I just want to talk to... my dad."

Cody nodded and stepped away without looking at John.

Bitty watched him uncertainly, then turned to John, somehow feeling incredibly guilty, though she wasn't sure why. She just knew John was mad and it was probably her fault.

Without thinking, or perhaps unconsciously trying to smooth things over, she hugged him gently.

He sighed and relaxed a little, hugging her back and kissing the top of her head. "Have a good day, babygirl," he murmured against her hair before inhaling deeply. A different kind of tension took hold of his body and Bitty felt her stomach drop. She knew that kind. She recognized what he wanted and she closed her eyes for a minute to make her heart slow down and the panic ease a little.

"I'll pick you up after school, okay? We'll go shopping for food you like after." He leaned back a little and cupped her face in both his large hands, smiling down at her tenderly. "I love you, babygirl."

She looked up at him in mingled bewilderment and wonder. No one in her life had ever told her they loved her. She felt her heart skip a beat for a completely different reason this time and she smiled. It was brilliant, shining, and utterly without reserve.

"I love you too, Jo-... Daddy," she replied in a breathless whisper.

He beamed at her, then kissed her forehead softly and stepped back. "Have a good day, babygirl."

She nodded and adjusted her crutches, smiling up at him for another moment before turning slowly and hobbling into the room with Cody.

***

Once again, Cody had her sit beside him in homeroom and stretched out in his chair casually, his hands behind his head again. He looked like some kind of model, artfully relaxed and skillfully careless.

Bitty just turned to the teacher when she started the announcements, missing the brief scowl on his face when she seemingly ignored him.

After announcements about the upcoming winter formal and reminders about parent/teacher conferences, they had a few minutes to relax before the bell.

"Hey, I'm pretty sure you're not going with anyone to the dance. Want to come with me?"

Bitty stared at him in surprise. "A... a dance? With you?" she repeated blankly. "I... my foot..."

He chuckled, flashing her his winning smile. "You don't have to dance, silly. You can just come to hang out. It'll be fun. I'll pick you up and drop you off. All you have to do is find a dress and be ready when I get there."

She considered him for a second, then looked down at the table.

'He wants into your pants. Don't go. Everyone knows that's all boys want at school dances.'

'Oh come off it, Bailey! That's ridiculous. That's only in movies and stuff. He's nice and he wants to help us fit in, that's all.'

'Bullshit. I can see where this is going. You'll see when he tries to grope her. Besides, John probably won't let her.'

'Why is it automatically Bitty who gets to go?'

'Oh for fuck's sake, Scarlett, don't be stupid. Besides, if you go, we will be fucking him by the end of it!'

'Shut up, Bailey! That's not fair!'

Cody's hand waved in front of her face and Bitty jerked and looked up at him. "What? Sorry. I was just... what?"

He grinned. "So? What do you say? Say yes. Come on. You'll love it."

She hesitated another moment, then nodded. "Okay."

He beamed at her and sat back a little more, looking confident. "Awesome. We can plan more later. Give me your phone number so I can call you," he said, pulling his phone from his pocket.

"I... don't know it."

He laughed. "Well, lemme see your phone and I can show you how to find it. It's in settings."

"I don't have a phone."

"Oh come on, Bitty. It's just a phone number. How am I supposed to plan stuff if I can't get a hold of you? Just give me your number. I won't pass it out or anything. It's only for me. I swear."

"I don't have a cell phone," she repeated.

He stared at her in disbelief. "You're actually serious?"

She nodded. "And I don't know... my dad's number. I'll have to get a card from him and give it to you tomorrow."

He sat back hard in his chair, still staring at her. "Who doesn't have a cell phone?" he muttered, shaking his head as the bell rang. "Okay, well, see you in social studies."

She nodded and stood up, slipping her arms into the backpack he held up for her, then tucking her crutches under her arms to join the throng of students hurrying to their next class.

Chapter Forty-Four

* Choice One *

Just like the day before, her first class—English—was a nightmare. She hadn't even started on the book and felt completely lost during the conversation. Thankfully the teacher didn't call on her; John's email must have reached her. That was at least a small relief. Yet again, however, she was given homework and more chapters to read. The panic began to build again as she tucked it into her backpack when the bell rang.

Cody was waiting for her at the social studies classroom and helped her with her backpack before sitting down beside her. She did her best to look like she was following along and tried to breathe through the fresh wave of panic at the latest piece of homework that was added to the pile but it was definitely getting harder.

Science was no better and nearly broke her control with the discussion and the subsequent homework assignment. It took everything she had in her not to break down and scream in sheer terror at the amount of work that was waiting for her. She had absolutely no idea how she would ever finish it, and wondered how *anyone* could after sitting in school for so long already. When did they have time to do it!?

P.E. gave her a breather at least, and she briefly thought about trying to get some reading done, but her anxiety was already at near breaking point and Sarah suggested just leaving it alone for now. Bitty had to agree; she was afraid even the sight of the contents of her backpack might be the last straw that would break the fragile containment of her panic. Instead, she just tried to imagine what it would be like to go to a school dance, with the captain of the football team no less! It was like something from another person's life, not hers. Bailey was still complaining, though. But then again, she'd been complaining and warning them about everything since they'd woken up in the hospital.

Cody met up with her again in the lunchroom and helped her with her tray, then found a spot for them both at the table with the rest of the football team. Bitty wished he had found somewhere in a corner where she could hide away and chill out for a while, but she followed him anyway. The boys were loud and rambunctious, and after a minute or two, Bitty just drowned them out, focusing on her lunch instead. She kept herself within her own little world until she was suddenly elbowed hard in the back and flung forward into her tray of food.

"Bitch," a tall blonde muttered as she passed by.

Before Bitty had time to think, Cody was on his feet.

"Kaylee!" he shouted angrily. "What the hell was that?"

She spun around to glare at him. "It was an accident. Your little bitch there was in the wrong place at the wrong time."

"Watch your mouth."

"I'm not your girlfriend anymore, remember? I do what I want when I want and you can't say anything about it. Go back to your little toy," she snapped, then turned on her heel and stalked away leaving Bitty staring at the table with burning cheeks. She'd done her best to wipe off the gravy from her shirt but there was still a greasy mark on her chest. It was probably ruined. The thought made her want to cry.

"Hey, you okay? Did she hurt you? I'm so sorry, Bitty. We broke up a while ago and she's pissed. You can probably see why we broke up, huh? I don't need drama like that. I'm sorry she was mean to you. I'll make sure it never happens again, okay?"

She nodded silently. Yet again, she was wishing she could go home before lunch was even over. This place was just too much!

The only thing that tided her over for the rest of the day was the promise of art at the end of it. If it hadn't been at the end of the day, she probably would have run out before now.

Somehow, she managed to struggle through the next three classes until it was finally time to make her way to the art room. The moment she walked in, the world seemed to fall away and she felt like she could breathe a little more. The art teacher smiled at her as Bitty took her lump of clay from the tray and headed for a table. She wished she could remember the teacher's name, but she'd never been terribly good with names. John would probably know or be able to find out.

The next fifty minutes went by far too quickly and Bitty nearly groaned when the teacher told them to start packing up their supplies and put their sculptures back on the tray. At least the day was finally over.

She flashed the teacher a small smile on her way past her to the door and eased her way into the flow of students to get to her locker. Once she had her jacket and gloves, she hobbled through the halls to the doors to meet John again.

Her heart rose when she saw him and she suddenly remembered his words from that morning; he loved her.

'He doesn't love you.'

"Stop it, Bailey," she mumbled, walking over to meet him as he came to get her. His smile made her stomach flutter and she returned it.

"How did it go today, babygirl?"

Her smile vanished and she looked down at the ground as they made their way to the car.

"Ah." He sighed and held the door while she got in. "I'm sorry, baby."

She stayed quiet as he shut the door and put her crutches and backpack in the back seat.

"Well, let's go pick out some things for meals. You can get anything you want. Within reason," he added with a wink. "I don't want my babygirl filling up on chips and candy instead of good healthy food!"

She just nodded and looked out the window as they drove to the grocery store, trying to keep the seemingly constant panic at bay. She felt like she'd been more stressed out in the last two days than she'd ever been in her life.

'You're not, Bitty. It just feels like it because it's a different kind of fear. We've always been afraid of being beaten or raped or murdered. It's normal. School stress isn't. It's completely different. Talk to John about it. He's there and he wants to help. Tell him how you feel.'

"I can't," she murmured under her breath when he got out of the car to come around and open the door for her.

"Alright, let's start in the produce section and work our way around to finish at the freezer section. I'll get a wheelchair once we get inside."

She just nodded in silence and followed.

~ Choice Two ~

Mrs. Barnes spent three hours with Bitty, working on math and reading. Despite Bitty's rapidly declining focus and concentration, she kept going until Bitty just couldn't control the pain. Without warning, she gave a strangled cry of agony and doubled over in her seat, clutching her stomach and sobbing.

Mrs. Barnes stared at her for a moment in shock, then stood up and hurried to her desk to call for help. She returned with the walkie-talkie in her hand and knelt beside Bitty, who had fallen to the floor and curled up in pain.

"Bailey? Bailey, can you hear me? What's wrong? Are you hurt?"

Bitty opened her mouth to answer, but threw up on the floor in front of the teacher's knees instead.

"Oh, god. Bailey, hold on. The nurse is coming." She gently stroked Bitty's hair back from her pale, pinched face and tried to soothe her until the nurse arrived a minute later.

"I don't know what happened! She seemed okay, just a little inattentive, and then suddenly she screamed and fell over! Is it food poisoning maybe?"

The nurse got to her knees on Bitty's other side and put her stethoscope in her ears to listen. She frowned and shone a light into her eyes.

"I don't know how, but it looks like she's detoxing from something. But I'm almost positive I saw her a while ago and she was going through it then. She shouldn't still be this bad."

She leaned over. "Have you been taking something while you've been here? I need to know what you've been on or I can't do anything."

Bitty tried to stop crying enough to answer. "Dope," she whimpered.

The nurse snorted in frustration and disgust. "Fine. We'll talk about this later. Can you walk?" she snapped.

Bitty shook her head and threw up again.

The nurse made a disgusted noise. "Damn junkies."

"Hey. She's just a kid. It's not her fault," Mrs. Barnes said, the look on her face as she regarded the nurse one of veiled anger and dismay.

"She's the one sticking needles in her arm to get by and I'm the one who has to clean up after them until the next time."

"She's a child," the teacher repeated. "She needs help, not judgement."

The nurse gave a throaty sigh of frustration and shook her head as she stood. "I'll go get the wheelchair. Stay with her."

Mrs. Barnes nodded and pulled a tissue from her pocket to wipe Bitty's face gently.

"Hang in there, Bailey. It'll be okay. If you can make it a few days, then you'll get it out of you and you'll feel a lot better. Can you do that for me? Even if you won't do it for yourself?"

Bitty just tried not to scream as a stabbing pain pierced her stomach. It felt like her insides were being cut to ribbons.

"Oh, kiddo. Hold on."

Bitty had never had an adult be so kind to her before, apart from Mildred who'd ended up hurting them anyway. It was like she actually cared about her. If she wasn't in so much pain, she would have been even more aware of the tenderness and concern the woman was showing her.

The nurse returned a few minutes later and the two women helped her into the wheelchair. Bitty expected the teacher to stay in the classroom and let the nurse take her out of her hair, but Mrs. Barnes walked alongside her all the way to the infirmary and stayed with her when the nurse and the N.P. helped her onto the exam table.

Bitty continued to cry in pain while the two of them stripped her and washed the mess off her, then put her in a gown and helped her onto a bed. Mrs. Barnes watched quietly, a look of sadness on her face.

"What are you going to do for her?" she asked.

The nurse practitioner looked up for a moment. "She'll have to stay here until it's out of her system."

"I know. But what are you going to do about her symptoms?"

"She'll have to ride them out."

Mrs. Barnes gaped at him. "You can't be serious? She's in pain! She needs help. I thought there were things you could give someone who was in withdrawals to help them?"

"I'd have to put in a request."

"Then do it!"

"She can wait it–"

"Fine, I'll call them myself. And I'm sure she has an advocate. I can call them, too. I'm sure they'd love to know what kind of medical care she's *not* getting in here."

The N.P. pursed his lips angrily, then huffed and went to the phone to call in the prescription.

Mrs. Barnes came over and stroked Bitty's hair again. "We'll get you some help, okay? We'll make it better. Just hold on for a little while." She took Bitty's hand and offered her a gentle smile.

Bitty squeezed it tightly and turned her face into the plastic pillow with agonized sobs.

The N.P. returned with a paper cup with a pill in it. "Take this. It'll help the withdrawals. Put it under your tongue until it dissolves."

The nurse beside him helped her to sit up enough to swallow the pill, then laid her down again and covered her with the blanket when Bitty started shivering badly again. The artificial orange flavor nearly made her throw up again, but she managed to keep it down, barely.

"You'll get another dose in a few hours."

After half an hour or so, Bitty's body began to relax, the pain went away, and her eyes closed as she drifted off into blackness for a little while.

Chapter Forty-Five

* Choice One *

John bought an entire cart full of food at the store, pulling it behind him as he pushed the wheelchair. Bebe made an appearance in the cereal aisle and the dairy section, begging for princess cereal and cotton-candy flavor yogurt. Jay was head over heels for the ice cream and chips, though John put his foot down at three bags of Cheetos.

"You'll turn into a Cheeto if you eat too many of those!"

Jay had laughed happily, his eyes shining with delight. "This is the best day ever!"

John grinned. "I'm glad you're having fun. I like to make you guys happy."

On the way home, Bitty decided to bring up the dance.

"Uh.. Joh-... Daddy," she began tentatively.

"Yes, babygirl?"

"Cody... umm... Cody asked me to go to the dance with him on Saturday. Do you think... do you think I could go?" She kept her eyes focused out the window, doing her best to keep him from getting mad.

"He did, huh?" he said quietly. "And, do you want to go? Or are you asking because you feel like you can't refuse?"

This time she did look at him. "I... I want to go. I think."

John nodded. "Would he be meeting you there, or is he planning to pick you up?"

She looked down. "He said he would pick me up."

John nodded thoughtfully for a moment before speaking again. "If I say you can go, I want you to promise me one thing."

She turned her face up to him again looking tense. "What?"

"If you want to come home, and he doesn't immediately stop whatever he's doing and bring you back, I want you to call me right away, okay?"

Her body relaxed. "Oh. Um... okay. I will."

"I want you to promise me, babygirl. And I'm going to trust that promise."

She nodded. "I promise."

He nodded too. "Okay. Then... I guess we need to get you a dress."

She stared at him for a moment. "A... dress?"

"Well, yeah. My babygirl's gotta have a dress for a formal."

"I... you don't... I can just wear what I–"

"Don't be silly. We'll stop at a store downtown and find something nice."

She stared at him in wonder, then looked down at her lap shyly. "Thank you."

He reached over and took her hand, giving it a gentle squeeze. "You're welcome."

***

After dropping their frozen things at home in the freezer, John drove downtown to the department store they'd bought her things at the last time and got her another wheelchair. An employee guided them to the formal wear section. John paused on the edge of the section.

"Alright, babygirl. Do you want to start looking for a specific color, or do you want to browse first?"

"Um... I guess... just... look around?"

He nodded and slowly pushed her into the maze of racks.

"If you see anything that catches your eye, let me know. Do you mind if I point out some things, too?" he added.

She nodded. "I don't mind."

They wandered up and down the rows, occasionally tugging out the hems of a dress to have a better look before moving on. After half an hour, they had collected five dresses of various colors and lengths.

"Okay, let's go try some of these on," he said with a smile.

Bitty hobbled into the dressing room while the attendant carried the dresses in and hung them on a hook for her. It wasn't going to be easy to dress and undress, but it didn't hurt as much as it had before, and she thought she could at least put a little more weight on it to give herself some stability.

Five minutes later, she limped out on one crutch to take a look at herself in the mirror and get John's opinion. He was waiting just outside the changing area and smiled when he saw her.

"Wow."

She smiled back and looked down at herself. The bodice of the strapless, royal blue gown slid down a little as she leaned forward and she held it to her chest. As she looked down, the short front hem of the dress lowered a little, but even so it was halfway up her thigh. It made her feel like she was wearing her old clothes. When she looked up at John, the look on his face doubled the feeling and her smile vanished.

His smile faltered at her expression. "You don't like it, babygirl?"

She shook her head very slightly and he nodded quickly.

"Then it's the wrong one. Go try the next one."

"You're not mad?" she asked softly.

He shook his head. "Of course not. If you don't feel like a princess, then it's not the right one. Go change."

She gave him a small smile and went back into the room.

The next dress was eliminated as soon as she got out of the dressing room because the red, mermaid style skirt tangled in the crutch and she nearly fell over. After that, she tried a pink, halter style floor length dress, but it, too, caught in the crutch and nearly tore. That had been a disappointment, but there were still two more dresses.

Second to last was another halter style with a red, velour top and a cream colored skirt that reached to her knees. The length seemed promising, but when she'd been zipped up, the plunging v-shaped neckline virtually exposed everything almost to her navel. She shook her head and John nodded in agreement.

Finally, when she tried on the last dress—a swingy seafoam color—she suddenly realized what John had meant by feeling like a princess. Though it was sleeveless, the bodice went all the way up to her throat and glittered with scattered rhinestones. The skirt was short, but went down to just above her knees so it didn't feel like she was on display as she had been with the first one, and it swirled and swung with her movements in a way that made her want to spin around in a circle just to see it flare out. When she came out to show John, she was beaming.

"Wow. That looks stunning babygirl," he said with a grin. "Is that the one?"

She nodded. "I really love it," she whispered.

"Then that's definitely the one."

She squealed softly with excitement and hugged him. "Thank you!"

He hugged her back tightly and kissed the top of her head. "You're welcome, babygirl. Now, go get changed so we can get home and eat. I'm starving."

She smiled up at him for a moment before hobbling into the changing room.

It was a peaceful, happy silence that filled the car on the way home, so unlike the silence that had weighed so heavily a few hours before.

~ Choice Two ~

When Sarah woke up a few hours later, Mrs. Barnes was sitting nearby reading. When she noticed Sarah's eyes were open, she stood up and smiled.

"How are you feeling?"

"Alright," Sarah mumbled.

Mrs. Barnes smiled sadly and nodded. "Hopefully the medication will keep helping. I have to go home, but I wanted to wait until you woke up so I could tell you."

"Why?"

"Well, I figured you could use the support. And I didn't want you to feel I abandoned you."

"Thank you," Sarah mumbled incredulously.

Mrs. Barnes stroked her hair. "I'll come see you tomorrow before classes. Take care, Bailey."

Sarah nodded and watched the woman leave with her book.

'She stayed the whole time?'

'She's a helper, isn't she? Is she helping us?'

"Yes, Jay. She's a helper," Sarah murmured, closing her eyes tiredly. The pain and nausea had faded, but she still felt like she had the flu and been beaten up.

"Oh good, you're awake."

Sarah opened her eyes to see a different nurse come in with two more paper cups, presumably water and a tablet.

"Here's your next dose. We're increasing it gradually throughout the day until we reach the maximum when it should really start to curb the cravings and keep the pain away."

Sarah nodded after letting the pill dissolve. "How long does it take to work?" she murmured, resting her head back heavily on the pillow again.

"Well, you should be feeling much better already. Once we reach your full dose, you shouldn't have any noticeable symptoms. You'll stay on that dose for a week or two, to make sure everything is out of your system and you'll have no more cravings once you're done. After that point, we'll start tapering you off it a little at a time."

Sarah nodded as she watched the nurse.

'She's lots nicer than the other lady. How come she couldn't be here all the time?'

'Yeah. She isn't mean. Do you think she'll get us some pancakes?'

The mention of pancakes made Sarah's stomach churn and she shut her eyes.

"If you're still feeling a little sick, there's a basin beside your bed. Do you want me to move it closer to you?" the nurse asked.

Sarah shook her head. "It's okay. Thank you."

"I'm Barbara, by the way. If you need me during the night, just ring."

Sarah nodded without opening her eyes. They felt too heavy to move right now. Without realizing it, she slipped into sleep for another few hours, waking only when the nurse brought her next dose.

***

Barbara was right. When Bitty woke the next morning, she felt better. Her pains had disappeared and she could actually think about food without wanting to throw up.

Mrs. Barnes stayed true to her word and stopped in to check on her. Bitty was rather shocked by that.

"You just came to visit?" she asked blankly. "Why?"

"To see how you were. I wanted to make sure you were being cared for and were coping alright. I said I would, and I do what I say I'm going to do. I'm sure there's been far too few reasons for you to trust anyone in your life, if you're like any of the other kids I've gotten to know in here, but I want you to know I'll do what I can to help."

Bitty nodded and watched her leave for the classroom. The teacher had seemed so brusque and uncaring when Bitty had first arrived in the classroom, but now she seemed to genuinely want to see how Bitty was doing. It was a novel experience and Bitty found she quite liked it.

'Hey, does this mean we don't have to do school?'

'Ugh, grow up, Jay.'

'He was just asking, Bailey. You don't have to be mean. Yes, Jay, I'm pretty sure we won't have to do school stuff today.'

'Oh whew. I don't want to do that anymore.'

'It's not a fucking choice. They like to make people feel stupid as much as possible.'

Bitty sighed and closed her eyes again. "I'm so tired," she mumbled.

The night nurse was gone and the woman from before was back. "That's what you get for dosing yourself with opiates. It'll mess you all up. Maybe next time you'll wise up," she snapped.

Bitty cringed and curled up again, trying to think of Mrs. Barnes' and Barbara's kindness. That was two people who had at least treated her like a person. She just had to keep her mind on that.

The rest of the day passed much as the night had; Bitty slept fitfully, waking for her medication and to drink something, use the bathroom, and sometimes just because no matter how tired she felt, her brain wouldn't stop.

The N.P. came in once or twice to check her vitals and speak to the nurse, but he virtually ignored Bitty. It was as if she was some kind of disgusting thing he wanted to avoid looking at or acknowledging. Then again, Bitty was used to that from most of the world, so she should have been accustomed to it; but it still hurt her to feel that way. She wished it didn't.

Mrs. Barnes stopped in again after school for a few minutes but said she had to leave soon because her son had soccer that afternoon.

'She's a mom! I bet she's an awesome mom.'

'She's probably the typical fucking soccer mom, screaming at the coaches when her precious son doesn't get put in.'

'Stop, Bailey. You can't really think she's like that, can you?'

'People can be completely different in different situations. You should know that Scarlett.'

'I do. It's just-'

'You can't buy into people's disguises all the fucking time. You're all like that, believing every fucking thing someone says or shows you about themselves. Why am I the only one who ever sees them for how they are?'

Bitty closed her eyes and rolled over miserably to try and sleep, hoping to block out the others' bickering. It was going to be a long night. Vaguely, she wondered if Rebecca would still be there when she got out of the infirmary.

Chapter Forty-Six

* Choice One *

When they got home, John took Bitty's new dress to her room and hung it carefully in the closet, then came back to unpack the groceries and start dinner. It was much later than he'd planned on being, so instead of the meal he'd originally planned, they settled for mac and cheese.

"I suppose you have homework?" he asked when they'd almost finished. As he'd expected, Bitty suddenly stopped eating and began pushing her food around on the plate miserably.

"Let's go get some of it done, babygirl. I'm sure you'll get caught up. Don't worry."

She stood up and tucked her crutches under her arms, then limped into the living room while he rinsed off the dishes and loaded them in the dishwasher. He came through with her backpack a few minutes later.

"Okay, let's see what we have." He went through her folders and sighed. "They're really piling it on, huh?"

She nodded, trying not to cry.

"Hey, we'll do it together." He reached over and squeezed her thigh and Bitty turned her face away unhappily, only turning back when he told her to look.

For three hours, they worked through the mound slowly, Bitty getting more and more frustrated and tired and Bailey getting more wound up because of it until she finally exploded to the front again and ripped up the paper before throwing it in his face with a furious scream. With a torrent of swears and curses aimed at him, Bailey stormed off once again.

John sat back on the couch with a sigh. "Well, we made it a little longer than last night," he said to the fireplace, then gathered up the books and papers. After carefully taping her homework back together, he tucked it all back in her backpack and headed for bed, but not before stopping outside her door and knocking very softly in case she was asleep.

"Goodnight, babygirl," he murmured quietly.

"Fuck off!" Bailey snapped, then added, "I'm not your fucking babygirl, you sick fuck!"

John sighed and went to bed.

***

The following morning, Bailey was still out and angry. She didn't speak a word to John except to tell him to 'fuck off' when he said good morning. He had simply nodded and got on with his routine in silence.

She glowered at him from her seat at the counter while she ate, frustrated that he wasn't giving her anything to fight him on. It was boiling within her and she needed a release. The night before had only given momentary relief from that particular frustration. It hadn't done anything to help the overall buildup of anger and confusion warring within her.

They gathered their things and got into the car in silence, and it carried over throughout the drive.

"Have a good day," he offered gently as she tucked her crutches under her arms.

"Fuck you," she grumbled without looking at him and hobbled away.

He sighed again, watching her go for a moment before getting back in the car and leaving for his office.

Cody met her outside the classroom with a big smile. It faded when she glowered at him and walked past without a word.

"Are you okay?" he asked, following behind her looking confused.

"Peachy," she snapped, sinking into the first empty seat she came to.

"Uh… you're not going to sit with me today?"

"I'm not your pet."

"I never said you were. What the hell is wrong with you today? You on your period or something?"

"Fuck off."

Cody glared at her, then stalked off to his regular seat as class began.

'Bailey! You're going to ruin this for Bitty! Please try to be nice to people. He's a nice guy. He's done nothing but help us and try to make Bitty more comfortable. Please don't drive him away.'

"Shut up, Sarah. He's only trying to get in her pants. I can see it. Now shut up so I can listen."

The rest of the day went about as well as the morning had. Bailey snapped and snarled at everyone who spoke to her, and Cody avoided her entirely at social studies. She sat alone at lunch and scowled at anyone who got near her until she ended up with a bubble of several feet around her as people began to steer clear.

Halfway through math, when the teacher began talking about their homework, Bailey had reached her breaking point. Without a word, she crumpled up the pages that had just been placed on her desk and tossed them straight into the trash from where she sat.

The room went silent.

She sat back and folded her arms, glaring straight ahead at the chalkboard.

'Oh, Bailey! What have you done? We'll be in so much trouble! Bailey, please!'

"Shut it, bitch."

The teacher's eyes went from wide with disbelief to narrowed and furious.

"I will not be spoken to or treated with such disrespect." She walked quickly to her desk and began scribbling on a notepad, then tore off the top sheet and frowned at Bailey.

"Principal's office, now! Hand this in."

"Make me."

There was a collective gasp from the entire room and the teacher's face went red.

"I can call security if that's the way you want to play this out, Miss Carter. I will give you one more chance. Take this to the principal's office or I *will* call security."

Bailey glared at her until the very last possible second, then stood up and stalked as well as she could on crutches to the front of the room, snatched the note, and left the silent, stunned room. Without looking back, she slammed the door closed so hard the glass cracked in the corner.

For a moment, she just stood outside the door, fuming with anger and frustration. She had no intention of going to the principal's office, but she wasn't quite sure where else to go. Maybe the girl's locker room? It was too cold to go outside and her locker with her coat in it was on the other side of the school.

Eventually, she settled on hiding out in the locker room and tucked herself into a corner out of sight.

'Bailey, why do you have to be so obnoxious all the time? Why do you have to make everything so difficult?'

"I'm sick and tired of the way they treat us and the shit they keep piling on. There's no fucking way we're gonna get any of it done and apparently they don't give a fuck about what John said about the damn homework, if he even *did* email them about it."

'He did. I'm sure he did.'

"What the fuck do you really know about him, Scarlett? You like the way he fucks? You like the whole Daddy bit? You think he's a fucking saint cuz he feeds us and lets us live in his damn house and he hasn't beaten us yet? You don't know anything else about him. You'll see. I'm right. You'll all be sorry you didn't listen to me. You'll see."

***

Bailey managed to stay hidden away in the locker room for another hour before another gym class came in. When she left and rounded a corner, she bumped right into the security guard who grabbed her arm before she could even spin to try and escape. Not that she would have been able to on the crutches anyway, but it was instinct.

"There you are! Come on. You're heading for the office."

His grip was like a vice and it made things very difficult trying to navigate with the crutches like that. But he didn't seem to notice or perhaps he didn't care.

Bailey was fuming by the time they reached their destination and she glared at the man when he pushed her into a seat to wait. Almost immediately, she was called into the office and she slumped down in one of the chairs in front of the desk, glowering at the principal as well.

Thousands of taunts and jibes ran through her head as she took in his round, bald head, tiny Hitler mustache and thick glasses. All of them wanted to escape and rain down on the supercilious bastard who was standing over her as if he could cowe her into submission.

She smirked. He had no idea how foolish he looked trying to act like the tough guy. The guy wouldn't last a second with Mack. The other man wouldn't even need to touch him to have the principal groveling at his feet. Yet here he stood, acting like he was a god Bailey should be afraid of and bowing to. She nearly laughed when he crossed his arms angrily causing his blazer and tie to lift like a fabric wall in front of him and he had to lower his arms again to get it off his chin.

"Do you think this is a laughing matter, Miss Carter?"

Bailey crossed her own arms, staring back at him without the slightest hint of regret or respect. "Is that a rhetorical question?"

He frowned and went to sit behind his desk. "I spoke to Ms. Bard and I am quite disappointed in your behavior. We expect respect and decorum at this school, and you have shown neither today. I understand you are a foster child?"

She simply glared at him with one eyebrow raised snarkily.

"I see. Well, given the situation and that this is a first incident, I will call your guardian and arrange for you to be taken home immediately. You may return tomorrow. But if you pull another stunt like today, your punishment will be more severe. I won't have hoodlums running around my school."

Bailey scowled at him, smirking when he looked away first, even if it was to dial John's number. She still won.

When John arrived, he gave Bailey a cautionary glance, then told her to wait outside while he spoke to the principal. A few minutes later, he emerged and took her arm gently to help her out of the chair.

"Let's go get your stuff and go home. I had to cancel my last two appointments and leave in the middle of one to come pick you up."

Bailey didn't respond.

Once they'd collected her coat and books, she followed him in silence to the car and sank down in the seat with her arms crossed.

"What happened?" he asked after a while.

"That bitch in algebra put more homework on my damn desk."

"What did you do?"

"I threw it away in the trash where it belonged. I'm not some fucking pencil pushing nerd. I'm sick of homework. I'm done. And if they think they can–"

"Bailey, that's enough. I understand you're frustrated, but this is serious. You could be in trouble if something like that happens again. And it will be Bitty who pays for it. They won't understand it's you. All they'll see is a moody teenage girl acting out and they'll punish her for it.

"If I can help you work through your anger, or find someone else for you to talk to, it will make things a lot easier on everyone. But you have to be willing to work on it. And right now, I don't think you *want* to let go of your anger."

He sighed and glanced sideways at her. "Your anger doesn't define you, Bailey. It's a symptom of your life, not a defining characteristic. You can still be Bailey if you're not hating the world. Let me help you."

"Fuck you."

He sighed again and drove home in silence.

Bailey went inside and straight to her room, slamming the door angrily. She didn't come out for dinner and threw a shoe at him when he opened the door to ask about her homework.

There was a flash of anger in his eyes for a moment before he got it under control. "Alright. I'll give you the night off. Tomorrow's Friday anyway and we'll have the weekend to work on it, except when you're at the dance. Goodnight."

There was no reply. He hadn't really expected one anyway. Perhaps one day…

~ Choice Two ~

By the next morning, Bitty was feeling much better. Her symptoms were gone and she wasn't even feeling the devastating emptiness that she'd felt other times with Mack when she'd gone a while without a hit.

She'd never been this addicted before and had never taken so many doses as she had in those days before she was arrested, so she'd never experienced withdrawals like she just had. But there was always that ache and need for something to fill the missing part of her.

It wasn't something she could define. It was more like not being able to catch her breath, but in a way that her whole body experienced. This time, she didn't feel that.

The nurse practitioner made a note that she should return each day for her maintenance dose, then sent her off to breakfast with the other girls.

"Bitty!" Rebecca cried happily when she saw her leaving the food line. "You're okay. You *are* okay, aren't you? What happened? Was it the drugs?" she finished on a whisper.

Bitty nodded sadly and sat down. "Yeah. I... Fowler wasn't here and–"

"Yeah, he's off for a couple days. I can't believe he did that to you!"

"So I started withdrawing pretty bad," Bitty finished when Rebecca stopped talking.

"God, I'm so sorry, Bitty. But you're okay now? They helped you?"

Bitty nodded. "Yeah, they gave me some medications that made it all stop. Mrs. Barnes pretty much made them. You should have seen her. I didn't hear all of it cuz I was hurting so bad, but she said she'd get them in trouble or something if they didn't do something."

Rebecca grinned. "I knew I liked her! She's so awesome!"

Bitty smiled too. "Yeah. She even came to visit me."

Rebecca beamed at her. "I'm so glad she helped. And I'm really glad you're okay."

When they had finished breakfast and put their trays away, Bitty walked beside Rebecca to the classroom. Mrs. Barnes smiled warmly at her and Bitty smiled back as she sat down.

Despite her inability to concentrate during her session with the teacher the other day, Bitty was surprised by what had soaked in during it. There was still a lot she was confused about, but it wasn't quite so overwhelming. This time, she was able to focus better on the assignments and actually completed half of one of the worksheets before it was time to switch subjects.

"I hope you're proud of yourself," the teacher told her when the girls were leaving.

Bitty nodded, smiling. For the first time in her life, Bitty *was* proud of herself over school work.

Nat was nowhere to be seen during lunch. Rebecca obviously understood Bitty's constant vigilance.

"She's not here. Nat, I mean. She got transferred to another facility. They caught her beating up another student and that was her last chance. She's in a more secure place now."

Bitty relaxed visibly and was finally able to enjoy her meal.

The rest of the day went by peacefully. Her time after lunch was spent watching another movie with some of the girls and she even got a chance to play four square with a few others in the gym. At dinner time, she was actually hungry again.

By the time she climbed into bed, she was almost smiling. Some of the weight of the world had lifted from her shoulders and she slipped into sleep quickly.

Maybe things weren't so bad anymore. Maybe what she'd thought was a horrible thing would actually give her a real chance at being free from her past. Maybe she could live a real life when she got out...

Chapter Forty-Seven

* Choice One *

Bitty woke up the following morning, completely unaware of Bailey's behavior the day before. She offered John a smile when she sat down to eat and he returned it like usual.

"We took the night off from homework last night, Bailey and I. We can work on it over the weekend; tomorrow before the dance and on Sunday."

Bitty hadn't realized the dance was the next day. Butterflies jumped in her belly and she nodded nervously.

"Okay. Thanks… Daddy."

John grinned at her. "You're welcome, babygirl. Would you like to go out after school and pick something pretty for your hair, possibly get some makeup?"

"Can we?" she asked hopefully.

"Of course! I wouldn't have offered if I didn't mean it."

She flushed and looked away with a nod. "Sorry, Sir."

He put a finger under her chin and brought her head up to look at him. "Don't be sorry for that, babygirl. I didn't mean to make it sound like I was upset. I meant it when I said I want to make you happy, though. I like to spoil my babygirls. Okay?"

She nodded.

"Now where's that beautiful smile?"

She couldn't help it. She smiled.

He chuckled and kissed her forehead before releasing her chin and taking a seat for breakfast.

****

Cody caught her eye outside homeroom when she limped to her locker, deciding to leave the crutches at home that day. When she smiled at him shyly, he smiled back and approached.

"Hey. You okay?"

"Yeah. It's only a little sore."

"What?"

"My foot. It's just a little sore to walk on. But it's easier to get around without the crutches and Daddy said since I'm sitting most of the day, it would be okay to try going without them today."

"Oh. Right." He eyed her uncertainly and nodded. "So… uh… you still wanna go to the dance with me tomorrow?"

"Is that okay?" she asked nervously, suddenly terrified that he'd changed his mind about taking someone like her.

"Of course. I just… yesterday you seemed to hate me… so I wasn't sure if you still wanted to. But yeah, it's cool. I'll pick you up at six. Text me your ad–," he broke off. "Oh, yeah, you don't have a phone. Can your dad text me?"

She nodded. "Can you write down your number?"

He wrote it down on a scrap of paper and handed it to her just as the bell rang.

The rest of the day went reasonably well except for the odd looks people were giving her, and the new pile of homework that was added to the old pile. The amount of it was ridiculous! It was better just to stuff it in her backpack and not think about it.

****

John picked her up as usual and chatted with her on the way home, asking questions about her day that she answered in monosyllables. She really hated school and it was not a topic she wanted to spend any more time on than she had to. But there was no way she would be able to tell him that. He seemed to get the hint after a few questions and fell to telling her about his own day.

He tried once again to help her with some of her mountain of homework, but yet again it ended in anger and frustration on her end and she went to bed in tears. John sat on the couch for a while, contemplating his options and what he could do for her. It was only two weeks until Christmas break, but it had only been four days since she'd been in school and it had been a nightmare. He wasn't sure what to do to help her, though.

After a while, he got up and packed away her things before heading for her room. She was already curled up in her bed asleep and he watched her from the doorway for a moment.

Part of him knew having her there was a bad idea. Now that he knew how old she was, it wasn't smart to keep tempting himself with her presence. It had been one thing being with her when he thought she was an adult, but now it was wrong, and he knew it. It wasn't all about the sex, and even when he'd been with his other 'little girls' they hadn't been in their 'little space' when they'd been together like that. That wasn't what turned him on. But there was no way to separate that from her in this situation, and it bothered him.

But another part wanted her again. She was the ultimate 'babygirl': someone he could care for, love, and spoil. And the sex had been amazing in the hotel. He could almost feel her again. What if it only got worse? Would it be fair to keep her around when he wanted her in more than a 'babygirl' capacity?

He sighed and stepped quietly into the room to tuck her in. After pulling the comforter up over her shoulders, he paused for a moment, then bent down and kissed her on the forehead before leaving the room quickly.

~ Choice Two ~

The following morning it was the same routine as all the other days. Bitty didn't even know what day it was anymore. It was even more monotonous than it had been when she was under Mack's fist. At least she'd seen different faces and different places. Here, there was nothing different; not in the routine or the company.

At least the food was different. French toast. It was actually pretty good. It reminded Bitty of a time she'd been taken to some kind of diner and given French toast in the manager's office in the back before the place closed and he got his fill of her.

That hadn't been too bad, actually. It had been air conditioned and there was a chair to sit on. She'd had food and drink for the hour she had to wait for him, and she'd been paid already, so she'd actually been able to relax. A friend of the guy had rented her for the evening for his friend as a birthday present or something. That had been one of her better experiences. He'd even given her some food to take with her. She wondered if French toast would always make her think of that john.

The medications Mrs. Barnes had insisted on were helping so much that Bitty almost didn't feel anything after she took it that morning. The N.P. hadn't even talked to her when she'd shown up, and she tried not to wonder why he seemed to hate her so much. At least she didn't feel sick or in pain anymore.

It turned out that the routine was a little different that day. There was no class in the morning after breakfast. Instead, afternoon chores were done early and the rest of the day was going to be free time. Bitty wandered over to the collection of lounge chairs and couches in the corner on the other side of the room from the tv where several girls were getting started on a group game of some kind.

For a while, she stood off to one side, watching them begin calling out answers to whatever the game was asking, their grins and laughter growing brighter and louder. Bitty didn't realize she was smiling wistfully as well.

'Go over and ask to play.'

'Yeah, Bitty! Let's go play! I wanna play the game! Can we? Can we?'

Bitty shook her head ever so slightly, her smile disappearing. "I can't."

'Why not? It looks like fun.'

"Cuz…. I… I don't know how," she murmured.

'Then ask.'

Bitty shook her head again and turned to leave.

"Hey. You wanna play?"

Bitty paused and looked back at the small circle of girls. "Me?"

The girl standing up nodded and gave her a smile. "You looked like you wanted to."

Bitty bit her lip and glanced at the other girls. None of them seemed to object. "If it's… if it's really okay…"

"Sure. You can be on Monica's and Daria's team. They're one short."

A tiny thrill ran through Bitty's heart and she actually smiled shyly as she went over and sat on the couch the other girl had indicated.

"Okay, so I call out a word and then you pick one of the cards from your hand," she said, handing Bitty some cards. "Keep them hidden! Okay, so I call out the word and then you pick the card you think fits best and put it facedown on the table. Remember your card cuz if it gets picked, your team gets a point. Got it?"

Bitty nodded and looked through her cards. After she'd had a minute, the girl began the game again and Bitty was soon laughing with the rest.

Chapter Forty-Eight

* Choice One *

When Bitty woke up and came out to the living room, John smiled widely at her.

"Morning, babygirl! I have something for you."

She cocked her head slightly and sat down on the couch, laying the crutches along the length of it out of the way. "You do?"

He nodded towards a wrapped box on the coffee table. "That's for you."

"For me? Now?"

He laughed and picked it up to hand to her. "Of course. Open it."

She took it from him with a cautiously excited smile and began to open it, barely holding back from ripping the paper to shreds while doing so. Inside was a box from a jewelry store. Her eyes widened and she looked up at him quickly.

He was grinning broadly and nodded in encouragement. "Go on. Open the box."

Carefully, she lifted the pretty white lid and stared down in shock. Inside, nestled on a bed of white padding, was a sparkling, choker style necklace of clear stones, a matching tennis bracelet, and small, matching earrings that hung down in a short tear-drop of the same stone. Her eyes widened in wonder and she looked up at him, speechless.

"They're not diamonds, I'm afraid, but they're just as pretty. I think, anyway!" he added quickly. "They're for tonight. They'll go with your dress. I went out during lunch yesterday."

She looked back at the jewelry for a moment, then burst into tears.

"What's wrong, babygirl!? Are you okay? Are they no good?"

She shook her head and turned to hug him tightly. "They're so beautiful! Thank you so much, Daddy!"

He let out a breath and hugged her back, resting his cheek on her head. "Oh, my babygirl. You're so very welcome. I can't tell you how happy you've made me already, and when you call me Daddy, it just makes my heart explode. It's the least I could do to show you how special you are to me."

He held her for a while until she finally sat up to look at the pieces again, gently taking them out of the box to examine with a smile.

"I was thinking," he continued, "that maybe we could go get your nails done or something? We'll get a little homework done, then go to the salon and take a breather. What do you say?"

She smiled up at him. "Really?"

He nodded. "Yeah. It would be a nice break, don't you think? Kind of like a reward for getting some work done."

She nodded. "I'd really like that. Thanks."

"Awesome. Well, let's get some breakfast and get started. The sooner we get some work done, the sooner we can go out and get you ready for the dance tonight."

She beamed at him as he helped her to stand, then followed him into the kitchen to start what promised to be a Cinderella day.

~ Choice Two ~

The game lasted over an hour, and by the time they tallied up the score, Bitty was exhausted. Her team didn't win, but that didn't even matter to her. She had been allowed to play with the group. No; *invited* to play. It was something she had only ever dreamed of. She was beginning to feel welcome in a way she'd never felt in her life. This was a place she had been so afraid of, a place she'd heard horror stories about. Certainly, her treatment by the infirmary day-staff and some of the guards had been bad, but it wasn't even the worst she'd been treated. And many of the staff had been decent enough.

Mrs. Barnes had certainly been an unexpected ally, and even some of the guards were kind or friendly. And now that Nat was gone, the rest of the girls seemed to be much nicer, too. She was out of the cold, had good food, a soft, clean bed, and for the first time in her life, she was being treated like a person.

'It's jail *Bitty! Don't be getting all mushy cuz a couple girls let you join their game! It's not a home or a family!'*

'Bailey, leave off. No one's saying it's a family. It's just not as bad as we thought, okay? Please just let us be happy for a while. Please?'

Bailey snorted in frustration and 'stormed' off into the back, leaving the others to bask in what was left of the good feeling that had washed over them.

***

Sarah was fronting during their 'work' time, helping serve dinner. There were no rude comments from anyone about her incompetence in their serving size and most people even smiled at her. It was a completely different place with Nat gone.

'We should have told on her. Someone could have helped us.'

'Oh, there's a genius idea! Get labeled a snitch and then get beat to death when they don't believe us and she finds out! Brilliant! Really, Jay. Grow up.'

"Stop it, Bailey. Leave him alone," Sarah mumbled.

"What?" asked a girl moving past.

"Nothing. Sorry."

The girl nodded, giving her a curious glance before heading to her table to sit down. Sarah finished up serving and took her own tray to the table Rebecca was seated at.

"I saw you playing that game earlier. You wanna play one tomorrow?" her friend asked.

Sarah smiled. "I'd like that, yes."

"Cool. Maybe we could even check out the Wii and play on it for a while. I love bowling."

"Bowling?"

"Yeah. The bowling game on the Wii. Have you played it?"

Sarah shook her head. "No. Maybe you can show me."

"Sure!"

Sarah smiled at the other girl and went back to her food in peaceful silence. After dinner, she took the book Mrs. Barnes had given her the day before back to her room and sat down on her bed. It was a child's book, but it wasn't so babyish that she couldn't at least try to enjoy it.

She sat quietly, sounding out the words carefully for almost an hour before the guard called lights out and came through to check in everyone's room. With a contented smile, she lay down and pulled the warm covers over her with a sigh.

It had been a good day.

Chapter Forty-Nine

* Choice One *

Bitty found it *much* easier to keep her temper and concentrate at home with John explaining things than she had when she'd come back from an exhausting day at school and then had to try to concentrate even more. The work was still hard and pushed the limits of her tolerance more than a few times, but Bailey never made an appearance and Bitty managed to hold it together as well.

After several hours of good work, John sat back and grinned.

"Look at that, babygirl! You finished all the homework for math!"

She looked up from putting her pencils away, her mouth open in shock. "I did? It's finished?"

He laughed and hugged her with a nod. "All of it! I'm so proud of you!"

She grinned back and hugged him. "Thank you."

"Alright, let's go get those nails fancied up!"

She giggled and stood up with him, a thrill coursing through her at the prospect.

***

John took her to a local nail salon and arranged for a full mani/pedi. Bitty felt like an actual princess. By the time she was picking her nail polish color, her cheeks hurt from smiling so much.

'I don't think we've ever smiled this much!'

'There wasn't anything to smile about, Scarlett.'

'Yeah, I guess not.'

John surprised her by getting his nails done too, sitting beside her the whole time, though he didn't choose polish for his. Bitty settled on a silver glitter polish that sparkled in the lights of the shop, her heart thrilling when John pointed out how nicely it would match her dress and jewelry.

He settled himself in the waiting area with a book while she got the polish applied, glancing over every so often to check on her and offer a reassuring smile.

Afterwards, they stopped at a diner around the corner and had lunch together. It was like a dream come true, and it only promised to get better.

***

When they got home, John helped her with a little more homework before leading her to the bathroom to get ready.

"Do you want to do your own makeup, or do you want help?"

"I can do it."

He looked slightly disappointed but nodded. "Okay. Let me know if you need anything." He gave her a smile, then softly kissed her on the lips and shut the bathroom door so she could shower.

She stood still for a moment, gazing at the door uncertainly. That was something she hadn't been expecting, though now that she thought about it, she probably should have. He was, after all, one of her johns. Just because he hadn't had her for a while, it didn't mean she was finished. It must have just been a break.

With a confused little sigh, she stripped and got in the shower, turning her thoughts to the dance ahead of her.

***

Two hours later, Bitty stood in front of the mirror in her bedroom, staring at herself in awe and disbelief.

"Wow," John said from the doorway.

She jumped and turned her head to look at him, her cheeks pink with shy pleasure. "Do I look okay?" she whispered.

He walked in and stood behind her, his hands on her shoulders as he met her eyes in the mirror. "Babygirl, you look stunning."

She beamed at him, then looked back at herself. Her long, brown hair fell in a silky sheet to her elbows, glowing in the bedroom light. The jewelry was delicate enough that it didn't seem to steal the spotlight from the dress that made her feel like a princess. For the first time in her life, Bitty truly felt pretty.

"You ready?" he asked gently.

She swallowed and nodded nervously. "I think so."

He squeezed her shoulders and kissed the top of her head. "I'll send you with some money just in case. And why don't you take my phone as well. I should have got you one days ago."

"Your phone?" she asked incredulously.

He nodded. "Yeah. Just in case you need to call me. I want you to call me if you need *anything*, okay? I won't be mad."

"Okay," she whispered.

He handed her the crutches and for a moment she felt some of the excitement slip. They ruined the effect quite a bit. But it only lasted a moment before she was on top of the world again.

Cody arrived to pick her up in a limo. Bitty's jaw dropped and she stared out at the driveway in shock, missing John's fleeting look of concern. It vanished when she turned to hug him and he hugged her tightly back.

"Be careful, babygirl. Call me if you need *anything*," he repeated seriously.

She looked up at him with a little nod. "Okay."

He kissed the top of her head before fixing her coat back onto her shoulders and helping her out the door.

Cody was grinning at her in appreciation and she smiled shyly.

"You look great. Ready?"

She nodded, smiled back at John for a second, then hobbled down the sidewalk to the limo and disappeared inside. She waved to John, who stood on the stoop until she rounded the corner, then settled back into her seat and gave Cody a nervous smile.

He reached out and slipped his arm around her shoulders, pulling her close against him, rather uncomfortably. Her nervousness changed into something different at the way he held her to him but she stayed silent.

He smiled down at her and she lifted her face to look at him, trying her best to smile.

"You're gonna have a great time. You're with me, so that'll make all the difference. When they see you with me, *everyone* is gonna know who you are."

She nodded slightly, still feeling uncomfortable.

'What's wrong with you? It's not like you've never been touched by a guy before. Want me to take over? I'll do it if you don't want to.'

Bitty shook her head very slightly. She wasn't nervous enough that she would let Scarlett or anyone else take over and make her miss this if she could possibly help it.

When the car stopped outside a hotel, Bitty frowned slightly in confusion. "I thought–" she began, turning to Cody. Before she got another word out, he held her head and kissed her hard. She froze in panic as he deepened it.

'See! See! I told you he would expect to be fucked! I warned you all! I knew it!'

He broke the kiss and smiled down at her, wiping her bottom lip with his thumb. "I knew your lips would feel so good."

Bitty felt like she couldn't catch her breath and she desperately fought the panic that was clutching at her chest.

Without waiting for her to respond, however, he climbed out of the open door the driver was holding, then leaned in to help her out.

"Let's go party."

In a daze of confusion, Bitty took his hand and carefully climbed out of the limo, then tucked the crutches under her arms. They weren't at the school like she thought! Cody had kissed her! Maybe she was supposed to have sex with him like Bailey had said. That was what happened in all the movies, wasn't it?

With her stomach in knots, she followed him inside in silence. Loud, thumping bass sounds assaulted her ears when they got inside and she suddenly realized the party must not be at the school like she thought.

Cody helped her get her coat hung up, then led her to a banquet hall where the music was coming from. It was much louder in there and added another kind of panic to Bitty's already high levels, but at least some of the confusion had gone when she'd realized why they had come here.

"Let's go over and meet the guys!" he shouted in her ear.

She nodded and began to follow him, her eyes wide with fear.

'You probably look like a damn deer caught in headlights. Suck it up, Bitty, for Christ's sake!'

She winced at the jibe and knew Bailey was probably right, but it was all so overwhelming it was hard enough just trying not to cry!

Cody led them to a group of five or ten guys on one side of the room and put his arm around her, drawing her against him almost hard enough to knock her over as he started joking with his friends.

Their eyes appraised her and her panic began to rise with their looks. After a minute or two, though, they turned their attention to the other girls there. For a while, they teased and goaded each other, scuffling playfully until some of them finally gave in and headed over to mingle.

"You wanna dance?" Cody yelled.

Bitty looked up at him skeptically. "I can't."

He shook his head, pretending he couldn't hear her as he pulled her to the floor. Without a word, he took her crutches and tossed them to the side, nearly tripping a passing student. Then his arms were around her and he was grinding against her to the music, grinning down at her.

She had no other choice. She couldn't exactly run away, and he *had* invited her and paid for everything. She really owed it to him. It was just a dance, after all. Her eyes fell to the floor slightly behind and to the right of him and she allowed him to move her body how he wanted to the music, trying not to let her panic overwhelm her.

'Let me do it, Bitty.'

'Yeah, there's a great idea. Let the whore out to grind with the horny teenage boy! She'll fuck him for you right here!'

Bitty barely heard the argument inside because the song ended and a slow song came on. Cody's arms tightened on her but he stopped rolling his hips against her. In surprise, she looked up into his face and found him smiling at her as he swayed side to side gently.

She offered him a weak smile in return and began to relax. Maybe it had only been that particular song. She hadn't been able to hear the words and she didn't know the song. Maybe what he'd been doing were the moves for it or something.

When the song ended, she tried to step back carefully.

"Can we sit down? My... my foot hurts," she asked, nearly shouting at him until he lowered his head to hear her.

He nodded and held her around the waist until they reached her crutches and she could walk on her own completely. For a few minutes, he sat with her and watched the rest of the students dance. Then one of his friends beckoned to him and he got up.

"Hey, I'm gonna go talk to the guys. I'll be back in a little while."

She nodded and watched him leave.

After forty-five minutes, he returned with a cup of punch.

"Sorry! I lost track of the time. Joey found a guy who agreed to buy us some bottles, so we went over to the liquor store. We're having a party at his place after the dance."

She looked at him nervously. "I'm... my... dad wants me home right after..."

His face fell and he looked at her darkly for a moment, then shrugged and sat back with his juice. "That's cool. I can find someone else to come."

A pang of regret and doubt tugged at her and she watched him uncertainly. "I'm sorry. I just–"

"It's cool. I get it."

She fell silent and went back to watching the others. Cody eventually got up again and went off with his friends. A while later, she spotted him dancing with a couple of girls, one of whom was the girl from the cafeteria, his ex apparently. Bitty sighed and looked away.

At ten to eleven, the DJ announced the last few songs and eventually Cody came back over to her. He grinned at her like a fool and held his hand out.

"Last dance, Bitty?"

'He's been drinking, I think.'

'No shit, Sherlock. I can smell the booze on him.'

'Be careful, Bitty.'

Bitty nodded slightly, acknowledging both his request and Sarah's warning as she stood and took his hand.

He led her back out onto the floor and tossed her crutches away again before pulling her to him and swaying to the music again. Surprisingly, he kept his hands to himself and only rocked slowly side to side, and she began to relax into his arms, enjoying herself once more.

The lights came up when the song ended and Cody retrieved her crutches, then walked her out to collect her coat and go home. When he pulled her to him in the limo again, she had a brief moment of worry that he was going to try something, but he didn't, and by the time they got back to John's house, she was actually smiling.

Cody leaned over with a smile.

"I had fun. Thanks."

Bitty tensed when he kissed her again, deeply like the last time, but he released her reasonably quickly and helped her get out.

"See you on Monday," he said with a wink as he got back into the limo.

She smiled with a nod, her good mood returned, and watched him drive away for a moment before turning to go up the path. To her surprise, John was standing on the front step watching her with a smile. He held the door open and she limped inside.

"Did you have fun, babygirl?" he asked softly as he took her coat.

"Yeah. They had a DJ and everything was decorated with silver snowflakes and it wasn't even at the school like I thought it would be. It was a hotel or something and the limo driver opened the door for us and everything."

"Sounds great."

She nodded and followed him to the living room to sit down.

"You want something to eat or drink?"

She shook her head tiredly and leaned against him when he sat down beside her. For a while, he asked questions about the dance, smiling and hugging her as she described everything, but when midnight came and went, he squeezed her shoulders one more time and stood up with a sigh.

"Alright, time for Cinderella to get to bed."

She gave him an exhausted but happy smile and followed him to the bathroom to wash off her makeup and brush her teeth, still talking about her evening while he stood in the doorway and watched with a smile. When she finished and limped into her room still talking, he laid out her pajamas on her bed, then stepped back to smile at her.

Her eyes met his, her face shining with happiness. She truly did feel like Cinderella.

Something in his eyes changed just then and her smile faltered a little as he stepped closer and took her face gently in his hands.

"You are so beautiful, babygirl."

Her smile faded and she stayed very still, her chest tight again. Then he kissed her. One hand slid to the back of her head to hold her mouth to his and his other slid down her back to unzip the dress.

The bottom fell out of her stomach and her breath caught in her throat. All the joy of a moment ago vanished and she closed her eyes against the tears that threatened to spill.

Without a sound, she stood where she was as he worked the dress off her and moved his mouth to her ear and neck, nibbling and kissing as he went. She squeezed her eyes more tightly and tried desperately to prepare herself. But it was so hard! She hadn't been expecting this, though she felt foolish not to have. It felt like she'd been punched.

His hands moved over her body, stripping her and pulling her against his obvious arousal, his breath hot on her suddenly cold skin. She obeyed his orders, moving her hands where he told her to, stepping her feet apart at his direction, all the while trying desperately not to sob with defeat and regret.

At last, his hand holding hers against his crotch as he rocked his hips, he lifted his head to smile at her and paused. She opened her eyes when he stopped moving and met his gaze miserably.

For a split second, she thought what she saw was anger in his eyes and she cowered away slightly, wondering what she had done to make him angry as he pulled away, but it vanished a moment later and left her confused and frightened.

John stared down at her in horror. The defeat and resignation, the sheer hopeless heaviness in her eyes had been like a punch to his gut. For a blinding moment, he had convinced himself she wanted this, wanted him. But the look in her world-weary eyes had shown him the ugly truth.

He was absolutely certain she would allow him to take her however he wanted, but not because she wanted it or him, but because that was all she knew. She would have done anything he said simply because she didn't know how to do anything else, no matter what she really wanted.

He was raping her. The sudden realization of that felt like a knife in his heart and he stepped back with tears in his eyes. She stood in front of him, naked and shivering, looking suddenly so very young and vulnerable, watching him in fear as if waiting for him to strike her.

"Oh, god. Bitty," he breathed.

She blinked at the use of her name, her nervousness increasing.

"I.... god, I'm so sorry. I'm so sorry. I...." He stared at her in utter horror, then stepped forward and hugged her tightly to him.

She went rigid with terror and bewilderment.

"You're done, Bitty. You're done. You don't have to do this anymore. I'm so sorry." He stepped back with tears in his eyes as he looked at her and shook his head, then held her cheeks in his hands and gazed down into her face.

"You're not here for that, Bitty. Do you understand?" The look in her eyes told him she obviously didn't and he sighed sadly, then kissed her forehead lightly and stepped back. "I'm so sorry. I'll never do it again." He closed his eyes and blinked at his tears, then tried to smile at her.

"Go to bed, babygirl. I'm not going to touch you. You're done. I'm so sorry." With that, he strode quickly from the room, leaving her staring after him in stunned silence, her mind spinning.

When he didn't return, she turned and put her pajamas on, then crawled into bed. After the light was out, she turned her face into her pillow and cried herself to sleep.

John had never hated himself so much in all his life as he did that night. He had ruined her wonderful day, and worse than that, he had betrayed her in the worst possible way.

~ Choice Two ~

Bebe woke up before the lights were on the following morning and was scribbling quietly on some blank papers with a pencil when they were finally called for showers and breakfast. She jumped up happily and followed the others to the shower room, doing her best to wash her hair and dry off.

During breakfast, she chattered excitedly to Rebecca about what game they were going to play and how good the sausages were. Her friend gave her a few puzzled looks but smiled anyway. What Bebe didn't notice was Fowler watching her from the other side of the room.

The day went much like the previous day had; she stopped at the infirmary to take her meds, chores in the morning, then free time in the afternoon. Rebecca was able to check out the Wii and showed Bebe how to play bowling and tennis. When their time was up, Bebe very nearly had a tantrum, but Sarah managed to soothe her just in time and Bebe flopped down on the couch instead, smiling at Rebecca.

"That was awesome."

Rebecca grinned and sat down beside her. "Yeah. I love those two games. Hey, you wanna play a card game now?"

Bebe nodded and followed the other girl to one of the tables. Fowler approached just then.

"Carter, come with me."

Bebe looked up and her eyes widened with fear. Rebecca seemed to understand and her face went white.

As slowly as she could, Bebe stood up, tears filling her eyes. Just as she began to follow him, panic rising in her chest, one of the other guards called out to him.

"Dave. Your wife is on line one."

He scowled and Bebe looked up sharply. He was married!?

'Of course he's married. Probably has kids too!'

To her relief, Fowler nodded and stomped away and Bebe returned to Rebecca.

Most of the day, she and Rebecca played various games together, sometimes joined by some of the other girls for a while.

By dinner, Bitty had returned, completed her dinner chores, and was sitting beside Rebecca and one of the girls who'd invited her to play the day before, Chan. It felt like she actually had friends and it was one of the best feelings in the world. Once again, she went to bed that night with a smile on her face.

Chapter Fifty

* Choice One *

The following day, things were awkward between them at breakfast until they sat down to eat. After a few bites, John sighed and put down his fork to look at her sadly.

"Babyg–... Bitty... I'm sorry for what I did yesterday. I'll understand if you want me to contact Jennifer and find you somewhere else to live where you never have to see me again. I promise you, though, that if you do choose to stay, I won't try to do anything to you again. It's your choice. I won't be mad no matter what you decide."

She watched him as he spoke, taking in the regret and pain in his face.

'Don't trust him. People don't change. He's a sick fuck. Get out of here.'

'He seems genuine, Bailey. And he's been good to us all along. Besides, he stopped last night. On his own. Bitty didn't say or do anything. He just stopped and apologized.'

'Plus, we don't know what kind of place we'd end up in if we left. We'd probably end up with someone who wouldn't stop. And I... I kinda like not having to fuck someone all the time...'

There was a stunned silence inside until Sarah murmured softly in surprise.

'You... are actually happy not to have to have to sex, Scarlett?'

'Yeah. It's fun sometimes, but I like the way I feel when I'm not just... a thing, Sarah. I'm tired of being nothing but a disposal system for guys to relieve themselves in and I'm tired of trying to enjoy it all the time because that's what everyone expects me to do. I like it here, and I want to stay.'

Bitty stared at John blankly, shocked by Scarlett's revelation.

'Who wants to stay, then?'

'I do, Sarah!'

'Me too! Me too!'

'Okay, Jay and Bebe do. And Scarlett. I'd like to stay. Bailey?'

'We're gonna get raped no matter where we go, and none of you are gonna listen to me anyway. Why even bother asking.'

John sighed and looked down at his food, misinterpreting her silence. "I'll call Jennifer after breakfast."

Bitty jerked to attention and shook her head quickly. "No!" She shrank back in surprise at the vehemence in her voice and the surprise on John's face.

"No?" he breathed incredulously.

"I don't... I don't want to go somewhere else. And neither does anyone else."

"Even Bailey?" he asked with a skeptical frown. She shrugged apologetically and he nodded with a sad smile. "It's okay, I understand. The rest of you really want to stay with me?"

She nodded.

He beamed at her as he stood and came around the table to hug her tightly. "I swear, from now on there's nothing between us like that again. If I do anything you don't like, tell me and I'll stop, okay?"

She nodded and he hugged her again, kissing the top of her head.

They finished breakfast in a much better mood than they'd started and went to work on some of her homework. For a few hours, they worked through reading and discussions, then took a break to watch a movie over lunch before going back for another hour of work.

John called it a day at about three and they spent the rest of the day together in comfortable laziness, watching movies and making dinner together.

That night, he tucked her in gently and kissed her forehead with a smile.

"I can't tell you how much it means to me that you're staying, babygirl. Thank you."

She smiled back and watched him leave, then rolled over onto her side and sighed peacefully. He really was the best thing that had ever happened to them, no matter what he had done or tried to do.

As she fell asleep, she began to imagine an actual future for the first time. A future with John.

~ Choice Two ~

The next four days were back to the routine she had been in when she'd first arrived; shower, breakfast, school, lunch, free time, dinner. She made sure to stop by the infirmary each morning for her dose of Suboxone. On Wednesday, the nurse practitioner informed her they would be tapering her off the meds for the next few days and then she'd be done.

Sarah was nervous about feeling the effects of the withdrawals, but by Friday when she took her last dose, Bitty felt reasonably confident that she would be okay. They'd gone off heroin before when Mack had just cut them off, though of course the amount in their system had been a lot less than it had been this time. Even so, they'd managed, so with the meds, she was sure they would be okay once they were gone, even if there were symptoms left over.

After lunch, Bitty was called to the office. She glanced fearfully at Rebecca who shrugged.

"Maybe you have visitors? Family? Social worker?"

Bitty shrugged back and headed down the hall. When she reached the office, Jennifer was waiting for her with a somewhat round, short man.

"Bailey, do you remember me? I'm Jennifer Wright, your social worker."

Bitty nodded.

"I'd like you to meet Mr. Knox, one of the assistant D.A.'s. He's working on a case of trafficking and we'd like to talk to you about your pimp. Let's go to the conference room."

Bitty nodded slightly, her throat dry with nerves as she followed them and sat down.

"First of all, how are you feeling?"

Bitty shrugged and looked down at the table. "Okay."

"That's good to hear. We have some questions for you, if you could answer them, please."

'You could have said it while bawling your eyes out and she would have said the same damn thing. She doesn't care."

Mr. Knox leaned back in his seat and regarded Bitty for a minute. "We've been following someone who we think is involved in sex trafficking and I'm looking for information. His name is Michael Granding, but he goes by the name 'Mack' on the streets." He watched her closely and Bitty felt her face pale in fear.

'He knows. He already knows. He just wants you to come out and say it.'

"I'm fairly sure he was your pimp but I don't have enough to put him away. I need your help; information, clues, testimony."

Bitty hunched up even more when he said 'testimony'.

'We should help him, Bitty. Then Mack can't hurt us anymore. This man will help us if we tell him stuff.'

'You're out of your fucking mind, Jay. Mack will get off cuz he always does and he'll have us fucking killed! No way in hell!'

'We should at least consider it.'

'Are you trying to get us beat to death?'

'No, but–'

'Then shut the fuck up and let me handle this.'

'No! Bitty is the better one to handle this. You'll make things blow up.'

'I handle it the way it needs to be handled.'

"...and it would help a lot of people if you would. What do you say?"

Bitty snapped her eyes to Jennifer. "What?"

Jennifer glanced at Mr. Knox, then back at Bitty. "I said we really need this information to add to what we have, and then we could put him away and it would help a lot of people. We really do need you, Bailey."

She stared at the table again, her heart racing.

"Was it Mack, Bailey?" Mr. Knox asked. "If you help us, he'll go away."

She shrugged, her eyes beginning to flick around the room nervously. She felt the need to run all of a sudden, she needed to get out from under their gazes, out of this certain death trap. She couldn't tell them anything or Mack would *know* it was her who had blabbed.

Knox sighed and crossed his arms. "Why did you stay with him? You could have left. Why didn't you call the police or tell someone? Did you want to stay? Did you like it?"

'Fucking BASTARD! I'll tell him where the fuck he can put his opinions!'

'Bailey, please. You're going to make things difficult.'

"I couldn't," Bitty mumbled. "He.... he hurt me."

"But you could have asked for help. We could have put you in foster care or arrested him. You were alone when we found you, weren't you? Why didn't you call for help then?"

Tears were filling Bitty's eyes and she hunched up tightly. Had she wanted it? Could she really have done more to get away from him? Was it really her fault after all? Doubt filled her mind and she barely heard the rest of what he was saying.

For an hour and a half, she sat silently in the conference room while Mr. Knox and Jennifer pressed her for information. But she just couldn't tell them. She would be in so much trouble. She knew it.

'But, Bitty, we don't have to go back to him anymore. We're in here, and when we get out, we don't have to see him again. He won't hurt us if we tell them.'

Bitty shook her head ever so slightly and the two adults sighed. Mr. Knox frowned in frustration and stood up, gathering his things angrily.

"Fine. But without your help, a lot of other girls are going to be in the same situation and it will be your fault."

"Brad! That's uncalled for."

"Well she needs to know the consequences of her decision. If she won't help us, there's no way we can hold him and he's free to go and do the same thing to other girls. But that's fine. As long as she's comfortable."

"Brad. A word outside. Now."

He scowled at her and snatched his briefcase off the conference table before walking out without looking back at Bitty.

Jennifer sighed and gave her an apologetic look before beckoning to the guard. "She's finished, thanks." She turned back to Bitty. "If you change your mind, tell one of the guards and they can contact me, okay?"

Bitty nodded and followed the guard miserably to dinner, taking up her position to serve again. At least by the time she had finished dinner and was sitting down beside Rebecca on one of the couches in the common room, she was in a slightly better mood, and after watching a movie with some of the others before bed, she felt almost like she had the last few days.

Chapter Fifty-One

* Choice One *

Bitty was still feeling overwhelmed at school even though she'd caught up with most of her homework over the weekend because at every class they just handed out more homework to be done. But having at least completed most of the old stuff made it a little less suffocating. Cody was with her at every possible moment during the day, holding her hand, hugging her, trying to kiss her at every opportunity. It was making her uncomfortable but she stayed quiet.

Each evening, John had set aside half an hour for homework and said they would do what they could in that time and anything else would wait. He had discussed things with the principal and they would do their best to ease her into things.

"We're going to start you on some easier classes after New Year's. That should help. We just need to get you through the next couple of weeks, okay, babygirl?"

She nodded and went back to her dinner in silence.

'Special ed, that's what he's talking about. You're gonna be in the loser class. Way to go, moron.'

'What's special ed?'

'It's just easier classes for people who need help, that's all, Jay. It's not bad. Don't listen to Bailey.'

'You wait. We'll be in with the losers and retards.'

'Stop it.'

'Yeah, stop, Bailey!'

"Stop!" Bitty whimpered miserably.

"What's wrong?" John asked in surprise.

She looked up at him, dismayed when she realized she'd said it out loud in an effort to stop the arguments about something that was already bothering her.

"Sorry. I… I don't know. Sorry."

"Babygirl, if something is bothering you, I want you to tell me. I won't be mad. I just want to help you."

She moved some food around on her plate and nodded. "K."

***

Friday afternoon, Cody put his arm around her outside the cafeteria and pulled her to him with a smile. When he tried to kiss her, she dropped her head and turned it slightly, her body tense.

"C–Cody... I don't..." she began, though her voice came out in a tight whisper of fear.

"Hey. Come with me."

She looked up nervously. "Where?"

He led her down the hall with a grin. "Somewhere a little more private."

She swallowed hard and stumbled along in his tight grasp.

'Something's wrong. He's acting weird. Bitty, tell him you're not going. Tell him you have to get to lunch.'

"Cody... I... I have to...."

"Shh," he whispered, grinning at her as he pushed open the door to the boy's locker room.

She balked. "I can't go in there!" she gasped.

Without a word, he shoved her in and shut the door behind him.

"I let you off on Saturday, but you owe me."

She shrank back as he approached her, her eyes filling with tears of dread. There was no doubt in her mind what he felt she owed him.

"Cody, please... I don't–"

He pushed her against a wall and started kissing her neck. "Shhh... let it happen. I'm good. You'll see. You'll love it."

Tears trickled silently down her cheeks and she closed her eyes as he started to remove her clothes. Instinct and training took over and she obeyed his directions without argument.

When he'd almost finished, the door opened and she looked up in horror to see three guys from the football team walk in on them. Cody didn't even stop. And even more disturbing, the others didn't look away or leave. They came right over!

Bitty's face burned hotly as she closed her eyes and looked away. Cody finished and got up, but before she could sit up properly, the others were surrounding her. Her heart stopped in fear and she looked up at him with wide eyes, waiting for him to stop them.

"Cody!" she gasped as their hands began roaming over her. "Please..."

"I knew you weren't a virgin, and any girl who isn't a virgin by your age is a slut. Just give them what they want."

Tears poured down her cheeks as they moved in like sharks who smelled blood in the water. It was like being back at work again and she tried to close her mind, hoping desperately that Scarlett or *someone* would take over and get her out of here. But it was devastatingly quiet inside.

She didn't bother arguing or fighting, or even begging. There was no point. She certainly hadn't been allowed to all her life, why should now be any different. Vaguely, she noticed there was now a line waiting for her, constantly changing faces and body parts, and yet they were all the same. She just closed her eyes and did what she was told, hoping it would be over soon.

It was impossible to tell how long she was there before the door opened yet again and a booming voice shouted loudly causing everyone to jump up. She opened her eyes and looked up into the furious face of the gym coach glaring down at her.

"Get your damn clothes on and get your ass to the office, *NOW!*"

She flinched violently and looked around for her clothes, finding them kicked under benches and crumpled in corners, expecting him to yell at the boys, call the police, *something*.

"Masters, Carter, Jackson, all of you, get out onto the field and start warm-ups! I want you ready to play when I get out there! And your minds better be on the game tonight!"

Bitty looked up at him in dismay. It sounded like the entire football team had been there, and he was just letting them go out to play football without a word!

When she'd slipped on her one boot, he shoved her crutches at her as if he was angry at *her* and practically muscled her out the door. She hadn't even had time to clean herself up a little and she could feel their leftovers oozing out of and over her. Tears still trickled down her face as they walked in severe silence to the principal's office. She glanced at a clock in the hall as they passed, shocked to see it was almost the end of school!

Her first clear thought since lunch was that she'd missed art.

The coach banged his fist down on the secretary's desk and she turned around with a start.

"Coach! Afternoon."

"I need to see Butler."

"Uh, okay." She got up and knocked on the principal's door, casting a curious glance at Bitty's tear-streaked face and sticky hair. When the door opened, she nodded to the coach and murmured something to the principal who nodded back and gestured for him to enter.

The large man practically knocked Bitty over shoving her toward the door and she hobbled in with her head down.

Once the door was shut, the coach pointed to a seat and almost shoved her down into it.

"I found her in the boy's locker room doing the entire football team," he almost shouted.

The principal's jaw dropped and he looked from the coach to Bitty. "Is that true?"

Bitty looked up at him miserably. "I was–"

"I walked in on her myself!" the coach interrupted. "Found her with five of them and more waiting. This is completely unacceptable!"

The principal sighed and nodded in agreement, glancing at the carriage clock on his desk. "I'll have to call your foster parents."

Bitty's face paled and she looked down at her lap. She was in so much trouble and she felt sick with nerves and a stomach full of…

She closed her eyes and tried to think of something else. Anything else.

"You can go. Thanks for bringing her in," Mr. Butler told the coach as he walked to his desk and sat down to call John.

The coach glared at her angrily as he turned and stomped out.

Bitty sat huddled in the chair, her arms around her waist and her head down miserably. They hadn't even let her explain. They didn't care anyway. Those boys weren't going to get into trouble. If they hadn't even been reprimanded when he walked in on them, nothing was going to happen even if she did tell them the truth. Boys just don't get into trouble for that; especially boys on a star sports team. No one would believe her.

Once Mr. Butler hung up the phone she was moved to a chair in the outer office where anyone passing could see her. She knew everyone would be talking about her on Monday. It was utterly humiliating. Tears continued to trickle slowly down her face. No one offered her so much as a cup of water while she waited for John.

Forty-five minutes later, John walked in and crouched down in front of her as soon as he saw her.

"Hey! What happened?" he asked gently, brushing the tears from her cheeks.

She didn't look up.

"Dr. Matthews, Mr Butler is waiting in his office," the secretary said.

He nodded and brushed at another tear on her cheek. "I'll be back in a few minutes, babygirl."

Soon after he went into the office, she heard his voice beginning to rise, joined by Mr. Butler's after a while. They seemed to be going back and forth and John was obviously not happy. Twenty minutes later, John stormed out of the office with Mr. Butler behind him, scribbled something on a piece of paper so hard she heard the pen crack a little, then came over to her.

"We're leaving."

She finally lifted her head to look at him and was shocked by the color and expression on his face. He was furious. She stood up nervously and glanced at the principal for a moment before hobbling out of the office with John behind her. She jumped when he slammed the door shut violently.

"Is your stuff still in your locker?" he asked, his voice shaking with anger.

She shrank back with a nod. "Yes."

He nodded and fell silent again. She was somewhat dismayed to see him pack *everything* from her locker into her backpack and leave the textbooks, but she was much too afraid of him in this mood to question him about it. He was so angry at her! She just stood off to the side and waited as quietly as she could until he'd finished, then followed him out of the building amid whispers and smirks. She didn't have to wait until Monday to be gossiped about, apparently.

The whole way home, John's fingers were white on the steering wheel and he muttered quietly to himself with a frown on his face. Bitty shrank down in her seat and looked at her lap in silence. He probably hated her now.

'I told you so.'

Now they were back? Bitty thought bitterly. At least, Bailey was back. If she'd been out, maybe she'd have gotten them out of there. Bitty had been useless and she hated herself for it.

John helped her out of the car as usual and seemed to calm down a little by the time they got their boots and jackets off.

"Want some hot chocolate?" he asked quietly.

She looked up at him nervously, trying to read his expression. If she said yes, would he be angry with her for being greedy? If she said no, would he be upset because she was being uncooperative? Every nerve in her was on edge, wary and fearful.

"I... I don't... If it's not... trouble..." she whispered.

He looked at her sharply and she shrank back in sheer terror. She'd said the wrong thing! She'd read him wrong! She'd made him angry again!

"I'm sorry," she breathed, hunching into herself. "I'm sorry. I'm sorry."

His entire body softened and he came over to her, pulling her rigid, anxious little body into his arms and hugging her tightly.

"Oh, babygirl. What happened?" he murmured, resting his cheek on her head, now crusty with the dried remains of her afternoon. "Because I don't think you went in there to seduce the football team, did you?"

The moment he touched her, Bitty's heart felt like it stopped and she held her breath in fear. But he didn't beat her or shout at her or tear her clothes off! He hugged her! He hugged her like he wasn't angry!

Suddenly, her emotions flooded out before she could stop them. She wrapped her arms around him and cried as the crutches fell away unnoticed by either of them. He stroked her hair gently and let her cry.

After a long time, when she'd stopped sobbing, he pulled away and gazed down at her. She was shocked to see his own eyes glittering a little in the light.

"Do you want to talk about it?"

She looked away quickly and shook her head, hunching up again. He sighed and hugged her close again for a moment, then released her and grabbed her crutches from the floor. With a sad smile, he went to the stove.

"How about that hot chocolate, babygirl?" he asked gently, but he'd already started the water. "You can go take a shower while I make it."

She gazed at his back for a long moment, her heart filling with love. He knew. He knew what she was feeling and she hadn't needed to say it. She nodded quietly and went to go clean the filth off her, wishing she could get it out of her, too.

The rest of the evening, neither of them spoke about the incident at school or, in fact, anything about school. He talked about a funny thing that happened at the sub shop, about the snow they were supposed to get over the weekend, and about what movie they would watch together. It felt almost normal, except for the fact that Bitty felt the return of an ache in her chest that had begun to fade over the last two weeks. It hurt. The whole time, she felt on the verge of tears and it was so very difficult to keep it together, especially when John tucked her close against him under his arm to watch the movie. She wanted to crawl further into his arms and cry until the pain stopped. But there weren't enough tears in the world to accomplish that.

After the movie was finished, she took another shower and dressed in her sweats and a long sleeve t-shirt. When she emerged, John was waiting for her.

"Can I brush your hair for you, babygirl?" he asked gently.

She gazed up at him with tears in her eyes, then nodded.

He smiled and grabbed the brush before following her to her room. Once she was sitting cross legged on the bed, he settled behind her and began gently brushing out her wet hair. After a while, he began humming a song to her.

She closed her eyes and sighed very softly, her body beginning to relax little by little until her hair was finished.

"Bedtime, babygirl," he murmured finally.

She nodded and crawled under the covers he pulled back for her. When she'd settled on her side in a little ball, he pulled them up and tucked them in around her gently before leaning over to kiss her on the top of the head.

"Sleep tight."

She nodded slightly and watched him leave before turning her face into her pillow to cry again. She couldn't remember it hurting this badly in a very long time.

***

It was Sarah who woke up the next morning. She found John brooding over a cup of coffee in the kitchen but he put on a smile quickly when he saw her.

"Morning, babygirl. You hungry? I was thinking French toast and bacon."

Sarah nodded and sat down at the table. "What's wrong?"

He met her eyes for a moment. "Ah. You're not Bitty, are you?"

She shook her head. "Sarah."

He nodded and gazed into his coffee for a moment before looking back at her. "Do you know what happened yesterday at school?"

She frowned. "I…" She gazed off to the side as if trying to remember something, then sighed and shook her head. "I'm afraid not. Why? Is something wrong?"

He shook his head and stood up. "We can talk about it later. I'll get breakfast started."

She watched him in some confusion, trying desperately to see if there was any shred of memory she could find about the previous day. But there was just nothing and Bailey wasn't talking. He obviously didn't want to discuss it with her, though, so she left it alone.

Sarah stayed out until after lunch when Bebe made an appearance to watch a cartoon that had flashed by as he scrolled through the channels for something Sarah might like, and she was happy to cuddle against him and enjoy the show with her typical child's wonder.

John found himself smiling again, even laughing along with her in parts. It was clear to him that Bebe certainly didn't know what had happened or she would be a mess.

When Bitty finally resurfaced it was dinner and he was talking about a picture Bebe had drawn for him.

"…such an artist!"

Bitty stared at her plate in confusion for a moment, then up at him. "I… what?" she breathed nervously.

He paused, then offered her a gentle smile. "Bitty?"

She nodded sheepishly.

"Are you okay?"

She nodded again, looking back at her plate. "Yeah."

"Are you ready to talk about it?"

Her eyes flickered up to his for a split second before she looked away again with a shake of her head.

He sighed and nodded. "Okay. Well, when you've finished eating, I made some jello for dessert. Bebe's request, I'm afraid. But hopefully you like it too."

She nodded. "Yeah, I do."

He smiled and they ate peacefully, talking about movies she'd heard of that she wanted to see. It was after he'd put a bowl of jello in front of her and sat down that he grew more serious again.

"Babygirl, yesterday, when I talked to Mr Butler… you were suspended."

She looked up at him in confusion. "Suspended?"

"You can't go to school for a while. Two weeks, actually."

Relief washed over her and she smiled. "I can't go for two weeks?"

He frowned. "That's not a good thing, Bitty. It goes on your permanent record. It'll affect scholarships or grants, it'll affect what colleges will even let you apply. What happened? *I* know it wasn't your fault, but if you don't tell someone we can't contest it."

Bitty looked down at her bowl of jello. Bailey had obviously filled the older ones in at some point because they seemed to know.

'Fuck that! We can get out of school for two weeks, Bitty! No one would believe us anyway and this way we're free for two weeks! No one looking at us or whispering about us, no homework, no having to be around those boys! Keep quiet.'

'Scarlett! We shouldn't get in trouble for what they did.'

'I fucking told you he wanted to get in her pants! I told you*! No one listened. Not that it matters anyway. There's no point in dragging it out. Just forget it.'*

Bitty had to agree with Bailey this time. They were already in trouble, no one would believe her, and, like Scarlett said, they didn't have to go to school for two weeks!

"Look, I know they forced you, Bitty. Even if you didn't fight it or tell them not to, I know you can't even do that. They *raped* you, Bitty. But I can't drag you in there and tell everyone that if you won't tell them, too."

"It wasn't any different than anyone else," she mumbled. "It was exactly the same as every other time. That wasn't rape."

John put his elbows on the table and held his head in his hands for a moment before sitting back up with a sigh. "Fine. It's your choice. I'm not going to push you anymore. It's about time someone gave you a damn choice in your life. If you don't want to talk about it, we'll move on."

For a moment, he looked across the table at her, then stood up and walked around to hug her, holding her head to his stomach and stroking her hair. "You have choices now, Bitty, and I'm not going to take them away."

He stepped back and smiled at her sadly. "Let's have dessert and go watch a movie."

She gave him a tiny, grateful smile and picked up her spoon. John had said she had choices now. And he was allowing her this one. She met his eyes and her heart thrilled. She loved him so much.

Chapter Fifty-Two

~ Choice Two ~

The weekend passed like the first one had; chores in the morning, free time in the afternoon. She had more friends now and seemed like she had so much more energy! She even noticed her clothes were getting tighter with the constant supply of good food. Fowler had been caught bringing drugs into the facility Saturday morning and been fired on the spot, so there was no more fear of him anymore. Bailey had criticized her for 'getting too comfortable', but the rest of them felt like this really wasn't such a bad place at all. Even school wasn't horrible.

Mrs. Barnes had been incredibly patient that past week, now that she knew where Bitty's education extended to, and Bitty had been reading a chapter book over the weekend. She couldn't wait to show the teacher on Monday morning.

After breakfast on Monday, however, Bitty was called to the office. A feeling of dread washed over her and her face went white. Jennifer was waiting for her.

'Probably come to grill you some more about Mack.'

Jennifer smiled at her. This time she didn't bother going to the conference room.

"Bailey, we've got a hearing in front of the judge soon. We'll be deciding placement options for you."

Bitty stared at her in dismay for a moment. "I... I'm not staying here?" she whispered.

Jennifer shook her head with a bigger smile, obviously misunderstanding Bitty's shocked expression for one of pleasant surprise.

"It's not likely. The judge will probably assign you to a foster home so you can get out of here and get back to a little more normal life."

Bitty suddenly felt sick. She didn't want to go to some foster home. She was finally settling in somewhere! She had friends and a room and she was learning things for the first time in her life! She didn't want to leave!

"Let's get going. I'll get you a jacket for the walk over," Jennifer continued, unaware of Bitty's internal agony.

All Bitty could do was nod and try not to cry.

'We're gonna get out of fucking jail, Bitty, for god's sake! How can you be upset about that? No one would want to stay!'

****

They waited in the hall outside the little courtroom until they were called, Bitty huddled in her loaner jacket as if clinging to the center itself. She couldn't remember if it was the same judge as the last time, but Sarah said it was. He smiled at her as she took her place next to Jennifer.

"You're looking *much* healthier, Bailey. Glad to see it!" he said cheerily. "Alright, let's see what else we can do for you." He glanced down at his desk where her file presumably sat, then up at Jennifer. "Ms. Wright, would you say Ms. Carter is ready to be released? I know we're packed full in the center, so if she's stable..."

Jennifer nodded with a smile. "Yes, your honor. She's been a model patient. I read about her detox and it went perfectly, her behavior has been good after the initial settling in period, and I think she's ready to be moved out."

The judge nodded and wrote something down.

'Say something, Bitty. Say you don't want to leave. Say you like it there.'

'Yeah, Bitty, I wanna stay. Please? Ask them to stay.'

"Alright, well, I'm sure you'd like to get out of there before Christmas, huh?" he said, smiling at Bitty.

'Say something, Bitty! Say something!'

Bitty swallowed down her terror and opened her mouth. But she was too late. The judge turned to Jennifer.

"Ms. Wright, have you got a plan in place for her situation yet?"

Jennifer nodded. "Yes, your honor. I've got a family waiting for her who can take her today."

Bitty looked up at her in horror. Today!

The judge nodded with a smile. "Perfect. Alright, it seems we have things settled. Bailey Carter will be transferred into the custody of the foster family Ms. Wright has arranged effective today." He smiled at Bitty again and Jennifer herded her out the door before she could catch her breath.

****

Bitty was taken back to the juvenile center where she returned the jacket. It was lunch time but for the first time in a week, she wasn't hungry. She felt sick, scared and miserable. Jennifer sent her off to have lunch while she arranged for clothes for Bitty to wear out, since she didn't have anything but the loaner clothes she'd been given when they'd picked her up at the hotel.

Rebecca was excited for her until she saw how upset Bitty was. Then she was confused.

"You *don't* want to leave?" she asked incredulously.

Bitty shook her head. "I like it here. It's the best place I've ever lived."

Rebecca stared at her in shock. "*This* is the best place you've ever lived?"

Bitty nodded, staring into her food with tears in her eyes.

"Wow," Rebecca breathed. "I.... Wow... I'm sorry, Bitty." With a quick glance at the guard, she gave Bitty a quick, tight hug. Thankfully, the guard didn't notice.

***

Jennifer had taken some clothes that mostly fit Bitty from the collection at the center for that purpose. They were well used and were a little big, but they were clean and big was better than small. There was no point in going back to her cell, since she didn't have anything besides the book she'd been so eager to show Mrs. Barnes that morning, and they could return that to the shelf for her. Tears stung at her eyes for a moment when she thought of not seeing the teacher again, but she clenched her jaw and pushed them down with all the other feelings that hurt too much to think about for long.

On the ride to the foster home, Bitty stayed silent and just looked out the window. She really didn't trust herself to speak even if she'd had something to say anyway.

Jennifer pulled up in front of a two story brick home with a little yard. There was a Christmas tree shining in the window. That surprised Bitty. Through all the stories she'd heard, she'd imagined a foster home as a den of misery or a different kind of prison, but this place looked like a regular home, like a family actually lived there.

When Jennifer got out, Bitty followed slowly, her stomach in knots as they approached the door and Jennifer rang the bell. She could hear footsteps on the other side and a moment later the door opened. A slightly plump blonde woman stood in the doorway with a bright smile and shining blue eyes.

"Jennifer, afternoon! Come on in!"

Jennifer smiled brightly back at her and stepped inside. "Good afternoon, Chelsea. Thank you."

Chelsea shut the door behind her and led them into a cozy looking living room. It was the room with the tree in it.

"Chelsea, I'd like you to meet Bailey. Bailey, this is Chelsea Archer."

Chelsea put her hand out to shake Bitty's. "Welcome, Bailey. Do you like to be called Bailey?"

Bitty shook her hand nervously. "I–I like Bitty, if it's okay?"

"Bitty. You can call me Chelsea." She looked over at Jennifer. "Pete is in his office. I'll give him a shout in a minute. Would either of you like something to drink?"

"I'm fine, thanks, Chelsea," Jennifer replied.

Bitty shook her head in silence and the plump woman nodded.

"Alright, I'll go get Pete and then we can talk. Have a seat." She bustled out and Jennifer gestured to the couch, sitting down beside Bitty.

"The Archers have two other foster kids living here, but you each get your own room. They both work from home most days of the week; Pete is an IT consultant, I think, and Chelsea does transcription services."

Bitty just nodded, looking at the Christmas tree. She felt like she'd never seen one so beautiful, except maybe in the store windows downtown sometimes when she happened to drive past there with a john.

Chelsea returned a few minutes later with a somewhat stocky man, his dark hair thinning a little, but his green eyes sparkling almost as brightly as his wife's. He came over to shake her hand too.

"Bitty, right?"

She nodded slightly and shook his hand uncomfortably.

The couple sat down on the couch opposite them and Jennifer started talking about Bitty. After the first few sentences, Bitty tuned her out and turned her attention to the Christmas tree again.

'Oh, Bitty! I wanna see! I wanna see! Please? Please let me see!'

'Stop it! We gotta be careful here. You can see later maybe.'

'Bailey, please? Please, Bitty?'

'I said shut up!'

"Bitty?"

Bitty's head whipped around and she looked at Chelsea with a nervous, guilty look.

Chelsea just smiled. "I was asking if you'd like to go up and see your room? Then we can go out and get you a few things that you'll need."

"Oh. Okay," Bitty said softly with a little nod.

Jennifer stood up with the couple and Bitty followed suit slowly.

"I'll check back in next week. If you need anything, you know how to get me," Jennifer was saying. She turned to Bitty. "If you need anything, don't be afraid to let them know. I have to get going since I have a couple more check-ins to do before five." She walked with Pete to the door and waved to Bitty and Chelsea as she went. Bitty heard her talking softly to Pete near the door.

"Alright, well, let's take you upstairs and let you have a look, then we can talk about what things you'll need while you're here."

Bitty nodded and climbed the stairs behind Chelsea, her insides roiling. On the one hand, she was terrified to be in a stranger's house with nothing but the clothes on her back and no idea where she was, but on the other hand they seemed like nice people, so maybe things wouldn't be horrible.

Her room was the farthest from the stairs, right next to the bathroom. It wasn't big, but it was nice. A twin bed against one wall boasted a pink comforter. The underside showed a little bit of blue where the edge was slightly bent up, so Bitty assumed it was so they could flip it over depending on who was staying in the room at the time. The sheets were a unisex green like the room, and there was a little bedside table beside it. On another wall stood a four drawer dresser beside the door to a closet. It was kind of like the room she'd had at the center.

"Jennifer said you don't have anything at all, so we'll need to get you a hairbrush, toothbrush and toothpaste, deodorant, underwear, clothes, winter things. It'll be fun, won't it? I don't usually get to go on a shopping spree, especially with a girl."

Bitty just nodded and followed her back downstairs. Pete must have returned to his office because Chelsea led her through to the back of the house and knocked on a half open door before peeking inside. He held up his hand and after a minute he said goodbye and hit a button on a headset before turning around to smile at them.

"I'm taking Bitty out to get her things. Will you meet the bus and get Sylvia?"

He nodded and checked his watch. "Sure. I'll finish up here and then I'll take a break for the day. Have fun, ladies!"

Chelsea led her back through the house to an attached garage off the kitchen. "I'll give you the official tour of the house when we get back, but

I think Sylvia would like to do the honors, so I figured we'll go get your things first. She's at school. So is Damien."

Bitty let the woman talk while they drove and headed into the thrift shop. To her amazement, she was allowed to pick out five whole outfits, choosing whatever she liked from the racks! When she'd made her choices and they'd checked out, Chelsea took them to a department store for socks, underwear, and boots; then to a drug store for her personal items before taking her back home.

When they got inside with her bags, there was a little girl and a teenage boy who looked to be several years older than Bitty sitting at the kitchen table with Pete.

"How'd the shopping go?" Pete asked.

"All set!" Chelsea said on the way through to the stairs. She and Bitty set the bags on the bed and went back downstairs.

"Bitty," she said when they returned to the kitchen, "this is Sylvia and Damien. Guys, this is Bitty."

Sylvia beamed at her, a few gaps in her teeth that may or may not have been loose teeth. "Hi, Bitty." She twirled her wispy brown hair as she watched Bitty take the seat beside her.

Damien looked up from his notebook briefly, then did a double take and regarded her with more interest, but still didn't say anything.

Dinner was punctuated by Sylvia's happy chatter as she recounted her day in great detail. When asked about his day, Damien simply grunted, "Okay." Thankfully, no one asked Bitty about her day.

Damien stayed at the table after dinner to do his homework and Sylvia was thrilled to be allowed to give Bitty the grand tour. The house was cozy and clean, and Bitty found herself relaxing as the little girl led her around with Chelsea bringing up the rear and mentioning things the child forgot.

"Alright, time to get ready for bed," Chelsea announced when they reached Bitty's room at the end of the hall. "No. No complaining or no story."

Bitty looked up at the woman in surprise as Sylvia sighed and went to the bathroom. "You... read stories to her?"

Chelsea smiled. "Every night. I can read to you, if you'd like?"

Bitty shook her head quickly even as Jay and Bebe cried out in delight at the prospect.

'Oh, Bitty! Why? Why don't you want her to read to us? Please?'

'Yeah, please? I want a story, Bitty!'

'Shut up, you two! Get over it."

"Alright, well, if you change your mind, you let me know, okay?"

Bitty nodded.

"You can watch a little TV if you'd like. I need to get Sylvia to bed and Pete is making sure Damien does his homework."

Bitty nodded again and followed Chelsea down to the family room with the TV. The woman turned it on for her and handed her the remote with a smile.

"TV rules are: no horror movies, no adult movies, no movies rated R without permission, keep it at a reasonable volume, and turn it off as soon as you're told. Agreed?"

Bitty nodded, earning her another smile from her foster mother before the woman bustled off to take care of Sylvia. Bitty sank down self-consciously onto the couch and began flipping through channels until she found a cartoon that looked interesting. In a few minutes, she was smiling and had relaxed.

By the time Damien came through from doing his homework, Chelsea had returned.

"Half an hour, Bitty, then bed, okay?"

Bitty nodded and glanced nervously at the older boy as he flopped down beside her, then turned her attention back to the next episode of the cartoon. It finished just as Chelsea came through again to tell her it was time for bed.

Damien took the remote and watched her leave, then began flipping channels.

"Off to bed?" Pete asked as he walked downstairs.

Bitty nodded.

"Alrighty, well sleep tight!"

Bitty half expected him to say something about bed bugs biting, but she figured maybe he knew that might be a little too close to home for someone like her. Chelsea made sure she brushed her teeth, then waited outside Bitty's bedroom while she changed.

Once she'd finished, Bitty opened the door again and climbed into the bed. Chelsea sat down on the end of it and gave her a gentle smile.

"I have a nightlight in here that's light sensitive, so it'll turn on when the other lights go out. If you don't want it, you can unplug it, but I haven't had anyone unplug it yet. If you need anything, our bedroom is just down the hall where Sylvia showed you earlier. You can come get me, okay?"

Bitty nodded very slightly.

"Alright, well, goodnight, Bitty. I'll see you in the morning." She stood and straightened the covers before leaving the room, shutting the door behind her. Sure enough, as soon as Bitty turned out the little lamp on the bedside table, a soft blue glow appeared near the floor by the door. It wasn't overly bright, and the little amount of light was nicely reassuring.

'I like it here, Bitty.'

'*Yeah. Me too.*'

'*They do seem nice...*'

Bitty had to agree. So far, anyway.

Chapter Fifty-Three

* Choice One *

John took the day off on Monday and they stayed home. He didn't seem angry that he'd had to stay home with her, but she felt like he wasn't very happy about it. Sarah suggested it was just guilty feelings and that he wasn't actually upset, but that didn't really lay Bitty's worries to rest. It wasn't a bad day on the whole, though. And not going to school was definitely a good point!

When he tucked her in that night, he told her she'd be coming to work with him again until the end of the year and he would find some online classes for her. She wasn't thrilled, but he promised her she'd still be coming in to the office with him and he'd help her throughout the day between patients.

Tuesday morning, Bitty packed some things to do for the day, since John still had to finish her enrollment in the online classes. Coloring books and crayons went in, along with a couple of easy-read books and some plain paper to color on. John also packed a book of stickers and Bebe's unicorn on the top of the bag before Bitty closed it up, and brought along his laptop.

Joan gave her a welcoming smile when they walked in, and said that she'd arranged the empty office for Bitty to use while she was with John. There was a couch that had apparently been in John's office before he got his new one, and a spare coffee table. John plugged in the laptop for her to play some games, and reminded her about the snacks in the breakroom, then gave her a hug and kissed the top of her head before going to meet his first patient.

The rest of the day was similar to the first day she'd spent there when he'd taken her in. Except this time she was more comfortable, both in the room and with John. She had relaxed around him now, especially since he'd stopped himself the previous week and promised that was the end of it. For several days she'd expected him to approach her again, but he had stayed true to his word. And Sarah had said she thought that since the incident at school, she truly believed he wouldn't try anything with her again. It allowed Bitty to rest some of her worries with someone for the first time in her life. It felt good.

John found some games she could play on the computer, and she spent the day coloring, drawing, playing games, and even taking a nap. She wasn't in the least bit sad to be out of school. As far as she was concerned, that was the best thing that could ever have happened.

John was smiling when it was time to go, and she could tell he had something to tell her. She was right.

"I finished getting you registered for online classes, babygirl," he told her as they pulled out of the parking lot. "You'll start tomorrow. You'll still have to come to work with me until the end of the year, because I can't leave you alone, but you'll have something constructive to do. And before you get too upset, I've arranged for the classes to be a little less rigorous. They'll work at the level you're at right now and try to catch you up gently." He reached for her hand and gave it a gentle squeeze. "It'll be better than the school. I've taken you out permanently, so you'll never have to go back."

She looked over at him in surprise. "Really?"

He smiled. "Really. You're finished there. And I'm looking into a different kind of school for you starting next year."

"What kind of school?" she asked nervously.

"I'll tell you more about it once I know how things are looking for getting you in."

She nodded and looked back out the window, turning the possibilities over in her head. If the online classes were going to be different than the school classes, then maybe it wouldn't be *so* bad. The only thing she'd really miss was art. She'd really enjoyed those classes.

With a sudden pang of regret that brought tears to her eyes, she realized she'd never get to see her sculpture. Yet another thing lost because of who and what she was.

'Whores don't need artwork.'

'Scarlett! That was uncalled for! It was special.'

'You know it's true, Sarah! That's all we are and that's all we'll ever be. We don't need art or school or anything else to let people fuck us. It's not like anything is ever gonna change. I thought things would be different now but they're not. They never will be. Every guy who looks at us just

wants to get inside us! There's no point in even wanting anything else. It just hurts, Sarah! It hurts *wanting to be something that you can't be and I'm tired of hurting! I'm so tired of hurting!'*

Bitty had never heard Scarlett being so hopeless before. She'd always seemed to be reasonably content with things as they were, as long as they didn't get hurt too badly. She'd thought she even *liked* sex. The only inkling she'd ever had that she didn't was the other week when she had said she was happy not to have to have sex with John. But that hadn't been the same as what Scarlett had just revealed. Scarlett sounded... hopeless. She didn't sound like she enjoyed it, or missed it, or had ever really wanted to be what everyone always thought she was. Suddenly, Bitty felt even worse about the cruel jibes Bailey was always making about Scarlett being a slut and a whore and nothing else. She'd always thought Bailey was being mean, but she realized now just *how* mean it had been.

"I'm sorry," she whispered.

John looked over. "Sorry for what? For asking about it? You can ask questions, Bitty. I may not always be able to answer them, but you're allowed to ask anything you want now. I won't get mad."

She shook her head. "N... no. I was just... nothing. Sorry."

He glanced at her curiously but left her to her thoughts.

Bitty found it hard to think about much else all through the rest of the evening. For the first time, she began to wonder if Bailey really liked being their protector, or if she felt she had to, to fill a role. Did Sarah want to care for them and love them like a mother, or was she just doing what she knew they needed? And what about that other girl they didn't know much about? What was she 'for'?

When John was tucking her in at bedtime, he sat down on the edge of the bed and considered her for a minute. "Babygirl, I'd like to get you in to see a therapist. It doesn't have to be me, probably *shouldn't* be me actually. But I want you to see someone. You don't have to talk about stuff you don't want to. You don't even have to talk about your past if you'd rather not. But it would help to have someone who could show you how to work with the others, communicate better, find ways to make everyone a little more happy with the situation.

"I'd love to be able to do that for you, but I think there might be things that someone else could do for you that you wouldn't feel comfortable telling me about. I'm not going to force you if you don't want to, but I do want you to go to *one* session. Just one. If you hate it, then we'll work on things together, okay?"

She picked nervously at the blanket and nodded a little bit. "K."

He smiled and stroked her hair back from her face. "That's my good girl. Thank you." He stood up and leaned over her to kiss her forehead, then tucked the blanket more tightly around her and left the room, leaving her to her thoughts again.

~ Choice Two ~

Bitty was terrified of going to school when she woke up the following day. She had managed not to think much about it the day before, but now that she had to get ready for a brand new school she was beginning to feel sick with nerves.

Chelsea and Pete both greeted her downstairs with their seemingly usual smiles and offered her three different kinds of cereal for breakfast.

Damien glanced up from his brooding to watch her sit down, then went back to scowling over his bowl.

"Hi, Bitty!" Sylvia cried in greeting when she came in. The child sat down beside her with a big smile, her blue eyes shining like gems. Bitty had never *seen* such blue eyes before. It was surprising she hadn't noticed them the day before, but then, she hadn't been sitting so close to the girl, and she'd been nervous about meeting them all as well.

"Bitty, I'm going to drive you to school today and get you set with the office. You can ride the bus home with Damien," Chelsea told her.

Bitty nodded silently and focused on eating her cereal. She had a feeling Pete and Chelsea would expect her to finish it and she didn't want to know how things would turn out if she didn't.

'They're not mean, Bitty. They won't mind.'

'You don't know that. They seem nice but you never know what makes a person snap. Wasted food could be their thing.'

'Bailey, stop. I think Jay is right, Bitty. Sylvia wouldn't be so happy all the time if they were mean.'

'Well Damien isn't happy.'

'He's older so he's probably got more problems than Sylvia. If things were bad, she'd be upset too. I think Jay's right.'

Bitty nodded unnoticeably but it got the message across to the others and they settled down again.

Chelsea drove both her and Damien to the high school. Bitty was surprised by that. She'd expected to be going to a separate school, since he seemed so much older than she was, but it seemed that the junior high was in the same building. Damien was in 11th grade. Bitty had been fairly sure he was older than her, but she hadn't realized he was that much older. She had guessed fifteen or sixteen at the most.

When they reached the school, Damien stomped off to his class without a word and Chelsea led Bitty to the office to get her things ready.

The secretary obviously knew Chelsea well and they processed her smoothly as if they'd both done it a million times. The lady was nice enough, though Bitty felt like one of the office assistants gave her the typical 'street trash' once over. It made her feel dirty again and she looked away with her arms around her waist.

Her class was just around the corner and she followed along behind the two women with her donation school supplies and backpack. Again, she got quite a few stares from the students when she was brought in and shown where to sit, and she slouched down in her chair as if she could hide from them. She found this room a lot different than the schools she'd been in before she quit going years ago, and far different from the cozy, almost reassuring classroom at the center.

When the bell rang after the teacher took attendance and passed out notes reminding everyone of a bake sale, Bitty looked around in confusion when everyone started standing up. She stood up and gathered her things slowly, watching the rest of the class file out. To her dismay, instead of all going in one direction, they split up and went in opposite directions down the halls!

"What am I supposed to do?" she breathed in horror.

'I don't know. Did the teacher say something? Was there something you were supposed to do?'

"I don't know!" she whispered back. "I don't know what to do, Sarah! What do I do?"

'Grow up, for a start. Just pick a direction or something. Figure it out, moron.'

Tears filled Bitty's eyes at Bailey's comment as anxiety took a tighter hold on her and she simply stood there, looking from side to side.

"What are you doing?" asked an impatient voice behind her.

Bitty spun and immediately cowered in fear, her eyes wide and her shoulders hunched. The teacher stood waiting with her eyebrows raised expectantly.

"You're supposed to be in class. What are you doing?" she repeated.

"I... I uh... I didn't... I don't... they all... everyone went different ways. I don't..."

"Well, what does your schedule say?"

"My... schedule?"

"Your *schedule*, yes! What does it say?"

"I..."

"Look in your folder," the woman said, snapping her fingers.

Bitty flinched a little and struggled to balance her notebooks, pencil box, backpack, and folders as she opened the top one.

"There, see? The top piece of paper with your schedule. What class does it list?"

"Oh... I..." Bitty stared down at the tiny writing in a table with weird, seemingly random times on one side and days on the top. 9:21, 10:05, 1:53. Bitty couldn't imagine why they were at such odd times. She also couldn't understand the first thing on the list.

"S–Sock... sock-ee... sock-eeaww-log-eye..." she mumbled.

"What?" the teacher asked blankly. "Let me see that." She took the paper from the folder and checked the schedule, then eyed Bitty suspiciously. "Sociology."

Bitty's face turned bright red and she looked down at the floor.

The teacher sighed. "Come on, I'll show you where to go."

Bitty nodded gratefully and followed the teacher down the hall. As they walked, she explained how to read the schedule and the room numbers beneath the subjects. Bitty was, of course, late for the class and slunk in with a red face to slouch in another chair.

The next class, she wasn't quite so late for, since it was just down the hall, and the one after that she asked the teacher for directions and so was finally on time.

Almost every class was ridiculously hard. Bitty couldn't even understand half of what was in the textbooks, and was given all the work she'd been unable to finish in class as homework. By the end of the day, her backpack was straining.

At least she managed to find the bus circle and get onto the correct bus. Damien slid in beside her, eyeing her backpack. His, too, was stuffed as full as hers. As usual, he didn't talk, though he kept looking at her throughout the ride. Bitty did her best to keep her eyes out the window.

When Damien stood up at one of the stops, she got up too and followed him off the bus. Pete was there and she headed over to him while Damien just stomped down the street to the house. She had been about to ask where Sylvia was when another bus pulled up and the happy little girl bounded off the bus into Pete's arms.

Bitty watched curiously.

'I thought she was a foster kid.'

'Me too. Maybe she's not. Maybe she's theirs?'

On the walk back to the house, Sylvia held his hand and told him about her day while Bitty trudged along behind them in the falling snow. She was exhausted. It had been tiring enough doing school at the center with Mrs. Barnes for a few hours every morning, but at least she had worked with Bitty at a level she could understand. Today had been more than twice as long as that, with work four times harder at least, and she'd been stressed and anxious and nervous the entire time. All she wanted to do was curl up in her bed and sleep.

"Do you have any homework, Bitty?" Pete asked as soon as they got inside.

She sighed and looked at the floor. "Yeah."

"Okay, well, let's get a snack and then we can do some of it before dinner."

Bitty just nodded and sat down at the table while Chelsea cut up some cheese and apples for all of them. She was beginning to see why Damien was grumpy. If he had as much homework as she did every night, there was no wonder!

The rest of the evening, it was all Bitty could do not to cry as she tried to work through her homework. Damien kept looking up to watch her with an inscrutable expression, especially when she stumbled over things he probably thought were simple. She wished she could go somewhere else and work on it, but Pete had simply told her to take her things out. He'd said nothing about being able to go somewhere else, and Damien had been at the table yesterday.

By the time it was finally bedtime, Bitty was too tired even to want to watch tv. She crawled into her bed and curled up with a whimper of misery. Once again, she was beginning to wish she was back at the center.

After Chelsea came in to say goodnight, Bitty turned over and cried herself to sleep quietly, dreading the rest of the week.

Chapter Fifty-Four

* Choice One *

Bebe limped into the kitchen the following morning in sock feet and sat down at the table with a smile for John. He smiled back in surprise.

"No crutches? Does your foot feel better?"

She nodded, rubbing her eyes. "Yup! And I'm tired of them. Can I be done with them?"

He turned back to the stove where he was stirring something. "I suppose so. You won't be walking around much, and I can just bring them along in case you need them later."

"*YES!*" she cried gleefully.

He laughed and took two bowls from the cabinet. "Do you want honey in your oatmeal?"

"Can I have raisins too?"

"Let me check." After searching through a cabinet full of random grocery items, he found a box of raisins at the back and held it up triumphantly. "TA-DAAAA!"

She giggled and waited for him to put the bowl in front of her, then added her toppings.

"Can I go to work with you again today?" she asked hopefully.

He nodded and swallowed his coffee. "Yup. You'll be coming to work with me for the next few days." After taking the seat beside her, he gave her a conspiratorial smile. "I have a surprise for you today after we're done at work."

Her face lit up eagerly. "What is it? What's the surprise?"

He shook his head and zipped his mouth. "Nope. Not telling. You'll just have to wait and see!"

"*Please*? I *have* to know! I'll *die* if I don't know! Please, please, *pleeeease?*"

"Sorry, babygirl. But I'll give you a hint. It's green... and it smells..."

She stared at him with an incredulous look. "It's green and smells?" she repeated.

He nodded and winked at her. "That's all you're getting outta me!"

Despite her pleading through the rest of breakfast and the drive, he only grinned at her and repeated his hint. Eventually, Bebe got frustrated and Sarah slipped back out again just as they pulled into the parking lot.

"Ready?"

She looked around quickly, then nodded. When he reached for the crutches in the backseat, she began to get out of the car and waited for him to hand them to her like he always did. This time he just shouldered his satchel and turned to her expectantly. Then she realized she was wearing two boots.

"I'm not... I'm not using crutches today?"

His eyebrows rose briefly, then he smiled. "Ah, sorry. Not Bebe?"

Sarah shook her head and was about to tell him her name when he held up his hand.

"Don't tell me." He considered her for a moment, then smiled. "Alright, I think I know... Sarah? Or is it Bitty?"

She nodded. "It's Sarah. How did you know?" she asked curiously as they began to walk slowly into the building.

"You each hold yourselves a little differently. Bitty sort of hunches up and keeps tucking her hair behind her ear. Bebe is just more flamboyant and Jay is sort of... I don't know how to describe it; he tugs at his shirt a lot, and he moves differently. Scarlett is kind of flirty, smoothes her hand over her clothes frequently. Bailey... well, I've only ever seen her ready to bite my head off, but she's more rigid and tense, and her eyes are different. And you, well, you're sort of calm and gentle, and you just have this sense of maturity, I suppose you'd call it."

She was watching him as they walked, fascinated by his descriptions of them all. She hadn't realized they were that obvious and it both worried and pleased her.

"I always thought we were discrete and no one could tell unless we said names or talked about Bitty like we weren't her, you know? I didn't know we were different like that outside."

He shook his head. "I think I can see it because I've spent so much time with all of you, and I know to look for the little things. I had another patient before like you. I could tell after a while who was out."

"Oh. What happened to her?"

"Happened?"

"You said 'had', not 'have'."

"Oh, right. She moved. After we worked together for a few years, she learned to manage her life a lot better and everyone began to work together much better, until she was organized enough to get a job. Her system didn't work as well together as yours does, so she was a mess for a long time before she came to me. It didn't help that other doctors didn't believe her or tried to medicate her for schizophrenia which made things a lot worse. So anyway, she put things together and got a job as a custodian for the university a couple of cities away."

"Why did she move so far away?"

"It was better pay than most jobs like that, and she saw it as a way to make a fresh start away from people she used to know. I referred her to a friend of mine and made sure to get her up to speed on my patient, and she's doing well."

They entered the waiting area and greeted Joan. Sarah mulled things over while they got things set up in the back office.

"Okay, I had Joan keep my first appointment open so I can show you the ropes on the school site. Some of it's online, a lot of it is offline, like reading a book or working out math problems to show your work, things like that. If you need help, or get lost, hang tight and I'll help you between patients as much as I can, okay?"

She nodded and sat down to watch as he gave her a quick tour of the site and explained some pages to get her started. Once he'd gone through things, he let her have the mouse to explore more for herself.

"I know you won't get much done today, it's just to explore, but if there's something you'd like to try, go for it! I'll check in with you in a little bit." He smiled at her from the doorway, then went next door to meet his first patient of the day.

~ Choice Two ~

Bitty woke up with difficulty the following morning. She wasn't just tired from the long day before, but it was the knowledge of what was facing her again that day. It had been mentally, emotionally, and physically exhausting and she was dreading going through another one. But there wasn't any choice.

'There's never been a choice for anything, Bitty. Why the fuck do you keep hoping for one? It's not like it'll ever happen and it's stupid to expect one!'

Bitty hunched up at the bitterness in Bailey's tone. She was probably right, but Bitty couldn't help hoping sometimes. It was stupid, but it was nice for that little moment the belief lasted.

She showered and dressed in silence before making her way to the kitchen for breakfast. Damien wasn't down yet but Sylvia greeted her with her usual smile which cheered Bitty up a little bit. At least she didn't feel quite so miserable as she sat down and began to eat the oatmeal in front of her. It wasn't bad, but she wished there were raisins to go into it.

'Damn, picky much? It's food! Just eat it!'

'She knows it's food, Bailey. She's not refusing it.'

'Well I don't see why the fuck she should be wanting more.'

"What?"

Bitty looked up at Chelsea. "What?"

"I thought I heard you say 'Asians'."

Bitty blushed a little and looked down at her bowl with a little shake of her head. "No. I... I was thinking about raisins."

"Oh. For your oatmeal?"

Bitty nodded with her head still down.

"I have some! Don't be afraid to ask!" She pulled out a glass canning jar of raisins and put it in front of Bitty with a spoon. "I almost always have raisins. Pete's favorite cookies are oatmeal raisin. And yet," she added with an amused look at her husband, "he doesn't like them in his *oatmeal!*"

She grinned back at Bitty and resumed packing Sylvia's lunch while Bitty spooned a few raisins into her bowl with a smile.

"Pete has a work meeting this afternoon and I'm taking Sylvia to the dentist, so dinner will be a little late. You can help yourself to some snacks and *try* to get started on your homework, you two. I'll be home as soon as I can to help you and get dinner on. Damien, I'm giving you my trust today, alright? You've earned it."

Damien looked up in surprise, then down at his bowl with a nod, though his face looked a little less dark than it had before.

That morning, Bitty was catching the bus with Damien. They were both silent on the ride again, but she didn't mind. There was too much squirming in her belly to be able to talk anyway.

The day went by the same as it had the previous day, though this time she was a little more familiar with how the schedule worked and it was only a matter of deciphering what each subject was and finding the rooms.

Once again, she was exhausted by the end of the day and slouched down in her seat on the bus. Damien slid in beside her again, which surprised her because, unlike the previous day, they were some of the first ones on the bus, which meant he had *chosen* to sit beside her. She had figured it was out of necessity the previous day.

They were still silent during the bus ride and the short walk to the house from the bus stop at the end of the street but Bitty really didn't mind. She was too tired for conversation and she actually sort of appreciated the chance to unwind.

Chelsea had left them a note on the counter with the phone numbers to reach her and Pete at, as well as a list of appropriate snacks and a reminder to do their homework. Bitty opened the fridge and took out a stick of string cheese and a little tub of yogurt for her snack. When she stepped back to shut the fridge, she backed into Damien who was standing right behind her.

"Sorry," she murmured, trying to move to the side so he could get what he was looking for.

He stopped her.

Bitty looked up at him nervously and shrank back at the look on his face. She knew that look. She hated that look.

Unconsciously, she began to shake her head and shift to the side, desperately trying to convince herself it was her imagination and he was just trying to get his own snack from the fridge.

He pressed forward, forcing her back until she almost fell into the open fridge as he began unbuckling his pants.

"You heard Chelsea. I'm in charge."

"Please," she whispered hopelessly, turning her face away.

"Don't act like you're not a slut. I can tell you want it."

Tears filled her eyes as he pushed her to her knees in front of him. There wasn't any point in arguing. It didn't matter anymore. She just obeyed as her snack fell to the floor.

Chapter Fifty-Five

* Choice One *

Sarah browsed the site for a while, trying out some of the educational games and poking around at the assignments.

'I'm bored.'

'Me too. Let's make paper airplanes again!'

'Why did he even bother signing us up for this stupid school stuff if it's almost next year already and he says he's got another school to send us to?'

"I don't know, Scarlett, but it's interesting. We'll make paper airplanes in a little while. I want to try some more of these quizzes. They're fun."

She smiled softly at the internal sigh of resignation and went back to what she'd been doing. They passed the day happily, taking turns at the things they wanted to do, though Sarah kept as much control as she could over the little ones when they were out after Jay began getting too excited about his paper airplanes and made too much noise. John had been very kind about it, but Jay had still retreated in tears for a while. The boy was much more cautious after that and they had no more incidents.

John had ordered subs again for lunch that day, allowing them each to make their choices for fillings. Bitty was beginning to feel a little bit grateful to Cody after a while. If he hadn't done what he'd done, she'd still be drowning in homework at school. And it really didn't make much of a difference having twenty more guys in her in the string of johns she'd already had; at least, that's what she managed to convince herself. Things were actually pretty good.

After his last patient, John came in with a smile and Bebe pounced on him in excitement.

"What's the surprise? What's the surprise? You said you'd tell me! What is it?"

He laughed and hugged her tightly to him. "Okay. Okay. I know." He stepped back to look at her face. "We're going to pick out a Christmas tree."

Her eyes widened so much they were completely rimmed in white. "*A Christmas tree?*" she shrieked in delight.

He laughed again as she began getting her shoes on and heading for the door.

"Hold on, babygirl! We have to pack up our things." He turned to look at the coffee table strewn with coloring books and crayons, then seemed to reconsider. "Tell you what, we'll leave everything but the laptop here until Friday. Then we'll bring it all home, okay?"

She beamed at him with an eager nod and he chuckled as he gathered up the laptop and followed her out, grabbing her crutches from next to the door as he passed.

Bebe could hardly contain her glee during the drive and it seemed that John was having just as much fun watching her. She talked non-stop the entire time and only paused when they pulled into the parking lot of the hardware store in front of the row of Christmas trees.

"Okay, rules."

She deflated slightly and turned her attention to him.

He held up one finger. "Number one, we can only pick *one*, okay?"

She grinned and nodded.

"Number two," he said, holding up two fingers, "it has to be the prettiest."

She beamed and nodded again.

"Number three," he added a third, "It can't be too big or we won't be able to get it home. Deal?"

She gave an excited squeal and nodded eagerly. "Yes, Daddy! Yes! I promise!"

He laughed and leaned over to hug her, then got out and came around to hold her hand.

Bebe spent half an hour walking up and down the rows of trees over and over again. By the end, she had narrowed it down to three trees: a spruce, a fir, and a pine. John looked up images of each kind on his phone so she could see what it would look like unbundled from its rope bindings and in the end, she chose the fir because 'it looked the fattest and happiest'.

Once they'd paid for it and John had strapped it to the roof of the car, Bebe thought they were finished. To her surprise, John didn't drive straight home. Instead, he stopped at another store a little further down and smiled at her.

"I want to buy you a Christmas ornament for the tree every year. You each get to pick one out, and then we're going to write a little note after Christmas saying what your favorite memory of that Christmas was, each of you. Then every year when we decorate the tree, you can read them and remember what everyone's favorite thing was."

'That is the most wonderful idea I've ever heard!'

'Bullshit. He's acting like we're gonna be around forever. Who says we're staying that long, huh? I'm sick of him taking it for granted that we belong to him.'

'He's not saying that, Bailey. He's giving us a home and memories and Christmas, Bailey! He's not bad. Why can't you see that?'

'And why can't you see that just cuz he's being nice doesn't mean he's not still a sick fuck.'

Bebe, however, had managed to completely ignore the bickering inside and was walking into the store hand in hand with him as if she were walking on air. As with the tree, it took her forever to finally settle on an ornament of a puppy in a package with a bow on its head. Then there were choices to be made by the rest of them. Only Bailey refused to pick something, though John seemed to have expected that, and with a wink to Bitty -who was out at that point after Bailey spurned his request for her to come out- he picked up the box containing a Grinch ornament.

Bitty giggled, her eyes shining with delight. "Perfect," she whispered.

John chuckled and put it in the basket as they made their way to the checkout. "Maybe next year it'll be Scrooge? Though, I like to think maybe she'll change her mind by next year."

Since it had taken so long to choose the tree and ornaments, John decided to stop for fast food on the way home, once again getting a combo for Bitty and a (thankfully gender neutral) kid's meal for Bebe and Jay to share.

"I'm afraid we'll have to decorate it tomorrow, since it's getting pretty late now. But we'll take it in and set it up tonight."

Bitty nodded, her smile no less glowing.

It took John a few minutes to wrestle the tree down from the roof and a few more minutes to get it into the living room. With an exaggerated swipe of his brow, he flopped down on the couch and closed his eyes.

"Whew! I'm done! I think we'll just have to leave it there for the night!"

Bitty sat down beside him, trying to hide her disappointment. "Okay."

He opened his eyes and looked over at her, then swiftly pulled her into his arms and kissed the top of her head.

"Oh, babygirl. I'm sorry. I was only playing. I forgot. Of *course* we're going to put it up tonight. You were supposed to argue and wheedle until I did what you wanted. I forgot you're not like my other little girls. I'm sorry." He squeezed her again and pulled back to smile at her, relieved to find her smile had returned.

"You can come with me to the garage to get the tree stand, or you can wait here."

"I'll come," she said shyly, following him out.

After a few minutes, John had loaded her up with some strings of lights and glittering garlands, and was lugging a large tree stand in behind her.

"Alright, babygirl. Where shall we put it?"

"I get to choose?" she breathed in shock.

"Of course! I bet you'll pick the best spot."

She smiled shyly and looked around. "M... maybe by the fireplace...?"

He nodded. "By the fireplace it is!" He put the base down a few feet from the mantle and grabbed a pair of scissors from a drawer in the kitchen. "You'll have to tell me which is the best side."

She nodded as he cut the ropes and the tree fell open. While he held it up, she peered around to the other side, trying to decide which side was the most perfect.

"I think this one is the prettiest," she declared, though with some reservation, since it was the back side.

John didn't seem to be bothered by that; he simply nodded, spun around with the tree, and lifted it up into the base. A few minutes later, they were both standing back to look at it with smiles on their faces.

"Alright, let's get the lights on."

Bitty looked up at him in surprise. "I thought we weren't decorating it today?"

"Hmm? Oh, no. Not with ornaments and stuff, but I think it would be nice to get the lights and garland on it at least. That way it's pretty when we go to bed, and when we decorate it tomorrow it's less hassle."

She grinned at him and began helping him by holding the neatly organized strings of lights for him. A long while later, he stepped back with a grin.

"Do you want to do the honors?"

"What?"

"Do you want to plug in the lights?" He shook his head. "On second thought, why don't you stay here and I'll plug them in, so you can see it better when it lights up. You just tell me when."

She nodded and watched while he dimmed the room lights, then moved behind the tree. When she was sure he was ready, she nodded again. "Ready."

He grinned and plugged in the lights.

It took Bitty's breath away. The soft yellow glow lit up the darkened room like a magical aura, catching the silvery reflective flecks in the garland and making the whole thing sparkle. John came up behind her and wrapped his arms around her shoulders, kissing the top of her head with a smile.

"What do you think, babygirl?" he murmured softly.

"It's…" She shook her head very slightly. "It's the most beautiful thing I've ever seen," she breathed.

He hugged her more tightly for a moment. "Tomorrow, it'll be even more beautiful once we put the ornaments on it."

Bitty didn't see how that was going to be possible, but she nodded anyway. When she went to bed a few minutes later, memories of the beautiful, glowing Christmas tree pushed aside the misery of the previous week and she fell asleep with a smile.

~ Choice Two ~

The floor was cold. But it was clean at least, Bitty reminded herself. She'd been taken in much worse places. Her eyes fell on the legs of the kitchen table and chairs as she lay with her head turned to the side. She began to imagine all the shoes that must have scuffed it, kicking happily while eating, being hooked around them during homework time, bumping against them, knocking into them as they went running by. It was a family table, marred and chipped in a loved and worn way instead of the battered and broken way her own family's table was, or Mack's, or any other number of table legs she'd seen over the course of her short life.

She had thought she could be happy here. She thought maybe this was one place she didn't have to be afraid. There were no guards, no pimps, no angry fathers. It had seemed safe. But of course, that was seeming more and more impossible by the day.

Did she have a big sign over her head that told every guy she met that she was a used and broken object to be taken at will? Sometimes she felt she must. Normal, regular, worthwhile girls didn't get used by every guy they met... did they? Surely not. After all, Rebecca had seemed so shocked. Rebecca was a normal, worthwhile girl. So what did that make Bitty...?

She brushed away a tear and closed her eyes, feeling that agonizing wrench in her chest that never quite seemed to go away. When would it end? *Would* it ever end? Could she ever get away from this kind of existence?

More and more, she was beginning to believe she couldn't. No matter where she went, people saw her as used and weak, and she didn't see how that could ever change. Her chest ached again and she choked back a sob before sinking into blackness, desperately trying to escape her fate for a few precious moments.

Her body went rigid with fear and Callie looked up at the man rocking above her, hurting her insides, making the noises Callie hated. Callie looked around wildly but she couldn't recognize anything. It was another strange place. With a whimper, Callie closed her eyes and covered her ears, blocking out the sounds. Callie couldn't block out the feeling though. Callie cried quietly, wishing everything didn't always, always hurt her.

***

Callie sat in the corner of the kitchen quietly, staring at the swirls on the pretty floor. Callie liked the patterns. They looked like clouds. Callie liked clouds when she was allowed to look out the window. She couldn't see out the window now. It was dark. But there were clouds on the floor to look at.

A lady with a smile came in. There was a little girl behind her. She looked like Callie's age. She was smiling too. Callie looked at the lady when she came over. She looked nice.

"Bitty? What's wrong?"

Callie just watched her, sitting small and quiet.

"Do you feel okay?"

The lady put her hand out and Callie ducked. Callie didn't like touching. Touching hurt. The lady frowned at her. Callie made the lady mad. Callie was scared. The lady looked at the man who hurt her.

"What happened?"

The man shrugged. "She was like that the whole afternoon. Maybe too much homework."

The lady looked back at Callie. Callie tried not to cry. Crying made people angry. Callie still hurt inside from the man. She didn't want to hurt anymore.

"Bitty? Let's go up to your room. We'll have some quiet time."

The lady put her hand out and Callie ducked before she got hit. But the lady touched her hand and Callie looked up again.

"Come on. Let's go upstairs."

The lady helped Callie to get up and held her hand when they went up the stairs to a bedroom.

"You can lie down for a while, Bitty. I'll come check on you in a little bit."

Callie lay down on the bed and curled up in a tight ball, crying quietly into the soft pillow. It smelled nice. It made Callie feel better. Callie went to sleep on the nice clean bed and nice soft pillow.

Chapter Fifty-Six

✳ Choice One ✳

Bitty really wished they didn't have to go to work that morning. She wanted so much to stay home and decorate the tree, but John promised that they would do it after dinner and that he'd make it special. If anyone else had said that to her at any other time in her life, Bitty would have thought they were lying, but she trusted John.

It surprised her how much she trusted him now. But no matter what Bailey said, he'd been the kindest, most trustworthy person in her life and she was beginning to love him.

John had breakfast waiting and after they put the dishes into the dishwasher, they headed for his office. It was becoming a lovely routine and Bitty found herself relaxing into it more and more. For the first time in her life, she didn't feel like there was a hand constantly at her throat, tightening and squeezing, making her heart race, making her feel sick and cold and constantly on watch.

Bitty passed the day with computer games and coloring, eating lunch with John at the cafe down the street. Only once, Bebe pushed out impatiently, getting upset when it wasn't time for the tree yet. John promised that he would save some ornaments for her if she didn't come out in time, telling her to let Jay know he would do the same for him, too.

Much to Bitty's frustration, John insisted they eat dinner before they decorate the tree, so to keep herself busy she helped him prepare it. It was actually rather nice once she got into it, the two of them working side by side peacefully as if they'd been doing it for years. She even managed to forget about the tree for a while (mostly).

Finally, after everything was put away, John put on some water to boil for hot chocolate, got some Christmas music going, and turned the lights a little dimmer to give the room a magical glow.

"Okay, I'll go get the boxes of ornaments. You get yours out of the packaging. It can be the first one on the tree."

She smiled at him as he left, though she stood staring at the tree for a moment longer before unboxing her ornament; a big snowman hugging a little snowman. The moment she saw it, she'd immediately thought of her and John. Her choice had been easy.

He came back in with a large plastic tub and placed it gently on the floor in front of the tree. "Luckily, my wife decided she didn't want the Christmas ornaments, so I have everything we need."

Bitty gazed into the box almost overflowing with colored glass balls, stars, snowflakes, and bells. It was like staring into a box of magic.

John broke her trance by pulling out a tree skirt and crawling under the tree to put it in place. When he stood up and beckoned her over with a wave of his hand, she approached with her ornament clutched carefully in her hands.

"Go ahead, babygirl. Hang up the first ornament of the year."

Almost reverently, Bitty hung the ornament on a branch at eye level and stepped back with a smile. A thrill ran through her heart and without thinking, she reached out to take his hand, tears in her eyes.

He squeezed it gently and smiled down at her. "Ready to cover the whole tree?" he asked softly.

She smiled up at him with a nod. "Yeah."

They spent the next hour hanging ornaments from almost every branch, sipping hot chocolate and listening to familiar Christmas carols lilting through the room. It was the most magical experience of her entire life. John reminded her to leave spaces at eye level for the others as well, making sure to give everyone an equal position on the tree.

Bebe finally got her chance about halfway through and it was all John could do to keep her from knocking the tree over in her excitement at hanging ornaments. When they had finished, Bebe declared it the most wonderful day of her whole life and hugged John tightly.

He hugged her back just as tightly, stroking her hair softly and kissing the top of her head. To him, it was worth everything he owned just to see that look on her face.

~ Choice Two ~

Scarlett woke up the next morning, showering and dressing as usual, though she wasn't looking forward to going to school. Bitty wasn't the only one missing Mrs. Barnes at the center.

"How are you this morning, Bitty?" Chelsea asked. The tone of her voice made Scarlett look up uncertainly. She sounded weird.

"I'm okay. Just tired, I guess."

"Do you want to talk about yesterday?"

Scarlett frowned slightly. Did Chelsea know how much trouble she was having in the new school?

"I... no. It's okay."

Chelsea watched her for a long moment, then nodded. "Okay. Let me know if you need anything."

Scarlett nodded and poured some syrup on the pancakes Pete put in front of her. Sylvia was also staring at her, though at least Damien seemed to be acting normally; at least, normal for *him*.

She sighed, wondering what had happened and whether it was something she should know about. In the end, she got distracted by the start of school and forgot about it for a while. What began to bother her a few hours into the day was the looks she was getting from some of the guys. Even girls were whispering as she walked by. The disgusting feeling of exposure grew as she began to wonder if Damien had told people something, probably painting her as a slut. She could never escape that label, could she?

A short while later, Bitty found herself sitting in English class trying to catch up on what the teacher was talking about. It was hard to find herself in the middle of something with no idea what was going on and still trying to act normal. She glanced at the clock to check the time, but they were the round ones and she couldn't tell what time it was. She was pretty sure English was the last class of the day, though.

Sure enough, when the bell rang, some of the other kids mentioned buses and she followed the stream of students to the bus circle. Damien came up beside her at the door and she felt herself go cold and tense. By the time she slid into a seat, she was shivering and felt sick. She didn't understand why, though. She'd been raped so many times before, but even Fowler hadn't made her feel like this. Maybe because she'd been hoping so much that things would be different.

Damien sat down beside her and she hunched up against the cold metal wall, staring out the window with her arms around her waist. He leaned over with his hand on her thigh to whisper in her ear.

"We're gonna have some fun tonight. Tell me you want it."

She yanked her leg as far away from him as she could, but it wasn't enough to dislodge his hand. He squeezed and shifted it up higher on her thigh.

"Don't even try to pretend I'm not the best you've ever had. I know you want it. Tell me you want it."

"Stop," she whispered.

"You will later."

By the time they reached their stop, Bitty was fairly sure she was going to throw up, and walked as quickly as she could back to the house without saying hello to Chelsea who was waiting for Sylvia. The moment she kicked off her boots in the mud room, she escaped into the bathroom and locked the door.

"I want to leave, Bailey," she whispered.

'What?'

***

Bitty suddenly felt Bailey's presence where she'd been absent most of the day. "I want to leave. He hurt me and he's not going to stop."

'Who hurt you?'

"Damien," she whimpered. She felt Bailey's anger flair and she closed her eyes. "I want to leave."

'It's a fucking blizzard outside and we're in the fucking middle of nowhere. We'll freeze to death. If he tries it, I'll kick his ass.'

Bitty put her head on her knees and cried softly for a while. When she finally got herself under control, she washed her face and left the room. Pete and Chelsea were in the kitchen, Pete cooking dinner this time and Chelsea helping with homework. They smiled at Bitty as she sat down in the chair furthest from Damien, carefully not looking at him.

It was hard to concentrate on her homework and just as hard to make herself eat something during dinner. She could feel Damien's eyes on her as much as she'd felt his hands yesterday. The moment she could get away with it, she asked to be excused to lie down for a while, pleading a stomachache.

Chelsea nodded and shot Pete a worried glance as Bitty left the table and escaped to her room. When she reached it, Bitty shut the door and curled up under the covers in her bed, wishing she had a lock on her door.

A little while later, she could hear Sylvia's voice coming up the stairs, talking about the book Chelsea was reading to her and about the bath bombs one of her friends at school had brought to show everyone and how much she wished she could have one. Bitty pretended to be asleep when Chelsea opened the door a little to check on her.

***

Bitty crept out of her room to use the bathroom much later. The lights were out in the hall. That meant everyone was in bed. Relief washed over her that they hadn't insisted she come down and finish her homework. She was also thankful for the lock on the bathroom door and wished for a moment that she could sleep in there for the night. But she knew that wasn't a good idea because she'd have to explain why she was sleeping on the bathroom floor and she had a feeling Damien would make her regret telling the truth about that.

Just as she got to her doorway, a hand covered her mouth and another wrapped around her waist, dragging her backwards and into one of the other rooms.

"Be quiet or they'll hear you. They'll find you in my room and I'll tell them you snuck in here."

Bitty whimpered and closed her eyes as he bent her over the bed and began tugging at her pants with his free hand. She began to give in, to keep quiet and get it over with, but before he could get her pants off past her knees, her body went rigid and her head shot up and back, cracking him hard in the nose.

He cried out in pain and shock and stumbled backwards as Bailey spun around with fury flashing in her eyes.

"Don't you EVER fucking touch me again! You son of a bitch!" she shouted, flying at him in a rage. Before he knew what was happening, she was kicking and hitting as hard as she could, taking out all the frustration, impotence, and wrath she'd been forced to hold back for so long.

She'd had the element of surprise and had gotten a few good blows in before he started hitting back. After the first two punches to her face and stomach, however, the lights burst to life and Pete yelled, thrusting himself between them to grab Bailey's fist that had shot out in retaliation.

"WHAT IN THE WORLD IS GOING ON IN HERE!"

Chelsea was standing in the doorway, her eyes wide in shock. Sylvia peeked out from behind her legs with terror in her eyes until Chelsea noticed and rushed her off to her room.

"SHE CAME IN MY ROOM AND TRIED TO GET IN BED WITH ME!" Damien shouted, glaring at her with rapidly swelling black eyes, his nose dripping blood. He was clutching his side with an obvious look of pain.

"HE'S A FUCKING LYING RAPIST!" Bailey screamed back, one of her own cheeks beginning to turn a dark purple.

"SHE'S BEEN AFTER ME SINCE SHE GOT HERE! I TURNED HER DOWN AND SHE CAME IN HERE AND TRIED TO GET IN BED WITH ME!"

"Woah, woah, woah!" Pete cried, putting his hands out to stop Bailey lunging at Damien again. "Bitty, pull up your pants, for God's sake! Damien, sit down!"

Bailey yanked her pajamas back into place, feeling another surge of outrage when she realized everyone in the house had now seen her half naked.

"YOU SON OF A BITCH!" she screamed again, rushing forward only to be grappled into a wrestling hold by Pete.

Chelsea appeared in the doorway again and Damien clutched at his side with a loud moan of pain. She rushed to him and lifted his shirt.

"He needs the hospital, Pete."

Bailey smirked at him, proud she'd done some damage.

Pete's arms tightened around her, triggering another flare of automatic anger at being restrained, trapped, helpless.

"LET ME GO! LET ME GO, YOU SON OF A BITCH! LET ME GO!"

"I'll take him," Chelsea said, helping Damien to his feet. "See if you can calm her down. We'll call Jennifer in the morning."

Pete nodded and waited until they'd gone downstairs before releasing her slowly. "Your room. Now."

Bailey glared at him and stomped down the hall to her room, slamming the door as hard as she could before throwing herself on her bed and trying to breathe. Anger and fury raged within her and she wanted nothing more than to fly down the stairs and finish the job on Damien. But she knew that would be impossible.

Pete showed up in her doorway, the deep frown still on his face. "What happened in there?"

"I told you!"

"No. You just called him names and tried to beat him up. What were you doing in his room?"

"He dragged me in there and started assaulting me, that's what!"

"I didn't hear anything, Bitty. If he dragged you into his room I would have heard. The only thing I heard was you screaming and beating him up. I really thought you were a very different kind of person than that, Bitty. And lying about it isn't going to help the situation."

"I'M NOT LYING! HE'S THE ONE WHO'S LYING!"

Pete frowned and rubbed the bridge of his nose. "Look, Bitty, we can't have you here anymore. Violence isn't tolerated in this house, especially to that extent along with the lying and the sexual assault-"

"I DIDN'T DO THAT!"

He held his hand up to stop her. "That's enough. You need to stay in here until morning, understand?"

Bailey crossed her arms and glared at him.

"*Understand?*" he repeated.

"*Yes!*" she snapped without looking at him.

He stood up with a nod. "Alright. We'll talk to Jennifer in the morning." He looked down at her for a moment, then sighed sadly and left.

After Bailey calmed down a little, Sarah was nudged out and curled up to cry quietly until she fell asleep. Bailey had ruined everything, she was sure.

Chapter Fifty-Seven

✱ Choice One ✱

Bebe was the first one up the next morning and John came out to find her still in her pajamas, cross-legged in front of the tree staring up at it in wonder. He smiled and squatted down beside her, stroking her hair.

"Morning, babygirl. How long have you been awake?"

She shrugged. "I don't know."

He chuckled. "Checking that the tree was still here?"

"I thought it was a dream," she replied shyly.

"Oh, babygirl," he murmured, hugging her gently. "It'll be here until after New Year's, okay? Let's go get some breakfast and dress. We have to go to work one more day, and then I'm taking off work for the next week. How's that sound?"

She grinned up at him. "Awesome!"

He kissed her on the forehead and helped her up so they could get breakfast.

By the time they got to his office, Bitty was out again. She settled in as she had the last few times, content in their routine. While he met with clients, she worked through a few things on the website, played a few games, and even began reading the book John had bought for her. Bebe and Jay came out for a while each, coloring and cutting things out of the paper they'd been given. Bitty was dreading the end of the year more and more. This was nice, and she didn't want to go to another school to be drowned with homework again.

***

When it was time to go, John came in with another smile like the one he'd had when they'd gone to get the Christmas tree and Bitty couldn't help smiling back a little bit. Something was up.

"Hey, babygirl. I thought of something I wanted to do with you today."

Bitty's face fell a little and she looked down at the crayons she was putting into their box. He wanted to do something with her. That probably meant in bed. She'd forgotten how their relationship had started and the stark reminder hurt a little bit.

"What's wrong?" he asked, his tone worried.

"Nothing."

"Don't keep it to yourself, babygirl. If something is bothering you, I want you to tell me. I promised I wouldn't get mad and I mean it. What's wrong?"

She packed the crayons for a moment in silence before answering. "You want to do things with me."

"Yes. I have a feeling you've never done it before."

She winced and hunched her shoulders. There was nothing she could think of that she hadn't been forced to do at some point.

"There isn't anything I haven't done before," she whispered miserably.

He stood in silence for a moment, then came over to crouch down in front of her. "What are you talking about?" he asked gently.

"Sex."

He sighed. "No, Bitty. I wasn't talking about sex. I wanted to take you to see Santa. I wanted to surprise you. Why on earth did you think I was talking about sex?"

She looked up at him in shock. "Santa?" she repeated softly.

He nodded. "Yes, baby. Why would you think I was talking about sex?"

She looked down, embarrassed. "You… you said there was stuff you wanted to do with me. I thought…"

"Oh, Bitty. No, baby. I told you I won't do that anymore, and I meant it, just like I mean everything I say." He hugged her tightly and kissed the top of her head. "If you don't want to go, we can skip it."

She shook her head. "No, I do. Please? I'm sorry."

He sighed and shook his head as well. "You have nothing to be sorry for. I know it's going to take a while to get used to your new life, and I'm right here to help." He hugged her again. "Shall we go?"

She nodded and looked up at him with a small smile as he finished helping her pack up her things.

"I don't suppose you wrote a letter to Santa, did you?"

"A letter to Santa?"

"Sure. To tell him what you want for Christmas."

"I..." She looked down at the ground. "Daddy, I don't really believe in Santa. I know he isn't real. But I still want to go see him," she added quickly, looking up at him.

He reached for her hand and squeezed as they left the room. "That's okay. I understand."

"Merry Christmas, Dr. Matthews."

"Merry Christmas, Joan! See you next year!"

She laughed and nodded, shoving her lunchbox into her shoulder bag while they left, humming Christmas carols to herself.

~ Choice Two ~

Sarah was still out when they woke up to the alarm the next morning. For a moment, she couldn't quite remember why she felt so anxious. Then she remembered and sighed. They were gone for sure. Pete had said they were going to call Jennifer. That probably meant they would be taken away. Maybe they would be taken back to the center. That might not be so bad. Or they'd be sent somewhere else with another family.

'That's probably more like it.'

'Shut up, Bailey. You got us into this. If you had just laid down and taken it we would still be allowed to stay.'

'Fuck you, Scarlett! I'm not laying down for anyone to rape! If you don't like it, then you should have been out to take the fuck like you're made for!'

"Stop," Sarah hissed when Scarlett gave a strangled, hurt little sob and ran away. "Bailey, please. Just leave things alone. You've done enough damage."

'Why the fuck should we be punished for not wanting that son of a bitch's dick in us? That's not fair and you know it!'

"Since when has life ever been fair? Besides, it happens all the time to girls. You know that as well as I do. No one cares. It's best just to take it and shut up."

'Fuck you!'

Sarah sighed when she looked in the mirror to do her hair and caught sight of the swollen cheek he'd given her, then finished getting dressed before slowly walking downstairs. She wasn't entirely sure she was allowed to be leaving her room, but Pete had only said she was supposed to stay until morning.

Everyone was sitting at the table and she looked away from the cold, accusatory stares. A surge of triumph from Bailey washed over her when she noticed Damien's broken nose, two black eyes, split lip, and the hint of a bandage under his shirt. She'd done some damage before he got his fists into her, too.

'Son of a bitch deserves it.'

Sarah couldn't deny that, at least. She had to admit, there was some satisfaction in the brief victory.

"Jennifer will pick you up after school to take you to your new foster home. We can't have you here anymore," Chelsea said quietly, her voice cold.

Sarah stared at the ground, biting back tears of regret and injustice, but she stayed quiet.

"Sit down and have some breakfast," the woman said, her tone slightly less chilly.

Sarah obeyed in silence, pouring herself some cereal and eating without looking at anyone. She could feel their gazes on her anyway, and she didn't want to see it. She could still feel Bailey's wrath burning in the background and she didn't want to lose control and give Bailey the opening she needed to slip out again.

This time on the bus, Damien sat as far away from her as he could. That was at least something. Whispers surrounded her, though, and she kept her head down, her eyes averted. Maybe they wouldn't have to come back to this school when they were taken wherever it was they would be taken. She had no doubt Damien was already spreading things about her.

The whispering only got more obvious as the day went on, until at lunch there was no doubt he'd been telling people all kinds of things about her. They gave her a wide berth but were no longer bothering to lower their voices. Bailey's rage began to grow again and Sarah had a harder time trying to hold onto her control.

The breaking point came right after lunch. One of Damien's friends came up to her, backing her against the wall.

"You like it rough, huh? I can give it to you rough. I'll give it to you like you never had before." His hand slid up her shirt and Bailey wasn't going to be held back any longer.

Her knee came up hard in the guy's crotch and as he doubled over, she shouldered him out of her way and ran. Before anyone knew what had happened, she was out the nearest door and didn't stop running.

'BAILEY! BAILEY WHAT ARE YOU DOING! WE'RE GOING TO BE IN SO MUCH TROUBLE! WE'LL BE ARRESTED FOR RUNNING AWAY AND HITTING THAT BOY! BAILEY, PLEASE STOP!'

"I'm not giving them the chance to stick us in another home with another asshole who thinks he can have whatever he wants from us! I'm done! I'm finished! We're leaving!"

Bailey had no idea how long she ran, but she was halfway across town before exhaustion finally overtook her and she collapsed behind a building to sob as the adrenaline seeped out of her body.

She didn't care anymore if the others saw her crying. She didn't care if they thought she was weak now. She didn't care if they didn't trust her anymore. They hadn't been listening to her before anyway. What difference did it make. It didn't. Nothing made a difference. They were what they were, and no matter where they went, it would never change. She was empty. She had nothing left to give. Her strength was gone and she just couldn't fight anymore. It was over.

When her tears finally ran dry and her mind went blank, she stood up and started walking. There was no real plan or destination, and she simply didn't care anymore. But it was cold just sitting there on the concrete and she'd run off without her jacket. So she walked. And walked. And walked. Until finally, she ended up on a street she recognized. Her heart sank and she stood at the end of it just staring down at the house she hated. What did it matter anymore? Where else was she going to take them? Everywhere was the same. At least here, she knew what to expect. At least here, she could get some relief from the needles he was all too happy to provide. At least here, she didn't have to pretend to anyone that they were more than what they'd always been.

With a shuddering breath, Bailey walked slowly down the street and up the steps of Mack's house.

Chapter Fifty-Eight

* Choice One *

"Maybe we should get you something pretty to wear before we go see him," John mused when they got to the mall. "It was a spur of the moment idea and I didn't really think about it, but if it's okay with you, I'd like to make it a tradition. Maybe we could dress up and get our pictures taken with Santa every year. Would you like that?"

'He's talking like we're going to be with him forever!'

'Oh, can we? Can we be with him forever, Bitty? I like him so much. I want to stay with him forever.'

'He's a foster home, moron. You don't stay forever in a foster home. Besides, I'm not staying with a pervert for any longer than I have to. I know what he is, even if you can't see it!'

'Bailey, stop. Just give him a chance. So far he's been wonderful.'

Bitty nodded. "Okay."

He smiled and squeezed her hand gently, then headed into the teen clothing store that had given him the idea.

Half an hour later, they emerged with her wearing her new sparkly Christmas dress and shoes and her regular clothes in a store bag.

"Are you excited?" he asked with a grin when they joined the line.

She nodded slightly, her nerves on edge. She knew he was extremely excited and she didn't want to ruin his happiness, but something was setting her off more and more the closer they got.

Finally, it was their turn. Her fingers were white with fear as they walked up to the man on the bench.

"Ho ho ho! Merry Christmas, young lady! Do you have a letter for me?" the Santa asked cheerfully.

Bitty shook her head in a minute gesture.

"We're hoping to get a nice picture together with you," John said quickly, noting her change in attitude.

"Of course! Take a seat."

John sat down and pulled Bitty into his lap, holding her in what he hoped was a reassuring way while the photographer focused the camera.

"Okay, smile!"

Though she felt like she wanted to throw up or scream, Bitty managed a miniscule smile for the second it took to take the picture before she simply couldn't hold on anymore. She had to run. She had to get away! But she couldn't! She was being pinned down, just like all the other Christmases!

Suddenly, Callie gave a terrified, strangled scream and cowered away, struggling to keep herself from trying to run away. Santa always hurt. Santa said she was naughty and hurt her so bad. Callie hated Santa. Callie wanted to hide. Callie tried so hard not to be naughty but Santa always said she was naughty. Callie couldn't help it. Callie didn't mean to cry when it hurt. Callie tried so hard not to run away from the beatings. But Callie was scared of the hurting. Callie didn't mean to be naughty. Callie didn't want Santa to punish her.

Callie couldn't do it. She had to get away from the hurting that was coming. With another terrified scream, she twisted away from the man holding her down and ran. Callie didn't know where she was. There were so many people. But Callie had to get away! Callie ran. Callie ran and ran and ran.

A policeman stepped in front of her and she screamed again. Callie almost fell down trying to run the other way but another policeman blocked her way and both of them tried to grab her.

"NO! NO! DON'T GRAB HER! JUST BLOCK HER WAY!"

Another man was running towards her. He looked angry. Callie was so scared. Two more men were coming and she didn't have anywhere to go! Callie looked around wildly, her eyes wide and terrified. There was no way out! Callie shrank down and huddled in a ball with her head on her knees, hunched up so the hitting might not hurt so much.

People were shouting around her, towering over her, getting ready to grab her and hurt her. Callie cried so hard.

"Hey. Hey there. What's your name?"

The man's voice didn't sound mean. The man sounded nice. Callie lifted her head a little bit to look at him without letting him get too much of her face to hit.

He smiled. It was a nice smile. His eyes were nice. Callie tried hard to stop crying so he wouldn't be angry with her and hurt her.

"What's your name?" he asked again.

Callie just looked at him.

"You're not Bitty, are you."

Callie stayed still and quiet. The man nodded.

"Are you Callie?"

Callie stared at him in surprise. The man knew her name. No one ever knew her name! Callie nodded.

He smiled a little more. "Callie, shall we go somewhere away from all the people? Somewhere safe?"

Safe.

Safe.

He wanted to take her somewhere safe. Would it really be safe?

Safe.

Safe.

Callie nodded.

The man stood up very slowly and Callie followed, watching the other people all around her, waiting for them to hurt her. They were staring at her. She followed the man. He talked to a policeman quietly, but Callie couldn't hear what he was saying. She stopped quickly. They were going to hurt her. They were talking about how to hurt her. Callie started to cry again. The man turned back to look at her and Callie wanted to run away again.

"Callie, we're going to go into a safe room away from all the other people, okay?"

Callie looked at the policeman. He stepped back away from them. Callie looked back at the other man.

"We're going into this room here. It's nice and quiet, and no one will come hurt you, okay?"

Callie looked where the man pointed and saw a room with a couch and some chairs. It wasn't so bright as it was outside where all the other people were, and it did look quiet. Callie looked at the man again and nodded.

He smiled his crinkly-eye smile and walked into the room. Callie swallowed hard and tried to stop crying as she followed him inside.

The man waited for her to come inside, then closed the door. It was suddenly so much quieter now and Callie felt a little bit of the scared go away. Then the man sat down in one of the chairs and crossed his legs. He didn't look like he was going to jump up and hurt her…

Callie looked around the quiet, dim little room, then back at the man. He smiled. Callie looked at the couch, then at the man, then back at the couch.

"You can sit down if you want."

Callie looked at him again, then slowly walked to the couch and sat down on the edge, looking around nervously. Her foot hurt so bad it felt like fire up her leg, but she tried hard not to cry. The man just sat quietly in the quiet, dim room. It was quiet. Quiet was nice. Dim was nice. The man kind of seemed nice too…

Slowly, the scaredness began to go away and Callie could breathe better. Callie relaxed a little bit. The man didn't try to hurt her. Callie thought maybe the man really wasn't going to hurt her. Maybe she really was safe in this nice little room. Callie thought maybe she would like to stay in the dim, quiet little room.

After a while, Callie sat back a little bit more on the couch, then slowly tucked her feet up beside her. When the man didn't get angry, she leaned against the armrest, tiredness trying to make her close her eyes. Callie wondered how long they had been in the little room. Callie wanted to sleep. Callie wondered if the man would be angry if she went to sleep. Callie didn't think the man would hurt her now. The man really did seem nice. Callie watched him for a few more minutes, then rested her head on the armrest and closed her eyes. Callie was so tired. Callie wanted to sleep. Callie slept in the quiet, dim little room with the smiling man.

****

Callie woke up when the man called her name. He was leaning forward in the chair across from her, still smiling.

"Callie?"

Callie blinked and sat up slowly, looking around again to see where she was. She was still in the nice, quiet room.

"Callie, I think we should go home. It's getting late and the mall is going to close in a little bit."

Home? Callie didn't want to go home. Callie got hurt at home. Callie wanted to stay in this nice room.

"We're not going to your old home. You're going to come to my home. There's a bedroom just for you there, and a Christmas tree. We can have something to eat. Are you hungry, Callie?"

How did the smiling man know what she was thinking? Callie watched him for a moment, then nodded.

The smiling man stood up slowly and held out his hand. Callie looked at it, then at him, then at his hand again, then took it nervously and stood up.

"My name is John," the smiling man said quietly. "I'll hold your hand while we go to my car. It's safe there."

Callie looked up at him, then looked around as they left the quiet room. It wasn't so loud anymore outside the room, and there weren't so many people. It wasn't so bright either.

A policeman and a man in a suit came over and Callie hid behind the smiling man, John, so they wouldn't see her. They talked about pictures and gave him a paper, and the smiling man John told them thank you and they all smiled. Then the smiling man John started walking again, still holding her hand.

They went outside to a parking lot and the man led the way to a nice looking car. He even opened the door for her and let her get in by herself. It smelled nice in the car. Callie liked the car. The car seemed safe. Callie got into the car and waited for the man to go around to the other seat and get in.

"Do you know how to buckle your seatbelt?" he asked.

Callie nodded and clumsily buckled the seatbelt. Then they were off. Callie looked out the window at the pretty lights. They looked like Christmas lights. Callie saw Christmas lights in a movie once. They looked like these lights.

It seemed like a very long time later the man drove the car into a neat, tidy garage. Callie looked around for the hurting things in the garage, but she didn't see any. The smiling man John opened the door and Callie unbuckled to get out of the car. Callie hoped the hurting things weren't in the house. But at least it would be warmer if they were.

Unless it was a basement. Basements were cold. And dark. Callie didn't like the cold and dark.

Callie followed the smiling man John into the house and took off her pretty shoes when he told her to. It was the first time Callie noticed them. They were the prettiest shoes Callie ever saw. Callie wished she could keep the shoes. They probably belonged to another girl, though. Callie thought that girl must be so lucky. Callie wished she could be that girl.

Callie kept following the smiling man John and stared around at the beautiful house. It made Callie sad. If it was a beautiful house like this, then Callie would be hurt in the cold, dark basement, not in the warm house. Girls like Callie didn't belong in beautiful houses with beautiful shoes. Callie belonged in the basement.

Callie tried very hard not to cry. Callie tried so hard to be good.

"Callie, I'm going to take you to your room, okay? You can eat in there if it feels safer."

Callie nodded quietly and peered into the room the smiling man John pointed at. Callie's eyes got wide and she looked from the beautiful room to the smiling man John and back. This was the room she would be in? It didn't look cold or dark or scary. It looked… beautiful. Why would the smiling man John put a girl like Callie in a beautiful room?

Callie went into the room and looked back at the smiling man John. He was smiling even more.

"You can get some pj's on if you want. They're nice and cozy. And you can get into bed, too." He was taking something from a drawer and laying it on the bed for her. When he finished, he knelt down in front of Callie and she looked at him, scared.

"You're safe here, Callie. I promise. Nothing is going to hurt you. I'm going to bring you some food, okay?"

Callie nodded and watched the smiling man John leave the room before she looked at the things he put on the bed. They were fluffy, snuggly, soft clothes. They were the coziest things Callie ever saw. Callie looked at the door quickly, then started to take off her clothes to put the cozy ones on. Then Callie saw the beautiful dress she was wearing. Callie almost didn't want to take it off, but she wanted the snuggly clothes on, so she took the dress off and quickly put the warm clothes on. Callie sighed happily and climbed into the soft, warm, cuddly bed. It felt good not to be on her burning foot. There was a beautiful unicorn stuffie on the bed. Callie wondered if she would be allowed to hold the stuffie. Again, Callie thought how lucky the girl who lived here was.

The smiling man John came back with some food for her and put it on the table beside the bed. Callie got ready for him to hurt her, but he moved away. Callie watched him, frightened.

"I'm going to go out to the living room, Callie. If you need anything, call me, or come get me, okay? If I'm not out there, then I'm in my room down the hall. You're safe. Have something to eat, cuddle the unicorn, and get some sleep, okay?"

Callie nodded a little tiny bit, watching the smiling man John leave. He really was leaving her alone without hurting her. Callie didn't understand. Why didn't the smiling man John hurt her? What was wrong with him?

Callie stopped wondering and ate some of the food, then lay down with the lovely soft stuffie to sleep in the beautiful room. Callie pretended *she* was the luckiest girl, instead of the girl who really lived here. It was nice to pretend. Callie fell asleep pretending.

~ Choice Two ~

"So, you came crawling back like the worthless snake you are, did you?"

"I never told them anything," Bailey mumbled, her head down, her defiance lost.

"Obviously, or I'd be in fucking prison right now. You think I'm a moron? So what took you so long to get back here?"

"I was in jail," she muttered.

"Hmph." Mack threw his empty beer can and it bounced off the side of her head. She flinched and turned her head slightly as the remnants of the liquid trickled down her cheek. "How do you expect to sell anything in clothes like that?" he snapped without looking away from the TV.

Bailey looked down at her sweater, jeans, and winter boots, then closed her eyes. She hadn't really thought about having to take off her nice clothes.

"Go sit in the corner. I'll set something up after this episode."

For a moment, Bailey's eyes flashed and she clenched her jaw, but it faded in a moment and she slunk into the corner and sat down.

'Bailey, I don't wanna be here again. Please can we leave?'

"Where the fuck are we supposed to go, Bebe?" Bailey muttered in a tired, empty voice.

'I dunno. I just don't wanna be here anymore. He hurts us, Bailey.'

"Yeah, well so does everyone else everywhere else. What's the difference?" She scowled as Bebe faded into the background crying. She was doing the right thing. It was the only thing. She had to remember that. At least this way, they knew what to expect. It wasn't a complete shock when someone took what they wanted.

Bailey closed her eyes and rested her forehead on her knees, trying to fight another wave of tears. She had broken. There was nothing left to fight with or for. It just didn't matter anymore.

After half an hour or so, Bitty found herself sitting in Mack's living room. Her eyes widened and fear choked at her throat. How had she managed to find herself back here! She looked around wildly, wondering if there was a way to slip out the door without him noticing. But he was on the phone, staring at her with that cold, calculating look that meant he was making arrangements for her. Her eyes filled with tears and she shrank down into herself with a barely contained sob. What had happened? How could she be back here!

All too soon, Mack had hung up and was hauling her to her feet roughly by the arm and dragging her out to his car. Bitty didn't dare argue or fight. It was just like it had been with Damien; fighting would only make it worse. What had happened with Damien? Had he brought her to Mack? Did he know Mack?

She was silent and terrified as Mack drove them through town to another motel and the dread and fear that had been gripping her throat moved into her chest.

Not again.

Without a word, she followed him inside when he hauled her out of the car and stood behind him with her head down when he booked the room. Just like always, the receptionist's gaze slid over her like she didn't exist as he handed Mack the key to the room.

The hotel didn't seem as seedy as the one he'd used the last time, but it wouldn't matter anyway. She wouldn't leave the bed.

Sure enough, almost the minute they got into the room, someone knocked on the door and a man walked in. Within minutes, she was naked on her back being used. Bitty closed her eyes and tried not to cry too obviously. How could she have come full circle?

The rest of the night, Bitty didn't sleep as man after man arrived, paid Mack, used her, and left. Nothing had changed. After all her budding hopes, nothing had changed. Maybe it had all just been a drug-induced dream. That was the only thing that made sense.

Chapter Fifty-Nine

* Choice One *

Bitty woke up and stretched before slipping out of bed to take her shower. She almost forgot it was Saturday and there was no reason to be out of bed in a hurry for a whole week. She smiled a little bit and went about her morning routine before heading out to the kitchen to greet John and inhale the delicious smell of waffles.

"Morning, babygirl," he greeted her after studying her face for a moment.

She smiled a little more and sat down. "Morning, Daddy."

He beamed at her. "How are you feeling?"

" Okay. My foot hurts today, though. Maybe I should use the crutches again for a while. I forgot we didn't have to be up early today," she added with a giggle.

He laughed too and nodded. "Yeah, force of habit. Well, I was thinking maybe we could make some cookies today? We'll make enough so everyone gets to decorate some. How's that sound?"

She grinned. "That sounds awesome."

After breakfast, John pulled out the cookbook, turned on some Christmas music, and began showing her how to make the cookies and frosting. Bitty felt like she was in a Christmas movie or something and her smile hardly left her face. The hardest part was waiting for the cookies to cool so they could be decorated and eaten, not necessarily in that order!

Bebe appeared just before lunch and began begging for cookies the moment she smelled them.

"*Please*!" she wheedled, gazing up at him with puppy-dog eyes.

John laughed and tousled her hair with a shake of his head. "It's almost lunch time! I don't want you spoiling your appetite with cookies."

"Just one. One won't spoil anything! I promise! Please?" A moment later, she found a cookie being held out in front of her with a wink from John. Bebe squealed and took it eagerly, then hugged him. "Thank you!"

He chuckled and kissed her forehead. "You're welcome, babygirl. But I expect you to eat a good lunch, okay?"

She nodded and sat down with her warm cookie, happily munching away while he finished putting the last few in the oven.

"When can we decorate them?"

"After lunch, when they're cool. If we decorate them too soon, they'll still be warm and the frosting will melt right off. Then we'd have a gooey puddle and no pretty cookies. Can't have that, can we?"

She shook her head quickly. "Uh uh."

True to her word, Bebe ate a decent amount of lunch and helped put the dishes away quickly so she could get to decorating.

"Okay, these six are yours to decorate however you want."

"Only six? But there's a hundred of them!"

He laughed. "There's a few dozen, but everyone needs a turn to decorate some, so you each get six. Six is a lot, young lady!"

She sighed but was smiling a moment later as she began spreading colored frosting on her cookies and covering them with sprinkles.

John took a few pictures and decorated two cookies of his own with her, reveling in the companionship and her simple, childish joy. Christmas had been losing its appeal the last few years, even when he was dating girls who lived his lifestyle. They were still wrapped up in adult worries and concerns and wants. Bebe, and most of the others, were completely different. Not only were they young enough to see it through a completely different viewpoint, but they had also never experienced a Christmas like he was trying to give them. It made everything so much more magical and for the first time in a long time, John found himself content with his life again.

As Bebe worked, her tongue pressed between her lips as she concentrated on getting the decorations just right, he mused about the incident with Callie the previous night. It was obvious by Bitty's behavior that morning, and by Bebe's as well, that neither had any idea what had happened. He recalled Jay mentioning that when Callie was out, no one was aware of anything. It also seemed, from what he'd seen, that Callie wasn't aware of anything until she was out, also.

A pang of sadness touched his heart at the thought of how terrifying that must have been for her. Santa seemed to have been a trigger in that situation and guilt joined the sadness as he tried not to imagine the cause of that terror.

"Bebe," he began casually, "Do you know who Callie is?"

She nodded absently. "She's a girl."

He smiled. "Yeah. Do you know anything else about her? Is she shy? Does she talk?"

She shook her head very slightly. "I dunno. Ask Bailey. Sarah might know," she added.

John nodded. "When you're done, do you think I could talk to one of them?"

"Maybe."

He smiled and held back a chuckle. "Okay, thanks."

Bebe had finished her cookies a few minutes later and obediently washed her hands when he reminded her.

"Daddy?"

"Yes, babygirl?"

She looked up at him shyly, some nervousness in her voice. "Could… I play some games on your computer?"

He smiled. "Of course. We really don't have any toys here for you, do we? Hmm… maybe Santa will bring you something nice."

She shook her head sadly. "Santa doesn't visit our house cuz we're too bad."

He sighed and knelt down, tucking his finger under her chin to lift her face to his. "Babygirl, you live in my house with my rules, and you follow all of them like a very good girl. Santa will definitely be bringing something for you."

Her eyes lit up with a hint of hope. "You think so?"

"I'm positive."

She grinned and hugged him.

He hugged her back and kissed the top of her head. "Alright, let's go get you settled on the computer."

The rest of the afternoon, Bebe played games on the computer until it was time for dinner. John told her they were making their own pizzas and she could add whatever toppings she wanted to hers.

"Can I have another cookie?" she asked as she loaded her pizza with toppings.

"After dinner. But we have to make sure we save one or two for Santa. He's coming tomorrow night, and you know he likes cookies, right?"

"*Tomorrow?*" she squealed, her hand frozen above the pizza, a fistful of olives clenched in it.

"Yup. Tomorrow night he'll be visiting to drop off some presents."

Her hand began to tremble with excitement and she was almost vibrating as she finished topping her pizza. The whole time, she talked non-stop about the things she'd heard about Santa and the things she'd seen in the movies she'd watched with John.

Unfortunately for Bebe, Sarah came out halfway through the baking time and helped John clean up the prep dishes.

"Hmm... Scarl– no... Sarah...?" he asked cautiously when her movements grew a little less clumsy.

She smiled and nodded. "Yes. Sorry."

He chuckled. "Hopefully I'll get better at telling sooner."

"I think you're doing a fantastic job."

He grinned and turned back to the dishwasher. "Sarah, I was wondering what you can tell me about Callie?"

"Hmm... not much. I only know that she's alone, quite completely. She doesn't know what happens when she's inside, and none of us know what happens when she's out. No one can talk to her, inside or out, and from what I've heard, she can't or won't talk to anyone even on the outside."

"I see. That's all you know?"

She nodded. "I'm afraid so. Sorry."

"No, don't be sorry. It's fine. I was just wondering what the best way to handle her would be. I'll figure it out. I assume she doesn't come out much?"

She shook her head. "No. Just in the worst situations, I think. Poor thing. I'm not sure there's any way to change that."

He nodded and shut the dishwasher. "I take it Santa is a bad subject for most of you?"

She looked down for a moment, then sighed and nodded. "There are men who..."

He held up his hand quickly, "I can imagine. Callie seemed terrified. Bitty is also one who's affected?"

She nodded.

"But Bebe isn't? What about Jay?"

"We've tried very hard to keep them as sheltered as possible, so for them, Santa isn't the monster he can be for Bitty and apparently Callie."

"Good to know. Thank you. What about Bailey?"

"I don't think she ever believed in Santa to begin with, so it's just another sick man in a funny outfit to her. I suppose for me, too."

He nodded sadly. "I'm so sorry, Sarah."

She shrugged. "Things seem to be getting better now, thanks to you."

He smiled. "I hope so. I'd like to show you life doesn't have to be the way it was. There are people who care. I know it's impossible to see from the streets the way you were living, but there are people out there who truly want to help."

She nodded without looking at him. "Thanks."

"What's wrong?"

"So many people think we're wrong for staying where we were, for going back to him, but it's hard to know who you can really trust to get you out, or even if there's any point. Sometimes it just seems like that's all life can ever be for someone like us."

He sighed, watching her sadly. "I understand. I'm sorry."

She looked up at him with a small smile. "It's not your fault."

"It is. I contributed to that by hiring you in the first place. I added to your hopelessness. I'm here now, trying to change that, but I can't imagine I helped things before. I'm so sorry, Sarah."

She looked down again. "It's okay."

After a long silence, he sighed. "Would you like to watch a movie while the pizzas finish? We could eat them while we watch once they're done."

She smiled at him. "I'd like that."

They settled on another Christmas movie and sat on the couch together, eating once the food was done and losing themselves in the Christmas-y story. When it was over, Sarah spread some frosting on her waiting cookies quickly before she headed for bed, a peacefulness washing over her as she drifted off to sleep.

~ Choice Two ~

Bitty found herself drifting in and out of sleep that night and into the next morning, until finally the stream of men stopped for a while and Mack came in. She managed to push herself up to sitting and looked up at him hopelessly. She hadn't had anything to eat since lunch the day before and her body had grown used to eating properly several times a day in the weeks she'd been free of him.

"Mack," she whispered miserably. "I'm so hungry. Could I have something to eat? Please?"

He threw a granola bar at her head and she ripped it open, devouring it and trying not to choke on it. Her throat was so dry. She'd barely been given the chance to go to the bathroom and get a drink from the faucet between clients. She wondered if she dared get up to get a drink now.

"You need to keep it quiet. I could hear you bawling out in the hall. If you don't shut up, we'll have the cops here again!"

She sniffed and looked down at the blankets. "I'm sorry. They hurt me so bad, Mack. I didn't mean to be loud. It hurts."

"I'll give you something to cry about if you don't find a way to shut your mouth."

"I'm sorry."

He pulled something out of his pocket and tied it around her upper arm. Bitty looked up in horror as he pulled a needle out as well.

"Mack, please don't! I... I just got clean. Please! I don't want any more. Please!"

He yanked her arm painfully towards him and took the cap off with his teeth. "You shut up. This will keep you quiet. You know you want it. You don't ever get clean of dope. You'll see."

She began to sob as he wrenched her arm and stuck the needle in. "Mack! Please! Please!"

Pleasure and relief washed over her in a tidal wave and her body instantly latched onto the wonderful, familiar feeling of the high. Her pleas faded away and her eyes closed with a whimper of defeat.

He released her and untied the band. "See? You ain't clean. Now keep quiet and spread your damn legs."

Bitty couldn't even cry anymore as the next man came in and climbed onto her. She'd forgotten how much less awful the drugs made everything feel. She could let her mind wander, let her body relax, the pain wasn't so bad, and the dirty words didn't stab at her heart. It was freedom, however momentary, and she gave herself to it in relief.

'Bitty! Not again! Please, Bitty! Fight it. We don't need it. Please, let's just get out of here. Bailey was wrong. We should never have come back here. We have to find a way out. Please.'

Bitty kept her eyes closed, losing track of how many men came through the door, blocking out the pleas of the others, letting go of everything that wasn't drug-induced pleasure. How could she have forgotten what a wonderful thing it was to be high?

Chapter Sixty

* Choice One *

The following morning, Jay woke up in excitement and dashed into the kitchen to find John, thrilled that his foot didn't hurt anymore.

"John! Is it Christmas? Is it Christmas?"

John laughed and looked up from his paper. "No, it's Christmas eve. Tomorrow is Christmas."

Jay sighed and plopped down on the seat beside him. "That's so far away. Bebe said Santa is coming this year cuz we were good. Is she lying?"

John chuckled and put his coffee cup down. "Jay?"

"Yeah?"

"Just checking. And no, Bebe's not lying. I know Santa didn't come before, but like I told Bebe, this is my house you're living in and my rules now, and you've been very good for me, so I made sure to tell Santa to come this year."

Jay grinned and reached for a banana. "Awesome! What are we doing today?"

"Well, since you didn't get to decorate your cookies yesterday, you can do that today, and we'll get our dinner things ready for tomorrow. Then we can watch some movies or I can read to you. Whatever you want."

"Okay!"

John grinned and stood up. "I didn't expect you up quite this early or I would have started breakfast sooner."

"Can we just have cereal? I want some of the chocolate kind."

John chuckled. "Sure. Cereal it is!"

***

Jay spent the morning decorating his cookies and playing computer games until Scarlett came out, hoping to decorate her own cookies. Bitty was the best decorator by far, but Scarlett's cookies were almost as good. Sarah had decided to let John decorate her cookies so he'd have something to decorate when the other ones were out, so the only ones left were Bailey's.

John hadn't really thought she would come out to do something as friendly as decorating cookies, but he'd wanted to make sure she had the opportunity to do so if she chose, and to show her that she was part of the family just as much as the others. Bitty was content to help John get the meal things ready for the next day so they would have less work to do, and he made it fun by singing Christmas carols as loudly and as badly as he could, urging her to join in when she knew the words. In an effort to make her feel less self conscious about not knowing many of the words, most of the time he sang the wrong words on purpose, making them up as they worked and substituting them with random words about what they were doing.

"Babygirl," he began once they had finished. "How would you feel about going out to see a movie tonight?"

"Like, to a movie theater?" she asked incredulously.

He nodded. "Yeah, I think there's a new Disney animation out that you'd like. We'll get popcorn and soda and all the good stuff. What do you say?"

She grinned. "Yes!"

He laughed and hugged her. "Alright, let me check the times and we'll go over."

Half an hour later, they were getting their boots and jackets on and heading for the cinema. Bitty was incredibly excited when they walked in, and she held his hand tightly as she looked around. It wasn't very busy since it was Sunday and Christmas Eve, so they had their choice of seats. He bought them a popcorn to share, two sodas, and a box of Junior Mints for her, cookie dough balls for him, though he promised to share them with her anyway.

John had been right. The movie was wonderful and Bitty was utterly entranced. Even John and the other adults in the theater were laughing and groaning throughout the show, and Bitty declared it the best movie ever.

"The best ever, huh?" he said as they left afterwards.

"Yeah. It was amazing."

He laughed and squeezed her hand. "I'm glad you enjoyed it. I did too."

Most of the way home, Bitty went on about the movie, telling him about her favorite parts and reciting lines she remembered from it. Eventually, her energy began to run out and she settled into her seat quietly, smiling out the window until they got home.

"Alright, young lady, bedtime. But first, we'll put out the cookies for Santa, shall we?"

Her smile disappeared and she looked at the floor. "He's coming tonight?" she whispered.

John knelt in front of her and lifted her chin. "Babygirl, this isn't the Santa that came to your other house. This is my house, and I won't let anything happen to you. This Santa is slipping down the chimney into the living room to leave presents and then he's leaving again. He's not even going anywhere near your room. You're safe."

She nodded slightly again. "K."

He tapped her softly on the nose with one finger and gave her a small smile. "Let's go get those cookies ready."

They worked in silence, putting two cookies onto a plate and pouring a mug of milk to set out on the coffee table.

"You know, when I was little, I put out cookies and milk for Santa and we'd also put out some carrots for the reindeer. Would you like to do that?"

She looked up at him in surprise. "Really? Did he take them?"

"He sure did." He grinned at her and rummaged through the fridge, pulling out some carrots. "Hmm… only four. Well, we could cut them in half, how about that?"

She smiled and nodded, looking more interested in feeding the reindeer than Santa. John cut them in half and she arranged them in a pretty fan shape around the cookies, then carried the plate into the living room while he brought the milk.

"Alright, babygirl, bedtime."

She looked down at the plate, then up at the tree and smiled a little bit before heading to her room.

When she'd finished brushing her teeth and getting her pajamas on, John came in as usual to tuck her in. He paused with a concerned frown when he saw the look on her face and the way she was curled up under the covers.

"Still scared, babygirl?" he asked gently, pulling the covers tightly around her.

She looked down and nodded.

"I see." He regarded her for a moment, then sighed and sat down beside her, resting his back on the headboard and putting his arm around her. "How about I sit here until he comes to make sure he doesn't hurt you?"

She looked up at him nervously. "Really?"

He nodded. "I'll be the nutcracker guard and keep you safe from the rats. How's that?"

She managed a smile as she thought of the story he'd read the other day and nodded. "Thank you, Daddy."

He smiled down at her, then leaned over and kissed her very softly on her forehead. "You're welcome, babygirl. Now, get some sleep and I'll keep you safe."

She smiled at him for a minute more, then closed her eyes and snuggled against him. In a few minutes, she was asleep.

John stayed beside her until he was sure she was asleep, then stood up carefully. It took him about an hour to finish his work and get ready for bed. When he was done, he stopped in her doorway and gazed in at her for a minute.

What could it hurt if he went back to her? What would it matter if he climbed in behind her and put his arms around her. What difference would it make if he stayed with her the rest of the night and protected her like he'd promised?

With a soft sigh, he walked in quietly and crawled into bed behind her, wrapping his arms around her waist and pulling her against him gently. He sighed again and kissed the top of her head softly, then closed his eyes. He knew he'd never be with her the way he'd had her in the hotel those first days and it was a sad thought, but then he thought of her face when they were decorating cookies, or when they'd gone shopping, or when he'd promised he would protect her, and he knew he could never betray her like that. She was happy, and that made him happy in a very different way. He was sure he could move past things that had happened with her and accept their new relationship. She needed a daddy, and he would be Daddy. It wasn't about the sex, after all. It was about the care and love he could give a little girl as a Daddy, and he was doing that right now. He didn't need sex to love her like that.

With a smile on his face, he kissed the top of her head again and went to sleep.

~ Choice Two ~

The drugs wore off far too quickly, bringing with it a tidal wave of agony that had been hiding behind the wall of pleasure. Everything seemed to hit her at once and she felt more miserable than she'd felt in a long time. She couldn't stop crying even when there wasn't anyone in her and she just wanted to curl up and disappear for a while. She needed more. She had to have more. She couldn't make it like this anymore.

Mack returned sometime in the morning and shoved her back in the car to take her somewhere else. As they passed a bank, she noticed the date: December 24th.

'It's Christmas eve, Bitty.'

'I miss the Christmas tree at Pete and Chelsea's.'

'Oh fuck off, you two! We were only there a couple of days! Don't act like we belonged there!'

Bitty hunched up in the seat, holding her stomach that was aching with emptiness and beginning to feel sick and crampy again. She needed another hit. She hadn't been hungry when she'd been high; even that pain had gone. She needed more.

Mack took her to an upscale home in the suburbs and led her inside. It was beautiful, but the man who met them led them through to a door off the kitchen which led to a flight of stairs going down.

Bitty swallowed down the dread as she followed between the owner and Mack. It was dark until he flipped on a switch and illuminated a furnished room. Bitty was surprised and looked around until he led her to the back and opened another door. This one led to an unfinished area that housed the boiler, electrical box, and a metal-post bed. There was a table with various 'tools' laid out and she just stared at it in horror.

She looked up to see Mack watching her, then looked away quickly.

"Be a good girl and you can have a hit when you're done. Be a bad girl and you'll be in a world of pain you didn't know existed, whore."

She nodded slightly and stared at the floor as the two of them talked details. Then Mack left and the owner got to work on her. Within minutes, Bitty wished with all her heart that Mack had pumped some dope into her veins before this man started his sick fantasies. It wasn't long before she was screaming, but she doubted anyone would ever hear her. Would they care, even if they did? Somehow, she didn't think so.

Chapter Sixty-One

* Choice One *

Bitty was suddenly very aware of the arms around her and the body pressed against her. She stiffened in fear, a thousand thoughts running through her head, not least of which was that John had lied and Santa had come for her after all. When her senses caught up to her panicking brain, she blinked a few times and frowned when she recognized John.

John was in her bed? John had his arms around her? Had John...

She looked down at herself, but she was still in her pajamas from the night before, and she didn't hurt anywhere. She looked back at his sleeping form with a little frown. Had he stayed all night to protect her like he'd said?

After a minute or so, she shifted uncomfortably and he opened his eyes. When he saw her, he smiled and moved his arms away from her.

"Morning, babygirl. Merry Christmas."

Her heart leapt and she blinked quickly. "It's Christmas? It's Christmas!" she gasped.

He grinned and nodded. "Shall we go see what Santa brought?"

"You stayed with me all night?" she whispered.

He nodded. "I'm sorry. I should have left, but I didn't want you to think I abandoned you. I also realize you probably got a totally different idea in your head. I only stayed so you wouldn't be scared, I promise."

She looked down at his chest for a moment, then looked up at him and nodded. "K. Thank you."

He kissed her forehead. "Let's go see what's out in the living room."

She smiled and slid out of bed, waiting for him to do the same before tiptoeing nervously to the living room. In the archway, she froze, staring.

It was still dark outside and the lights on the tree were twinkling with their soft yellow glow. The ornaments and garland sparkled in the warm light and beneath the branches there was a pile of gifts. Actual, beautiful, wrapped gifts. On the couch was a bulging blue quilted stocking beside a beautiful matching pink one almost overflowing with candy and more gifts.

John's hand on her back made her jump and he snatched it back quickly. "Sorry. Do you… uh… want to go see what's in them?"

She looked from him to the tree and back. "They're… they're really for me?" she breathed.

He smiled and nodded. "Yes, babygirl. Well, some of them, anyway. I'm sure there's some for everyone else, too. Shall we go look?"

She gazed at the tree for a moment longer, then nodded and gave him a small smile.

He grinned back and took her hand as they entered the dim room, sliding the light dimmer switch up a little to give them some more light without taking away from the magic of the tree.

"Which first? Stocking or tree?"

She glanced at the couch. "Let's do stockings."

He smiled and sat down with her, waiting for her to reach into hers. "Go on," he urged when she simply sat there. "See what's in it."

She looked at him nervously for a moment, then smiled a little bit and began pulling things out; a pair of fluffy socks, a couple of candy bars, a pack of cards, an apple and orange, a tiny can of soda, and at the bottom, a small envelope with a gift card inside. Her eyes nearly bugged out of her head and she held it up to show him.

"It's… it's for… It says… $50!" she gasped.

He grinned and hugged her. "I guess Santa thought you needed some back gifts. You can spend that however you want, babygirl."

She stared down at the little plastic card in her hands, unable to speak.

"Would you like to open your other gifts, or should we have some breakfast first?"

She lifted her eyes to the pile of presents under the tree, then glanced at him with a nervous smile. "Can we open the other ones?" she whispered.

~ Choice Two ~

Scarlett had no idea what time it was when he finally took a break. She could hear him stomping up the stairs, his footsteps tired and heavy on the floor above her. She couldn't move; he'd left her strapped to the bed in the dark. Every inch of her hurt beyond belief. She'd never been through something like this before. Mack must have been punishing her for disappearing, even though there was no way it was her fault.

Her tears refused to stop until he came downstairs and shoved a gag in her mouth.

"Shut up. My kids are visiting!"

She looked up at him in misery and disbelief as he turned the light out again and shut the door. Desperately, she wished for some kind of relief, even just getting out of this position. She couldn't remember much, but what she did was worse than any nightmare she'd ever had. How could he keep her strapped up and gagged down here, bruised and bleeding while he entertained his *children*? At least it sounded like they didn't live with him. They were lucky enough to escape the monster. Why could she never be that lucky?

Eventually, Scarlett blocked out enough of the pain and withdrawals to slip into a semi-sleep. In the background, she heard Christmas carols, laughter, smelled delicious food. Her heart ached as much as the rest of her to hear it. It was a lot easier when she could pretend Christmas wasn't happening, but to be trapped under a happy family doing happy family things while she was starting to wish she could just die, it was too much.

Eventually, she heard the door slam and the house was quiet. Part of her hoped he would come down; she needed the bathroom so badly and her throat hurt with dryness. But the sane, logical part of her knew that there would be no reprieve when he returned, only more pain.

To her surprise, he returned and removed the gag and restraints, then offered her a glass of water which she finished almost immediately.

"I've got you for another hour," he murmured in her ear and she shuddered, tears filling her eyes.

An hour of what he'd been doing to her! She didn't know if she could make it! A few minutes later she was screaming again, wishing Mack would come back and take her away. Anywhere would be better than this. Why did people seem to think that she had no feelings, either physical or emotional? Why did they do things to her they would never dream of doing to someone else? Why was she just an object to sate their desires, expected to keep quiet and take it like she wasn't in agony? Why?

Once again, she drifted in and out of consciousness until finally there was nothing. Eventually, she realized she was alone and it was dark. She slipped into blackness with a sigh of relief until she felt herself hauled roughly to her feet and dressed. The clothes against her wounds was excruciating and she cried out. That earned her a backhand to her cheek and she tried to curb her whimpers as much as possible as she was virtually dragged out of the house.

Every position she sat in on the drive hurt some part of her throbbing body and her vision blurred as they drove through streets decked in Christmas lights. People were taking gifts out of cars, greeting family and friends, laughing and playing. Christmas trees decorated just about every window. It was something she could only ever dream about. Scarlett closed her eyes against the miserable sights of real life and tried to escape from the pain.

"I'm having people over for Christmas. You'd better behave and be quiet."

She barely heard him and certainly couldn't even answer. Her lips were chapped and bleeding, her throat was raw and dry and she tasted blood in the back of it along with other things. Her clothes were damp with red stains, and Mack didn't even seem to care. How could he not care? Why did no one care? She let her mind wander, trying to slip back inside, into the dark of her room where nothing hurt, away from everything for a while.

Bitty gave a gasping cry as she was pulled out of the car and a tidal wave of agony hit her like a brick wall. Mack hauled her inside, smiling and greeting his friends who were gathered already. Several of his girls were huddled in corners but none looked as worse for wear as Bitty felt. It seemed Mack was taking a break for Christmas. Maybe Bitty would be able to rest and nurse whatever wounds were tormenting her. Maybe she would get a Christmas miracle.

He tossed her towards the wall and her legs gave out causing her to hit her head on the baseboard. Blood began to drip into her eyes and she saw points of black floating in her vision for a long time. She was so cold but it even hurt to shiver. Huddling up just put more pressure on her wounds and there was nothing she could do about her damp clothes. Whatever they were wet with, Bitty didn't want to know. Eventually, she lay down on her side on the floor and closed her eyes, crying as quietly as she could. Why had they left? Nothing could be worse than this. She didn't understand why she had ended up here again.

Chapter Sixty-Two

* Choice One *

John grinned at her and nodded. "Of course. How about we open three, then take a break and have some breakfast before doing the rest?"

"There's more than three for me?" she asked incredulously.

He laughed and beckoned her over as he sat on the floor beside the tree. "Sit over here so I can get a picture quickly."

She obliged, moving beside the tree and giving him a shy little smile as he held up his phone. When he'd finished, he nodded at the pile.

"Go ahead."

She stared at the pile for a long moment, her eyes moving from each one to the next in wonder. Finally, she reached for a small rectangular box, and two medium sized boxes with her name on them. After glancing at him to make sure it was okay, she began peeling the paper off the first medium sized box. A smile spread over her face when a ceramics painting kit appeared. It held a little piggy bank and several colors of paints. Taped to the outside of the box was a penny.

Bitty looked up at him in sheer joy. "I can paint this? Myself?"

He nodded. "Of course. However you want it to look. And the penny is to go into it when it's done. It's good luck to have a penny in a piggy bank."

She examined the box—front and back—for a moment before setting it aside and reaching for the next one. John snapped a few pictures as she opened them, hoping to capture the magic of her first real Christmas.

The next gift turned out to be an instant-print camera and film which he helped her open and set up. Bitty's excitement was through the roof and as soon as it was ready, she took pictures of the tree, the gifts, him, and -with a shy smile- a selfie of them both in front of the tree.

As much as John was dying to see her open her presents, he was willing to be patient and let her enjoy each one on its own. The joy in her face was almost overwhelming and he felt he could just watch her all day.

Her final gift was an iPod and a gift card for iTunes. Bitty stared at it in wonder. The other things had seemed extravagant, but she had no real idea of their cost. An iPod, however, was something she had heard about.

She lifted her face to him in shock. "This is really for me?" she breathed.

He smiled warmly at her and nodded, then leaned over to hug her. "Yes, babygirl. Merry Christmas."

She hugged him back, tears shining in her eyes as he stroked her hair softly. "Thank you for bringing me here. Thank you for everything."

His arms tightened on her and he kissed the top of her head. "It's been my pleasure, babygirl." With a sigh, he leaned back a little bit and smiled at her. "Shall we go get some breakfast?"

She returned his smile and nodded, taking the hand he offered to help her up, then followed him into the kitchen. John had insisted on eggs and bacon because they were going to have enough sweets the rest of the day and he wanted to combat the sugar with something more substantial.

Bitty really had no objection. She loved the good, solid food she'd been getting since she came here, and he had promised she'd be allowed to eat her candy afterwards anyway.

John turned on some Christmas music to listen to while they ate and they talked about what colors she might paint the piggy bank and what music she would like to try. Bitty had never really explored music before. It wasn't as though she'd ever had the chance to delve into anything that wasn't pure survival. She'd heard radios and things, of course, but it had never really been anything but background noise. Now John was excited to suggest things she might like to try out and musicians he liked that she might enjoy too.

When they'd finished eating, they returned to the living room to open a few more of the gifts. Bitty was surprised to see that not all of them had her name on them; there were gifts for Bebe, Jay, Sarah, Scarlett, even Bailey and Callie.

"How did he know?" she whispered in awe.

"Who?"

"Santa. How did he know about everyone?"

John smiled and shrugged. "He's Santa. He knows a lot of things." His face suddenly lit up. "Hey! We didn't check the milk and cookies!"

After a nervous glance at the table, she looked to him for reassurance, then took his hand and followed him to the table. Sure enough, the milk was gone and there were only crumbs left on the plate, along with what looked like some kind of gooey liquid.

"Reindeer slobber!" John declared, and Bitty couldn't help but laugh.

Beside the plate was a note.

"Why don't you try reading it, and I'll help you with any words you don't know."

She eyed him doubtfully but picked it up and sat down on the edge of the couch to read.

Dearest Bitty, Bebe, Jay, Sarah, Scarlett, Bailey, and Callie,

I can't thank you enough for the carrots and cookies. The reindeer loved the tasty treats, and they're so much healthier than cookies for them! I'm sorry about the drool, but reindeer will be reindeer.

I'm also sorry I never came all those other years. It wasn't your fault, dearest, and I hope you will understand that some day. There has to be a little bit of magic in every house I visit or I can't get in, and I'm afraid I couldn't get into your old house. But from now on, I'll be visiting you at your new house every year.

I hope you enjoy the things I brought for you, and maybe next year you'll want to write me a letter to tell me all the things you want. I know that might take some time and I have all the time in the world to wait until you're ready. Merry Christmas, dearest.

Love,

Santa

Bitty sat still and silent for a long time, staring down at the letter in her hands. He hadn't skipped her every year because she'd been bad. John was right. He couldn't get in because there was no Christmas at her house. It wasn't her fault. He'd said so.

Eventually, she looked up at John, tears spilling down her cheeks. "You were right," she whispered.

"About what, babygirl?"

"That… that I wasn't too bad for Santa to come. He's really real and he explained why he never came."

He smiled and hugged her tightly. "You were never bad, Bitty. I'm sure you were never bad a day in your life. Not any of you."

'Bullshit! He's not real! Santa's nothing but perverts and sickos dressed up in a red suit to use little kids how they want! John wrote that note! It's the only thing that's possible.'

'Bailey! Stop it! You don't know that at all. Leave her alone and let all of them have their Christmas. Bitty, you know how Bailey is. Don't let her ruin everything. She doesn't believe in anything good, you know that. Santa wrote you a letter to explain everything, and that's what you should believe.'

Bitty looked down at the note in her hand, torn between believing Bailey and listening to Sarah's reassurances.

John's arms tightened around her, and once again he seemed to know what she was thinking. "The Santas you knew before, Bitty… They weren't Santa. They were just people who didn't care about a wonderful, precious little girl. This is so much different. This Santa, the real Santa, would never, ever hurt you."

She sniffed softly and wiped her eyes, then looked up at him and managed a small smile. "Really?"

"Honest to god, cross my heart, really." He smiled at her and she smiled back a little more widely. With another quick hug, he leaned back and grinned at her. "How about we set up that iPod?"

She nodded, her happiness flooding back into her once more.

~ Choice Two ~

She had no idea how long she lay on the floor shivering, slipping in and out of consciousness while Mack and his friends laughed and drank and ate. Neither she or any of the other girls were offered anything and she heard more than just her own stomach rumble with hunger. She wondered vaguely how many of his friends knew about what he really did and how many girls were shut in a room without food, water, or anything for a toilet. Some, at least, because they'd used her, but perhaps not all.

She just couldn't stop shivering and her eyes refused to open. She was so very tired, but every time she heard footsteps outside the door she jerked back into consciousness as fear gripped her again and again. The front door slammed a few times, and then the talk and laughter grew more rowdy and lewd. One by one, he or some of his friends came in and hauled one of the girls out of the room. These must be the friends who knew. Maybe the girls were Christmas gifts for his friends.

The moment Bitty had been dreading arrived when heavy boots stopped right in front of her. Her aching body protested violently when his hand wrapped around her upper arm, causing her to scream in pain. When he pulled her to her feet the sudden change in position felt like her brain had splattered against the inside of her skull and she threw up at his feet. Before she could even gasp for breath, a fist knocked her brain back the other way and she threw up again.

"Fucking disgusting bitch!"

Through the fog in her head, she thought that might have changed his mind about taking her, but she was dragged along behind him anyway. Her vision was so blurred she could hardly see more than a few fuzzy shapes around her and she stumbled the whole way on shaking legs.

With another sharp jerk, whoever it was tossed her on a mattress on the floor but the movement again caused her to vomit, though what she had in her stomach to throw up was a mystery. Another fist to her face brought a rasping scream of pain from her dry, bloody throat.

"Keep your fucking guts inside you! You're making a mess! What the fuck is wrong with you!"

Bitty kept her eyes closed, hoping and wishing that someone would switch in, give her a respite, take some of the agony for even a few minutes. She couldn't breathe or think or move. She needed someone to let her escape. But she was alone. There was no presence or voices, everyone was hiding from the nightmare. She could hardly blame them. She didn't want to be out for this either.

Whoever it was obviously wasn't *that* bothered by her 'mess' because they were quick enough to strip her. He paused for a moment when he uncovered the damage the other man had done, then gave a low whistle and stepped back.

"Mack! Come take a look at this."

Heavy footsteps thudded but Bitty couldn't open her eyes anymore. They were just too heavy and she hurt too much. The light in the room was like knives in her head.

"Fuck. He ruined her. What a waste. I should have had him pay more. Bastard."

"Well, I don't want one that looks like this! Gimme one of those others."

"Fine," Mack growled angrily. "Go get a different one."

The other man left and suddenly there was a heavy boot slamming into her side. She heard a rib crack and she screamed again. That earned her another kick.

"You're worthless! Get back in the other room!"

Bitty tried to move, she really did. But all that happened when she made the effort was a twitch of her fingers. Even that seemed like it took every ounce of strength she had.

"Mack, please," she croaked, still unable to open her eyes.

"You fucking lazy whore!" His fist wrapped around and through her long hair and he began to pull her off the mattress. She screamed and desperately tried to move to ease the pain but her body just wouldn't work anymore. Yet again she threw up and her whole body shook violently. She couldn't keep going, she couldn't make it stop. She needed to rest. She had to rest.

Bitty's body went limp and all she could do was whimper as she was kicked into the corner of the room. When he stormed out, Bitty finally let her body go completely limp, slipping into unconsciousness once more.

Chapter Sixty-Three

* Choice One *

After lunch, Bebe was suddenly bouncing around the living room with cries of joy and excitement.

"There's presents! There's presents! Daddy! There's presents!"

He laughed and took her hand, pulling her to the tree and sitting down with her on his lap.

"There's some for you," he told her, picking up some of the gifts and putting them in front of her.

"For me?" she squeaked.

"Yup, just for you, though maybe you'll still share with everyone else anyway?"

Bebe, unlike Bitty, tore into the wrappings wildly and shrieked with delight at the baby doll in the box. She moved on to unwrap a feeding set for the doll, then a Barbie set, then a stack of picture books.

"The last one you'll have to stand up for," he told her with a grin as he pointed to a huge box tucked slightly behind the tree.

"That's for me?" she breathed, jumping to her feet and running to it.

"Yup. Go ahead."

Once again, the paper tore away in long strips to reveal a deluxe dollhouse. Bebe could only stop and stare at it in awe for several long moments before she spun around to look at him in excitement.

"It's really for me?"

"Really truly. You want to open it and set it up?"

"Yes! Yes! Yes!"

He laughed and began the job of unboxing and building the house, stopping every so often to help her extricate a doll or an accessory.

The excitement must have been spreading through her like wildfire because it wasn't long before Jay came over with a shy, hopeful expression and John took a break from the house to sit with him to open the gifts with his name on them.

Jay started opening them slowly, like Bitty had, but when the train set came into view, the wrappings were torn off like Bebe had done. The same thing happened with the toy cars and the Xbox.

"I think Santa probably got you a few less than the others because the Xbox is a pretty expensive gift. But there's some games we can play together on there, if you'd like."

Jay beamed at him and John returned it. He had to admit it had taken him a while to adjust to seeing the eyes and soul of a little boy in the body of a young teenage girl, but now he could see them each for who they were and the outside had begun to slip away when the others were out.

Scarlett had been a little more difficult to shop for. He knew she was—in her own mind—a twenty-something young woman who was not shy about her sexuality, but his first thought of lingerie had quickly been shoved aside by his practicality and reason. While Scarlett saw herself as an adult, Bitty was still a child no matter what she'd been through or done in her life, and there was just no way he could justify giving her something like that.

He had been quite unsure of his choice for her, but she seemed to be more than happy with her makeup kit, necklace and earring set, and gift card. She had immediately asked him to put the necklace on her and had put the earrings in right after.

Sarah had been even more difficult to shop for, since he knew very little about her besides her desire to comfort and care for others, specifically those in their system. In the end, he had bought her a fluffy decorative pillow, a velour blanket, and a gift card for herself, too.

When it came to Bailey, John had wondered whether he should even try to get her anything at all or if she'd smash it into his face. But he found he couldn't get the others something and not her. Not entirely out of sarcasm, he had found her a black uni-sex shirt that read 'Final Warning! If you don't want a sarcastic answer, don't ask me a stupid question' and a maroon young-miss shirt that said 'I hate everyone'. Whether or not she'd even make an appearance was another thing he wasn't sure about, and was surprised when he looked back at the couch before dinner and found her sitting on the couch with her arms crossed and a scowl on her face.

"Bailey, Merry Christmas."

"You can't buy us off, you know."

"I know. I'm not trying to. You guys just deserve better than you've had. I got you a couple of things too, if you'd like to see them. I swear I'm not expecting anything from you if you decide to keep them. It's Christmas, and I like to give people gifts."

She glared at him for a long moment, then gave a heavy sigh and got up to snatch them from him. After returning to the couch, she scowled over at him again, then ripped open the first one.

John began to get nervous as she stared down into the box in utter silence, but a moment later, he thought he caught the shadow of a smile at the corners of her eyes. Without a word, she opened the second one and this time he was sure he could see a smile carefully hidden behind her hard face.

"These are rude as fuck," she snapped, but she hadn't taken her eyes off them.

"Yeah, I know. But I figured this way you don't even have to say anything to anyone. They'll just leave you alone."

She looked up at him with an unreadable expression. "You got these for me?" she asked finally.

He nodded. "If you don't like them, I can return them. It's fine."

"No!" she snapped quickly, then caught herself and looked down at them again. "I... guess I may as well keep them."

John smiled, though he tried not to show it too much. From her, he felt that was a huge compliment.

Even more than his doubts about Bailey's appearance, John felt sure Callie would be a no-show. If she only came out at the most traumatic times, he felt there was no way she would be around today, and he certainly wasn't going to try to trigger her out.

Bitty switched in just after dinner and they snuggled on the couch under Sarah's blanket to watch a Christmas movie. John eyed the last gift under the tree somewhat sadly and wondered if Callie would ever get it.

Part of him felt that was a wonderful thing and it would mean life had improved for Bitty and her system, but another part felt like Callie had been cheated somehow. She had only ever lived to experience terror and pain, and she knew nothing of what the world could be without it.

His eyes filled with tears and he tightened his arm around Bitty for a second. She looked up at him with a big smile before turning back to the movie.

As he was tucking her into bed that night, he sat down and stroked the hair from her face.

"I forgot to tell you, I heard back from the school I wanted to send you to. They accepted you based on the sculpture you made at the other school. It's a school of the arts, so you'll be surrounded by art, music, and dance."

"My… my sculpture?" she asked in confusion. "But I never finished it. I didn't even get it back."

He smiled. "I contacted the art teacher and she went ahead and fired it anyway. She took a picture of it and sent it to me, and I sent it to the other school with an explanation that it wasn't finished. They decided it showed enough talent for someone who'd never done anything like it before that they would allow you in. You'll get the piece back once school starts. I'll pick it up."

Her eyes filled with tears and she sat up to hug him. "Thank you, Daddy!"

He beamed and hugged her tightly to him. "I love you, Bitty. Not in an 'I want to have sex with you' way. In the 'I want to be your Daddy forever' way; if you'll let me."

She smiled and hugged him again with a nod. "I love you too."

Chapter Sixty-Four

~ Choice Two ~

Bitty didn't know how long she'd been asleep but the sun was just setting out the window. Maybe it was still the same day; Christmas day. A desperate, aching wish swam through her throbbing head that maybe God and Jesus were truly real and would send her a Christmas miracle.

It didn't seem likely. After all, she'd wished and hoped and prayed her whole life for a way to escape her existence, but nothing had ever come. The closest she'd been to an escape was the few wonderful days in the detention center after she'd detoxed and Fowler had been arrested. But even that had come to an end. She just wasn't meant to live a life like other people. She would never escape, never be free.

Pain radiated through her thin, broken little body. It hurt to breathe, it hurt to think, it hurt to simply be.

Mack's boots stopped in front of her and she found her head lifted by his fist in her hair once more. She very nearly threw up again but all that happened was a dry heave; there was just nothing left. She hadn't even had a few sips of water since that morning.

"You're pathetic. Look at you, bitch, lying in your own filth, turning my friends off with your disgusting body. I don't even know why I let you stay in this house. You're useless to me. You have until tomorrow to rest and then I'm getting my money out of you."

He dropped her head and it cracked heavily on the floor causing another wave of nausea to roll through her. His boot landed twice more in her stomach and chest and she felt something else send a spike of agony through her body from her gut.

Then she felt it, them. All of them. Bebe, Jay, Scarlett, Sarah, Bailey, and another small, terrified one she'd never felt before. Everyone was with her.

'Please, God. Please help us get out of here.'

'Jay, there is no God. There never was. No one is gonna send us a miracle.'

'But it hurts, Bailey. It hurts so, so bad.'

Bitty felt another kick to her stomach as Mack walked past on his way out.

And then it happened. A Christmas miracle.

A syringe dropped from his pocket and landed quietly on her arm before sliding off and rolling a few inches away. She opened her eyes enough to see Mack's fuzzy shape walk out the door; he hadn't noticed.

She looked back at the full syringe and summoned every shred of strength she had in her to reach for it.

That small cylinder held hope, relief, freedom.

Her hands shook violently as she tried to bite and pull hard enough to get the cap off and she had to rest for a moment once she did.

'Bitty, what are you doing?'

Jay's voice sounded nervous, confused.

"It's God, Jay," she replied in a bare whisper. "It will make the hurt stop."

With another great effort, Bitty lifted her hand to her elbow and pushed the needle in but she was too dehydrated. Her veins had almost collapsed. It took her three tries with rests in between before she managed to hit the vein.

'Bitty... there's too much in there...'

Sarah's warning didn't even sound like she meant it. It seemed more like a token resistance.

"I know," Bitty whispered as she pushed the plunger down. "But it'll stop hurting, Sarah. I won't hurt anymore."

Relief flooded through her, her body relaxed, the pain seemed to float away. Bitty felt the arms around her that had been the only loving arms she'd ever known, Sarah holding them, comforting them. Even Bailey had sunk down into Sarah's comfort.

For a brief few moments, it was warm, loving, almost as if she were safe. Tiredness crept over her; a tiredness that would not be pushed away anymore. Bitty felt her body relax, release, slow down.

She sighed and let it take her away from the pain forever.

She was free.

Epilogue

* Choice One *

Five Years Later

"Bailey Matthews."

Bitty smiled into the audience in the direction of the ridiculously loud whistle before turning back to the principal to collect her diploma and pose for a picture.

She had done it.

The new school had proven to be a life changing place. She had needed remedial classes in everything, but her art skills had flourished. Her teachers had worked with her patiently and tirelessly to bring her reading and math to her grade level. It had taken years of work, but John had been there every step of the way to hold her up when she wanted to give up, to reassure her when she felt like she was failing, and to cheer for her when she met each goal along the way, just like he was doing now.

A year after she'd gone to live with him, John had formally adopted her and she had been quick to drop her former last name of Carter to take his. He had been a wonderful father to her through the years.

She'd made friends eventually and her counseling had been going well. Her past still haunted her often, but it was lessening with every year and every step away from that existence.

"I can't believe we're done!"

Bitty turned to grin at her friend Emily as she looped her arm through Bitty's.

"No more school until fall, and college is way different than high school! You sure you don't want to go to college?"

Bitty nodded. "I'm sure. Maybe later, but I need to be done with school for a little while. I have things to work through."

"You're so lucky your dad is so laid back about it. My parents freaked out when I even suggested taking a year off!"

Bitty met John's proud gaze from the other side of the stage while she waited for the rest of her classmates to collect their diplomas.

"Yeah," she murmured with a smile, "I'm so lucky."

The moment the ceremony was over, John was rushing to her with the proudest look out of any of the parents there. He swept her up into his arms and spun her before setting her gently back on her feet with a laugh.

"I'm so proud of you, babygirl! But more important, are *you* proud of you?"

She grinned and nodded. "Yeah. I am."

'Me too!'

'And me!'

'Yes, we should all be quite proud of ourselves. We've come a long way.'

'Did you see me turn down sex with Ben the other day!'

'Oh for fuck's sake, Scarlett, get over that already. That has nothing to do with graduating high school!'

'It's a graduation of its own, Bailey. She has every right to be proud of that, too.'

Bitty laughed and both John and Emily grinned back at her with curious expressions.

"Everyone says they are, too!"

"Even Bailey?" Emily asked in surprise.

Bitty laughed and shrugged. "Well..."

They all laughed again and Emily hugged her quickly before excusing herself to greet her parents.

Bitty had been terrified when Emily began to notice the changes in her behavior the more they hung out, but when she and John had explained things to her, Emily had been quick to go with the flow and accept everyone. It felt wonderful.

"Well, babygirl, what do you say we go out to dinner and celebrate?"

She grinned and nodded. "I'd love to."

As John hugged her again, Bitty closed her eyes and held onto him tightly, almost not wanting to let go.

"What's wrong, babygirl?" he asked gently.

"Nothing. Nothing is wrong. You changed everything for me, Daddy."

He chuckled and squeezed her tightly. "No, babygirl. You changed things for yourself. I only gave you the opportunity to get out of there that you needed to do it."

She smiled against his chest and sighed. He was right; he'd given her an escape from the clutches of trafficking and the tools and counseling to recover, but she'd done the rest. There was still a lot of healing to do, but now she knew she could do it.

She was free.

Author's Note

Bitty's story may seem unreal or far-fetched, but all too often it is the real existence of many children and adults trafficked across the globe, many times in your own backyard. Boys and girls of all ages, races, and nationalities are subjected to unthinkable acts because they simply don't have the resources or help they need to escape.

Not all trafficking is physically violent like Bitty's story is. Sometimes it's a threat to someone they love, or the lack of other options, or simply because they don't know how to live any other way. It's not only women and girls who are forced into service; it is a crime that involves many men and boys as well.

Trafficking isn't something that happens across the ocean in undeveloped countries. Trafficking happens every day in thousands of cities across North America, Europe, Australia, as well as those of more impoverished countries.

It isn't even always something that a person is forced into initially. Many times someone will think they are being offered something that will make their life better, just as Bitty did when she met Mack; a way to escape or better their lives, only to find out once they're trapped that there's no way out. Blaming the victim of human trafficking only makes it worse and harder for them to seek help.

While sex trafficking isn't the only form of trafficking, it is one of the biggest and fastest growing industries, pulling in about $99 BILLION every YEAR. It is estimated that there are about 25 million men, women, and children trapped in slavery across the globe.

Another part of Bitty's story is her Multiple Personality Disorder, now known as Dissociative Identity Disorder. Again, it may seem like a plot point to a horror movie, but it is another real condition, usually a side-effect of childhood trauma as a way to cope. While Hollywood has exaggerated DID in almost every representation of the condition, it is nothing to be afraid of and alters are rarely violent towards other people.

Studies show that as many as 1-3% of the population meets the criteria for a dissociative disorder. That is the same percentage as those with Bipolar disorder or Schizophrenia. It differs from Schizophrenia in that the 'voices' are not hallucinations but rather separate identities within the mind and is not a condition treatable with medication.

Bitty's system of alters consisted of six others, though other systems can have anywhere from 2-100 alters and may include men and women, children and adults. Every DID system is unique and as varied as the alters themselves.

Sometimes, DID can cause problems in everyday life when alters switch and don't know what's going on. Not everyone can communicate with their alters, much like Callie was unaware of the others and they could not communicate with her. With help, counseling, and support, many people with DID can go on to learn techniques to live a fairly normal life.

This story is, of course, fiction, but the theme is not. It is all too real, even though shown at the extreme. You can help by spreading information, helping form support groups in your area, donating to rescue organizations like Polaris, educating law enforcement, and petitioning lawmakers to take a different stance on victims of trafficking. They shouldn't have to pay for the crimes of others when they need help and understanding.

A detective on a trafficking task force in Washington put it in a way that may help people understand.

"If a child on a soccer team is raped by their coach, they don't arrest and punish the child. But as the laws stand now, if a child is picked up for prostitution, they are treated like a criminal for the same thing."

So please, be aware, spread the word, and fight for those who can't fight for themselves.

Everyone deserves to live free.

ABOUT THE AUTHOR

Arden has been reading and writing since an early age, happily losing herself in fantasy, science fiction, and contemporary fiction throughout her life. Having started her own company creating audiobooks for other authors' works, she finally achieved her dream of publishing a book of her own. Arden lives in Wisconsin with her husband, four children, five cats, multiple tanks of tropical fish, and an umbrella cockatoo. When she's not working, Arden enjoys playing flute, violin, and piano; cross-stitch and coloring; playing Halo with her son; watching K-dramas and anime with one of her daughters; and playing Dungeons and Dragons with her other two daughters.

Resources

211 (United States quick-dial)

Polaris Project - PolarisProject.org

love146: love146.org

National Human Trafficking Hotline :
humantraffickinghotline.org

Shared Hope International: SharedHope.org

National Coalition for the Homeless:
nationalhomeless.org

Shatterproof - Stronger than Addiction:
shatterproof.org